What's Left of Kisses?

Out of the Blue – France, 1916

Grieving over the death of his lover, British flying ace Bat Bryant accidentally kills the man threatening him with exposure. Unfortunately there's a witness: the big, rough American they call "Cowboy"—and Cowboy has his own price for silence.

The Dark Farewell – Little Egypt, 1922

It's the Roaring Twenties and Prohibition has hit Little Egypt where newspaper man David Flynn has come to do a follow-up story on the Herrin Massacre. But the massacre isn't the only news in town. Spiritualist Medium Julian Devereux claims to speak to the dead—and he charges a pretty penny for it. Flynn is convinced Devereux is as fake as a cigar store Indian, but when Julian begins to see bloodstained visions of a serial killer, the only person he can turn to for help is the cynical Mr. Flynn.

This Rough Magic – San Francisco, 1935

Wealthy playboy Brett Sheridan thinks he knows the score when he hires tough guy private eye Neil Patrick Rafferty to find a priceless stolen folio of Shakespeare's The Tempest before his marriage to a society heiress is jeopardized. What Brett doesn't count on is the instant and powerful attraction that flares between him and Rafferty.

Snowball in Hell – Los Angeles, 1943

Just back from the European Theater, reporter Nathan Doyle is asked to cover the murder of a society blackmailer—a man who, Homicide Detective Mathew Spain believes, Nathan had every reason to want dead.

What's Left of Kisses?

HISTORICAL NOVELS, VOLUME ONE

JOSH LANYON

VELLICHOR BOOKS

An imprint of JustJoshin Publishing, Inc.

WHAT'S LEFT OF KISSES? Historical Novellas, Volume I
Copyright (c) 2016 by Josh Lanyon
Cover Art by Kevin Burton Smith
All rights reserved.

ISBN: 978-1-945802-55-3
Printed in the United States of America

JustJoshin Publishing, Inc.
3053 Rancho Vista Blvd.
Suite 116
Palmdale, CA 93551
www.joshlanyon.com

This is a work of fiction. Any resemblance to persons living or dead is entirely coincidental.

What's Left of Kisses?

HISTORICAL NOVELS, VOLUME ONE

"The human race tends to remember the abuses to which it has been subjected rather than the endearments. What's left of kisses? Wounds, however, leave scars."
— **Bertolt Brecht**

Out of the Blue

FRANCE, NOVEMBER 1916

CHAPTER ONE

"*D*on't be too hasty, Captain Bryant," Orton warned. "Not like I'm asking a king's ransom. Not like you can't find the ready, eh? What's a couple a bob 'ere and there? Could 'ave gone to the major, but I didn't, did I? Not one word to 'im about what you and poor Lieutenant Roberts used to—"

Bat punched him.

He was not as tall as the mechanic, but he was wiry and strong, and his fist connected to Orton's jaw with a satisfying crack. Orton's head snapped back. He staggered, tripped over something in the shadowy darkness of the stable, and went down slamming against the side of the stall.

The elderly dappled gray mare whickered softly. Leaning over the stall door, she lipped at Orton's fallen form.

For a second, perhaps two, Bat stood shaking with rage—and grief.

"Get up, you swine," he bit out.

Orton's head lay out of reach of the uneven lamplight, but his limbs were still—and something in that broken stillness alerted Bat.

"Orton?"

He moved the lantern and the light illuminated Orton's face. The man's head was turned at an unnatural angle—watery eyes staring off into the loft above them.

Bat smothered an exclamation. Knelt beside Orton's body.

The mare raised her head, nickering greeting. The lantern light flickered as though in a draft. He could see every detail in stark relief: the blue-black bristle on the older man's jaw, the flecks of gray in his mustache, oil and dirt beneath his fingernails.

There was a little speck of blood at the corner of his mouth where Bat's ring had cut him. But he was not bleeding. Was not breathing.

Bat put fingers to Orton's flaccid throat and felt for a pulse.

There was no pulse.

Sid Orton was dead.

Bat rose. Gazed down at the body.

Christ. It seemed…unreal.

He was used to thinking swiftly, making life-and-death decisions for the entire squadron with only seconds to spare, but he could think of nothing. He'd have to go to the CO. Chase would have to go to the Red Caps…

Bat wiped his forehead with his sleeve. First he'd need to come up with some story—some reason for what he'd done. Gene mustn't be dragged into it. No one could know about Gene and him. Wasn't only Gene's name at stake. There was Bat's own family and name to think of. This…just this…murder…was liable to finish the old man.

He couldn't seem to think beyond it. Disgrace. Dishonor.

He ought to feel something for Orton, surely? Pity. Remorse. He didn't. He hadn't meant to kill him, but Orton was no loss. Not even an awfully good mechanic. And Bat had killed better men than Orton—ten at last count—for much worse reason.

A miserable specimen, Orton.

But you couldn't murder a chap for that.

Gaze riveted on the ink stain on the frayed cuff of Orton's disheveled uniform, Bat tried to force his sluggish brain to action. Yes, he needed a story before he went to the major. More, he had to convince himself of it—get it straight in every detail—in case he was cross-examined. Mustn't get tripped up.

If only he had ignored Orton's note… Why the devil hadn't he?

"You waiting for him to tell you what to do?" a voice asked laconically from behind him.

Bat jerked about.

Cowboy leaned against the closed stable door. His eyes glinted in the queer light. Bright. Almost feral as he watched from the half shadows.

"P-pardon?" Bat asked stupidly.

"If you don't plan on getting jugged by the MPs, you better get a move on."

It was as though he were speaking to Bat in a foreign language. Granted, Cowboy was a Yank—a Texan, at that—and did take a bit of translation at the best of times.

Bat said, "I don't—what d'you mean? I-I shall have to report this."

"Why's that?" Cowboy left his post at the door and came to join him. Oddly, it gave Bat comfort, Cowboy's broad shoulder brushing his own. Together they stared down at Orton's body.

Already he had changed. His face had a waxy, sunken look. The smell of death mingled with kerosene and horse and hay.

Bat's stomach gave a lurch and he moved away, leaning over a rusted harrow. But there was nothing to vomit. He hadn't eaten since yesterday. Hadn't eaten since Gene bought his packet and crashed in flames in the woods of the estate his family once owned near Hesdin.

Instead, he hung white-knuckled onto the rough metal frame heaving dry, empty coughs and nothing coming out but a few exhausted tears. Not for Orton. For Gene.

"You better pull yourself together, boy," Cowboy told him when the worst of it was over. Listening distantly to that terse voice, Bat knew he was right. He shuddered all over. Forced himself upright, blinking at the American.

Cowboy was a big man. Several inches taller than Bat. Broad shoulders and narrow hips. Long legs. Must be the way they grew them in Texas. Cowboy certainly fit Bat's notion—based entirely on the works of Zane

Grey and Max Brand—of a man of the West. He'd been attached to the RFC for about two months. Which was a bloody long time in this war. Several lifetimes, really.

The old mare stretched her long neck and nibbled at the collar of Cowboy's tunic. He patted her absently and drawled, "Orton was a side-winder. A low-down, miserable piece of shit pretending to be a man. He wasn't even a very good mechanic. Whatever else you might be, you're one hell of a pilot. And the RFC is running short on pilots these days. Let alone aces."

Bat blinked at him, wiped his face again. He felt hot and cold, sick and sweaty. He felt as though he were coming down with something—something fatal. He was unable to think beyond the thing at their feet. "What are you saying?"

"I'm saying what the hell's the point of you going to jail for killing that skunk? Anyway, I saw what happened. It was an accident. You slugged him and he fell and hit his head."

"It's still…" But he didn't finish it. He felt a flicker of hope. "You'll back me up then? When I go to Major Chase?"

"I don't think you want to do that."

Too right there. Bat didn't. But…

"How are you going to explain what he said that got you so mad you punched him? Or what the hell you were doing in the stables this time of night?"

Before Bat thought of an answer—assuming he'd have come up with one—Cowboy added, "I guess Orton ain't the only one who ever noticed you and Lieutenant Roberts were kinda sweet on each other."

Bat lunged, and Cowboy sidestepped, grabbing him and twisting his arm behind his back in a wrestling move they never taught in any offi-cer's training course Bat had received. It was fast and efficient. Pain shot through his shoulder and arm and he stopped struggling, sagging against Cowboy. The American was so big, so powerfully built, it was easy to underestimate how fast he was when he needed to be. Not least because he never seemed to be in a hurry. He spoke in a lazy drawl and moved with easy, loose-limbed grace. Even when he flew into battle, he picked off enemy planes as though he were potting birds off a branch with a rifle. As though he had all the time in the world.

Listening to the calm, strong thud of Cowboy's heart, Bat thought dizzily that this was the closest he'd come to being in a man's arms ever again.

Cowboy's voice vibrated in his chest as he intoned, "Never realized you had such a temper, Captain Bryant. One of these days it's going to land you in a fix you can't get out of."

Bat yanked free and Cowboy let him go.

"Not tonight, though."

Bat rubbed his wrist where Cowboy's fingers had dug into the tendons. "What d'you mean?"

"I mean, if you can simmer down long enough to listen, I'm going to help you."

"Help me how?"

Cowboy wasn't looking at Bat. He stared down at Orton's body. Thoughtfully, as though only making his mind up to it, he said, "I'm going to get rid of him once and for all."

"How?"

"Never mind how. It'll be better if you don't know. Go back to the mess, and make sure everyone sees you. Close the place down. Then head up to your quarters. Understand?"

The flicker of hope flared. Bat knew a cowardly longing to do exactly as Cowboy instructed. Leave it to him, go get blind drunk, then retire to bed and forget any of this happened.

He forced himself to say, "Awfully good of you, old chap, but you must see I can't...can't let you do this."

Amused, Cowboy retorted, "You don't even know what I'm going to do, *old chap*, so why argue about it?"

He was staring at Bat, smiling that funny crooked grin of his. Bat had never noticed how blue Cowboy's eyes were. Blue as the sky—back when the sky was empty of anything worse than clouds—light and bright in his deeply tanned face. His hair was soft gold. Palomino gold.

Helplessly, Bat said, "Why should you do this? Why should you help me? I haven't been…it's not as though…"

"You've acted like a stuck-up sonofabitch since the day I arrived, is that what you were going to say?" Cowboy asked easily. "Not a member of your old boy's club, am I? Well, I guess it could be that I like you anyway. Or it could be having you around makes my life easier—'cept days like today when you seem bent on getting yourself blown out of the sky."

His gaze held Bat's, and there wasn't anything Bat could say. *Today.* Yes. What a long time ago it seemed.

If Cowboy hadn't been there today…Sid Orton would still be alive.

"Git," Cowboy said softly. "I'll find you later."

And so…Bat got.

* * * * *

No. 44 Air Squadron was stationed at an old château outside the village of Embry near Calais. The château had withstood the French Revolution and the Napoleonic Wars—and it wasn't doing too badly against the 44th although the piano in the former grand salon would never be the same.

Bat heard the voices before he pushed open the door: shouts and laughter and singing. He felt a wave of grief—a longing for Gene so fierce that he stopped in his tracks, resting his head against the carved wood of the mess entrance.

Never again. Never hear his voice, never taste his mouth…

He had told himself he was prepared for it. They had spoken of it many times in that hard, light way they all spoke of the inevitable. But he had not been prepared.

He smoothed the emotion from his features and went inside.

The room was long and handsome with forest-green walls and large windows facing the gardens and the aviaries that had once been stocked with exotic birds. The birds had been set free or eaten long ago, the shutters were closed and the blackout curtains drawn tight. There was an ornate marble fireplace reputedly designed by Leonardo da Vinci. The fire in the grate crackled merrily and threw warm shadows. Of the original furnishings only the piano, several needlepoint chairs, and a few watercolors had survived. They were all but invisible in the fug of tobacco smoke. The mess was packed. West and Rowbothom were tucking into eggs and bacon beneath the Iron Cross Gene and poor old Sandy had wrenched off a downed Fokker. Elliot was sleeping, a letter crumpled in one hand, an overturned glass by his elbow. Varlik and Heath were at the bar bellowing "Roses of Picardy" in accompaniment with the gramophone.

Roses are shining in Picardy
In the hush of the silver dew
Roses are flowering in Picardy
But there's never a rose like you
And the roses will die with the summer time
And our roads may be far apart
But there's one rose that dies not in Picardy
'Tis the rose that I keep in my heart.

"Bat, old son," shouted Ambrose. "Where the devil have you been all night?"

"Oh, you know," Bat said vaguely, dropping into the chair across from him.

Ambrose blinked at Bat over his pint. He was lanky and fair and Bat had known him since Eton, which no doubt entitled Ambrose to a few liberties. Difficult, after all, to keep any distance with a fellow with whom you'd shared smuggled bull's-eyes at midnight, toasting your slippers on the fire grate, and bemoaning the general barbarity of Latin masters everywhere.

Ambrose said solemnly, "Don't want to brood, old bean. Owl wouldn't want that."

What did any of them know what Owl had wanted or hadn't wanted?

"No, of course not," Bat said. He nodded thanks as MacArthur, the mess steward, brought him a pint. Mac began to mop up the new recruits, sending them off to their quarters with brusque kindliness. Dawn patrol was only a few hours off.

For a time Bat sat there listening to but not taking in the comfortable and familiar ack-ack of voices. Ambrose began to quiz him about the small mirror Bat had rigged to the cowl of his plane three days earlier. The mirror offered a lovely view of the tail of his plane—and anyone coming up on it. They all experimented with ways to give themselves some edge. No secret Jerry had better planes and better-trained pilots. Gene had said— No. Better not to think of that.

Instead, Bat nodded and drank and wondered what the devil Cowboy was doing.

"Roses of Picardy" went for another spin on the gramophone.

The last hour felt increasingly unreal. Bat wondered if he was by chance even now dossed down and dreaming. He must have been mad. Mad to meet Orton at all, mad to lose his temper, mad to strike him. What had possessed him? It was not like him. At least...not like he had used to be.

"I mean, you take all the sport out of the thing, old son," Ambrose was telling him quite earnestly.

Bat started to laugh. He caught himself up sharply. If he started, he was liable not to stop.

Tubby yelled across the room, "Bat, we're drinking to Owl."

Bat's hand clenched on his glass. He relaxed it consciously. The room fell silent—except for Elliot's snores.

Varlik rose, drink in hand, steadying himself. He had a fine speaking voice—even three sheets to the wind. He pronounced carefully, "Here's a toast, now! Fill the cup! Though the shadow of fate is on the wall, here's a final toast ere the darkness fall. Fill the cup."

There was a rumble of acknowledgment.

Bat lifted his glass, drank deeply. Managed to keep smiling.

Gradually, one by one, the other fellows began to drag themselves off to their beds. Ambrose bade Bat good night and Tubby took his place across the table. Tubby—The Right Honourable Thomas Lovesby—had also been at Eton with Bat. They had roomed together, in fact, and if anyone knew Bat, it was the man who had cheered him with contraband cigarettes when he was homesick, assured him with bold-faced lies that no one noticed that little stammer when Bat was upset, and thrown pillows at him when he snored too loudly. Not that anyone ever *really* knew anyone else, according to Gene. In the end they were all alone. Flying alone, dying alone—

Leaning forward, his elbow missing the edge of the table, Tubby just managed not to slam his chin on the tabletop. He fastened an earnest if bleary eye on Bat and said, "Thought you were done for today, old man. Fritz nearly had you. Lucky thing Cowboy moseyed along when he did."

"Yes," Bat replied. "Johnny-on-the-spot, wasn't he?" He watched the steady slow sweep of Mac's broom on the marble floors.

"Bat, you mustn't…"

Bat leveled a look at him and Tubby's round face reddened. "No use giving me that look, old man. I know you. Best pilot in the fuckin' squadron. We can't do without you."

"Tell it to the brass hats," Bat said, and despite his best effort the bitterness crept into his voice. "Two patrols a day with odds only five out of seven planes returning at the end of it. Has a single man in this last batch of replacements more than eighteen hours in the air? We're all for it eventually. It's only a matter of picking the when and where."

"That what you were doing today? Picking the when and where?"

Bat used his sleeve to wipe away the ring of wet his glass had made on the table. "Lost my head for half a mo, I suppose," he said grudgingly. "It won't happen again."

"Owl wouldn't—"

"Don't."

Tubby broke off uncomfortably, and Bat summoned a smile.

"I'm all right, Tubby. Truly. No need to fuss, old thing. Just need a good night's sleep, that's all."

Tubby grinned and checked his watch. "Better run to catch it then."

"On my way." Bat stood up, steadying himself with an unobtrusive hand on the table edge. All at once he was dead tired. Running on nerves and will for…how long was it now? Even before Gene, really. But somehow, with Gene, it had been bearable.

"Shall I tag along and tuck you in?"

"Tongues will wag, Tubby darling. Tongues will wag." Bat squeezed Tubby's shoulder and left the mess.

The fliers were quartered upstairs in the old château. No question pilots lived well—certainly better than the Poor Bloody Infantry. Better housing, much better food, and an enviable degree of freedom. They didn't live *long* as a rule, but…a short life and a merry one, eh?

Bat went up the wide marble staircase and down a long hallway punctuated by occasional snores from behind carved doors. He had the "blue room" which looked over the shattered wreckage of what had once been the conservatory. The château had been bombed twice so far, though that was before the RFC had taken up residence.

He let himself into his quarters and went over to the bed without bothering with a lamp. It was a nice enough room: threadbare blue velvet furnishings and pale squares and ovals marking where pictures had once hung on the azure walls. It was a long time since he'd spent a night at the château. Gene never could reconcile himself to the noise and rough-housing of life on an aerodrome, and had taken lodgings in a ramshackle former hunting lodge not far from the airfield. His widowed landlady was elderly, somewhat deaf, mostly blind, and grateful for the small income. Most nights Bat had stayed with Gene in the room that had once belonged to Madame's son—killed in the first summer of the war.

Bat tugged at his left boot, but any effort seemed too much, and he let himself fall back on the tapestry-draped bed and covered his eyes with his arm. True what he'd told Tubby; if he could just sleep…

Once again he saw Gene's plane descending down in long swooping curves.

At first he'd thought it was all right…Gene wasn't hit. He knew what to do. Bat had survived being shot down twice. Then Gene had looked up and waved at him. Just…casually. *So long. I'll be seeing you.*

Bat had registered part of Gene's tail was gone, shot away, and by the time his machine dropped out of the clouds, it was in pieces and Gene was falling…falling…

His eyes flew open and Bat sat up, breathing hard. Sleep? Not bloody likely. Not when every time he closed his eyes he saw Gene plummeting to his death.

He shouldn't be sleeping anyway. He should be dealing with the business he had funked last night. He rose, eased open the door to his room, and listened. All was quiet. Everyone sleeping—or lying awake dreading the swift approaching dawn. He shrugged back into his leather jacket, making his way softly, silently down the hall—past the bad paintings of irritable-looking French counts and countesses. Not an attractive bloodline, the Molyneuxs, but they were all done now. There was only a daughter left— fled to London.

Bat ran lightly down the grand staircase, marble steps and marble balustrade. For a second or two he stood outside the open door of the mess. Tubby was still chinwagging with Mac. Good old Tubby. He could hear the clink of glasses, the clatter of dishes.

He turned, went out the entranceway beneath the enormous Molyneux crest, down the steps into a damp night perfumed with the scent of roses and wood smoke. High above, the stars blazed on indifferently like beacons on a faraway airfield, burning as they had burned since man first crawled out of the ooze. Man's first bloody mistake.

Slipping through the herb garden, he dodged the sentries without much effort, and cut across the parkland of overgrown lawns and tangled rosebushes to the road. He'd stolen this way many times and did not need the moon—that big, bright bomber's moon—to show the way.

In the meadow that now served as airstrip, the planes waited, shadowy and ghostlike in the moonlight. A crust of frost sparkled on the ground like broken stars and a hint of cordite drifted on the breeze.

Bat headed automatically for his plane. Oh, she was a little beauty! A DH-2 with 100-horsepower Monosoupape engine and a cockpit large enough to shift around in and get a good look at the sky. Not like the old crates they flew at the beginning of the war. This girl could go eighty-six miles an hour at 65,000 feet in the air.

He stroked the bat insignia—the malicious pointed grin—painted on the forward part of the fuselage, and examined the neatly mended stitching of bullet holes. The chill of metal beneath his fingertips brought it all back, and he was in the clouds once more feeling the shock of bullets punching into the left side of her. Not a feeling one ever quite grew accustomed to—assuming one survived getting hit the first time, and that was as often luck as skill. This afternoon it had been luck that had saved Bat. Knocked sideways in the sky, he'd yanked the stick, pulling her up into a steep climb as he emptied his drum into the belly of the Fokker blasting over.

He had to have hit it but the Fokker rolled out and came around again as Bat was completing his half loop. He reached the top. Spun her back into upright position only to spot—with a sickening jolt—that grinning bastard in his mirror, waiting…

The end then. That was what he'd thought. It had felt like destiny—but he dived anyway, plunged into the blue emptiness below him like a swimmer striking into deep water. Every moment he'd expected to feel machine gun fire tearing into him, thinking that at least it would be quick.

No time for regrets. No time for anything but the recognition that his number was up.

But like the U.S. cavalry, Cowboy was there, coming in fast, spitting bullets.

Bat banked sharply, gave Cowboy plenty of room, and the American sat on the Fokker's tail and strafed it.

The Fokker seemed to melt right out of the air. One minute it was there, the next it was hurtling downward amidst the long white streamers of machine gun tracers.

Cowboy drew up beside Bat and gave him that little nod. Bat nodded back and then veered right, and Cowboy sheared off to the left. But despite his brisk demeanor there was cold sickness in Bat's belly, and his hands shook on the stick. It was the shock of it, the unexpectedness of it. Not of the attack—of surviving it.

Now, remembering, it felt a very long time ago. Years ago. A lifetime before Orton. Before he had killed Orton.

He stood motionless absorbing that.

He had killed Orton.

It was unbelievable. The entire night was like some ghastly never ending nightmare.

He thought again about finding Orton's note in the pocket of his flight jacket, the scrawled slip with its misspelled demand to meet in the stable. He should have ignored it. Followed his first instinct to burn the note and forget about it. Why, *why* hadn't he? Curiosity? No, more than that. Unease. There had been something in Orton's manner for some time. Something that wasn't quite open insolence, and yet... Yes. Something knowing and contemptuous. Instinctively, Bat had recognized it and feared the mechanic might have some evidence, some proof.

But what? They were careful. Always.

There had to be something, though. Something damning, or Orton wouldn't have dared approach a superior officer in such a manner.

Something had emboldened Orton. Perhaps he'd gone to Madame's last night—last night while Bat was drinking himself insensible. And if that was the case, it was Bat's own damned fault. He should have faced it then. If he'd had the sand last night, perhaps none of this need have happened.

Instead, like a bloody fool he'd struck Orton—killed him—before finding out what the man knew. It was only too likely at this very instant a piece of incriminating evidence sat awaiting discovery by the military police when they went through Orton's personal belongings. Perhaps Orton had the proof on him when he died? Either way it was too late. Nothing to be done now.

Too late.

Leaving the airfield, Bat located Gene's battered bicycle beside one of the huts. He walked the bike to the road, mounted it, and skimmed along through the moonlight until he came to the black mouth of the tunnel of trees. As darkness swallowed him, he closed his eyes, holding the bike to the unseen road, feeling the dank cool breeze against his face, whistling in his ears. He flew along, the tires skipping off the ground here and there—

He was almost startled by the bright wash of moonlight. Opening his eyes again, he saw before him the old hunting lodge where Gene—and, unofficially, Bat—had lodged for the past year.

He'd had no real plan when he left the aerodrome—he simply needed to be moving, not thinking, not remembering—but now he was focused on the things he must do—and do quickly. Time was against him now.

He propped the bike beneath an arbor sagging under the heavy shroud of pallid roses. He unlocked the side door. Digsby, Gene's French Bulldog, waited in the warm darkness, wriggling and whimpering as Bat stood trying to find his bearings.

Old Madame Fournier would be long in bed. The house smelled of rising bread and other pleasant things that triggered memories of a different time, of a different life.

"Hullo, Digs," he whispered. The dog darted past him looking for Gene, snuffling at the bottom of the door.

"He's not here."

Digs sat down, eyes gleaming in the shadows, and stared at him per-
plexed. Bat knelt, tugging the dog's ears, making a fuss of him as Gene
would have done.

Madame must have been expecting him after all. She had left some
kind of pie wrapped for him on the stove—squirrel or rabbit, no doubt. The
woman had an astonishing way with vermin. She could probably make rat
taste like fine cuisine, but he was not hungry. It was hard to imagine ever
being hungry again.

Dog at his heels, he made his way silently into the sitting room. The
blackout curtains were drawn, the hearth laid. He lit the tinder and as the
flames caught, went to unlock Gene's desk. The clock on the mantle tolled
the hour with silver chimes, a peculiarly civilized tone.

He reached into the desk drawer and pulled out Gene's journal and the
long leather-bound ledger where he had jotted down his poems. Opening
the journal, he flipped through the pages. Gene's writing—that firm,
graceful script—was as familiar to him as his own. The words blurred and
he blinked fiercely.

For a time he read by firelight. Read about the boredom and monotony
of life on the aerodrome when they weren't flying. Read about the exhil-
aration of when they were in the air hunting. Read about that final leave
together in Arras. A faint smile touched his mouth. They had walked a
lot that weekend, exploring the ruins outside the village and the caves
they called "Baume aux pigeons." Gene had talked about Diogenes and
St. Vedast and the Vikings and the Benedictines. In the evenings they had
stayed in the grand old hotels with their faded grandeur—lace-trimmed
sheets and muted tapestries of noblemen hunting boars and lions and uni-
corns. They dined in the restaurants on chipped china and mismatched
polished silver and watched each other's faces in the candlelight. For that
brief time the front had seemed far away although not a night passed that
they did not lie in each other's arms and listen to the distant thunder of
guns.

Bat read about himself. Gene saw too bloody much. His smile faded, remembering Orton, but there was nothing here that anyone else could not read.

A photo fell out: him standing beside one of the old BE-8s.

Bat studied his own cocky grin and tried to remember being that young. Tried to remember what had amused him so. It was like looking at a stranger. He turned back to Gene's papers. What had Orton found? They were always careful, always circumspect. Always guarding their words, schooling their expressions. And shuffling quickly through the papers, Bat resolved he would not be careless in this; it was the only thing left he could do for Gene. He rose and put the journal and his own photo on the fire. The flames leapt with a hungry *whoosh*.

Quickly, he went through the poems.

> *Somber is the night...*
>
> *A broken roof whence the rain drip, drip, drops...*
>
> *Flung toward heaven's flowering rage...*

He knew them all, knew every one of Gene's poems. Knew them from Gene's bellyaching about rhythm and meter and his pains to find the exact word to the final, astonishingly lovely results. Not that Gene ever considered any of these "final" results. Bat had no idea if they were any good. He wasn't sure he'd really even understood them—but he'd liked them…very much. Anyway, if Bat didn't understand half of them, surely this lot could safely be sent back to the maiden aunt in Quebec?

He heard the drone of a plane and looked ceilingward. Digs, too, raised his head listening.

One plane.

B Flight arriving home? He listened, automatically counting. But there was only the one plane—and it was too early for B Flight to be returning to the roost.

Odd. They were sharing the drome with 19 Squadron. Perhaps it was a pilot from the other squadron returning from reconnaissance? Archie kept silent, so it wasn't enemy aircraft.

The engine faded away into silence. Digs lowered his head to his paws. Bat returned to sorting papers.

Major Chase would write the official letter. There was only the aunt left. Aunt Monique. "Aunt Moneybags" Gene had called her. Bat would have liked to write to her as well, but he couldn't seem to think of any-thing that an elderly woman in a faraway country would wish to hear. *You should have been kinder to that small boy. He grew up to be a fine man, a decent, brave, generous man—he should have had longer. We should have had longer...*

His fingers lingered on the fragile paper of the poem Gene had been working on that final night.

The lamps are lit and there is the thunder of guns in the east

You lay your head upon my breast and smile...

The words blurred. Christ, he was tired. He pinched the bridge of his nose.

When he opened his eyes, Digby, settled before the fire, was watching him with the steady intent regard of a dog who knows something is up.

"It was over before I knew he was in trouble," Bat told the little bulldog. "That's some comfort, I suppose."

Digs continued to stare at him, as though requiring further explana-tion. But there was no explanation. Nothing made much sense anymore—hadn't for a long time. The only thing that had made sense was Gene—the way they felt about each other—and most people wouldn't think that made sense either.

Quickly now, Bat went through Gene's books, and stacked them neatly on the desk. Unlike his own motley collection of paperback west-erns and detective stories, Gene's library mostly consisted of history and philosophy books and a few "Georgian" poetry collections. Bat tied the books with string and picked up the photo of Gene.

Most people would have thought it a good likeness, but you couldn't tell from the photograph that Gene's eyes had been brown, not black, or that there were red glints in his hair or a pale smattering of freckles across his nose. You couldn't tell any of that. You couldn't tell from the steady way he stared back at the camera that he had a trick of raising his left eyebrow, giving him a quizzical look. You couldn't tell from his photo…how funny he had been; how he could always make you laugh. You couldn't tell the way his hands had felt on Bat's body or the way his hair had smelled or the way he used to whistle when he was happy.

Bat put the photo with the books, rifled through the drawers one last time, but there was nothing left. Empty wooden boxes. Nothing to hurt or disappoint here. He gathered the photos of Gene's family and the few letters from home, bound them neatly and put those with the rest of his things.

The poems…he waited till the last. He didn't want to put them in the fire. When he read them he could hear Gene speaking each line.

Well, what do you think about this then? 'Unlucky as magpies…'

What the hell could anyone make of that? But Gene would have feared someone reading between the lines. And Bat had given his word. He rose, gently laid the thin pages across the logs and watched them catch, watched the flames turn blue and the papers blacken.

Digs raised his head and watched them go, panting softly as the papers went in a blaze, then turned to regard Bat.

His task finished, Bat stood unmoving. Was there something left to do? He couldn't think what it might be. If he'd only thought to do this last night it might have made a difference—or had it even then been too late? No use thinking of that now. In any case it would almost be a relief to put paid to all this. It seemed an awfully long time since he had truly slept. Days. The last time he'd slept, Gene and he had held each other through the night.

It seemed strange that they had no presentiment, no foreshadowing…

At last he turned, put the keys to the desk atop the stack of books, and pulled his revolver out. All the while Digs watched with bright, intelligent eyes.

"I don't think there's a way around it," Bat told him. "He'd never have tried it on if he hadn't proof, you know. It's bound to come out—and then what?"

Digs' bat ears twitched.

"Too right. If they don't hang me for murder, they'll court-martial me for conduct unbecoming."

As though the dog had put forward some argument, the man said, "You know as well as I do it's the honorable thing. Be much worse the other way. Worse for everyone."

It didn't take much to pull a trigger, yet he stood unmoving as the china clock ticked away long minutes.

Madame Fournier was three parts deaf. Still, not a pleasant sight to come down to in the morning.

No. He couldn't do that to Madame Fournier who had been so kind to him and Gene.

He turned from the desk and made his way quietly through the dark house. Digs followed at his heels breathing in his enthusiastic asthmatic way.

In the kitchen Bat knelt, ruffling the silky ears.

"Cheerio, Digs," he whispered, rising. "Behave yourself."

The dog began to whine and scratch as soon as Bat locked the door behind him.

"*Quiet*, you," Bat ordered.

The grass sparkled wetly in the moonlight as he started across the lawn toward the old hexagonal gazebo.

He tried the door. It wasn't locked and it swung open onto a mostly empty room. Melancholy moonlight spilled through the broken slats in the roof illuminating a few pieces of wicker furniture and some faded cushions. The room smelled of dead leaves and dry summers. It smelled of the past. Of people and times gone forever.

"This is beginning to feel like a lost cause," someone said behind him, and Bat nearly leapt out of his skin.

Cowboy stepped out of the shadows of the surrounding trees. Bat tried and failed to think of a thing to say.

"I thought I told you to wait for me," Cowboy said, and Bat finally found his tongue.

"What are you doing here?"

"Looking for you."

"Why?"

"Told you I'd see you later."

Had he? Perhaps he had. It all felt like a very long time ago.

Bat said, "I did as you said. Then I remembered—"

"What? You had an urgent appointment with your Maker?"

"Sorry?"

"The pea shooter. Or were you planning on sittin' in the moonlight and bagging a few trench rabbits?"

Bat looked down at the Webley. He'd nearly forgotten he still held it.

Cowboy waited.

Bat jerked out, "Did you—?"

And Cowboy said easily, "Said I would, didn't I?"

He must have been more strung up than he knew because the old schoolboy stammer returned. "W-what did you do?"

"Don't fret. I took care of him."

Proof of how tired he was, Bat couldn't seem to think how to frame the question he needed to ask. Finally, he said, "I sh-shouldn't have let you. I'm grateful of course. But it was a mistake to drag you into it. I should have gone to Chase straightaway. This doesn't change anything."

Cowboy laughed. "Now there we disagree."

Bat couldn't see the joke. "Tonight," he began. "Earlier. *Why* were you following me?"

He felt Cowboy's scrutiny, although the gloom did not allow a reading of his expression. "Guess I thought you might be feeling lonesome," Cowboy said, adding as Bat opened his mouth, "and blow your brains out."

Bat's throat closed. "That's a…a bloody extraordinary thing to say."

"Ain't it, though?"

He heard the irony and was reminded that he was standing there clutching his service revolver.

It stung something back to life inside him. "Surely even you can understand…"

He stopped—hearing the priggishness of that—before Cowboy repeated quietly, *"Even me?"*

"I don't m-mean it that way," he said quickly. "I apologize. You've been kind in your way."

Cowboy's laugh was genuine. "That's your idea of an apology, is it? And you folks say Americans are rude!"

Bat put his hand to his eyes. "Look, I put that badly. I mean only that…this is my problem. Despite your…help, I shall have to deal with the consequences."

"By blowing your goddamned fool head off?"

"Oh, leave off, can't you?" Bat cried. "I didn't ask you to involve yourself. I'm sorry it happened. Damned sorry. It doesn't change anything. If you want the truth, I can't face the disgrace. It isn't only me—my name. It's my family. Gene's name. Gene's memory. Can't you understand?"

"I understand Roberts is dead. His feelings don't come into it. Are you afraid of being hanged as a murderer or going to prison for being homosexual?"

"Either. Both, goddamn it!"

"What happened to keeping a stiff upper lip? Okay, okay," Cowboy said quickly as Bat drew himself up. He seemed to be thinking. "So you can't live with the shame or whatthefuckever. But that doesn't explain what the hell you were doing today, does it?"

"Perhaps you know what you're talking about. I don't."

"Today. Before you tangled with Orton. What were you doing up there in the clouds this afternoon?"

Bat stared. He couldn't understand everyone's preoccupation with one bloody dogfight.

Cowboy said, "You didn't know anything about Sid Orton trying to blackmail you when you were doing your damnedest to get yourself blown out of the sky."

"That's the fucking *job*."

"The fuckin' job is to patrol inside enemy lines and knock down anything that gets in our way. And to do that we need every plane and every pilot."

True enough—as far as it went.

"Not going to be a hell of a lot of use to anyone in prison, am I? Or hanged."

"You're not going to prison—if you can keep your head. Which, I will admit, appears to be harder than I'd've thought given what a cool bastard you always seemed to be."

The futility of it all overwhelmed Bat for an instant and he groaned, "What possible *difference* can it make? Today or tomorrow, the end will be the same."

What possible difference could it make to *Cowboy*? And yet, apparently it did. He said stubbornly, "Every man counts. You know that. That's why they keep sending up wet-behind-the-ears kids in planes made of sticks and wires. If you're going to throw your life away, at least go out fighting. Take a few Jerries with you."

Neither of them spoke.

On the other side of the lodge, a rooster began to crow. Better than an alarm clock, that bloody bird. It would be light in less than an hour.

Another night got through; Bat felt a twinge of relief. The nights were the worst. Sunrise meant dawn patrol, and if he'd made it this far…

Cowboy said, "I'll tell you what I think. I think you're grieving for your—for Gene. You're looking for a reason to pack it in."

"That's fucking ridic—"

"And I think if you show some of the steel you use to hold this outfit together, you'll discover pretty quick being alive is a hell of a lot better than the alternative."

Bat opened his mouth but he simply hadn't the energy to fight Cowboy, and Cowboy was still waiting. Bat said slowly, "I never thanked you for today."

"I'm not looking for thanks." Cowboy added as Bat started to speak, "Not for that. But you're right. You do owe me, and I do plan on collecting."

Bat gaped as Cowboy moved toward him in the darkness, pulled him into his arms, and kissed him.

Despite his harsh words and rough hands, it was the briefest of kisses—a warm brush of lips—like a sun-warmed blossom skimming Bat's mouth. Had it been anything else, he'd have reacted violently. As it was… for one bewildered moment he couldn't move.

Then he drew in a sharp breath and kissed Cowboy back fiercely, wanting the feel of that hard hot mouth on his own—needing to feel, to be touched—craving it. That desperate hunger for physical contact took Bat aback, shocked him, but he couldn't help himself.

The kiss seemed endless. Cowboy's hand went to the back of Bat's neck, fastening, drawing him closer.

When he suspected he was about to die of suffocation, Bat pulled away, gasping. His heart was racing violently.

"Are you mad? What are you doing?"

"You seemed to have a pretty good idea."

Bat wiped his mouth—wet from Cowboy's hot kisses. Cowboy grabbed him and kissed him again, hard and brief. Like the final word in an argument.

"And don't forget it," he said.

They stood there breathing hard, and Bat felt raucous laughter well in his throat. The knot that had wedged itself there ever since Gene went down kept it from escaping in hysteria.

"See you at five," Cowboy said.

After the sound of his footsteps in the fallen leaves died away, Bat walked slowly back to the lodge, unlocked the door, and went inside. It wasn't until he closed the door behind him, leaning weakly against it, that he realized Cowboy had walked off with his revolver.

CHAPTER TWO

*O*ne of the best pieces of flying advice Bat got was from his brother Algernon who flew reconnaissance at the start of the war.

"Think down to the gunners," Algie had said. "Treat it like a game. You're pitting your skill against theirs. It's a kind of sport, really. And remember, a chasse machine is rarely brought down by Archie. You're too fast for them. There are plenty of ways to outfox them. The best pilots are the best sportsmen." He'd ruffled Bat's hair, adding grimly, "Or the chaps who learn to stop feeling anything at all."

At the time Bat couldn't imagine what he meant.

The first two weeks were the most dangerous to a new pilot. They didn't see anything—and what they did see, they didn't understand. Shell fire scared the devil out of them and the Hun pilots they ran into were all hardened pros with several weeks' experience in Russia or the Balkans. By 1916 the RFC was losing nearly a pilot a day; Gene worked it out once and told Bat the average life expectancy of an allied aviator was eleven days. Of course there were the old hands like him and Gene who defied the odds. But no one defied them forever.

Bat knew Jackson was for it from the minute he was up in the air. Bat had given orders to rendezvous two thousand over field and once they assembled, he'd headed northeast with the rest of A Flight falling into formation behind.

The new fliers got the oldest machines, and Jackson was in one of the battered Spads. It climbed slowly. Tubby and Varlik did their best to shepherd him along, diving under and climbing up again to keep him aligned. Ambrose was on Bat's left, in Gene's former position. Cowboy was a dark silhouette on his right as they reached the cloud bank and began to climb.

As they rose into the crystalline air and the rising sun gilded the fleecy floor of clouds beneath them in amber and rose gold, Bat felt an echo of the old joy to be airborne once more. All around him the rest of A Flight surfaced at widely scattered points through the rolling cloud cover. Cowboy crested and gave him that little nod.

Bat nodded back. His revolver had been lying on the seat when he climbed into the cockpit that morning. Color warmed his face and he was grateful for the distance between their machines.

A Flight formed up once more and turned northward. Far below them were the green valleys, dark forest, shining rivers of France… Then they were over the lines. Although they were too far up to hear anything one could see by the thousands of tiny bursts of light that the day's business had already begun. Shell bursts and muzzle flashes winked and sparkled miles beneath them. But they weren't crossing over enemy lines until the replacements had a chance to get the lay of the land; instead A Flight headed west along the sector.

The twinkling lights faded and the battlefront—a jagged, winding scar of desert slashed through the green and pastoral land—lay directly beneath them. They were now four kilometers within the French lines. Clouds of smoke bloomed like scarlet-edged roses—interrupted at intervals by puffs of black-and-white shell bursts.

A Flight turned northward and then back. Bat glanced in his mirror and Jackson was gone.

Just like that he had dropped out of the sky.

Bat swore without heat. That was all the time to react there was for at that moment a patrol of Spads and Fokkers came out of the sun like a swarm of hornets out of their hive. The air was alive with the deafening roar of engines as aircraft maneuvered for position, climbing and dropping while all the while the webbing of white streamers from machine gun bullet tracers wound around A Flight. It was a kind of deadly ballet—spinning, diving, banking—as they dodged each other's machines and tried to make sure they fired at black crosses and not the roundels and tail cockades of their own planes.

Bat spared a quick glance for his altimeter, temperature, and pressure dials, and when he looked up again a Fokker was coming at him, looming up like a freight train on a motion picture screen. It drove straight toward Bat, firing as it came. It was a tactic that would have succeeded with a new pilot, whether the bullets struck home or not. Bat responded with the familiar surge of cold resolve, opening the throttle and hurtling forward—and he'd have rammed the other plane if the German hadn't lost his nerve and dived.

Making a tight turn, nearly on his wingtip, Bat shot after him and managed to settle on his tail, firing five or six rounds while the Fokker zigged and zagged until he finally lost control and plummeted down, engine smoking.

Bat looked around and saw Ambrose in hot pursuit of a Spad, machine guns blazing. Tubby was doggedly chasing another into the blue distance. Varlik was still in one piece, and Heath…

Fuck.

He caught movement out of the corner of his eye. Cowboy glided into place beside him and nodded. Bat tightly nodded back, part of his mind still on bloody Heath. But he was surprised. Generally Cowboy preferred to hunt on his own. He'd stayed with the pack today. Expecting a repeat of Bat's shaky performance of the day before? He needn't have worried. Bat had resigned himself to facing down whatever the day brought.

He looked again for young Jackson, hoping that he had missed him in the maelstrom of the battle, but there was no sign of the khaki and tan Spad.

Already the dogfight was breaking up; the Boche planes out of ammunition and raveled out by the wind were fleeing back to their lines. Most aerial battles didn't last longer than two or three minutes as they only carried enough ammunition to fire for about fifty seconds. But Bat's fuel tank was still a quarter full, he had plenty of ammo and, unlike Cowboy's bullet-scarred machine, his plane hadn't sustained any new damage.

Bat signaled to Cowboy to make for home with the rest of the patrol, and gave her full rudder, heading back to see if he could spot where Jackson had gone down. There was always a chance the boy had managed to land safely.

The wind was kicking up now—rain clouds rolling in from the north. He rode the buffeting, scanning the green expanse below.

Cowboy stuck to Bat's machine—irritating as a burr beneath one's saddle—but Bat knew he couldn't endanger the other pilot or risk losing his plane by trying to shake him. In any case, it wasn't necessary for he quickly spotted Jackson's shattered plane in an open field. It was in flames.

Bat circled round once more to see if there was any sign of life. Unsurprisingly, there was nothing but fire and smoke. He glanced back at Cowboy, but what he could see of his face beneath the goggles was unrevealing.

He turned homeward once more, Cowboy trailing after.

* * * * *

"So your daddy's a duke," Cowboy said, blue eyes watching Bat over the rim of his glass. He drank, set the glass down. His lips were wet from the ale, and Bat had a sudden, uncomfortably vivid recollection of what that firm mouth had felt like pressing his own.

"An earl, actually," he replied quellingly.

Cowboy was not quelled.

"So what's that make you?"

"The youngest of five sons."

Cowboy grimaced. "What do they call you? What's your title?"

"The Honourable, but no one calls—"

"What kind of a moniker is 'Bat'?" Cowboy interrupted. "What's your *name*?"

"Aubrey."

Undisturbed by Bat's terse response, Cowboy offered that wide, white grin. "Aubrey? That's sweet."

"Go. To. Hell."

Cowboy laughed.

They had arrived back at base after first crawl without further incident. Bat had made his report to Major Chase, grabbed a quick kip, and taken out the afternoon patrol for an uneventful foray behind enemy lines. Now A Flight was done for the day. Bat had walked into the mess with the intention of drinking himself slowly and steadily into oblivion. If Gene were alive they would have—but Gene was not alive, and somehow Bat had to unwind that screaming pitch of tension that had kept him moving for the past two days—unwind without pulling apart because in twelve hours he had to lead A Flight out again.

Captain Sears, broad-shouldered and dark with a long seam of scar down his tanned face, stopped by the table. "Hard luck about…" He trailed vaguely. These days it was always hard luck about someone or other.

Sears was 19 Squadron's A Flight commander. He shared a friendly rivalry with Bat—Sears currently down two kills. Three if—once—Bat's morning's work had been confirmed.

"Jackson," Bat supplied automatically.

"Replacements?"

"By tomorrow, according to Chase," Bat said.

Two patrols a day, two hours each patrol. Now and again they put in as many as six hours, but Wing discouraged it. Pilots at the front were burning out fast enough and someone had to be in shape to go up every single day weather permitting.

When they weren't flying, they slept. Or drank. Or read. Bat had grown very familiar with the works of Zane Grey and Max Brand. Some chaps played cards or wrote letters, but mostly they slept a good deal.

Sears moved off and Cowboy said, as though there had been no interruption, "So what are your brothers doing these days? One of 'em's a big muckety-muck in the War Office, right?"

"Archie," Bat said reluctantly. He didn't feel like chatting with Cowboy. He didn't want to spend any time with him at all if he could help it. He didn't want to think or answer questions. He simply wanted to get drunk enough to sleep—to sleep too deeply to dream. "Algie and Cyril are gone—since the first year of the war. Dorian is with the Grand Fleet in the North Sea."

"And you were at Cambridge when you decided to join up?"

"Magdalene College, yes."

Christ. Picnics with pretty girls and punting on the Cam. Taking tea with dons and playing cricket. A lifetime ago.

"What were you studying?"

Bat shrugged a negligent shoulder. "Suppose I was eventually headed for the Foreign Office. That's what the pater wanted."

"You always do what the pater wants?"

Fastening a cool eye on him, Bat said, "Clearly not."

And Cowboy grinned. He seemed—as usual—very relaxed. Bat had a reputation for being unflappable, but in fact, he lived on his nerves, and his nerves had been strung far too tight for far too long. He found this… insouciance of Cowboy's grating. And bewildering.

He said, "You haven't yet told me what you did about…him."

Cowboy's white grin broadened. "You don't really want to discuss it *here*?" He glanced meaningfully around the crowded mess.

No one was paying them any mind. Varlik was once again singing "Roses of Picardy" in duet with the gramophone. Ambrose and Heath were engaged in some drinking game. Tubby was busily cheating at solitaire.

Everyone else seemed riveted by the antics of a half-starved monkey that B Flight's Berckman had brought back from leave.

Bat said slowly, "According to Sergeant Lamb, Orton is supposed to have scarpered. AWOL."

The smile faded from Cowboy's face. "You didn't question Lamb about Orton?" he demanded.

Bat shook his head. "Orton was assigned to my bus. Lamb had to fill in for him. He happened to mention it."

Cowboy was eyeing him with a dark and doubtful gaze. "You know to keep your trap shut, right?"

Bat smiled tightly, containing the flash of hostility he felt. The unpleasant idea occurred that he could not afford to quarrel with Cowboy. Could not afford to fall out with him. Not given the secret they shared.

Perhaps some similar idea cropped up in Cowboy's mind. He said, "Why don't we get out of here and go someplace we can talk."

It was not a suggestion. He stood, waiting. Bat stared up at him—and realized that here too he had no choice.

He followed Cowboy out of the mess, and the last notes of "Roses of Picardy" died behind them as the door swung shut.

"Let's walk down to the lodge," Cowboy said. "You look like you could use some shut-eye. When was the last time you slept? Really slept, I mean?"

"How is that your affair?" Bat spoke tersely, his resentment of this high-handedness growing momentarily.

Cowboy's big hand wrapped around Bat's upper arm, warningly. "It's my *affair* because if you make some stupid mistake 'cause you're too tired to think straight, we're both sunk."

Bat roughly freed himself, uncaring of who might be watching—even knowing as he did so, that Cowboy had a point. He was too weary to be careful, his emotions dangerously near the surface, and now he was more than a little foxed. After months of hiding his feelings—from even himself—the cracks were beginning to show.

He said, "I can't stay on at the lodge. Those were Gene's digs, not mine. Not officially."

"The old lady won't care, will she? Could probably use the extra dough."

He thought of Madame Fournier's kindness—most likely due to the infirmities of age. A God-fearing woman, Madame would not knowingly have sheltered Gene and him if she'd any notion of what they got up to in that little room where her son once slept. There was always a foolish—dangerous—temptation to believe that there was understanding, perhaps sympathy, in silence when in fact all there was, was ignorance.

"I don't know," he said. "I don't care. I can't stay there now."

"Don't be too hasty," Cowboy said cryptically, in an uncanny echo of Orton's threat. When Bat stared at him, uncomprehending, he added, "A little privacy would be useful."

For what? But Bat did not ask the question. He was increasingly certain he did not want to know the answer.

They walked down to the lodge in silence filled only by the crunch of their boots and the occasional song of a woodlark.

"You think the birds talk to each other in French?" Cowboy asked, and that bit of whimsy won a smile from Bat. The walk in the cool air had helped clear his head. He forgot his earlier annoyance.

"Possibly."

Cowboy was also smiling. His eyes slanted Bat's way, and Bat felt himself coloring though he wasn't sure why. He looked away hastily. Luminous white mushrooms grew at the roots of the ancient trees forming the leafy tunnel overhead. Wild berries lined the road, glossy purple and scarlet in the gloom. It smelled richly of damp earth and moldering leaves—and the leather of Cowboy's jacket and the soap he used.

"It's a lot like home," Bat said. Or at least the home of his boyhood. "Like Kent. Feels different, though. Feels…French." Gene had said you could see the Flemish influence in the village names and architecture. Gene would have been an architect if not for the interruption of war.

"Doesn't feel like America, that's for sure."

The red roof of the hunting lodge appeared before them, smoke drifting from the white stone fireplace. Cowboy touched Bat's arm, and they left the path and cut across the field to the gazebo where they could be assured no one would overhear their conversation.

"I shall have to think what to do about Digsby," Bat was saying as Cowboy pushed open the rickety door. "Gene's dog. I suppose Madame might keep him on—"

He broke off as startled doves took wing through the holes in the roof. The door slammed shut behind them, closing them in with the musty scent of decaying wood and dead leaves and bird nests. Cowboy's arms went around Bat.

Shocked into immobility, Bat recovered fast and shoved him away. Cowboy eyed him narrowly and then shoved back—harder—pushing Bat against the rough wall, big fists locked in Bat's tunic, one knee thrust between Bat's long legs.

"Just settle down, Aubrey. We're going to do this." His face was dark, filled with a ruthless intensity that started Bat's heart rabbiting.

"Like hell." His simmering resentment crackled into life, but beneath the anger was excitement. Part of him welcomed the idea of fighting Cowboy, part of him…

"N-no," he got out.

"Y-yes," Cowboy mocked—but there was a bewildering thread of gentleness, as though he were simply teasing, as though they were playing.

It was confusing. He told himself what Cowboy needed was a good thrashing, and what Bat needed was to deliver it, but…as his eyes met that dark blue gaze, he felt strangely irresolute. A peculiar languor gripped his body. Cowboy's breath was warm against his face. His mouth tingled recalling the feel and taste of Cowboy's, and he wondered what would happen if he let Cowboy put his hands on him. Cowboy's groin ground against his own, Cowboy's muscular thigh pressed against Bat's genitals. Cowboy's big hands moved over Bat's chest, smoothing his uniform, feeling for the buttons.

The idea alarmed him—but not nearly as much as it should have. In fact, maybe he wasn't alarmed so much as…stimulated. He put his hands on Cowboy's to stop him, but instead he was pressing those big hands closer, wanting to be fondled, caressed.

Cowboy pulled Bat close again, and Bat knew a kind of relief that he wasn't being given a choice, that this choice was being taken from him; all he had to do was not fight too hard.

He closed his eyes, raising his face, and Cowboy began to kiss him hotly, his mouth bruising, his teeth biting Bat's lips. Bat groaned into Cowboy's mouth as the other man's big hands ran over the long lines of Bat's body, tugging at his tunic, and Bat began to tug at his uniform, wanting the bulk of cloth removed from between his arching, trembling body and the warm weight of Cowboy's hands. His cock felt swollen, heavy, constricted within the confines of his clothing.

"Easy, easy," Cowboy murmured, like he was soothing a nervous colt, undoing the fastening at Bat's tunic collar, fingers warm against Bat's throat.

Bat swallowed hard as Cowboy pressed a soft kiss in the naked hollow of his throat. He opened his eyes and Cowboy's face was absorbed, grave. His lashes rose and he met Bat's gaze. He seemed to be waiting for something.

What?

Seemingly of their own volition, Bat's hands rose and he responded in kind, shoving aside Cowboy's heavy jacket, working the fastenings of Cowboy's tunic—careful of buttons, careful with His Majesty's property— they couldn't afford to explain untoward damage. Through the coarse wool of their uniforms, their groins ground urgently against each other, and then their hot mouths met again in frenzied hunger.

The night before Bat had been too startled to truly acknowledge what was happening, but now…he was almost stunned by the intimacy of it, the silky rasp of Cowboy's jaw against his own, the pressure of two mouths, the mingling of breath and saliva, the unaccustomed taste of another man, the slick surprise of tongue—

He was gasping for air beneath the impact when Cowboy tore his mouth away, breathing equally hard. His hands slid down Bat's long, thinly muscled back, finding his way to Bat's waistband and fly. His hand slipped inside, rough but caressing, feeling Bat up with gentle but thorough expertise. Bat hissed but didn't speak, didn't say the words, even as Cowboy worked his way through layers of cloth to bare skin. He was longing for Cowboy to free him, to wrap his hand around Bat's rigid prick, but instead Cowboy's hard, unsteady fingers found the entrance to Bat's body.

Bat jumped. "No," he said hoarsely.

"Hell, yes," Cowboy retorted a little unevenly.

"No." And Bat started to fight him.

Cowboy let him go so abruptly Bat staggered, falling back against the wall.

"He's dead," Cowboy said. "You're still alive, whether you like it or not."

Rage washed through Bat's body. It was followed by astonished realization. "You don't understand," he said. "Gene and I weren't—we never— did that." The very idea of it made him feel very odd indeed, made his mouth dry and his legs weak.

Cowboy went so still he merged with and vanished into the shadows, leaving Bat feeling as though he were alone. It was an unexpectedly grim feeling. He managed to control his voice.

"Are you going to say something?"

"I'm not sure what to say. You must have done more than hold hands."

The bubble of emotion that never seemed to leave Bat's chest expanded and he couldn't seem to breathe. He struggled with it.

So it was mostly relief when Cowboy's powerful arms folded him close once more. "I'll never understand the English," Cowboy muttered. He bent his head and his lips grazed the nape of Bat's neck. Bat shivered and pressed his face into the strong column of Cowboy's throat.

Of course they had done more than hold hands. Eventually. Given their natural reticence—and fear—he sometimes wondered how they had got together at all. How they had ever moved from lingering glances and long talks about navigation and topography. But they had. They'd held each other, they had kissed, they had—but *this*, no. Bat, even less experienced than Gene, had suggested certain things, but Gene had been very clear. And that had been all right by Bat—he'd been slightly ashamed for suggesting it.

Heat flooded his face, which he kept buried in Cowboy's neck. "We tried to keep to the…the Platonic ideal."

"Jesus."

"I mean, we tried—"

"I know what you mean," Cowboy said amazingly. "I read the *Symposium*. I went to Harvard."

And it was Bat's turn to be speechless. He raised his head, staring at Cowboy's face in the gloom.

Cowboy laughed. "What did you think? I rode in from the plains on Old Paint?"

Frankly…yes. Hadn't Cowboy rather acted that way? Was it merely a pose? Or perhaps his strange sense of humor?

"Why'd you let us all think—what we thought?"

"What do I care what a bunch of English stuffed shirts think?"

Bat tried to throw him off, but Cowboy held him in place, back to the wall, and despite the cool words his hands stroked the other pilot in long tremulous caresses, warm hands sliding down Bat's flanks and back.

Bat's body responded with a treacherous weakness. He had to bite his kiss-swollen lips against the moans threatening to tear out of his throat.

"Not you. I care what you think," Cowboy's voice was low.

"Oh, bully for me," Bat drawled thickly. But it felt good. Very good to have Cowboy touching him. Despite his suspicion and resentment, Bat clutched Cowboy tightly, not wanting it to end, and when Cowboy's hand slid down over his taut buttocks, palming him, he tried not to tense, tried to relax. The brush of fingertips on bare skin felt startlingly nice and started a peculiar ache in his chest.

This was something he had not foreseen. That he might enjoy Cowboy's sexual trespass. That he might welcome it. He struggled with guilt and pain and loyalty to Gene while Cowboy stroked him and whispered soothing things like he expected Bat to start bucking and biting.

"Yeah, you're beautiful, aren't you? Sharp and shining like the edge of the sun." He kissed the corner of Bat's mouth, his erection thrusting aggressively into Bat's groin.

And Bat began to move against Cowboy, longing for—needing more. Cowboy's finger slipped right inside his body and an odd thrill shot through Bat. He shuddered all down the length of his body and half swallowed a protest.

"Easy, easy," Cowboy whispered hotly against his ear. "You want it and you need it. Hell, we both need it. It doesn't have to mean anything more than that. Why should it?"

He kissed away any objection Bat might have made while all the time his finger kept stroking inside Bat's body, nothing tentative about that touch, fingering Bat up with tantalizing expertise while he kept him pinned against the wall, not letting him move. And Bat turned his mouth from Cowboy's and heaved in great gulps of air like he'd flown far too high, putting all thought away and opening his thighs to give Cowboy greater access.

*Dear God that felt...*it made him melt inside, made him ache, made his body keen silently, desperate for more—much more. Embarrassing sounds escaped him, abject sounds, and Cowboy kissed them all away, smiling, seeming pleased as Bat grew more frantic pushing down instinctively against Cowboy's hand, trying to take his finger deeper.

When Cowboy withdrew his hand Bat was aware of stinging disappointment. But then Cowboy guided him around to face the wall, and Bat planted his hands against its splintered roughness, spreading his legs, instinctively readying himself. He was shivering in a kind of terror, knowing what must happen now, fearing it—and craving it.

He heard the rustle of cloth and then Cowboy's fingers were back but now they were slippery with oil. Blunt fingers cupped his balls, cradling them, caressing, and then one blunt finger traced the quivering entrance of Bat's body once more.

"Ready as you're going to be," Cowboy said. "Just relax…that's it…"

Bat swallowed dryly. He knew a moment of dizzy alarm. What was he surrendering to? What liberties was he allowing Cowboy? Allowing? Too late to stop it now. He knew that.

The big American was warm and solid all down the length of his back, the open flaps of his tunic tickling Bat's bare skin as he leaned over him, his breath hot on the nape of Bat's neck, his knees pressing into the back of Bat's, hard hands locked on his hips. Cowboy's cock lanced lightly between the cheeks of Bat's arse—a trace of sticky wet—and the implicit threat, the tease of alarmed pleasure, focused Bat's thoughts. This was no betrayal of Gene. This was lust. Animal lust. Nothing to do with what had been between himself and Gene, and perhaps he did need it—this disconcerting proof that he was still alive. He didn't care if it hurt; he rather hoped it did.

Bracing himself as Cowboy's cock pushed slowly into him, Bat was astonished to find his body grudgingly accommodating the larger man's organ, though he had to grit his jaw to keep from crying out. It did hurt. Not unbearably so, however, and the pain freed him of guilt.

Slowly…so very slowly Cowboy shoved deep into Bat's body until Bat could feel the softness of hair against his buttocks. Cowboy thrust against him once, and Bat quivered. They were locked so tight that he could feel Cowboy's heart hammering against his back.

"You want this, don't you?" Cowboy whispered against Bat's ear.

In answer, Bat wriggled, pushing back a little, trying to find himself a bit of room to breathe. To think. But one of Cowboy's hands moved its grip from Bat's hip, coming beneath his belly and finding his cock, closing around it with easy expertise, pumping as though caressing a rifle. That helped, and again Bat's body responded eagerly, his cock filling and lengthening once more.

Cowboy kissed the back of Bat's neck and it was sweet. Bat relaxed into Cowboy's hold, resting his forehead on the wall, smelling the biting pungency of wood and sweat.

Cowboy was thrusting into him now, slow, steady, rhythmic thrusts, his heavy cock like a piston pushing into the cylinder of Bat's body. In. Out. In. Out. It was unbelievable—unbelievable that Bat would allow this, and yet he was standing docilely permitting Cowboy to take him. Cowboy was grunting fiercely in Bat's ear and oddly it began to excite Bat: the honesty of that rough animal pleasure. He groaned into the knotholes of the paneling.

"Yeah, that's right, Aubrey," Cowboy rasped. "That's right, sweetheart. You know it, don't you? You know you belong to me now."

Bat shook his head. "Y-you're…fucking mad," he jerked out as Cowboy shoved into him, but Cowboy laughed.

"You're only fooling yourself." He used his knee to push Bat's legs farther to give himself better access, making Bat take him more deeply, and staggeringly, Bat acquiesced, pushing back on Cowboy's engorged cock with a helpless moan.

He let Cowboy fuck him, submitted to Cowboy's rough and thorough possession until his legs felt too wobbly to support him. Then Cowboy changed his angle, drove into Bat one more time and it was like lightning striking.

A white blaze lit up Bat's body, nerves igniting. His breath caught, he shuddered all over, releasing his seed over the larger man's hand, the wall, the floor...flooded with physical sensation—and unexpected emotion. At nearly the same instant, Cowboy groaned deep down in his chest and grabbed Bat tight against his torso, spilling blood-hot semen into him. That splash of liquid heat recalled Bat to himself.

What had he done? He had given into the basest of desires. He had let Cowboy use him, mark him like a wolf spraying its territory. He knew only too well what Gene would make of such brutish behavior, and yet...he felt very little. Perhaps he was simply numb.

Bat slumped against the wall, panting. After a time Cowboy's cock slipped out of him.

Bat's limbs were trembling—hands too—and his cock was suddenly unbearably sensitive. The odd thing was Cowboy seemed to understand that and he became tender—almost woman-tender so that Bat could have wept with humiliating gratitude. It was unmanly but he wanted this, wanted to be gentled, cared for. He breathed quietly against his arm as Cowboy cleaned him off with his soft linen handkerchief and then tucked him back inside his trousers. Then he drew Bat against him and they sat down—half collapsing on the faded old cushions of the dilapidated furniture.

For a time they sprawled there and Cowboy rocked Bat against him in a funny soothing way. Bat closed his eyes. The traitorous wish occurred that he and Gene would have done this, and then, even more traitorously, he realized he wanted nothing more than to sleep against this strong warm body and not think anymore.

Cowboy kissed his hair and his face and rocked him some more and Bat let himself drift.

He must have fallen deeply asleep because the next thing he knew Cowboy was saying softly, "Rise and shine, Aubrey. I gotta get back and you need some real sleep."

Bat blinked at him, nodded, and sat up. He ran a hand through his hair.

"All right?" Cowboy asked, and though he spoke brusquely, there was some remaining trace of that unexpected tenderness in his voice.

Bat nodded again. He had no words to express his confusion, his astonishment at what he'd done—what they had done.

They rose and dressed quickly, and then Cowboy went back to the airfield and Bat returned to the lodge.

Madame greeted him with pleasure and Digsby with outright joy. It was not until Bat had been persuaded into sitting down and eating a bowl of hot stew that he realized that Cowboy had still not told him what he had done with Orton's body.

CHAPTER THREE

There was no dawn patrol the next morning. The early morning rain rumbled down drowning the distant thunder of the guns and turning the château windows silver.

Bat had walked back from the lodge at first light, Digs trotting beside him. He breakfasted in the mess on croissants and hot coffee then spent the rest of the morning in the blue room napping and reading *Riders of the Purple Sage* while Digs snored next to the bed. Having slept deeply and dreamlessly the night before, Bat felt strangely peaceful now.

Just before noontime he went down to the mess. The lads—already restless with inactivity—were smoking and talking and playing cards; "Roses of Picardy" was playing as usual but for once no one was singing along.

Bat was both a little relieved and a little disappointed that Cowboy was not there. Not that he had much time to think about it. Mac was pouring him a drink as Ambrose approached with two uniformed youths in tow.

"Replacements," Ambrose told him, with a jerk of his head. "Burns and Pickering." To the shining-eyed fliers who snapped twin salutes and gazed at Bat with near awe, he said, "Captain Bryant. A Flight's leader—and the best fuckin' pilot in 44 Squadron."

"Gentlemen," Bat said. "At ease. We don't stand on ceremony here." Immediately the replacements began chattering about what an honor this was and how eager they were to begin showing the old Huns…

Bat glanced inquiringly at Ambrose who, interpreting his look correctly, said, "Eighteen hours for Burns. Pickering has sixteen."

"But we're fast learners, sir," Pickering put in quickly. "Top of our class."

"We will go up tomorrow, won't we, sir?" Burns added anxiously.

"You'll be going up this afternoon if the weather clears," Bat said.

The replacements beamed and Bat nodded pleasantly, took up his glass and moved down to the end of the bar where Tubby joined him a short while later.

"You know, old man, you're going to have to do something about Heath," Tubby informed him.

Bat looked up from *The Sunday Times*—collected and posted faithfully from home each week by Lady Edith Rowe, the girl he supposed he would marry if he survived the war. Since that was highly unlikely, he didn't worry much about it. Besides, Edie was a nice enough girl. A bit… aggressive, perhaps.

"What about Heath?" Bat inquired.

"You know damn well what about it. He's loafin' up there. We all know it. I can't think why you've let him off the hook this long."

Bat's jaw tightened. Yes. He knew. He could feel Heath's fear every time they went up. He knew that sick dread well—had gone through something similar after the first time he'd been shot down.

The trick was not giving yourself time to think about it.

And of course Bat was far more afraid of letting down his family, his name, his country than of being killed. Heath—well, things were rather different for Heath.

"Are you saying I'm not doing my job?" Bat asked coolly.

But Tubby wasn't intimidated. "You know what I'm saying."

Bat finally sighed. "Right. I'll have a word with him."

Tubby nodded, and they sat for a time lost in their own thoughts.

"Have you heard from Janet?" Bat inquired, shaking off his preoccupation.

Tubby opened his mouth to answer, but broke off to swing to his feet as Major Chase entered the room with a tall, gray-haired man of about sixty in a French uniform. Bat followed suit.

"At ease, gentlemen," Chase said. "This is Colonel Reynard of the National Gendarmerie."

A rare and watchful silence fell in the mess, broken only by Berkman's monkey, which apparently didn't hold a high opinion of the National Gendarmerie.

The colonel smiled faintly at the monkey's chatter. Berkman tossed his cap over the beast and it sat down, putting tiny pale hands on the sides of the cap and shifting it to see.

"Colonel Reynard has a small mystery for us," the major announced. "It appears that sometime after oh twenty-three hundred on Monday night, the nude body of a man fell from the sky and crashed through the henhouse roof of a Monsieur Dubois. Although the man wore no identity disc, he had a couple of tattoos. A skull with a dagger through its eye on one arm and a British lion on the other. I'm told these match the description of tattoos borne by Airman Mechanic 3rd Class Sidney Orton who went AWOL on Tuesday last."

There was dead silence and then someone—Tubby—began to laugh, jarring the shocked hush.

"Lieutenant Lovesby," Bat said automatically.

Colonel Reynard had been watching them all with his grave, rather sad blue eyes. His gaze fastened on Tubby.

"Sorry," Tubby muttered. "It's the thought of old Orton crashing in on the hens. They'll be off their egg-laying for the duration."

There was an uneasy ripple of laughter—Orton had not been well known—and those who knew him did not particularly like him, but the fellow was dead after all. Perhaps murdered. And by one of them. No one had missed the implication of a naked corpse dropping from the sky.

"Quite," Major Chase said. "No flight was logged for Monday night; however several people heard an aeroplane take off and land perhaps forty-five minutes later."

The door behind them opened, and Cowboy walked in.

"Did anyone s-see this plane?" Bat asked at the same instant. To his chagrin, his stammer was back. Years without a fucking problem and now he was chewing up words.

Major Chase eyed him—as did the Frenchman.

"Not that we have been able to discover so far," Major Chase said. "The colonel is asking whether anyone remembers anything that might prove helpful in his investigation."

"*His* investigation?" Bat said. "Sir, isn't this a matter for the military police?"

"Colonel Reynard began investigating this as a civilian death, but he's made remarkable progress in two days. And as we are guests in this country, Wing has directed that we work in conjunction with the civilian constabulary."

Bat felt the weight of another's gaze. He looked up and Cowboy stood by the piano watching him. And he could practically hear Cowboy telling him to shut it.

And perhaps Cowboy was right. The Red Caps would not take kindly to civilian interference. They would probably work against this old French fox with the shrewd blue eyes.

"This mechanic, Orton," the colonel said. "He was well liked?"

No one said anything.

"His sergeant can give you a better idea of the company he kept," Major Chase said.

"He was a lousy mechanic," Cowboy remarked.

"You did not care for him…*monsieur*?"

"Like I said, he was a lousy mechanic. Good mechanics can mean the difference between life and death to pilots."

Bat felt the floor dip beneath him as it did when one had flown too many hours in a high wind. What was Cowboy doing? He'd warned Bat off only to bring attention to himself. Attention neither of them could afford. It was obvious that Colonel Reynard had already drawn the conclusion that Orton had been dumped by a pilot in the squadron he serviced.

Bat questioned, "Was he dead?"

"What is that you say?" asked the colonel.

"Did the fall kill him?" Bat asked. "Or was he already dead?"

"Ah. A very good question, Captain…?"

"Bryant," Major Chase supplied. "A Flight's squadron leader."

"He reads detective stories," Ambrose offered jovially. "Sherlock Holmes. Nick Carter."

The colonel said measuredly, "It is possible that Orton was killed in the fall. His back was broken when he crashed through the henhouse roof. However, he sustained a blow to the head which might also have killed him."

"I don't suppose it could have been an accident?" Tubby suggested. "A couple of mechanics out joyriding?"

Colonel Reynard said smoothly, "This we will attempt to ascertain from the Sergeant of Mechanics. In the meantime, would it be possible for you gentlemen to account for your whereabouts on the evening in question?"

"I say," Varlik spoke up. "Surely no one *here* is under suspicion?"

The colonel made one of those broad Gallic gestures.

"We expect your full cooperation, gentlemen," Major Chase remarked. "The sooner we get this matter cleared up, the better for all of us."

There was an awkward silence.

"Your whereabouts, messieurs?" Colonel Reynard probed.

"We were all here," Tubby said, looking around for confirmation.

"B Flight was on maneuvers. We were all here," Rowbothom clarified. There were nods, murmurs of assent, agreement between them all. Even the monkey seemed in concord. Was it going to be that simple?

"Not Bat," Heath said.

"Certainly he was," Tubby said instantly. "Chatted with him for hours."

"He didn't come in until late. Nearly midnight, it was."

"Well then? He couldn't be in two places at once, could he?"

The French colonel turned to Bat. A battery of eyes seemed to swing his way.

"If you want the truth, I don't remember," Bat admitted. "I'm usually here but…"

"It was right after Owl went down," Ambrose said. "The next night, wasn't it?"

There was an uncomfortable pause. The colonel looked his inquiry. Bat said calmly, "Lieutenant Roberts and I were close friends. His plane went down Sunday in the Hesdin woods."

"Ah," the colonel replied.

"I never saw Cowboy that evening," Elliot put in.

"That's because you spent the evening sawing wood in front of the fire," Cowboy retorted laconically, and there were chuckles. "You can bet I wasn't flying loop de loops and dropping passengers on farm animals."

More laughter, but Reynard queried, "You are not well, monsieur?"

"*I?*" Bat said coolly. "I'm perfectly well."

The colonel nodded thoughtfully, still inspecting Bat. "This Monsieur Orton, he gets along all right with everyone?" he asked again.

Everyone nodded and shrugged it off. Orton was all right, that was the consensus.

"Not much of a mechanic, really," Ambrose opined, and there was agreement.

"But one does not kill a man for that," Colonel Reynard said genially.

"Depends on just how bad a mechanic he was," Cowboy said.

The colonel smiled, looking, in Bat's opinion, more like a fox than ever. "*Oui*, Monsieur…?"

"Cooper," Major Chase supplied.

"Monsieur Cooper, it is apparent to all that you were no admirer of this man, Orton."

Cowboy smiled genially.

There was further discussion of putting together a timetable of the squadron's movements. Bat missed much of it as he was running over all the things he wanted to say to Cowboy—none of them flattering. He surfaced when Major Chase said, "I suppose you'll want to go through Orton's things?"

"Mais oui, certainment."

It took every ounce of Bat's self-control not to look at Cowboy.

The door to the mess opened. Sergeant Smythe looked in. "Wing's just telephoned. The clouds 'ave lifted, sir. Four enemy planes 'eaded our way!"

"A Flight," Major Chase said to Bat.

"On it, sir," Bat said, and indeed they were already scrambling for their flight jackets and racing out the door, boots pounding on the wet earth as they ran for the airfield.

Bat found himself loping alongside Cowboy ahead of the others. He glanced at the hawkish, hard profile and said, "Was there anything on Orton to connect him to me?"

Cowboy shook his head, once, curtly.

"He must have had some sort of proof, though. They'll find it—"

Cowboy stopped, grabbing Bat's arm and halting him as well. They were oblivious to the men running past them, shooting curious looks their way. "What proof do you think he had?"

"No idea. I can't imagine what it would be."

"I think Orton was bluffing. I think he was trying to rattle you while you were off-balance. Why else would he have waited till Owl was dead?"

Bat shook his head. "Why in God's name did you drop him onto a henhouse?"

"I was aiming for the pond!"

Glancing back toward the château, Bat saw Major Chase and Colonel Reynard coming out the door. He freed himself from Cowboy's grip.

"Don't lose your head," Cowboy growled. He turned and sprinted toward his plane.

Bat headed for his DH-2. A thought struck him and he cut across to Pickering and Burns who were trying to convince Sergeant Lamb that they were supposed to be going up with A Flight.

"Burns, you're up," Bat called.

"What about me, sir?"

"Next time, Pickering."

"Sir!"

Bat ignored the wail of protest. To Burns, he said, "Listen, old son. Stick close to me. Remember, don't fly in a straight line. Make yourself a difficult target. And short bursts of machine gun fire are best. Don't spend everything you have in the first minutes."

Burns nodded eagerly, eyes bright. Bat squeezed his shoulder fleetingly before racing back to his own plane. He swung himself up into the cockpit, fixed his goggles as the mechanic swung the propellers.

The mechanic—a replacement for Orton—yelled, "Switch off!"

Bat echoed him, cutting the switch. He grabbed for his fur-lined gloves, shoved his fingers into their soft warmth.

The mechanic shouted, "Contact!"

"Contact!" Bat snapped the switch back on and heard the tigerbelly rumble of the Monosoupape engine.

The plane trembled all over with an illusion of anticipation, and then they were jogging, bouncing down the rough dirt runway, propellers moving in a shimmering blur until the spinning wheels left the ground and Bat was airborne again climbing toward the black-lined clouds.

It was cold, but the rainswept wind felt good on his face, cleansing. He looked to the right and Cowboy was there, his profile grim. To Bat's left, Ambrose was fiddling with his Lewis machine gun.

The pack was on the hunt once more.

* * * * *

Bat didn't start out hating the Germans. He'd been at school with a couple of German boys, and he'd been dismayed at the idea he might one day come face-to-face with Karl or Gerrit at the front.

Even after Algie had been killed, Bat tried to look at the situation impersonally. It was war, after all. That had been Algie's attitude, and Bat tried to adopt it as his own. It had grown more and more difficult as time went by, and more and more of his friends died. But was that the fault of the German pilots he came up against? Or was it the fault of the corrupt old men who determined such things?

The solution Bat came up with was to avoid getting too close to anyone. Of course that was impossible when it came to old chums like Ambrose and Tubby—and Gene—well, that had been something entirely different. The queer thing was he couldn't remember the first time he'd seen Gene. They'd transferred in around the same time, perhaps that was it, but Gene had simply always seemed to be there.

No, he couldn't help feeling the way he had about Gene.

But long before Gene's death, Bat had faced up to the fact that one couldn't cherish one's comrades too dearly without imperiling one's own effectiveness and the job at hand.

Varlik's death hit him hard, though—mostly because he felt it was partly his fault. If Heath had been in position instead of hanging back from the fight, Varlik quite likely would have made it. Made it through that skirmish at least. But Heath had circled and dillydallied out the edge of the fray until he'd caught the attention of one of the Boche pilots, and then he'd turned tail and ran for home.

Varlik had gone down—in flames—less than two minutes later.

Back at the aerodrome, the other pilots were no longer speaking to Heath—which in Tubby's case, was a good thing. And Bat didn't trust himself to haul Heath on the carpet until he'd reported to Chase and had a drink. Or two.

Cowboy joined him as he was down to the suds, and watching that lean, hard body move onto the stool next to him, watching the movement of muscle and long, strong limbs beneath the khaki tunic, Bat felt a jolt of lust that appalled him.

Gene had been right. This was the lowest kind of animal passion, and having given into it once, Bat now craved that physical release unceasingly. It unnerved him, the way he looked for Cowboy—on the ground and in the air. He wanted Cowboy despite the risk, and he knew from the steady look Cowboy gave him—his eyes dark blue like the approaching night—that Cowboy wanted him too.

And this was madness. *Madness.* Because even if there had been no risk at all, he couldn't afford to need anyone again. Not for anything— except, perhaps, support in the air. This was all any of them could afford to give.

"Why don't we get out of here?" Cowboy asked under his breath.

"Can't."

Cowboy raised an eyebrow. "Can't? Or won't?"

"Same thing," Bat replied, still curt.

"Not exactly," Cowboy replied. "But I won't insist." He added gently, "This time."

Bat's gaze met Cowboy's. *"Insist?"*

"Yep."

"Planning a spot of blackmail yourself, are you?"

Cowboy grinned, unperturbed. "Not a very friendly way to put it. You weren't exactly fighting for your honor yesterday."

True, but hardly tactful. Bat managed a chilly smile and an indifferent lift of his shoulder.

"Throw a dog a bone," he said.

Cowboy's expression tightened, then he laughed. He said softly, "You're just kidding yourself. You'll be begging me for it before long."

After delivering a long withering stare, Bat rose unhurriedly from the bar. "Pardon me," he said.

Cowboy drawled, "That's right. Git along little doggie. We'll chat later."

Bat froze and then laughed derisively. He crossed to Heath who stood by himself at the end of the bar.

Someone had turned on the gramophone. "Roses of Picardy" was playing, and it seemed to Bat that Heath lost color as the first notes began.

He turned as Bat reached him, saying fiercely in an under voice, "Do they think I don't know? They blame me!"

Bat fastened a hand on Heath's shoulder, guiding him toward the door. "Step into my office, old boy."

Heath resisted, then allowed himself to be towed outside.

They walked around the side of the house to the garden that was mostly sticks and dead leaves and brambles at this time of year. Perhaps at any time during a year of war. It was nearly dusk, and the good smells that issued from the mess kitchen were at odds with the dark, musty smells of the herbs growing between cracked paving stones.

Bat lit a cigarette for himself and one for Heath who ranted for several minutes about the injustice of it all. Bat said nothing until even Heath seemed to have tired of the sound of his voice.

Into the sudden silence, Bat expelled a long stream of smoke. Heath was watching him warily. Bat said calmly, "Look here, there's no use beating around the bush. I'm not saying Varlik's death is on your head, but you're funking it. And you have been for some time now."

Heath stood stone still. His eyes looked black in his white face. "Are you saying you think I've lost my nerve?"

Bat drew a lungful of smoke. "Have you?"

"No, I bloody well haven't! I just haven't been lucky in my hunting that's all. I'm out there same as everyone else, risking life and limb."

Bat was silent.

"Oh, I know what this is about," Heath said bitterly. "Not part of the club, am I? I don't have some fancy fucking public school education. My father isn't a viscount or an earl."

"Don't be an ass," Bat said wearily.

"I don't see you giving Ambrose a pep talk every time he fails to bag his Fritz. Or Tubby. I'd like to see you drag bloody Tubby on the carpet like this. I don't see you trying to make an example of fucking Tubby!"

Exasperated, Bat bit out, "I don't see Tubby or Ambrose hanging back from a scrap, watching a comrade—" He broke off as Heath flung away from him. "Right," he said more calmly, "If it helps…I know what you must feel. The first time I was shot down—"

He'd told the story a number of times. Told it for laughs in the mess, although in fact he'd had nightmares for weeks about it. Enemy fire had hit his fuel line. He'd run out of petrol on his way back to base, tried to make it back across the lines, and hadn't managed. He'd tried to bring the plane down in one piece and hadn't quite managed that either. He'd broken his leg and dislocated his shoulder. When he'd been lifted out of the wreckage he'd told the German soldiers they spoke excellent French—which, since these Germans had actually been French soldiers, amused them all heartily.

"You've no idea what I feel! None of you have." Heath glared at Bat, his eyes bright with tears. "It's just a game to you! And if you die, fuckin' *Per ardua ad astra*!"

"It's not true, Heath." Bat reached out, but Heath shook him off and strode away down the uneven pathway.

With a dismal sense of failure, Bat watched him go.

"Maybe you ought to work on that bedside manner of yours, Aubrey," Cowboy said lazily from behind him.

Bat managed not to start. He flicked his cigarette away and turned unhurriedly. "What do you want?"

"You," Cowboy said. "Now."

Bat's heart began to race meeting that shadowy, hungry look. He shook his head.

"Aren't *you* forgetting something?" Cowboy inquired. "You're not in any position to tell me no."

So he hadn't imagined the tacit threat in Cowboy's words. Bat swallowed, said thickly, "Aren't *you* forgetting something? You can't go to Chase or the Red Caps without implicating yourself in a murder."

Cowboy's grin widened, very white in his bronze face. "Well, I wasn't planning to tell *everything*. I wouldn't have to. See, I wasn't totally honest about not finding anything on Orton's body to connect you to him."

Bat opened his mouth but found his brain empty of words.

Cowboy continued cheerfully, "So all I've got to do is make sure that little piece of evidence finds its way into the right hands…"

The paving stones seemed to shift beneath Bat's feet. He reached out to steady himself on the marble foot of a statue of Diana.

"No need to look like that," Cowboy told him kindly. "I'm not going to hand you over to that old Frenchie—or the Red Caps. I like you, Aubrey. I'm not going to hurt you, but I am going to have you whenever I want you."

Bat was shaking his head.

"Sure I am," Cowboy said. "No use pretending you don't want it too. I can feel the heat coming off of you every time you look at me. You want it just as bad as I do, and this way you don't have to feel bad about Owl or your lordly ancestors or that little gal who faithfully mails you *The London Times* every week."

Edie. Funny thing that Cowboy should mention her in this context. The one time Bat had tried with Edie…well, it hadn't gone terribly well. Edie had been lovely about it, but, embarrassing as it was to admit, she flustered him. Whereas Cowboy—

A strange shivering heat crackled through Bat's nerves as he met Cowboy's gaze. He felt feverish. Hot and cold, hungry and sick all at the same time. *He had no choice.* He was going to have to submit to Cowboy— whenever Cowboy wished. The thought appalled him, and it filled him with frantic excitement. His erection was already swollen and rubbing painfully against the binding cloth of his trousers.

"What proof do you have?" he managed in a voice that did not sound like his own. "What did you find on Orton's body?"

"Maybe I'll tell you one of these days," Cowboy said, "but right now I don't want to waste any more time talking. We get little enough time as it is. Let's go someplace we can be private." He turned and walked the other way through the garden, not bothering to ascertain whether Bat followed or not.

After a wavering, undecided moment, Bat started after him—uncomfortable and unspeaking—until they came to the huge old aviary now overgrown with vines and shrubbery both inside and out of the cage.

The metal gate clanged dully shut behind them, and Cowboy turned to draw Bat into the shelter of a thicket of cypress.

"You know what to do," Cowboy told him as he stood there, staring.

It was actually a great relief to drop his trousers and free his constricted cock. Unmoving, barely breathing, Bat waited while Cowboy unfastened his own uniform and then turned his attention to Bat's tunic, taking his time, kissing the side of Bat's throat, the curve of his bared shoulder…

The head of Cowboy's thick rigid cock brushed Bat's naked belly.

"Just do what you're going to do," Bat ordered through dry lips. "Don't turn it into a performance. How do you want me?"

Cowboy lifted his head and smiled faintly, wryly. He put his arms around Bat and kissed him again, and his mouth was tender and soft, coaxing Bat's lips apart. Unwillingly, Bat began to respond. He liked it. He couldn't help it.

Cowboy's mouth was warm, the taste rich and mellow as sun-split fruit or golden ale. His eyes glittered, and Bat responded to that fever-bright sheen with a rush of aggressive hunger, his hands hard and demanding as he grabbed Cowboy back—grinding his mouth against Cowboy's, making an assault of hot mouths and grasping fingers. Everywhere Cowboy touched, Bat's taut body seemed to leap into clamoring life.

It was not like their previous coupling; Bat was dimly aware that his anger was driving them both. They wrestled for control, locked together and grappling. Their tunics were undone, trousers around their ankles and then they were lying in the soft moss. Cowboy kicked free of his trousers and his muscular legs fastened viselike around Bat's narrow hips. They bucked and heaved, arching hard against each other, pushing away even as they struggled to be one. This time Bat refused to give Cowboy entrance, and Cowboy's stiff cock seemed to joust with his own, scraping and stabbing.

It ended with jarring suddenness, Bat's body erupting in incandescent release that tore through him, leaving him shaking and stunned. From the crown of his head to the tips of his toes…every atom of his body seemed to spark and snap in the wake of that firestorm.

Cowboy came a few seconds later—with a funny little sob. He continued to clutch Bat tight as little ripples moved through his powerful body.

At last he opened his eyes and studied Bat's closed expression.

"Did I hurt you?"

Bat curled his lip. "Do you think you could?"

"Sure," Cowboy said. "But that's not what I want." He levered himself up, getting to his feet in one lithe move, reaching a hand down.

Bat ignored it, rising and dragging up his trousers. He brushed himself off finding with distaste his belly sticky. This had been more on the lines of assault than genuine invasion, and he felt almost…disappointed to be getting off so easily.

He could not understand himself. Even less could he understand Cowboy who reached out to brush his mouth with an almost hesitant touch. "You look like the kid Santa Claus forgot. Wasn't it all right?"

Bat jerked his head away, turning to button up his tunic. "What proof against me did Orton have?" he asked shortly.

There was a pause. Cowboy said, "We better get back before someone notices we're gone."

"Does it matter?"

"We're spending a lot of time together. These boys pay attention to everything you do."

"A little late to think of that, isn't it?"

Cowboy said nothing.

Bat finished buttoning his tunic. He stared at Cowboy in the failing light. "You're not going to tell me, are you?"

Cowboy said slowly, "How about this? How about I tell you what you want to hear after you tell me what I want to hear?"

"What is it you want to hear?" Bat snapped.

Another pause.

"I'll let you know when I hear it." And Cowboy grinned that wide, white grin.

Chapter Four

$\mathcal{B}$at had hoped to spend a little time training Burns and Pickering in something beyond map reading and flight theory, but Heath was shot down the following morning, and Burns had to replace him. Burns was shot down that afternoon, and Pickering was assigned his place in A Flight.

"Awful run of luck we're having lately," Tubby said when he and Bat stood outside smoking that evening.

"Yes."

"At least Heath went out like a man in the end."

Bat drew on his cigarette and released a long stream of smoke into the chill night. The scent of rain was in the air again. He hoped it would rain. He hoped it would come down in sheets and ground them for a day or two. It would be a rare delight to look forward to a day without funerals.

Into his silence, Tubby said, "Hope you're not brooding over Heath, old man. You know as well as I do he was responsible for Varlik's buying it."

"Christ, Tubby. The bloody Boche are responsible for Varlik." Irritably, Bat flicked his cigarette away.

"Heath—oh well. True enough. No point speaking ill of the dead." Tubby puffed thoughtfully. "Heard from Edie lately?"

Bat felt another flare of annoyance. What was the matter with him? Nerves apparently shot to pieces. "Yes," he said. "I get a letter every week. She's joined the Women's Defence Relief Corps."

Tubby laughed curtly. "Has she. Little Edie."

Bat glanced at his profile. "Why?"

Tubby shrugged. "No reason." Still not looking at Bat, he said neutrally, "You seem to have changed your mind about Cowboy."

"What d'you mean?" Bat inquired, equally colorless.

"You had no use for him at first, but you seem fairly tight now."

Bat closed his eyes, glad of the concealing darkness. *Tight.* Yes, that was one word for it. He thought of that morning. He'd deliberately stayed at Madame Fournier's the night before, but Cowboy had been waiting for him in the tunnel of trees when Bat started for the airfield just before dawn.

Cowboy had gestured for Bat to go to the gazebo, and silently, Bat had obeyed. He had intended to stay unmoved and unresponsive—they were taking fearful risks. Gene would have been appalled. Bat was appalled—but apparently helpless to resist. And though he wanted to pretend otherwise, his appetite was as fierce as Cowboy's.

So he had let himself be ordered to the gazebo, knowing full well what would happen but telling himself he would be an unwilling partner to it. They'd had to move swiftly, changing out of their flying clothes. Bat had not struggled when Cowboy turned him to face the wall, following the silent directions to spread his legs. But despite his determination to remain stoic, when that slick oily finger pierced him, his breath caught harshly, and he began to pant as Cowboy stroked and teased him in that strange seductive way.

It felt like nothing on earth. An outrageous intimacy, and yet unbearably sweet to have Cowboy touching him so. He began to cry out softly. Cowboy whispered hotly against his ear, "Tell me what you want, Aubrey."

He had shaken his head, but what was the use with excitement and pain spiraling beyond his control. "Please…" he'd ground out. "Please."

Cowboy murmured, *"Please?* You sound like you're begging me. Are you begging me to fuck you?"

There was a friendly mockery in his voice, and his fingers were moving with delicate expertise, pressing and pushing inside Bat's arse.

Bat had nodded, then said hoarsely, "I do want it. I want you to fuck me again."

"I thought you would," Cowboy said dryly.

And he withdrew his fingers and pushed his cock inside Bat's body. It was so much more intense than the fingers—more satisfying too, that warm weight shoving into him inch by inch, forcing him to accept, submit—it was a relief to be taken over like that.

"This what you want?" Cowboy asked.

Face to the wall, the rough wood against his face, Bat had nodded frantically. Yes. Please. Yes. This was what he wanted. To be fucked, to be taken, to be mastered—just for these few minutes before he had to be in charge again of so many men, so many lives. He was trembling as Cowboy slid the rest of the way into him, slow but steady until they were standing balls to arse, and Bat heard his own whimpers.

"Shhh," Cowboy soothed. "I'll give you what you want." He'd kissed Bat's hair and he kissed him behind his ear, and then he had fucked him briskly, hard and businesslike while Bat mewled those helpless shaming noises. Cowboy thrust into him deeply, held Bat as he writhed and twisted in sweet abandon until he had come in shuddering waves of release. Then quiet and obedient, Bat had stood trembling while Cowboy continued to thrust into him again and again, feeling it intensely as Cowboy pressed home, and then Cowboy had come too.

It was over and they were dressing quickly, not speaking, not looking at each other. They left the gazebo, cut across the field past the incurious gaze of a brown-and-white cow.

They had walked in silence to the airfield, climbed in their planes as the sun came up red and molten as Mars.

And a few hours later Heath was dead—and then Burns.

What did it matter really? Both he and Cowboy could also be dead the next day—within a few hours really. Any of them might be. No wonder if they all felt that terrible compulsion to grab every second of life, to make some brief human connection, feel something even for a few minutes.

Eat, drink, and be merry for tomorrow we die. It was even in the Bible, wasn't it?

Bat having failed to answer, Tubby examined the tip of his own cigarette. "Any word on what that French colonel turned up on Orton?"

Bat stared at him then. "No."

Tubby put his cigarette to his lips, pulled on it thoughtfully, and said, "Orton was no loss. Whoever dropped him out of that plane must have had good reason. Ruddy useless as a mechanic."

Bat made a noncommittal sound.

* * * * *

Bat slept in the château that night. He fully expected Cowboy to come to him—and braced himself to repel all boarders—and Cowboy did come, but he sat on the foot of Bat's bed and shared the contents of a package from home, apparently content to smoke and chat and divvy up small, silver-wrapped chocolates.

The red tip of Cowboy's cigarette wagged in the darkness as he said, "Henderson says the prevailing theory is some French pilot might have killed Orton."

"Henderson?" Bat asked around the bite of milk chocolate.

"One of the mechanics assigned to my bus." Cowboy studied Bat through the veil of cigarette smoke. "Turns out Orton was something of a ladies' man."

"You're joking."

Cowboy shook his head. "Nope. Furthermore, it seems our Sidney was no respecter of the sacred vows of marriage."

Bat unpeeled another chocolate thoughtfully. "But this is the opinion of the ground crew. No reason to believe that old gendarme fox subscribes to that theory."

"No," Cowboy agreed.

Neither spoke for a time. Then Bat asked reluctantly, "Why *did* you help me that night?"

But at the same time Cowboy said, "So what do you plan on doing after the war?"

"After the war?" Bat stared as though Cowboy had gone mad.

"Sure. You still planning on going into the Foreign Office like your daddy wants?"

"Oh, you bloody… *Yank*," Bat retorted, and Cowboy gestured for him to lower his voice.

"What are you on about now?" he asked.

"You blighters come along and you're so sure of yourselves. So arrogant and all-knowing. It's only a big game to you. A great bloody adventure. *After the war!* I suppose it's no wonder—not even your fight, is it?"

"It will be," Cowboy said. "Eventually. Better fight 'em here than in England. Or at home."

Bat made a sound of disgust which seemed to amuse Cowboy all the more. The moonlight softened his face, made him look younger—as young as Burns or Pickering. "Now don't go gettin' riled, Aubrey. I'm just making pleasant conversation with you."

"Don't," Bat said.

Cowboy snickered, unperturbed, and tossed Bat another chocolate. Watching Bat irritably undo the silver foil, he remarked, "Some people are going to live through this war. Someone always does. I plan on being one of them."

"You will be," Bat said, and managed to make it sound like something Cowboy would do out of spite.

Cowboy said evenly, "And so will you."

Bat laughed without humor. "I shall be more than happy if I manage to get away with murder."

"Shut that kind of talk. It was an accident, and we both know it."

"But you're still threatening to go to the Red Caps if I won't let you—" Bat swallowed on the words as the mental image of what he had already permitted—what he longed to do with Cowboy again—came into his mind. And if he was honest, the dreadful part was not that he had no say in the matter; it was that he didn't *want* a say.

Watching the emotions flicker across the other pilot's features, Cowboy said calmly, "That's right. I like what we do together. And so do you, although I know you don't think you should. Maybe because you're still in love with Owl's memory. Or maybe because you just don't have a lot of imagination."

Bat gaped at him, and Cowboy leaned over and kissed his mouth. He tasted like chocolate and the cigarettes he had been smoking. He tasted warm and alive and sweet. Before Bat could respond, Cowboy drew back.

"You like those?" He glanced at the chocolate Bat held in nerveless fingers.

Bat nodded.

"They call 'em kisses," Cowboy said.

Bat found his voice at last. "They look like tears to me."

* * * * *

First crawl passed without incident.

In the middle of the afternoon A Flight was assigned the task of bringing down an enemy balloon near Sailly-sur-la-Lys. The observation balloons made the miserable conditions of ground warfare even more unpleasant for the PBI, for here too the Germans were better equipped and better trained.

The terrain itself was already difficult thanks to the scenic hills, forests, and rivers of northern France. The bland German eye in the sky was the final straw.

Unfortunately Varlik had been 44's most successful balloon strafer. He had developed his own method of making one straight dash through the circle of Archie and firing a single long burst of incendiary bullets into the balloon. Varlik had scorned the prevailing tactic of repeat sorties through the black barrage of anti-aircraft guns as nothing more than a showy means of suicide.

But now Varlik was dead, and it fell to Bat to decide who should be the balloon killer's successor. As he mulled over his fliers, it occurred to him that if he really feared exposure by Cowboy, the means of putting a halt to it was at hand.

He rejected the idea instantly, but still the notion persisted. If Cowboy was a threat to him, Bat could eliminate the threat by simply sending Cowboy out on difficult mission after mission until one of them finished him.

Horrified, he sat with the map before him unseeing of the grids and lines…picturing instead Cowboy's death. Picturing an end to that arrogance and domineering—an end to manipulation and coercion. He could have his life back. For whatever time was left to him.

Not only would it mean the end of this degrading physical blackmail, it would be the end of his own ignoble desires.

He sat unmoving at the spindly desk in the blue room. Easiest thing in the world. But his heart was beating like a wild bird trapped in a cage.

An end to that lazy tiger's grin; an end to those midnight-blue eyes that saw far too much; an end to the powerful body that overwhelmed and ravished his own. His arse was still sore from the most recent pounding he'd taken. And perhaps he did lack imagination, but all he had to do was close his eyes and he could smell again the scent of sex and leather and bare skin, feel the burn and scrape in his violated channel, hear Cowboy's harsh breaths against his ear—and his own voice crying out for more.

Quickly, he folded up the map and rose. When he went out to give the day's orders he assigned Ambrose the honor of puncturing the balloon, and tagged Elliot to be his picador.

* * * * *

Bat had his pilots set their watches to match his own, issuing orders to cross the lines precisely at 14:15 and fly intercept between Ambrose and Elliot and any hostile aircraft. He took every man of A Flight with him, fully expecting to find Hun planes guarding the airborne enemy observation post, and in this he was not disappointed.

As the patrol continued in formation on the safe side of Allied lines, Ambrose and Elliot left the pack and positioned themselves a good distance the other side of Sailly-sur-la-Lys. So far they had spotted not a single pair of German wings, but Bat was wagering the Jasta would be making an appearance as soon as A Flight approached the gasbag.

As his watch neared the hour Bat prowled closer to the point of attack. Scanning the fields of blue ahead, he spotted two DH-2s four or five miles ahead streaking toward the dun-colored balloon.

"Oh, *Christ*." Bat checked his watch. 14:10. In their eagerness to bag the balloon, Ambrose and Elliot had disobeyed orders and had gone in several minutes ahead of the stated time. Bat looked around. The rest of A Flight was coming into formation right on schedule, but now instead of offering cover to their balloon killers, they were left in the position of running to catch up.

Bat signaled smartly and the machines of A Flight opened up in pursuit of the two pilots. In the pale distance Bat spotted a formation of six Albatros moving to cut off the de Havillands' approach.

One lone Spad seemed to burst from the clouds, swooping in to engage the Albatros fighters. Cowboy.

That was the last clear thought Bat had for some time as two things happened at once. The balloon burst into flames indicating that either Ambrose or Elliot had succeeded in reaching the target despite the best diversionary attempts of the Albatros fighters. At the same instant the towering clouds behind Bat seemed to spew out a stream of Fokkers and Halberstadt Ds which swarmed down on A Flight's Spads and DH-2s.

Bat, who had started to Cowboy's aid, found he was distanced from the rest of A Flight with two Fokkers on his tail. Flaming bullets wove a deadly web around his aeroplane as he zigged and zagged. Meanwhile the ground crew was sending up "archers" and "onions" and they blazed through the knots of planes like fireballs. But the Fokkers would not be shaken, and Bat took more drastic evasive action by means of the Immelmann Turn, a sharp rudder turn off a vertical zoom—followed by a steep dive.

As he completed his half loop he was on the tail of one of the Fokkers, but the other had executed a half loop himself, and was still on Bat's tail. He could feel the impact as machine gun bullets tore into his craft, and figuring that he was lost, he determined to take the pilot in front of him down with him. He kept the DH-2's nose pointed at the tail of the Albatros which was now diving steeply downward in an attempt to escape, and his thumb firmly on the trigger. As the distance closed to fifty yards, Bat saw his bullets pierce the back of the pilot's seat.

The enemy plane fluttered and then began to fall, and Bat pulled his stick back nearly to his seat and began a sharp ascent in the hope of shaking the second fighter off.

As he climbed he recognized one of his own patrol on the tail of the Fokker—Pickering—emptying his drum into the Hun. A waste of ammunition, but Bat was grateful for it as the second Fokker grew preoccupied with his own fight for survival. Bat shot up and away. With a little time to breathe, he began to scout for Cowboy.

Had Cowboy made it—outnumbered as he had been? It had been a gallant effort distracting the Albatros fighters from Ambrose and Elliot—and fucking unnecessary if everyone had only followed orders.

Bat couldn't see the American pilot anywhere; the air was humming with bullets and tracers as black crosses and gold cockades, blue and brown planes wove in and out, darting forward and back in the ferocious flurries of a dogfight.

Many twisting, turning combats were in progress as Bat once more gained the sunny blue fields above Sailly-sur-la-Lys. Several machines had fallen but whether friend or foe was impossible to tell at that great height. The Spads and de Havillands were scattered far across the sky; A Flight's formation was destroyed. There was nothing for it. Bat determined to call them together and head back across the lines. The balloon was in flames, the mission was successfully completed, and to continue fighting across enemy lines was foolhardy.

The Boche seemed only too happy to see them go. Bat collected his pilots and made for home, and the enemy planes lost no time in putting further distance between them. Bat dropped back a bit noting that the last of his flock were well on their way. Out of the corner of his eye, he spotted action over the Somme, and detoured to investigate.

He found Cowboy engaged in attack on a German Albatros. It became rapidly clear that his gun had jammed because he was firing at the German pilot with his pistol. Bat began to laugh, giddy with relief he had no intention of examining. However, his amusement was short-lived. The German pilot, having belatedly figured out that his attacker was in a vulnerable position, swung about to turn the tables on the gadfly American.

Cowboy was reloading his revolver, cool as could be, when he spotted Bat. He gave that nod, that aggravating cool little nod, and Bat signaled him out of the fray in no uncertain terms. Cowboy turned on wingtip and moved out of harm's way, and Bat came diving down at full speed, guns blazing.

With his first burst of machine gun fire he saw the petrol tank of the enemy machine rupture into fire. Bat pulled up as the other plane began to spin like a Roman candle.

The enemy plane descended rapidly, the wind fanning the flames into a fiery furnace. Bat hoped the pilot was dead for he would have been burned to a crisp long before he hit the ground. He watched till the final impact. There was a great explosion and all that remained of the aeroplane was a black cloud of smoke and dust that ascended a few yards and was scattered across the bones of the battlefield.

Bat turned for home once more, Cowboy falling into position beside him.

* * * * *

"That was close," Cowboy said once they were on solid ground once more. He poked a finger through the bullet hole in the leather sleeve of Bat's flight jacket. "You sure you're not hit?"

"Fritz can't shoot to save his life," Bat said, although his arm stung where the bullet had grazed him. In fact, it was little short of a miracle he was standing there, but then it was a miracle either of them was standing there. Thinking about how close you'd come only gave you a case of the screaming wobblies. Much better to keep one's thoughts focused on the here and now.

He said, "Speaking of not able to hit the broad side of a barn, I thought all you cowboys were supposed to be expert marksmen?"

"You've been reading Max Brand again. The wind velocity threw me off."

"Wind?" Bat scoffed. "You call that little zephyr dancing up there a wind?"

Something flickered in Cowboy's eyes, and he whispered huskily, "When can you get away? I want you, Aubrey."

That was all, but Bat had to fight the wave of heat rising inside him threatening to melt bones—and brain. He said stiffly—stiff being the operative word, "I shall have to make my report."

"I'll see you afterwards. The gazebo."

"I…" Bat swallowed. He had to get control of this thing. "I don't know that I can."

The lines of Cowboy's face were taut with hunger—and something else. He said flatly, "You can and you will. I'll see you down there." And he turned and walked away.

This was…this had to stop. This was madness. Utter, absolute madness.

Heading for Major Chase's office, Bat pulled off the white silk scarf that protected his neck from chafing against the leather collar of his flight jacket.

He rapped briskly on the closed door. The murmur of voices beyond stopped.

"Come," called Chase, and Bat stepped inside.

He hesitated before closing the door. The old gendarme, Colonel Reynard, was sitting in the chair before Chase's desk. The office smelled pleasantly of pipe smoke. A bottle of scotch sat on the desk between the two officers.

"Captain Bryant," Major Chase greeted him. "Well done! Wing has been on the line. Your mission appears to have been a success."

"Sir," Bat said automatically. His attention was on Colonel Reynard. He did not like the light of recognition in the old officer's blue gaze. But then everything about Colonel Reynard made him uneasy.

He made his report succinctly. Major Chase nodded, approvingly. Colonel Reynard sat sipping his scotch and listening, apparently cleared for this kind of debriefing.

Bat finished his chronicle and waited for dismissal.

Major Chase looked at Colonel Reynard and Colonel Reynard nodded infinitesimally.

Something was up all right.

Major Chase said, "As you know, Bryant, Colonel Reynard has been looking into the death of mechanic Sidney Orton. Orton was assigned to your crate, wasn't he?"

"Yes, sir," Bat said.

"How did you get on with him?"

"Sir?"

"What was your private opinion of the man?"

Bat thought over his response. He said, "Never noticed him much. That is…"

Colonel Reynard leaned forward slightly. *"Oui?"*

Bat said without expression, "I'm afraid he wasn't an awfully good mechanic."

Chase snorted. Colonel Reynard leaned back in his chair.

There was another look between Chase and the Frenchman. Colonel Reynard said, "You had not personal dealings with this man Orton?"

"I?" Bat said in the tone perfected through generations of applying the foot firmly to the neck of the dear old proletariat. He hoped the mildly affronted tone helped disguise the fact that his heart was hammering with fright.

The colonel said in his nearly flawless English, *"Eh bien.* Can you explain, Captain Bryant, why this man Orton should have had in his personal belongings a letter from you to the late Lieutenant Gene Roberts?"

CHAPTER FIVE

That sick, jarred feeling: it was much the same sensation as when one made a particularly rotten landing.

"I've no idea, sir," Bat answered, and he must have sounded suitably bewildered.

The colonel opened an attaché case, took out an envelope, and unfolded the letter inside which he proffered to Bat. After a hesitation, Bat took it.

It was a letter he had written to Gene from England the previous summer. After he'd been shot down over Verdun, he'd been invalided home to Kent to recover. It had seemed to take a bloody long time, and he'd written to Gene once or twice, although he was not, in the general way, much for letter writing.

He felt the blood drain from his face as his gaze raced line by line through the missive.

And yet…it was a harmless enough letter. He came to the end of it— that stilted schoolboy signing off—and began to read it again more slowly. There was nothing in these neat, guarded lines to give them away. Bat's fretting to get back to the front was clear—as was his fear for his friends, though he hid that a little better behind the usual raillery. He had even mentioned Edie in passing.

Feeling the eyes of both men upon him, he did his best to keep his expression impassive as he refolded the letter and handed it back to Colonel Reynard. He looked the older man straight in the eyes.

"I don't understand," he said.

"What is it you don't understand, Captain Bryant?" Colonel Reynard inquired.

"I don't understand why Orton should have such a thing in his possession." He glanced at Major Chase, but Chase said nothing. Apparently this was Reynard's show.

Colonel Reynard said with a mildness Bat didn't much like, "You can think of no reason this man Orton would retain a letter that belonged to you or Lieutenant Roberts?"

"Perhaps Owl dropped it and Orton intended to return it to him."

"I think not," Colonel Reynard said.

Bat held his tongue.

"Perhaps Monsieur Orton spoke to you about this letter?"

"No." Bat made an effort. "If he'd mentioned it to me, I should have asked for it back." He added, deliberately casual, "Why not?"

"Suppose there was a price attached to its return?" Colonel Reynard suggested.

"Sir?" Bat turned to Major Chase.

Major Chase said, "Answer the question, Captain Bryant."

Bat said frostily, "Are you suggesting this Orton was a blackmailer?" The old earl couldn't have put more hauteur into it.

After all, what was it but a stupid, boyish, and rather innocent letter? Quite innocent as he compared what had been between Gene and himself to the things Cowboy had taught him. There was nothing in this letter to give them away...beyond the fact that Bat had written to Owl while home on leave. And what was extraordinary about that? A lot of chaps wrote from home. No, the extraordinary thing would be that Orton had apparently believed the letter worth hanging onto. Perhaps when combined with whatever proof Cowboy had found on Orton's body it added up to something more damaging.

What had Cowboy found? Bat had to know. Another letter? A more damaging letter? He remembered only too well the pain of being separated from Gene, wondering if Gene was even alive when he wrote. It had been unbearable being apart. Knowing Gene was flying into danger every day without Bat to watch his back.

Unmoved by Bat's show of indignation, Colonel Reynard said, "We have found a number of articles in Monsieur Orton's belongings that would lead us to believe he perhaps…augmented his pay with blackmail."

"Blackmail?" Bat forced a laugh. "I say. What a rum thing. He'd have had to come up with something better than that, you know." He nodded dismissively at the letter and waited, hoping he wasn't giving himself away by so much as a tremor. If they had a more incriminating communication, they would have shown it to him, right?

Right.

They were bluffing. And as he met their twin gazes, Bat knew that they realized he now recognized this—recognized that they had lost this hand. He did not allow his relief to show by so much as a twitch.

"Thank you, Captain Bryant," Major Chase said, and dismissed him.

* * * * *

Cowboy rose as Bat slammed into the gazebo.

"Started to think you weren't coming," he said gruffly, and there was a funny note in his voice that Bat didn't stop to analyze.

He crashed into Cowboy, hands digging into his shoulders as he pinned him against the wall. "What did you find on Orton's body?" he demanded furiously. "What was it? *Tell me,* goddamn you or I'll kill you myself!"

Bat had the advantage of surprise, but Cowboy was by far the larger and stronger. He could have broken Bat's hold, could have thrown him off. Instead he put his arms around him, pulling him closer.

"What is it? What happened?"

Something strange and terrible was happening to Bat. As those powerful arms locked around him, drawing him still closer to Cowboy's hard, muscular form, his control seemed to slip. His hands fisted helplessly in Cowboy's tunic, he butted his head against Cowboy's—and he could hear the steady thump of Cowboy's heart against his own—Cowboy was talking to him, but Bat couldn't hear the words because he was crying. Crying for Gene, for himself, for all of them—all the chaps who had died, all the chaps who were going to die—crying for the bloody, goddamned uselessness of it, pointlessness of it. A ripping crash of emotion like a wing folding up, like the entire spread of canvas over the top wing tearing away in the wind and disappearing behind him.

It had happened to him just that way—not long after he'd returned to the front after being shot down the first time. He had been so sure he was going to die. After all, he'd already had his lucky escape. He could not believe he would survive again as his right wing tore away and the plane went out of his control as slowly, then faster and faster, its tail began revolving.

Around and around it had whipped like a top—he felt that same horrifying helplessness now, as though he was caught in a tailspin, plummeting toward the ground, toward the inevitable smashup.

Except that Cowboy was holding him up, speaking quietly to him. "Tell me. You've got to tell me. What's happened?"

Bat shook his head. He had to get control, but...so far no luck.

Cowboy stroked Bat's back, kissed his face, kept murmuring. After a time the soft, foolish words sank in.

"You're all right, Aubrey. I won't let anything happen to you. Tell me what's wrong."

I won't let anything happen to you? That would have been funny enough even if Cowboy wasn't half of what had happened. Bat lifted his head, wiped his face on his sleeve, tried to pull free. Cowboy kept his hold.

Bat said, "They've found a letter from me to Gene in Orton's kit."

Cowboy was very still. "You said there wasn't anything for them to find."

Bat wiped his face again. "It's not…in itself it's nothing. I wrote after I was shot down last summer. The only real…significance is that Orton kept it. They think he was supplementing his pay with blackmail."

"They?"

"Chase and that old French fox. He knows. I can feel it."

"Shhhh…" Cowboy seemed to be thinking.

Bat sniffed. Already he felt calmer. After all, what were a few tears given the things he and Cowboy had done?

He said, "I can't face being arrested. *Court-martialed?*"

"This is where I came in." Cowboy's eyes slanted his way. "Look, you're not going to prison and you're not going up in front of a firing squad. You're not going to be arrested, so shut up."

"I tell you, they *know*."

"They *don't* know," Cowboy said with certainty. "They're fishing. You're one in a sea of possibilities. Don't you see that?"

Bat stared. Cowboy's mouth was a breath away from his own. He could see the gold glint on his jaw and the blue gleam of the eyes gazing deeply into his. He had a compulsion to cover Cowboy's soft mouth with his own.

Instead he said, "You think Orton was trying it on with some of the other chaps?"

"If all Chase and this colonel found was your letter, they wouldn't be jumping to the conclusion that Orton was a blackmailer. Especially if the letter is as innocuous as you say. He's got other victims in this camp, you can bet on that. Which means Chase and the Frenchie have other suspects."

Bat wondered why he didn't try to free himself. He continued to stand in the circle of Cowboy's arms. He said, "Colonel Reynard knows. I don't know how, but he knows. I could see it in his eyes."

"Well, he's an old copper," Cowboy replied. "I guess he's got a nose for it. It doesn't matter. If worse comes to worst, I'll tell 'em I'm the one who dumped Orton."

"What?" Bat freed himself then. "What are you saying?"

Cowboy said coolly, "I'll tell 'em I killed Orton. They'll believe it once they know I dumped Orton's body."

At last Bat said, "Why…would you do such a thing?"

For the first time, a certain self-consciousness crossed Cowboy's hard face. "I told you. I like you, Aubrey." He shrugged. "I guess it's more than that."

Bat couldn't seem to think of a word to say. In fact, he wasn't sure he remembered how to coordinate his tongue and lips.

"Yeah, that's what I figured," Cowboy said, watching him struggle. "You think you're still in love with Gene."

"I…"

Cowboy said gently, "Maybe you are. But you like what we do together, even if you can't admit it. You're aching for it right now. Rigid as a tent pole." He smiled faintly, glancing down at Bat's crotch.

Bat didn't have to look down.

"It's okay," Cowboy said in a deep velvety voice. "I'm going to take care of you."

It was the best it had been thus far: long and slow and loving. They stroked and caressed as though they had all the time in the world, and then Bat lay on his back in the faded cushions and Cowboy knelt between his legs, pierced him through the tight crack of his arse with agonizingly sweet deliberation. Bat had pulled Cowboy down to him. Their bodies rested hot and humid against each other in the chilly room, and then Cowboy began to move, the deep thrusts seeming to keep time with the beat of their hearts.

They kissed, and stroked each other—*pleasured* each other, that was the word—and Bat came right away in shivery jets. Cowboy's cock jerked and strained, trying for the very heart of him—a few more urgent thrusts and Cowboy was spilling into him.

Afterward they lay in each other's arms smoking, kissing, and occasionally talking.

"First time I saw you," Cowboy said. "I thought…" He laughed softly.

"What did you think?" Bat turned his head, rubbing his nose at the dust that puffed up from the old cushions.

He remembered the day Cowboy had turned up with the other new recruits—all dead now. He remembered the confident swagger, the cool way Cowboy had sized them all up, the lazy, deep voice as he introduced himself—everything about the big American had annoyed Bat, all the more because he knew it was an unreasonable reaction. Later, down at the lodge, he and Gene had joked about the Seventh Cavalry.

Cowboy said reminiscently, "I thought you were cute as a newborn foal."

"Cute?" Bat was truly appalled.

"Sure. Tall and quiet and sort of shy."

"Shy?"

"Well. The fact is, I mistook your natural limey repression for something else."

Bat muttered, "Ridiculous."

Cowboy continued dreamily, "And then those pretty gray eyes of yours looked right through me and you said in that god-awful snooty accent, *"I say, another cowboy here to save the day."*

"Did I?"

Cowboy was grinning reflectively. "Yep. Just that dry sense of humor of yours."

Bat winced.

More seriously, Cowboy said, "It was the same day Sandy MacIntosh got shot down and you were feeling raw. I know you better now. I know why you keep a distance from the replacements—why we all do, I suppose."

Bat grunted.

"Anyway, the nickname stuck."

"What *is* your name?" Bat asked.

"Aloysius Cooper."

Aloysius. Awful. It suited him. "And what do you plan to do after the war, Aloysius?"

"I expect I'll be a lawyer like my daddy and his daddy before him." Cowboy squinted up at Bat through the flickering light of the trees moving above the broken roof of the gazebo. "You ever been to the States?"

Bat shook his head.

"You never know," Cowboy said.

* * * * *

There was the promise of snow the next morning when A Flight set out for first crawl. Bat could taste it in the wind whipping his face, smell it in the bitter cold.

Ambrose was on his right, Cowboy sailing along on his left, the two biplanes shimmering in the first light like golden stars. After the losses of the day before, they planned nothing more strenuous than a learn-the-line for the two new replacements Hutchinson and Close. A stroll in the park, Bat told his new boys, and he hoped it was true.

It was on their way back to the drome that they came upon a squadron of Fokkers flying low beneath them. Excitement rippled through A Flight like a tailwind, for the German pilots had failed to spot them. For a few seconds they traveled in parallel, then Bat stuck the nose of the DH-2 down and dived for the tail of the nearest Fokker.

Belatedly realizing his peril, the pilot of the Fokker tried to outdive Bat. A second Fokker came to his assistance, settling on Bat's tail. Cowboy peeled off, zooming down and fastening his teeth on the heels of the second Fokker. And just like that, the skies were a battleground once more, every machine pouring streams of tracer bullets into the craft before him, an argument punctuated by the black-and-white puffs of Archie down below as the anti-aircraft guns of both sides joined in.

Bat's targeted Fokker dropped like a stone—an account almost too easily settled. Two of the other enemy planes streaked for home, the pilots wounded or their machines crippled. Bat scouted for Cowboy and spotted him far down below with three Fokkers on his tail.

He swore and dropped down rapidly, watching as Cowboy turned and rolled, firing three short bursts at his opponents before climbing again in an effort to turn the tables.

Mad as wasps, the Fokkers buzzed after him, keeping up their pursuit and maneuvering to try to reposition on his tail once more. One of the pilots spotted Bat, and behind him, Tubby and Ambrose rushing to catch up. They moved to engage, and a short fierce fight broke out. Machine gun bullets cut through the air while the pilots swerved and climbed and dived, narrowly missing each other—sometimes by only a few feet. One of the Fokkers went down and the remaining two ascended steeply, once more speeding for home and the protection of their own landing field. Tubby and Ambrose gave chase.

Bat watched the retreating planes go with grim satisfaction. Looking down, he was dismayed to see Cowboy sinking to earth. The Spad's propeller was turning slowly, and Bat knew instinctively that Cowboy's plane had been struck in some vital part of the engine.

Cool as ever, Cowboy put his machine at an angle and went volplaning down. Bat sped after, quickly overtaking him as he calculated the distance that separated the American from the far-flung trenches. Cowboy was only seven or eight thousand feet above the ground and the lines were some six miles distant. There was no sign of panic or alarm from the American, but he could hardly fail to be aware of the tightness of his predicament as he coaxed his powerless craft along, gliding like a drunken swallow.

Bat was the one quietly, fervently swearing as he sailed along overhead. In most circumstances an aeroplane might potentially skim along for a mile or so without losing more than a thousand feet altitude. There was a chance Cowboy could make eight miles without engine power provided he managed to stay eight thousand feet above ground. Provided, too, that no ill wind blew against him—and that no enemy bullets found their mark as he sank nearer and nearer to the ground.

Bat flew above the wounded bird, ignoring Cowboy's attempts to wave him off. Archie joined the serenade, and both planes were peppered with shrapnel.

The best-case scenario was that Cowboy might land safely and be taken prisoner. The worst—

But Bat refused to consider the worst. He didn't ignore the miniature eruptions around him so much as he was simply oblivious to them, his entire focus on Cowboy's battle for the lines. The American was gauging speed and distance with the precise judgment of a trick rider—Bat was the one whose hands were wet with perspiration, whose heart tripped. There was simply nothing he could do—nothing but keep Cowboy company until the end. Whatever the end might be.

The ground drew closer and closer to Cowboy's hanging wheels. Bat spied the rear trenches of the Germans, saw shocked white faces staring up as they passed above. Cowboy was doomed to strike the next trench, three hundred yards ahead.

Bat dropped into line beside Cowboy, firing at the trenches, spraying bullets in an attempt to keep the soldiers occupied with something besides taking potshots at RFC planes.

The second row of German trenches appeared below the sinking Spad which skimmed lightly over them.

With rising hope Bat saw that the fields ahead were open and relatively smooth. If Cowboy could land…

He had to land there. There was no other option for him. At the rate he was dropping, if he continued to coast along he would be rolling up at the front line trench of the Huns.

At that moment the Spad touched earth with a teeth-rattling jar, rebounded lightly, and struck again some thirty feet ahead—bouncing over the narrow front line trench and rolling some thirty or forty yards across no-man's-land.

Then there was silence but for the drone of Bat's circling plane and the twang and ping of Cowboy's engine coming to rest.

Cowboy was up and out of the Spad, and setting fire to it before it had stopped quivering. Soldiers from both sides spilled out of the trenches. The air whistled with bullets and yells.

Bat swooped down and landed a hundred yards away. He whistled— not that there was much chance Cowboy had missed his arrival. The Germans certainly hadn't. The Allies were doing their best to cover him which mostly increased the odds of Cowboy getting shot.

Boche bullets kicked up little clouds of dust and weed as Cowboy covered those hundred yards in less than ten seconds.

Reaching the DH-2, Cowboy gave Bat's props a good hard swing, and scrambled onto the fuselage as Bat took off again.

Cowboy's face was black with smoke and oil beneath his goggles, but he was grinning. Bat had never seen anything more beautiful.

EPILOGUE

It was snowing the day of Tubby's funeral, grounding all flights.

Bat stood next to Cowboy and listened to the chaplain while the soft silent snow feathered the hard ground. He was glad of the snow. Glad it would be a day or two before they could fly again—maybe longer if the snow lasted. For the first time he wished that he might never have to fly again. Funny to think how he had dreamed of flying from the time he was small; he'd only been six years old when man first took to the sky. Now he was twenty-three, but he felt nearer a hundred.

But Day shall clasp him with strong hands,

And Night shall fold him in soft wings

His eyes met Cowboy's and though they were not touching, he felt as though Cowboy's hand brushed his cheek. Inexplicably, he felt comforted. But perhaps it was not so inexplicable after all. Maybe there was some truth to that poem of Tennyson's. *Better to have loved and lost than never loved at all.* Gene would have understood that.

In the mess that evening, Ambrose made Varlik's toast for Tubby.

"Here's a toast, now! Fill the cup! Though the shadow of fate is on the wall, here's a final toast ere the darkness fall. Fill the cup."

A nice enough toast, but Bat was thinking of the vulgar verses they all knew—and at one time found quite comical. There was a rumble of acknowledgment as Ambrose finished speaking. Everyone drank. The new recruits—even Berkman's monkey.

Cowboy sat down next to Bat at the bar, his shoulder brushing Bat's, and said, "What did Chase want this afternoon?"

Bat met the midnight-blue eyes, and his tension lessened. They would be together tonight and he could grieve for Tubby then—grateful for one more sunrise—and one more night. They were lucky to have this, he knew that now; lucky for as long as it lasted—as long as they managed to live.

He said, "Chase told me that…perhaps God works in mysterious ways."

"What the hell does that mean?"

"Some of those letters they found in Orton's things were Tubby's."

Cowboy frowned, not quite following.

"Apparently when he first came over he managed to get a French girl pregnant. He married her, but…I don't know what happened. He abandoned her. No one knows the full story. No one ever will now. But somehow Orton found out and was threatening Tubby with exposure."

For a long time, Cowboy was silent. Then he said, "They think Tubby killed Orton?"

Bat smiled without humor. "I don't think so. Not really. He couldn't have dumped Orton's body. He never left the mess that night. Only you and I were unaccounted for at any part of that evening. But we're doing valuable work here, you see. And the French appreciate it, and Chase needs every pilot."

"And," Cowboy said thoughtfully, "Orton wasn't a whole hell lot of use as a mechanic."

"Quite," said Bat. He drank and then said quietly, "What was the proof you found on Orton's body?"

"What's that?"

"The proof you threatened to take to Major Chase. What was it?"

"Oh." Cowboy stared down at his drink. A faint smile touched his mouth. He said, "There wasn't anything."

Bat stared at him. At last, frowning, he said, "What are you saying?"

Cowboy said calmly, "There was no proof. Nothing that could be used in evidence against you. Nothing at all. I made it up."

"Why?"

"Because I wanted to keep seeing you, and for that to happen I knew I needed some hold over you. At least until you got used to the idea."

Bat didn't know what to say. Cowboy looked at him sideways, gave a tiny, sheepish smile. "I told you. I liked you. A lot. I knew you were still in love with Gene. But…I figured I had something to offer you too, even if you didn't want to admit it."

Bat stared down at his glass.

"Now you know," Cowboy said after a time.

"Yes."

"So that's it then. I guess I don't have a hold on you anymore."

Bat looked up. He held Cowboy's gaze with his own. "I wouldn't say that," he said.

The Dark Farewell

Little Egypt, 1922

Chapter One

The body of the third girl was found Tuesday morning in the woods a few miles outside Murphysboro. Flynn read about it the following day in the *Herrin News* as the train chugged slowly through the green cornfields and deep woods of Southern Illinois. The dead girl's name was Millie Hesse and like the other two girls she had been asphyxiated and then mutilated. There were other "peculiarities," according to the newspaper, but the office of the Jackson County Sheriff declined to comment further.

The peculiarities would be things about the murder only known to the police and the murderer himself. At least in theory. Flynn had covered a few homicides since his return from France three years earlier, and it wasn't hard to read between the lines. But there were already rumors flying through the wires about a homicidal maniac on the loose in Little Egypt.

Flynn gazed out the window as a giant cement smokestack came into sight. The perpetually smoldering black slag heap, half-buried in the tall weeds, reminded him in some abstruse way of the ravaged French countryside. His lip curled and he stared down again at the newspaper.

He didn't care much for homicide cases; he'd seen enough killing in the war. And reading about poor, harmless, inoffensive Millie Hesse and her gruesome end in the dark silent oaks and elms of these lonely woods dampened his enthusiasm for the story he was there to cover, a follow-up on the Herrin Massacre the previous summer. Not to write about the massacre itself. More than enough had been written about that.

It had been a big year for news, 1922, between the 19th Amendment giving women the right to vote and the discovery of King Tutankhamen's tomb, but you'd be hard-pressed to find anyone in the States who hadn't heard about what had happened in these parts between local miners and the Southern Illinois Coal Company. Flynn wanted to write about Herrin one year later; the aftermath and the repercussions. Plus, it was a good reason to visit Amy Gulling, the widow of his old mentor Gus. Gus had died in the winter, and Flynn hadn't made it down for the funeral. He didn't care much for funerals, either.

The train had been warm, but when Flynn stepped down onto the platform of the old brick station in Herrin, humidity slapped him in the face like a hot towel in a barber shop. It reminded him of summer in the trenches, minus the rats and snipers, of course.

He nodded an absent farewell to his fellow passengers—he couldn't have described them if his life had depended on it—and caught one of the town's only cabs, directing the driver to Amy Gulling's boarding house. Heat shimmered off the brick streets as the cab drove him through the peaceful town past the sheriff's office, closed during the violence of that long June day last year, and the hardware stores where the mob had broken in to steal guns and ammunition which they had then used to murder the mine guards and strikebreakers.

The cab let him out in front of the wooden two-story Civil War-style house on the corner. Flynn paid the driver, picked up his luggage and headed up the shady walk. He rang the bell and seconds later Amy herself was pushing open the screen door and welcoming him inside.

"David Flynn! I just lost a bet with myself."

"What bet?" He dropped his bags and hugged her hard.

"I bet you wouldn't come. I bet you'd find another excuse."

Amy was big and comfortable like a plushy chair. She wore a faded but well-starched flowered dress. Though her hair was now a graying flaxen, her blue-green eyes were as bright as ever. They studied him with canny affection.

Flynn reddened. "I'm sorry, Amy. Sorry I didn't make it down when Gus…"

She waved that away. "The funeral didn't matter. And you're here now. You must be tuckered out from that train ride."

She led him through to the parlor. A fat woman in a blue dress sat fanning herself in front of the big window, and in another chair a small, slim girl of perhaps twenty was reading a book titled *The Girls' Book of Famous Queens*. She had dark hair and wore spectacles.

"This is Mrs. Hoyt and her daughter Joan. They're regular boarders. They've been with me for two months now, since Mr. Hoyt passed."

"How do," said Mrs. Hoyt. The fine, sharp features of her face were blurred by weight and age. When she'd been young she probably looked like Joan. Her hair was still more dark than silver.

The girl, Joan, gave him a shy smile and a clammy hand.

"David's an old friend of my husband. One of his former journalism students. He's going to be spending the next week or so with us."

"Are you a newspaperman, Mr. Flynn?" asked Mrs. Hoyt.

"I am, but I'm on vacation now." Flynn knew this old beldame's breed. She'd be gossiping with the neighbors—those she considered her social equal—in nothing flat. And he wanted the freedom of anonymity, the ability to talk to these people without them second-guessing and censoring their words.

There was plenty for people to keep their mouths shut about considering Herrin had a national reputation for being the worst of the bad towns in "Bloody Williamson County." The trials of the men who had murdered the Lester Mine Company strikebreakers and guards had ended in unanimous acquittals, shocking the rest of the nation.

"David was in France," Amy said with significance.

"My son was in France, Mr. Flynn. Where did you see action?"

"I went over with Pershing's American Expeditionary Forces, ma'am."

"As a soldier or a journalist?"

"As a soldier." He had been proud of that. Proud to fight and maybe die for his ideals. Now he wondered if he wouldn't have done more good as a reporter.

"My son fell in the Battle of the Argonne."

The girl bowed her head, stared unseeingly at the book on her lap.

Flynn said, "A lot of boys did."

"My son was the recipient of the Medal of Honor."

"I'm afraid I didn't win any medals."

"Well, let's get you situated," Amy said briskly, breaking the sudden melancholy mood that had settled on the sunny parlor. "I've got David in the room over the breezeway."

"That's a mighty pleasant room in the summer," agreed Mrs. Hoyt. The daughter murmured acknowledgement.

Flynn smiled at Amy. "I remember."

He nodded to the ladies and followed Amy. She was saying, "I've turned Gus's study into a library and smoking room for the gentlemen."

Flynn asked unwillingly, "Has it been tough since Gus died?"

"Oh, you know. I manage all right. I keep the boarding house for company as much as anything. I never was happy on my own." Amy paused in the doorway of another room. "Here are our gentlemen. Doctor Pearson, Mr. Flynn is an old family friend. He'll be staying with us for a few days. Mr. Devereux, Mr. Flynn."

The gentlemen appeared to have been interrupted in the midst of writing letters. Doctor Pearson was small and spry with snapping dark eyes and the bushy sideburns and whiskers that were popular before the war. Mr. Devereux was older than the doctor, but he dyed his hair and mustache a persevering jet black. He had the distinctive features—aquiline nose and heavy-lidded eyes—Flynn had grown familiar with in France.

"Pleasure to meet you," Dr. Pearson said, putting aside his pen and paper and offering his hand.

Devereux was equally polite. "A pleasure, sir." He had a hint of an accent, but it was not exactly French. French Canadian perhaps? Or, no, French Creole?

"Mr. Devereux is a regular contributor to a number of Spiritualist periodicals," Amy commented.

Mr. Devereux livened up instantly. "That's correct. I'm penning an article for *The Messenger* in Boston."

Flynn nodded courteously. Spiritualism? Good God.

Perhaps Amy sensed his weary distaste because she was soon ushering him out of the room and down the hall.

They started toward the long blue-carpeted staircase. A quick, light tread caught Flynn's attention. He glanced up and saw a young man coming down the stairs. He was tall and willowy, his black hair of a bohemian length. His skin was a creamy bisque, his eyes dark and wide. Flynn judged him about nineteen although he wore no tie or jacket. He was dressed in gray flannel trousers, and his white shirt was open at the throat, the sleeves rolled to his elbows like a schoolboy.

"This is Mr. Flynn, Julian," Amy said.

Julian raised his delicate eyebrows. "Oh yes?"

"He's an old friend of my husband and me. He's going to be staying with us for a time."

Julian observed Flynn for long, alert seconds before he came leisurely down the rest of the staircase. He offered a slender, tanned hand and Flynn grasped it with manly firmness.

"Charmed," Julian murmured. He gently squeezed Flynn's hand back and studied him from beneath lashes as long and silky as a girl's. It was a look both shy and oddly knowing. Flynn recovered his hand as quickly as he could. He nodded curtly.

Julian smiled as though he read Flynn's reluctance and was entertained by it. It was a sly sort of smile, and his mouth was soft and pink. A sissy if Flynn had ever seen one.

"Julian is Mr. Devereux's grandson." There was something in Amy's voice Flynn couldn't quite pin down. Either she didn't like the old man or she didn't care for the kid—or maybe both.

Julian said slowly, "You're a…writer, David?"

"How the hell—?" Flynn stopped. Julian was smiling a smug smile.

"I know things."

"That's a dangerous habit."

"The philosophers say that knowledge is power."

"Sometimes. Sometimes it's the fastest way to get punched in the nose."

Both Amy and Julian laughed at that, and Flynn realized that he probably seemed a little hot under the collar.

Julian nodded pleasantly and sauntered away to the smoking room *cum* library.

"What in the blue blazes was *that*?" Flynn inquired of Amy as she led him up the staircase.

She laughed but it sounded forced. "*That* is The Magnificent Belloc. He's a spirit medium."

"You're joking."

Amy shook her head. "He's giving a show over at the Opera House every night this week except Friday and Sunday. Friday the high school is putting on *A Midsummer Night's Dream*."

"Spiritualism," Flynn said in disgust. He came from a long line of staunch Irish Protestants.

"Oh sure, there are a lot of fakes and phonies around. But the war changed a lot of people's feelings about spiritualism and mediums," Amy said. "When you lose someone dear to you, well, I guess you'd do anything to be able to talk to them one more time."

Flynn glanced at her and then glanced away. "I guess so."

"I don't put stock in spirits and that sort of thing, but from what I hear young Julian has a knack for knowing things."

"I'll bet."

Amy said mildly, "He called it right with you. I didn't tell him your first name was David or that you were a newspaperman."

"No, you didn't. But you did mention it to Mrs. Hoyt and her daughter." Flynn added dryly, "I'm guessing that The Magnificent Belloc's bedroom is the one over the parlor. Is that right?"

Amy looked chagrined. "That's right."

"I thought so. That kid's as phony as a three dollar bill."

"Oh, he's not so bad. A bit of a pansy, I guess. It's the old man I don't like. Whatever that boy is or isn't, it's that old frog's fault."

Flynn didn't argue with her, but he didn't agree either. Devereux younger wasn't anyone's victim. He recognized that jaded look. Whatever the racket was, The Magnificent Belloc was in it up to his shell-like ears.

Amy continued up the narrow staircase to the second level. Flynn's room was in the former servants' quarters on the far side of the house's breezeway. The roofed, open-sided passageway between the house and the garage was on the east side of the corner property, the "cool" side shaded by a big walnut tree, but there was nothing cool about that sunny box of a room that afternoon.

After Amy left, Flynn unpacked and then washed up next door in the closet-sized bathroom that had once served as a storage room.

Back in his room, he changed his shirt and examined himself closely in the square mirror over the highboy. What had that punk seen? Dark, wavy hair, blue eyes, strong chin and straight nose. Regular features. He was a regular guy. He looked all right. He looked like everybody else. Girls liked him fine. That girl, Joan, she didn't see anything wrong with him.

He shook his head impatiently at the troubled-looking Flynn in the mirror.

It didn't matter what that pansy thought or didn't think. Flynn didn't have to have anything to do with him. He was going to get his story and then he'd be heading back to New York City where people had a little discretion, a little subtlety.

He could smell fresh coffee and frying ham, and he followed the aroma downstairs where his fellow boarders were having a big noontime dinner of fried eggs, ham, sausage and golden brown potatoes. "Luncheon" they called it in New York, although you wouldn't get anything like this for lunch.

Flynn took a seat at the table across from Joan. He noticed—to his relief—that the disturbing Julian was absent. There was a lively discussion going on about the recent murders in the neighboring county.

"Perhaps someone could ask the Comte about them," Joan said, with a self-conscious look in Flynn's direction.

Doctor Pearson snorted. The older Devereux was shaking his head.

"Who's the Comte?" Flynn asked.

"The Comte de Mirabeau. Julian's spirit guide," Joan replied primly. "He was a French statesman, orator and writer. He died during the French Revolution."

"You're not a believer, young man," Devereux said severely, watching Flynn.

"I believe in plenty of things," Flynn said. "What did you have in mind?"

"Julian is a medium," Joan said.

"A medium what?"

Mrs. Hoyt gave a breathy laugh and scooped up a mouthful of eggs.

The conversation briefly languished, and Flynn decided to ask about the trials of the miners accused of murder last year and the winter. That revived the discussion, but mostly what he heard about was how the KKK and the local ministers were trying to persuade the government and the law to do something about the bootleggers and their roadhouses springing up like toadstools. The massacre was old news. It appeared nobody wanted to think about it.

Astonishingly, these civilized, decent folk seemed to think the best bet for the lawlessness plaguing their county was the Ku Klux Klan. Flynn found it hard to credit. He kept his mouth shut for the most part and listened.

"Thank goodness for Prohibition!" exclaimed Mrs. Hoyt, shoveling in fried potatoes.

Dr. Pearson shot back, "The only thing Prohibition helps is the gangsters and the damned Ku Klux Klan."

"It's kept a lot of boys off the liquor," insisted Mrs. Hoyt thickly.

"Ah baloney," growled the old doctor. "More of those kids are trying booze out now than they were before Prohibition. Forbidding it makes drink seem exciting."

"That's because the sheriffs don't enforce the law!"

Amy said to Flynn, "Mrs. Hoyt is right about that. We've got a poor excuse for a sheriff. He's great pals with half the bootleggers in the county."

"I'm surprised that you, a doctor, would take that view," Mrs. Hoyt said to Pearson. She seemed indignant, but Flynn had the idea this was not a new argument in this household.

Pearson was unmoved. "When drink was legal these kids weren't allowed in a saloon, but these damned bootleggers don't care who they sell their hooch to or who they sucker into gambling away their paychecks. Why, I was tending a poor kid over in Murphysboro just last week who died of that damned bathtub gin."

Joan's gaze met Flynn's and slid away.

"But that's exactly what the Klan and the ministers are saying," Mrs. Hoyt insisted. "If the law won't clean this mess up, then the people have to."

Devereux chimed in, "People? Which people? A bunch of anti-union kleagles and clowns dressed up in spooky robes doing their mumbo-jumbo and burning crosses out in somebody's pasture."

The old guy sounded pretty heated. Flynn was willing to bet that with their complexion and coloring, he and the kid had been mistaken for Italians or worse on more than one occasion.

"You're a fine one to talk about mumbo-jumbo," Mrs. Hoyt said tartly.

Devereux bridled. "I assure you, Madame, Spiritualism is as valid and respectable a religion as any other. We simply believe that the door between this world and the next is accessible to those who hold the key, and that through the talents of one gifted with the power to communicate with spirits, we may learn and be advised by our loved ones who have gone before us."

"Speaking of those gone before us," Flynn remarked, "I see your grandson isn't at lunch."

"Julian rests in the afternoon," the old man said stiffly. "He is not strong, and his efforts to act as conduit to the other side tax him greatly."

Flynn managed to control his expression. Just.

There was not a lot of chat after that. When the meal was finished, Flynn excused himself and went back to his room. He wanted to start looking around the town as soon as possible.

He found he had a visitor. Julian Devereux was seated on the bed, idly flipping through his copy of *Bertram Cope's Year*. Flynn had left the book in his Gladstone.

He paused in the doorway, the hair on the back of his neck rising on end. "What are you doing in here?" he asked sharply.

Julian jumped—so much for psychic powers—though his smile was confident. He tossed the book on the green-and-white Irish chain quilt, leaned back on his hands.

"I thought we should get to know each other, David."

Flynn studied Julian's finely chiseled features coldly, taking in the angular, wide mouth and heavy-lidded, half-amused dark eyes.

"Why's that?"

Julian arched one eyebrow. "You know."

"No, I don't. And I'm pretty sure I don't want to."

Julian tilted his head, as though listening to an echo he couldn't quite place. "I didn't figure you for the shy type," he said eventually.

"I'm not. I'm not your type either." Flynn was careful not to look at the book on the bed. "Now if you don't mind—?" He held the door open pointedly.

A look of disbelief crossed Julian's face. He rose from the bed and slowly moved to the door. For an instant he stood before Flynn. He was so slight, so lithesome that Flynn kept picturing him shorter than he was. In fact, he was as tall as Flynn, his doe-like dark eyes gazing directly into the other man's.

"Have it your way," he said.

"I intend to."

"But if you should change your mind—"

Flynn inquired dryly, "Wouldn't The Magnificent Belloc be the first to know?"

CHAPTER TWO

"*T*hose scabs and strikebreakers got what they asked for." That was the view of big Tom McCarty.

"Bullets and pick handles?"

Flynn was genuinely curious about that kind of reasoning, and McCarty's weathered face tightened. He was a young mine hoisting engineer with powerful arms and shoulders, a long-time member of the United Mine Workers. He didn't say he had been at Crenshaw Crossing or Harrison Woods. He didn't say he hadn't been. "The miners were striking for safe working conditions and decent wages. They deserve that. Anybody deserves that. But Lester and the other mine owners shipped in them strikebreakers and scabs and gave away the striking miners' jobs. I stand by what I say. They deserve what they got."

There were mutters of agreement from the other men at Skeltcher's Tavern. Except that Skeltcher's wasn't a tavern anymore. Theoretically it was a soft drink parlor. Every town, every wide-spot-in-the-road now had a small, weather-beaten saloon currently known as a soft drink parlor though the clientele hanging around those joints didn't much look like sody pop drinkers to Flynn.

"What about these stories about cutting the throats of the wounded men?"

"Don't believe everything you read in the papers, pal."

"I won't," Flynn said gravely.

An older man with the cough that came from too many years of ciga-rettes—or coal dust—chimed in, "If rich, blood-sucking mine owners like Lester get away with using thugs and scabs to break a strike down here in a union stronghold, then the UMWA and the other unions are finished in this country."

McCarty agreed. "Those miners were acquitted by a jury—two juries—of their peers. That's justice."

Flynn nodded politely and stood McCarty to another "root beer." Maybe it wasn't justice, but it seemed to be raw democracy in action. Flynn had read the trial reports and one thing was clear—local sympathy had been unwaveringly with the miners. An initial inquest concluded that all the strikebreakers were killed by unknown individuals, and recommended that Southern Illinois Coal Company and its officers be investigated in order to affix appropriate responsibility on them. Eventually two trials were held, the first on November 7, 1922, the second that very same winter. Only six men had been indicted for the massacre, and both trials ended in acquittals for all the defendants. At that point the prosecution had given it up as a lost cause. The remaining indictments were dismissed. The pros-ecutor had summed up the defense's case as "These men were justified in what they did; and besides, they didn't do it!"

You could still hear the echo of that sentiment in Skeltcher's soft drink parlor. It was like the entire town of Herrin, maybe Williamson County, were suffering from a kind of hysterical blindness and couldn't see what the rest of the world saw. Old General Black Jack Pershing himself had shown up in Marion and pronounced the massacre as "wholesale murder as yet unpunished."

And that was very much the mind Flynn had been in when he had boarded the train in New York. How could it be anything else? But listening to these men talk he was startled at their certainty, their lack of remorse, their continuing and abiding anger at the rich men who they believed had forced them to take violent action. Little as he liked it, Flynn couldn't help but suspect there was a grain of truth in the miner's comments about whether Lester and the other mine owners would ever be held to account for the unsafe working conditions in their properties or the men killed in the explosions in their mines.

$\mathcal{I}$t was still early when Flynn left Skeltcher's. His thoughts were restless, and he wasn't ready to return to the stuffy quiet of the boarding house, wasn't ready to hear more about how the KKK was going to save western civilization, wasn't ready to talk to Amy about Gus. Instead, he walked along the mostly empty streets trying to reorganize his thoughts, trying to quell his own turbulent needs.

It was all the fault of that young fakir, the sham mentalist with the lithe body and ancient eyes. That kind of thing was dangerous even in New York where people were cosmopolitan and sophisticated and where there were clubs where a man could go for drinks and the company of men like himself. In Harlem, Greenwich and Times Square there were restaurants, cafeterias, cafés and speakeasies where the city's intellectuals and artists and bon vivants gathered.

Little Egypt was a cultural wasteland in comparison. And Julian Devereux stood out like a tropical flower.

So Flynn strode along the brick streets, waving the gnats away, watching the fireflies winking on and off. It was still uncomfortably warm, though the yellow stars were high in the pink and violet sky now.

A poster in a shop window caught his eye, and he stopped to examine it. Fancy swirling script announced The Magnificent Belloc's public exhibition on Tuesday, Wednesday, Thursday and Saturday night at the Opera House on West Franklin Street.

Flynn snorted at the flowery sketch of Julian in the garb of an Indian prince. He was surrounded by highly stylized zephyrs—or maybe ordinary working draughts—with faces both mournful and gay. The spirits he communicated with? Yet even in that strange drawing Julian's mysterious dark eyes seemed to gaze out at Flynn, seemed to hypnotize him.

Amused at himself, but curious nonetheless, he caught the little streetcar and made the journey across town to the Opera House. It was a grand-looking building with a wide arch entrance, terra-cotta trim and sour-looking gargoyles.

"You're just in time," the freckle-faced girl in the ticket booth told him. "We got strict orders to lock the door after the show starts."

"Is it much of a crowd?"

To his surprise, the girl said, "Oh, yes. The Magnificent Belloc impressed a lot of folks last night, and they told their friends and families."

Flynn raised skeptical brows, but he went inside the lobby which was startlingly ornate with dark wood and gilt fixtures and red carpets. An usher held the door for him and Flynn slipped inside the darkened theater. The door closed firmly after him.

Through the darkness, he found his way down a row of plush seats, located an empty seat near the back and sat down. It was only then that he actually looked at the stage. There was a small table with a crystal ball in the center. Behind the table, The Magnificent Belloc was sitting in a large gold throne. Presumably it belonged to the Opera House since it was hard to picture gramps and Julian lugging that piece of furniture all over the Midwest. It was a nice prop, though, and it suited the occasion and the man sitting in it.

Julian looked like one of those French aristocrats from the time right before the people got tired of eating cake and started lopping heads. He wore dark blue leggings and a silver and powder blue brocade frock coat over a soft shirt with bunches of lace at the throat and cuffs. He had caved to the fashion of phony mediums and donned a turban, but it was relatively simple, creamy pale silk fastened with a giant sapphire. There were jewels on his slender hands and pinned at the lace at his throat; they flashed in the footlights every time he moved. The crowd seemed spellbound, and Flynn was not surprised. Julian looked beautiful and exotic and mysterious. He looked unearthly.

Flynn had already missed the introductions and preliminaries, whatever they were. Julian's eyes were shut and he was mumbling to himself, but the acoustics of the old building were excellent and Flynn recognized the occasional French word. Not French as he knew it. It was probably supposed to be the French of Paris at the time of the Revolution, but it was more likely French Creole. Then again, French Creole was supposed to be an older variety of French, wasn't it?

Someone shouted out from the crowd, "What about these here murders we're hearing about? What do the spirits say about them?"

The Magnificent Belloc shook his head, gave an impatient flick of his jeweled fingers and kept concentrating.

There were hisses and shushing from the crowd for the man who had interrupted the mystic's train of thought. He subsided, abashed.

Belloc—it was hard to think of him as Julian in this context—sat up straight and opened his eyes. He had a distinctly French inflection as he said, "Her name is Marie. No. *Mary.* A pretty child. *La pauvre petite.* She was very young when she crossed, yes?"

Reaction rippled through the crowd but no one spoke up.

"She was…confused at first," Belloc said gravely. "The young ones often are, but they…what is the word? Habituate the most quickly." He looked out over the sea of faces, although he probably couldn't see anything beyond the front of the stage. "Mary. She is all right now. Everything is all right now. Who is here for Mary?"

There was a smothered sob as though torn unwilling out of some grieving breast, and an elderly woman stood up, handkerchief pressed to her mouth.

"Ah. *Grand-mère,*" Belloc said kindly. "Mary wishes to tell you something. She wishes to tell you that she is all right. She is happy. She is playing with the little lambs and baby angels. She is strong and she is well again."

The woman sobbed into her handkerchief.

"Non, non, Grand-mère," Belloc said quickly. "Mary wishes you to be happy for her. She has joined us with one purpose tonight and that is to tell you that she thanks you for all your love and your care, and that she is in a better place now, *oui?"*

The woman buried her face in her handkerchief and sank back into her seat.

Belloc nodded, well-satisfied with his chicanery, and relaxed in his throne. He closed his eyes.

Already the murmurs were running through the crowd impressed with the evening's entertainment so far.

Belloc mumbled some more French words. He dipped his head as though agreeing to something the spirits were saying. Listening a few seconds more, he held up a graceful hand, bidding the spirits to shut it for a sec.

"Joe…Joseph…he is very excited to speak tonight. Who is here for Joseph?"

Four different people rose throughout the audience, and a nervous titter went through the crowd.

Belloc laughed too. *"Eh bien!* We must narrow this down." He turned to consult with Joe for another few seconds, but again it appeared Joe was overeager and a little incoherent.

"Joe was a miner? Is that correct?"

All four members of the audience remained stubbornly standing.

Flynn began to enjoy himself.

Belloc returned to listening to Joe. He cast the audience an apologetic look. "It is a little hard to understand. Joe, he is not…was not…much for conversation on this side. Except perhaps when he had a bit of the…how you say…*moonshine?"*

Laughter rippled through the audience and three of the four standing sat down. Pointedly.

Belloc smiled encouragingly at the fourth. "What is your name, Madame?"

"Mable Gabbay. I was Joe's second wife."

"Oh yes?" Belloc hesitated a fraction. "And the first Madame Gabbay, she is…?"

Mable said grimly, "Joe was nine years a widower when I met him."

Belloc turned back to Joe, who appeared to be requesting a quick word. He listened attentively to Joe, then turned back to the widow. He said with charming simplicity, "He misses you, Madame. There is no doubt of this. He misses you greatly."

"What I want to know," Mable said, "is whether *she's* over there with him?"

The audience burst into nervous laughter. Surprisingly, Belloc laughed too, although he quickly sobered.

"Madame Gabbay," he said seriously, "it is most important that you understand that it is different on the other side. Joe has returned to us tonight for two purposes. The first is that he wishes you to understand that on the other side the feelings and thoughts that trouble us on the earthly plane are gone. They are no more."

Mable bridled at this but didn't argue.

"The second purpose for Joe's presence here tonight is that he wishes you to understand that he loves you. He wishes he had told you this more often. But though he did not say the words, he was not a man for words, he felt for you *la passion grande.*"

Mable did not seem to have an answer for that. She stared with a sort of hard, anxious longing at the empty space on the stage next to Belloc's throne before taking her seat again.

Flynn felt faintly nauseated. This was nothing more than base manipulation of people's deepest, most cherished feelings. Belloc was skilled enough, though the act was much simpler than others Flynn had seen. No floating lights or musical instruments, no weird noises or showy stagecraft, no assistant moving through the crowd and feeding him code words and signals. Belloc was doing it all through, no doubt, painstaking research of the community: reading the obituaries and social pages of the local paper, checking the local cemetery, exploring the town and picking up useful bits of info—all that plus using what was no doubt a wily intuition. Given how very at ease he was, Flynn guessed he'd been involved in this mystical fraud one way or another since childhood. It was sickening and it was fascinating.

After the success of Joe and Mary, Belloc moved into high gear. He kept the names flying, kept the audience eagerly supplying him with the cues and information he needed.

He kept up his reassuring prattle about the idyllic happiness on the other side and the beauty and joy of being dead. And the suckers ate it up, every word.

Had it been a different time and place, Flynn would have taken time and pleasure in writing a searing exposé of His Magnificence. But he didn't have time and this was not a town to be trusted when angered. Flynn didn't need more blood on his hands.

"Henrietta, Orrin says that you must look in the cellar. There is something valuable there. You will know it when you see it. Peter, Dolly says you must remarry. *Vraiment.* You do not honor her memory with loneliness and grief, but with joy and love. Maggie, your brother Glenn sends his greetings and wishes you to know that he is happy and well. David, Gus says you must not waste time on regret. He is happy that you are here. Your presence will make a difference in the days to come."

Flynn caught this last in frozen disbelief. "You phony little sonofabitch," he muttered. His words carried with unexpected clarity in the pause that had followed Belloc's last remark.

People glanced around looking for the heretic, and there were murmurs of displeasure. On stage, Belloc had fallen silent, fist to his forehead, ostensibly concentrating hard.

"Angela," he said slowly, "I have a message from Bill." He raised his head and stared out beyond the glare of the footlights. "Is Angela in the house tonight?"

A tall woman stood midway up the sea of red velvet chairs. "I'm Angela. Bill was my father. William Robert Tucker. He passed nine years ago." She looked around smiling, and others were nodding affirmation.

In that same tired voice, Belloc said, "Angela, Bill says that you must not feel guilty for going out tonight. He was teasing you, that is all."

Angela seemed to recoil. She said falteringly, "What does he mean? What is he saying? Who was teasing me?"

"Bill…was teasing you." The fakir must have been tiring because he wasn't bothering with the accent anymore.

"*Bill?* My husband Bill? Is that what he means? What does he mean? What is he saying?" She looked around as though expecting answers from the audience, but the people around her were deathly still.

"Bill says he loves you…you must not grieve for the…you must not."

"What are you *saying*?"

The voice dragged on. "When you see the music box he made you—"

"My father never did!"

"When you listen to the tune 'By the Light of the Silvery Moon'…"

Angela screamed, her voice ringing shrilly off the rafters and walls. "It's not true. It's not Bill. It's my father. It's *not* Bill!"

There was stricken silence in the auditorium. Flynn could almost pick up the soft, tired breaths of Belloc. The spiritualist was gripping the arms of the throne with white-knuckled hands, his eyes were closed, his face tense and pained. Alarmed whispers rustled through the spectators like a fox running through tall grass. The whispers picked up volume and velocity as they flowed through the aisles.

Angela made her way through the row of seats, still crying and protesting, "You're lying. You're trying to frighten me. It's not true. It's not

Bill. It's not true…" She ran up the aisle followed by her companions, and they hurried out through the double doors, leaving them swinging.

In the wake of her panicked flight a hushed alarm hung over the spellbound audience, all gazes fixed on the man in the golden throne.

After very long seconds, Belloc's eyes flew open and he seemed to recover himself. He offered a tired smile.

"You have questions, no? Let us see if the spirits have answers. Arthur, Madeline says that you must take the time to eat a proper supper…"

Relieved laughter from the crowd. Flynn rose and made his way down the narrow row of chairs and out of the Opera House.

A fake and a phony. That summed up The Magnificent Belloc. But a smart one, a shrewd one. The Bill incident had been eerie, no doubt about it. It had spooked Bill's wife. That was probably no accident. Whether the story was true or not, it would set tongues wagging, and tomorrow night more people would show up at the Opera House and pay their hard-earned pennies to hear that charlatan babble his clever concoction of spooky stories and platitudes.

Flynn walked briskly, lost in thought, and eventually he reached the boarding house. He let himself inside the airless house with the key Amy had given him and went quietly upstairs.

It was still uncomfortably warm in the room above the breezeway, a hot, still night. The crickets chirped merrily and in the distance a dog was howling. Flynn undressed and stretched out on the cotton bedcover. He closed his eyes.

He heard the clickity-clack of the train wheels again, miles and miles of it, and soon he drifted into dreamless sleep, leaving images behind like smoke from a train: bloodied miners, white-sheeted klansmen, and a slim dark man in the rich costume of a doomed aristocrat.

CHAPTER THREE

*T*hursday Flynn woke to the sound of voices.

He opened his eyes and blinked at the glare of bright sunlight on wall-paper. It took him a few seconds to place himself, to remember that he was in Herrin, in his old room at Gus and Amy's.

He winced, remembering the things Julian Devereux had said during his show at the Opera House the evening before.

David, Gus says you must not waste time on regret. He is happy that you are here. Your presence will make a difference in the days to come.

Nothing would give him greater pleasure than to punch that wiseacre in his wide, smirking mouth. But he had to give Devereux credit. He was good at reading people, good at ferreting out the truths people tried to hide even from themselves. In that sense he was like a smart investigative reporter, but he used his skill for making fools of others rather than edu-cating them with the truth.

Flynn rose and went to the window, gazing down. He could see the breezeway below and the striped awning of the old swing as it rocked gently. Someone was sitting in the swing: he could see a flannel-clad bent knee and the flash of smooth brown arm as the swing moved in and out of sunlight. A radio played noisily through the kitchen window.

Flynn went next door and had a quick bath using three pots of water, two hot and one cold. The day was already hot and by the time he'd shaved and dressed he was nearly as sweaty as when he began, but he smelled more civilized.

At breakfast it was Flynn, Mrs. Hoyt and Joan.

Joan was talking about the murders in Jackson County, although she broke off when Flynn entered the dining room.

"Publishers make things up to sell more papers, isn't that true, Mr. Flynn?" Mrs. Hoyt inquired.

Flynn shook his napkin out and said, "Respectable publishers don't."

Mrs. Hoyt's expression indicated she believed the respectable publisher to be right up there with the dodo bird.

Joan, keeping her voice down as though afraid of being overheard, said, "The papers say that the bodies of the women were prepared as though for Egyptian burial. Do you suppose that means they were wrapped like mummies?"

According to Flynn's pal in the AP, the women had been left naked, their bodies crudely carved up, their internal organs wrapped in linen bandages and left in mason jars like the hearts, lungs and kidneys of ancient pharaohs had been placed in canopic vases for burial. Of course that could be a rumor, and even if it wasn't, Flynn wasn't about to share it with the ladies over breakfast.

Mrs. Hoyt said in shocked tones, *"Joan."*

Joan turned scarlet and explained, "I enjoy murder mysteries."

Mrs. Hoyt was shaking her head at her unnatural offspring. Flynn smiled at Joan. She blushed more.

"I suppose you've covered a few murder cases in your time, Mr. Flynn?" That was Mrs. Hoyt again.

"A few." To Joan, he said apologetically, "They're mostly sad, sordid affairs. Not like the things you read in books. Most murderers aren't that smart. If they get away with it, it's more luck than anything."

"That's what Julian says."

"Julian?"

"Mr. Devereux. I suggested that perhaps he could use his talents to help the police like they say Mr. Edgar Cayce has done."

"And what did he say?"

"He said that the spirits didn't like to get involved in such sad, sordid affairs. Those were his exact words. That the spirits came to us to teach us about how to live better lives so that we can safely reach the blessed hereafter."

"Did he?" Flynn said dryly.

Amy came out of the kitchen with a great platter of pancakes. She had always been a wonderful cook, although she employed a woman to help her now. It had interested and surprised Flynn, the relationship between Amy and Gus. Gus had been a New York intellectual and radical. Amy was… the salt of the earth. Not the kind of woman anyone would have pegged for Gus. Maybe it was true about opposites attracting. Amy and Gus had seemed as happy as two people could be with each other. Not that Flynn was an expert on such things.

"Did you have a nice time last night?" Amy asked Flynn, forking a stack onto his plate.

Flynn nodded. "It was educational. I caught part of young Julian's show at the Opera House."

"Oh my."

Joan caught her breath and said, "I want to see Julian's show. Mama doesn't approve of spiritualists."

"You're not missing anything." Catching their expressions, Flynn qualified, "I guess I'm not much for spiritualism myself."

Amy said quietly, "There's talk that he foretold the death of a member of the audience."

"No." Reluctantly Flynn added, "It seemed like he might have foretold the death of a woman's husband." He shrugged as the ladies gasped.

"It's the devil's work," Mrs. Hoyt exclaimed.

"But what if it's true?" Joan asked.

"There are things we're not meant to know."

Flynn devoted his attention to his pancakes. He wondered why Joan wasn't married and starting a family of her own. But the war had probably put paid to a lot of women's hopes for that. Over a hundred thousand dead American soldiers meant a hundred thousand fewer husbands and sweethearts.

"Where *is* The Magnificent Belloc?" he asked.

"Julian doesn't eat breakfast. He can't the morning after a performance."

Joan seemed to know an awful lot about Julian, given he and gramps couldn't have been staying at the boarding house long. If she was sweet on Julian, that really was a shame.

Flynn raised polite eyebrows, and she continued, "Mr. Devereux rarely rises before noon. And Dr. Pearson is always away by this time of the morning."

"That's because he's the only doctor in this county who knows his business," Mrs. Hoyt said briskly. "I don't hold with those boys fresh out of the university. I don't like a doctor younger than me."

"Now, Mrs. Hoyt," Amy said briskly, "that young Dr. Anson in Carbondale is very pleasant and very knowledgeable."

Mrs. Hoyt was unswayed, and Flynn went back to eating his pancakes and trying not to listen to them. He had a lot planned for the day. He wanted to hurry and finish this story; he could no longer remember why he thought traveling to Illinois was a good idea. Murders and mystics…

*W*hen breakfast was over, Flynn nodded good-bye to the ladies and walked out to the breezeway to have a smoke.

Most of the houses in town were single story, designed with a front porch where people could sit on their swings in warm weather, fan themselves and say unkind things about their neighbors in relative comfort. The boarding house swing was at the west end of the breezeway making it a shady and fairly pleasant place to sit in the hot afternoon. Cream-pink roses wound up the walls of the arbor.

Julian Devereux sat idle in the swing. He looked up at Flynn's approach and offered that sly smile. "Good morning."

Flynn nodded curtly. He leaned against the wall and lit his cigarette, studying the younger man with a level eye.

"Did you enjoy the show last night?"

"Not particularly."

Julian chuckled. "Why not? I heard I was very good."

Flynn said evenly, "You want to know what I thought? I thought—think—you're a two-bit four-flusher in fancy dress. You winkle out people's deepest, most treasured feelings and you use that knowledge to take advantage of them."

"No, I don't," Julian said calmly. "I give them hope. And reassurance."

"Hope and reassurance? Is that what you were feeding that woman last night when you hinted her husband was dead?"

Julian's smile faded. He stared out at the street where two women were strolling along with shopping bags. "I don't remember that."

"I bet everyone else does."

Julian raised a negligent shoulder. Flynn puffed on his cigarette and eyed the younger man's sharp profile.

"I notice you don't deny it's all a bunch of hocus-pocus."

Julian's dark, wide gaze turned his way again. He said mockingly, "Deny it to a smart big-city reporter like *you,* David?"

"Why did you tell that woman her husband was dead?"

"I told you I don't remember that." He sounded mildly irritated.

"That's convenient. How long have you been in this racket?"

Julian smiled with disarming sweetness. "Oh, I come by my trade honestly. I was, as they say, born in a trunk. The only offspring of Count Amadeus and Zaliki the Seer. In fact..." his voice dropped for apparent dramatic effect, "...my mother foresaw my father's death during her final performance."

Flynn's smile was sardonic. "The Astral Plane by Louisiana way?"

Julian cocked his head inquiringly. "I'd think with the things you must have seen in the war you'd want to believe there was something more, something better waiting for us."

"You don't know anything about it."

Julian continued to stare at him with an intensity that made Flynn uncomfortable.

"What was that book in your luggage?" he asked unexpectedly.

"You saw it," Flynn said shortly.

"I saw you turn white."

"I don't like people going through my things."

"You don't like people." Julian was smiling again. "You'd rather write about them, turn them into characters like in a book, than have to deal with flesh and blood."

Flynn dropped his cigarette on the walkway and ground it with his heel. "You better stick to fortune-telling and leave the psychoanalyzing to the experts."

Julian's laugh was suggestive. "I'll tell *your* fortune if you like, David."

It irked Flynn the way the pansy kept saying his name, *David*, with that certain knowing intimacy. He had no right to take that tone. He didn't let his irritation show as he replied, "I thought spiritualists didn't predict the future."

"I'll make an exception in your case."

"Thanks. I'll work it out for myself."

Julian said quite seriously, "All right. But don't take too long, will you?"

Flynn gave a dismissing laugh and walked away. He was annoyed with himself for going out to the breezeway in the first place. He'd had a pretty good idea Julian was sitting out there, but as much as he disliked the other man, he'd headed straight out there after breakfast. It was peculiar. He understood part of the uneasy draw. He and Julian did have one thing in common, but that only made it worse. Julian was the kind of twilight lover that embarrassed men like Flynn. It was only when he saw sissies and pansies like Julian that he felt ashamed of what he was.

*T*he Hoyt mother and daughter were back when Flynn grabbed his coat and hat and left for the soft drink parlor and pool hall. With Amy's permission he borrowed Gus's Model T and drove into the center of town rather than walking in the bright shimmering heat.

Milo's place looked exactly like it was: a rundown, old pool hall. Flynn walked down a narrow hallway dividing a small office from a storeroom. A scrawny, squint-eyed man sat in the office, watching the back entrance. A well-chewed cigar was clamped between his teeth and a double-barreled shotgun lay on the big desk in front of him.

Beyond the office was another room with two card tables and a door on each end leading to the front. The right door led to a couple of beat-out pool tables set off from the bar by a five-foot curtain divider. Two men lackadaisically knocked colored balls around with pool cues and cursed each other amiably. The left door opened on the front of the soft drink parlor. The tall wooden bar was scuffed and battered but someone had made it their business to keep it and the tall stools before it well-polished and gleaming.

The bartender was a Hungarian named Earl. He asked what soft drink Flynn wanted, and Flynn ordered a Dr. Pepper. The Dr. Pepper turned out to be half a soft drink bottle full of fine Canadian whisky. He drank it and ate salty Georgia peanuts while he talked to the natives. For a bloodthirsty lot, they were surprisingly good-natured and frank.

"People around here are sick and tired of Williamson County being called Bloody Williamson," said a man the others referred to as Monty. "We're sick of being called murdering hillbillies by newspapers all over the country."

"Twenty-one men dead, two trials, and not one conviction," Flynn pointed out.

"That should tell you something right there."

It did, but apparently not the same thing it told the gentlemen of Herrin.

"I tell you what I feel bad about," said a man with a long scar down the side of his face. "I feel bad that W.J. Lester didn't get what his boys got."

The other men gave him warning looks, but he ignored them. "Hell, this is the strongest union area in the entire country, but Ole King Coal thinks to hell with that and he brings in a bunch of scabs, mine guards and hoodlum strikebreakers from Chicago. Pride goeth before a fall. That's what the Good Book says. If anyone should have reaped what he sowed, it was that bastard. But he walked away scot-free like the rich always do."

"The coroner had it right when he said the real criminals were the officials of the Southern Illinois Coal Company."

There was a muttered chorus of agreement.

Monty said, "The miners stood their trial and they were acquitted fair and square, but you'd never know it to hear these bastards talk. Look at that union-hating jackass Harding and his baloney about 'free Americans have the right to work without anyone's leave.' He and the big-shot mine owners figure if they can bust the UMWA in Illinois then they can bust any union in the country. Or that other bastard Pershing and his bullshit about 'inoffensive people having the right to earn a livelihood.' Inoffensive, my ass! It's easy to stand in judgment when you've never been hungry or had to see your kids go hungry."

Flynn was silent. He had a lot of respect for Black Jack Pershing, but he'd covered a mine disaster in his time. And he remembered hearing Gulling talk about the mine conditions before the unions: working in water up to your hips, gas-filled rooms, cave-ins, and all that for a buck fifty a day—a buck fifty if you were lucky.

Rough justice. That was the consensus of Milo's pool hall and soft drink parlor and a couple of hours of talk and drink didn't sway them an iota. They were resentful but not remorseful. And there was still a lot of bitterness and hatred boiling not far below the polite surface.

When he figured he'd learned all that there was to learn at Milo's, Flynn got in the Model T and drove out to Moake Crossing, about half a mile from where on June 21st the previous summer, the miners and a mob of about five hundred—and growing—had finally forced W.J. Lester's mine to shut and the workers to surrender.

This was the road the miners had marched their prisoners down after their surrender. This was the place where McDowell, the mine boss, had been taken off the road and shot to death.

It was a harmless-looking place on a sunny July afternoon. Nothing but farm fields and forest. It seemed a long way from town. The sky was cloudless and the air so still you could hear the hum of every insect.

Flynn put the flivver in gear and continued on. He had read the accounts many times. The prisoners were walked along the railroad tracks, their arms in the air until they came to the powerhouse. Then, the story went, the Union President Hugh Willis supposedly drove up and warned the miners not to kill their prisoners on an open road where women and children might see.

Maybe that part of the story was the fantasy Willis and others claimed. Certainly nothing had been proven against Willis. But it was no fantasy that the strikebreakers and guards had been herded north of the powerhouse, across the tracks to a narrow strip of wood and brush. The mob pushed their captives into the trees, and about a hundred yards from the treeline they came to a fence with four strands of barbed wire. A big bearded man in overalls yelled out, "Here's where you scab bastards run the gauntlet. Let's see how fast you gutterbums can run all the way back to Chicago."

And then the mob had opened fire.

When Flynn came to the spot, he pulled to the side of the road and got out, walking across to the dense woods and green brush. The pound of his shoe soles on the dry ground sounded unnaturally loud in the unfriendly silence. He was not a superstitious man, but the place had a queer, haunted feel. The barbed wire glinted barbarous and cruel in the unforgiving sunlight. It reminded him of other barbed wire and other blood-drenched ground.

The undergrowth crackled, but when he glanced around, nothing was there.

High overhead on a tree branch, a black crow called out in its harsh, raucous voice.

CHAPTER FOUR

On the way back to the boarding house, Flynn stopped and bought an electric fan at the hardware store. He parked the Model T in the garage and carried the fan inside the house. In the parlor he could hear Mrs. Hoyt complaining; he didn't catch the words, but he knew the tone. Her daughter's voice murmured in acquiescence.

Farther down the hall, in the study where Gus had typed his Pulitzer prize-winning series of articles on the national coal strike in 1919, he could hear Dr. Pearson and Mr. Devereux bickering, but it sounded mostly amiable.

"David," Amy called.

Flynn glanced around. Amy was coming his way, a fair-haired, broad-shouldered man in tow. The man carried a suitcase in each hand. For one shocked instant, Flynn thought the man was Paul. Then reality reasserted itself. Aside from the light hair and the broad shoulders, the man didn't resemble Paul at all.

"David, this is Mr. Lee. He works for the Queen of Egypt Medical Supply Company and stays with us regularly." To Mr. Lee, she said, "Mr. Flynn is an old family friend."

Mr. Lee's tilted green eyes met Flynn's briefly. He looked away then his gaze returned and locked. He shifted his samples bag and offered his hand and a smile. David shifted the fan he was carrying and shook hands. He smiled back. Mr. Lee was blond and boyishly handsome.

"Casey."

"David."

"Well now, I'll leave you two to get acquainted. Mrs. Greer helps me out in the kitchen, but her daughter is ill and she had to leave this morning." Amy was already turning. "I need to get back to work." She hurried away, and Flynn and Casey Lee were left to climb the stairs to the second level on their own.

"Medical supplies?" Flynn asked. He thought he recognized a fellow veteran. It was the way Casey held himself and the quick, no-nonsense way he'd sized Flynn up. During the war there hadn't been time to waste.

Casey laughed. "Yep. I'm the original snake oil salesman. We sell everything from elixirs to remedies for warts and asthma." He gave Flynn a sideways smile.

"You must travel around quite a bit."

"I'm on the road pretty much all the time these days. I was in Marion yesterday." He grimaced. "Day before that I was in Murphysboro."

"Yes?"

"The whole of Jackson County is talking about those murders. People are pretty worked up."

"I bet."

They reached the second level. Casey said, "Amy lays a mighty fine table. I always eat too much. I was thinking of going out for a walk after supper."

"I have the same problem," Flynn said. "Maybe I'll join you."

Casey smiled. He turned left to go down the hall to his room and Flynn turned right.

He was still smiling as he opened the door to his room. The smile vanished at the sight of Julian Devereux lying on his bed.

Julian wore a sumptuous plum-colored dressing gown. At the squeak of the door hinges, he turned his head and looked up under his lashes, smiling with deliberate seduction. "I knew you were back."

Flynn closed the door and leaned back against it. "What the hell are you doing in here?" he asked, keeping his voice down.

"Waiting for you."

"You're wasting your time."

"It's my time to waste." Julian sat up, the purple robe falling open to reveal a sleek, honey-colored body. "Although I shouldn't want to waste much more of it."

Flynn shook his head in disbelief. "You must be insane." He truly didn't know what to make of this young maniac. He had neither scruples nor morals. Worse, he didn't appear to have any commonsense. He added deliberately, "Or stupid."

As it slowly sunk in on him that Flynn was serious, Julian's smile faded, lost its confident curve. His bold gaze darkened with something like hurt. "Why would you say that? The moment I saw you I saw that you were just like me. That you wanted this too."

"I'm *nothing* like you," Flynn said with quiet intensity. "Now get out of my room."

Julian continued to stare at him with those wide, dark eyes. "I'm not wrong." He spoke with a stubborn sort of dignity. It was almost disarming.

Flynn, however, had no intention of being disarmed. "You damned fool. You're going to get us both arrested. Or killed."

Julian shook his head. "People don't notice unless you bring attention to yourself. They see what they expect to see."

He said it quite seriously, and Flynn had to laugh. "*The Magnificent Belloc?* I hate to break it to you, Devereux, but you have a way of bringing attention to yourself." He tipped his head toward the doorway. "Get the hell out. I won't ask you nicely again."

"Fisticuffs would draw the attention you're trying to avoid," Julian pointed out, but he rose from the bed, straightening his dressing gown without haste. Flynn had to hand it to him; he wore his own skin with a panache most men only managed when fully and expensively clothed.

Flynn stepped away from the door, intending to open it. Instead, he found his arms full of Julian. He pressed his slender, taut body to Flynn's and wound his arms around Flynn's neck. Flynn could feel the other man's sizable erection poking through the silk of his dressing gown, and his own body automatically responded.

That was biology. It was pointless to argue with it. He tried, though, opening his mouth to blast Julian. The sound that escaped him was surprisingly without force, and then Julian's lips, soft and honey-sweet, touched Flynn's. It was a delicate kiss, skilful but subtle. The body in Flynn's arms felt slight and almost feminine, but the aggression, the hunger, was all male.

Flynn's own body tingled with uncomfortable awareness. It was all he could do not to respond to that kiss with a blaze of hunger. Instead, he grabbed Julian's wrists, forced his arms from about his neck, and thrust him away none too gently.

Julian staggered, but caught himself. He glared at Flynn. His chiseled nostrils actually flared.

"I don't understand you, David."

"I'm making it as clear as I can. I'm not interested."

"No one will know—"

"I'm not interested in *you*," Flynn cut in. "I don't even like you."

Julian considered this, blinking, puzzled. Flynn opened the door, glanced down the empty hallway. "The coast is clear. Go."

Face averted, Julian went without another word.

Flynn closed the door. He was tempted to lock it, but that would be ridiculous. He made room for the new fan on the dresser top, plugged it in and waited for the sparks to fly. But the fan came on smooth and quiet, the metal propellers flying fast enough to chop an unwary finger off, and a wonderful breeze washed through the warm room, erasing the faint spicy scent of Julian's cologne.

* * * * *

The entire household gathered for the simple, hearty supper of navy beans cooked with chunks of tender ham. There was fresh cornbread and cold, tangy coleslaw. Plenty of everything. David still vividly remembered the deprivations of the war years, and he gave thanks with everyone else at the table. He noticed that even Julian and Mr. Devereux politely murmured along with the mealtime prayer.

As though feeling his gaze, Julian's lashes lifted and he gave Flynn a long, silent look. Flynn looked away.

"Were you in the war, Mr. Lee?" Mrs. Hoyt inquired.

"Yes, ma'am. I was in France with the 5th Marine Regiment."

"Belleau Wood?" Flynn asked.

Casey met his eyes and nodded.

"My son fell at the Battle of the Argonne."

"Sorry to hear it, ma'am."

"My son won the Medal of Honor."

"I'm sure he was a very brave man."

Mr. Devereux cleared his throat noisily. "Even if Julian's health had permitted, we are firm believers in nonviolence."

Casey raised his brows. "Well, Julian's only a kid," he said politely.

Flynn glanced at Julian. He was very quiet, his face expressionless as he replied, "I'm twenty-six."

"That so?" Casey said, showing the surprise Flynn felt. "No offense intended."

Julian did not respond, his attention focused on his plate. Flynn felt an unexpected stab of sympathy for him.

"Lordy, I know what it is to suffer from ill health," Mrs. Hoyt said, and she proceeded to describe in detail her many physical woes.

Joan sank lower in her chair, and Julian had apparently removed himself to the astral plane, but Amy listened politely and made sympathetic comments although she had surely heard all this a hundred times. Dr. Pearson contributed with his own occasional acerbic advice, and Casey cheerfully recommended several Queen of Egypt products with miraculous healing properties.

He was personable and quite a talker; Flynn bet he was a great success in his line of work.

When Mrs. Hoyt had worn out the topic of her own ill health, she asked about the news around the county, and Casey admitted he had been in Murphysboro two days earlier.

"Why that was right around the time of those brutal murders," Mrs. Hoyt exclaimed. Joan brightened and the rest of the table eyed Casey expectantly—except for Julian who continued to stare at his plate as though he could foretell the future in the navy beans.

"Well, I was only there when they found the last girl, Millie Hesse," Casey hastened to say. "Although the whole county's been talking about it ever since the first murder."

"Anna Spiegel," Joan said eagerly. "She was the first. Then Maria Campanella, then Millie Hesse."

"I knew Anna," Casey said. "That is to say, she was a regular customer of mine."

"Was she in ill health?" Mrs. Hoyt asked with interest.

"No. Not that I know of. Anna used our beauty products. Our lip salves and rouge papers and kohl eyeliners. She was a very pretty girl." He smiled at Joan. "We carry the finest all natural and all quality beauty products."

Joan blushed and reached for her coffee.

Casey grinned at Flynn who tried not to grin back. Casey had an irrepressible good humor that was hard not to respond to. Looking away from him, Flynn happened to catch Julian's eye and his smile faded. Gramps might be a pacifist, but the expression in the back of Julian's eyes was definitely violent. He looked from Flynn to Casey and his mouth tightened.

It seemed he wasn't kidding about his instincts.

"Was she a nice girl?" Mr. Devereux asked with what appeared to be unwilling fascination.

"Not if she used cosmetics," Mrs. Hoyt retorted.

Casey objected to this. "Sure, she was a nice girl. At least as far as I could tell. They were all nice girls from what I heard. Not the kind of girls to get themselves into trouble. That's what no one can understand. How this fiend could get close to them. He must be very clever."

"Or very evil," Devereux added.

"Excuse me," Julian said, rising. "I have to prepare for this evening."

"There's peach cobbler for dessert," Amy told him.

He shook his head.

"I'll save you a piece for later," she promised, and he smiled at her. It was a genuine smile, warm and friendly and uncomplicated. It surprised Flynn.

Nearly as much as the realization that he was aware of every move Julian made.

When Julian left the room there was a pause and then Mr. Devereux said, "My grandson is very sensitive to the vibrations of evil."

Dr. Pearson snorted. "What that young man needs is fresh air and sunshine and exercise. A few early nights wouldn't come amiss either."

"He has always been most delicate."

"What's wrong with him?" Casey inquired with interest, no doubt mentally running through the catalog of Queen of Egypt remedies and elixirs.

Mr. Devereux shook his head. Casey said, "Sorry if I offended him. I guess he's got one of those baby faces. Must have been hard on him not being able to serve his country."

Mr. Devereux opened his mouth, seemed to consider the company, and said, "My grandson has been called to a higher purpose."

Mrs. Hoyt sniffed disapprovingly.

$\mathcal{A}$fter the peach cobbler, Casey mentioned that he was going for a stroll and Flynn said he'd join him.

They grabbed their jackets and hats and stepped out into the warm twilight.

"I know a place we can get a real drink," Casey said, lighting a pipe.

Flynn nodded.

They talked about the war and France. "Do you miss it sometimes?" Casey asked as they watched the street lamps blinking on all down the long silent blocks.

"Miss it? No," Flynn said.

"I do. I never felt as alive as I did in the war." Casey gave him that wide, friendly grin. "I guess that sounds peculiar."

"No, I think I know what you mean." Flynn added, "You never feel as alive as in those first seconds after you just miss getting your head blown off. I just wonder what the hell it was for. I lost a brother, an uncle, and two of my best friends in that war. I miss 'em every day." And Paul. He'd lost Paul too, but he couldn't talk about that. Not to anyone. Rarely did he even let himself remember.

A sniper's bullet on a sunny day. One second Paul had been warm and alive, the next he was dead. *Dead.* No warning, no reprieve, no deferment. Dead and done.

"Yeah. I know. I lost a lot of pals too. Every one of the guys I joined up with went during that damned war."

"It changes you," Flynn said quietly. "It changed the men here. Were you around last year?"

"You mean the so-called massacre?"

Flynn nodded.

"I saw a damn sight more than I wanted to," Casey said grimly. "But you know, my granddad worked in the mines back before the union. Things were different back then—harder, meaner. My granddad worked for fourteen hours a day in a shaft that was only three feet high, sometimes up to his ankles in water. He spent all day bent over, loading coal onto mule carts. The mules used to go blind from so much time in the dark. Granddad died in the mines from bad air."

"Everyone died back then," Flynn agreed. "From the bad air, or collapses, or shaft fires."

"That's right. The lucky ones who survived the mines ended up dying of black lung. It's not that long ago. People still remember those days."

Flynn thought of the stories he'd heard: a man using his pocketknife to cut the throat of the wounded, a woman holding the hand of her child as she led him to see the dying, a man urinating on the corpses. As bad as anything he'd seen in the war. But then this *had* been war—or at least a battle in an ongoing war.

"You know," Casey said, "a lot of those people on the road and at the cemetery where it all ended, they weren't miners. They weren't even from Herrin. They were the no-account trash that gathers any time there's trouble."

Flynn nodded. It was something to take into account, true enough.

"Why do you care?" Casey asked. "You're not from around here. You're from…where? New York?"

Why *did* he care? Why was it so important to understand what had happened? Understanding it wouldn't change it. Probably wouldn't even prevent it happening again someplace else.

Flynn said, "They took dynamite and blew the draglines and the shovels and bulldozers of the Lester strip mine. They blew that mine apart. It'll never operate again."

"Maybe that's a good thing."

They had reached the Lafayette Hotel. It was one of Herrin's nicest lodgings, designed to recall European splendor before the war. It had done a brisk and lively business before Prohibition, but now, like a lot of businesses, it was struggling to stay afloat. Small iron balconies and window boxes decorated the outside. Inside, the walls were paneled in a red wood, ornate amber chandeliers hung from the ceiling, the carpet was an elegant pattern of fruit baskets and flowers on a field of black.

They went inside and ordered "soft drinks" which they sipped while they continued to talk, although they steered clear of such serious subjects as the war or the massacre. Casey was easy to talk to and Flynn found himself opening up in a way he rarely did anymore. He bought the second round. Their conversation grew less focused.

By the third round, Flynn was impatient for what would surely follow—the reason they had both walked out that evening. He was already trying to calculate the logistics of it. This was not New York where they would find a sympathetic club or speakeasy.

They would need to find a quiet alley or a deserted building or a corner of the park.

It had been a while since he had to sneak around like that. He lived in a Greenwich Village brownstone, and while he was cautious, he didn't have to exercise the kind of care necessary in a small town like Herrin.

He wondered what it was like for a man like Casey. The war had probably simplified a lot of things for him. No wonder he missed it.

"Another?" Casey asked, half-rising.

Flynn didn't want another drink. He wanted Casey's body which was enough like Paul's body to fill him with a fierce hunger. A hunger that had sparked, oddly enough, when Julian had pressed his slim, hard form to Flynn's.

He hesitated, but Casey was giving him a meaningful look, so Flynn nodded. Maybe Casey had to get drunk to do it. That was sad, but it wasn't uncommon.

They had a fourth round of "soft drinks" and then, finally, Casey said, slurring a bit, "We oughta start back, ya think?"

They rose and went out, down the front steps and started walking back. At first Casey was whistling softly, "Ain't We Got Fun," but then he fell silent, seeming increasingly morose.

Their footsteps echoed loudly down the quiet street. Flynn was all but positive he hadn't misread him, but wondered if Casey had changed his mind.

But as they came to the set of stairs leading to the small corner park, Casey grabbed his arm and they ran up to the iron gate. It wasn't locked and they slipped inside, easing the gate shut behind them. It closed with a ghostly clang.

The park was dark and shadowy. The street lamps didn't reach beyond the tall maple trees lining the spiked fence, and they made their way down the dirt path to the small, open-air gazebo. Flynn started to climb onto the gazebo, but Casey pulled him back.

"No. Not there. Over here." Casey led him behind a great flowering barberry bush and unzipped his trousers, freeing himself. Flynn unfastened his own trousers.

The fact that they'd had a good deal to drink, and that Flynn had been craving this release since…anyway, it made it easier. Made it simple to push aside the faint dismay that their joining was so blunt, so businesslike. What was he looking for? This was not Paul, this was not romance, let alone love. He didn't look for that at home, why should he look for it here?

They stumbled together, and Flynn could feel the heat coming off Casey through his clothing. They were both perspiring with excitement—and humidity. He could feel Casey's heart thumping against his own as though he were scared to death. They clutched each other like drowning men. Casey's hardness jutted against his hip. His hands were going to leave bruises; his mouth was like a cave, dark and empty. It opened to Flynn's and their tongues slid together, wet and hot and slick.

Strangely, in that moment, Flynn remembered that delicate, expert kiss Julian had pressed upon him in his room. He remembered how Julian had felt in his arms: light and ardent as a raw flame.

The impression was gone in the next instant. The tang of Casey's sweat and the sweet scent of his hair oil mingled with the sharp, acidic scent of the barberry bush. Casey's fingers dug into Flynn's buttocks, urging him closer. Flynn pushed against him, rubbed against him, hunting eagerly for the release he knew was coming.

Casey's mouth opened wider, his tongue pushed deeper. Flynn drew back from that fever heat, from the bite of the whisky and the unfamiliar taste. He didn't want kisses, he just wanted the relief. He slicked his palm with spit, reached down, got both their stiff cocks in one hand and began to work them, rubbing them together.

Casey groaned into his mouth and then tore away, tipping his head back and gulping great lungfuls of night as Flynn rolled them forward, shoving them along. They humped and fumbled against each other, nearly overbalancing in their thrusting, grinding, frantic…like two stags rutting.

A roiling blaze of heat soared between them, and Casey made a sound like he was choking to death. Hot wet come spattered between their bodies. Breathing hard, they hung onto each other—mostly to keep from falling over.

Then the hasty, limbs trembling, business of wiping off, doing up the zippers and buttons, moving quickly, putting it behind them.

They looked each other over, not that there was much to see in the uncertain light, and they moved in accord down the dirt path back to the iron gate. They stepped through it, the gate shutting with a faint chime behind them. They walked down the steps to the pavement.

To his horror, Flynn realized there was a man a few feet in front of them. He must have just passed by the park as they were reaching the gate. Flynn felt an unexpected, guilty alarm that they would be discovered— what the hell explanation could they give for being in the park at that hour?

Casey realized their danger at the same instant. He stopped in his tracks. The man must have sensed their presence, for he glanced over his shoulder and jumped visibly.

"Didn't see you behind me," he said. His hat brim hid his features, but he sounded nervous. "Were you in the theater too?"

Casey appeared struck dumb. Flynn said, "Yes."

"Wasn't that the damnedest thing?"

"I—"

"Not that I believe in that superstitious mumbo-jumbo." The man gave an edgy laugh. "But it was strange, certainly."

"Yes."

They were now all three of them walking in a small herd, Casey bringing up the rear. Moonlight shadowed the beautiful old houses and the churches as they stepped briskly along their way. Warmth still radiated from the bricks of the buildings and road.

"The rest of it, well, any good huckster could come up with that pabulum. Your Auntie May wants you to wear a scarf in cold weather, your grandpapa still loves you." The man snorted in amused disgust. "But predicting Bill Doyle's death? And that thing about the murders."

Flynn felt a chill slither down his spine. He knew that the man had been to the Opera House and that he was talking about Julian.

He said carefully, "But maybe we misunderstood him? Maybe that's not what he was saying at all?"

"What else could he have meant?" the man said. "He said—she said— whoever that was supposed to be said that she was lost on the far side of Crab Orchard Creek. That the other girls were with her. Four girls. And one of them doesn't know she's dead yet."

CHAPTER FIVE

*W*hen Flynn and Casey reached the boarding house they found everyone out on the breezeway, drinking lemonade and talking. It was clear that the news of Julian's announcement had already, in the mysterious way of small towns, reached home.

The three ladies sat on the wide swing, their shadowy faces lit by the street lamps a few yards away. Their paper fans fluttered like the wings of dying moths, languidly waving back and forth. Dr. Pearson sat smoking at the edge of the brick walk, the red tip of his cigar glowing in the darkness.

Amy instructed them to bring chairs outside and pour themselves a glass of lemonade. Casey and Flynn obeyed. They sat a few feet away from each other on the breezeway, sipping their cold drinks. Casey sniffed discreetly a couple of times, and Flynn was tempted to elbow him in the ribs.

Mrs. Hoyt made a disapproving noise and said, "I don't need to ask where you gentlemen have been this evening."

For a paralyzed second Flynn thought she meant…but then he realized she was talking about the alcohol they had consumed earlier.

"Are the Devereuxs back yet?" he asked, ignoring her.

"No," Amy replied. "Any minute now, I expect. We heard the show ended early."

"Did it?"

"They're saying it was true about the man whose death he predicted, that his wife came home and found him dead."

Joan's shadow shivered in delighted horror. Mrs. Hoyt exclaimed, "Table tilting and spirit writing. Bell ringing and levitation and invisible hands playing musical instruments. At worst it's blasphemy and at best it's nonsense!"

"It's harmless nonsense, I guess. And it's fun," Casey put in, and Flynn saw the white flash of Joan's grateful smile turned his way.

Mrs. Hoyt said, "From what we've heard from the neighbors, I don't think people found it much fun tonight."

"How can that be Julian's fault?" protested Joan. "Anyway, he doesn't deal in spiritualistic phenomena."

"How would you know, missy?"

"I asked him. He said that's for people in traveling shows and carnivals."

"And what is he? The child of a fortune-teller and a vaudevillian."

"Now, Mrs. Hoyt," Amy remonstrated amiably, "the Devereuxs are my guests. I don't want you speaking ill of them. I don't have any complaints about either of them. Julian's a sweet enough boy."

Casey gave a derisive laugh as he lit his pipe.

Flynn stared at him, at the handsome features looking mask-like and foreign in the brief illumination of the pipe bowl. He asked, "Is it true he prophesied another murder?"

"He didn't prophecy," growled Dr. Pearson from the gloomy corner of the breezeway. "He announced she was dead. According to Mrs. Muenster next door."

"He must have heard it on the radio," Mrs. Hoyt said. "Or he simply made it up to frighten people. To get more people to come to his show."

"The radio wasn't on when he came back," Amy said.

"When he came back from where?" Flynn asked.

"I don't know where. He was gone most of the day. He goes out every day. Of course they only arrived on Monday. He said he went to the dime museum today."

"Where were he and the old man before they came here?"

"Cairo."

Joan said, "Cairo, Illinois that is."

"Where else would it be?" Mrs. Hoyt retorted. "Those two are home-grown hucksters."

Amy said, "According to Mr. Devereux they traveled the Continent before the war."

"There is only one continent worth traveling and that is the United States of America," Mrs. Hoyt pronounced.

Flynn asked, "How long were they in Cairo?"

Mrs. Hoyt laughed jarringly. "It's easy to see you're a reporter, Mr. Flynn. You ask so many questions."

"A reporter," Casey repeated in a funny voice.

"Well, well." Dr. Pearson sounded amused.

David flicked his cigarette butt in the damp grass and slapped at a mosquito. "Reporters take vacations too."

"But you're not on vacation," Dr. Pearson said shrewdly.

"No," Flynn admitted. "I'm writing a story on Herrin one year later."

"Not much of a story there." Pearson didn't sound troubled about it, but then who in this godforsaken town did?

"Most people I've talked to seem to see it your way. The rest of the country still wonders whether what happened here could happen some-place else."

"Of course it could. People forget about Ludlow now because that was before the war mostly. But women and children died in that one. And that time it was the mining companies doing the shooting."

"Gus covered the Ludlow story," Amy said quietly.

"I remember." Flynn looked her way although he couldn't read her face in the dim light. Gus had helped dig out the dead women and children killed in the fire set by the Colorado National Guard.

"These are evil, godless times," Mrs. Hoyt pronounced.

"It's not the gods who've forgotten—" Dr. Pearson broke off at the sound of voices inside the house.

"I don't want to talk about it anymore." Julian's irritated voice carried clearly through the open windows. Behind the lace curtains they could see his silhouette and the silhouette of the old man as though they were watching a *Punch and Judy* show. Devereux senior had a fierce, unforgiving profile. Julian had taken off his turban, and his longish hair and ruffled collar gave him the aspect of a prince in a fairytale.

"You're going to ruin us with that kind of prophesying," the old man snapped.

"It wasn't a prophecy."

"Whatever it was, it has to stop. You're frightening people. You're frightening *me*. Prophesying is for…for lowlifes and scallywags."

"It wasn't a prophecy."

"People walked out. People left the theater tonight."

"I know. *I* left the goddamned theater."

"Cursing and blaspheming. What devil possesses you?"

Julian said with sudden anguish, "Leave me alone, can't you?"

Their voices faded as they went up the stairs.

"Well!" Mrs. Hoyt said at last.

"That guy's nuttier than a fruitcake," Casey observed.

"Maybe he's telling the truth," Joan said defiantly. "Did you ever think of that?"

Silence followed her words, so perhaps no one had.

*C*asey went upstairs when Flynn did.

"You didn't say you were a reporter," he said softly, as they reached the top of the stairs at the second level.

"Does it matter?"

"I guess not." But Casey was giving him a funny look.

"What?"

"I don't know." Casey shrugged his wide shoulders.

Abruptly, Flynn was fed up with Casey, fed up with the evening, fed up with himself for ever traveling to this hick town. "Good night," he said curtly, and went down the hall to his room.

He opened the door, stepped inside, closed the door. It was difficult to see in the silver-edged darkness. Was he alone? He stood still, waiting, but no one spoke. No one moved. He turned on the lamp, and the room was empty, the bed neatly made, the window open to the hot, still night.

He was conscious of disappointment.

What had he expected?

Perhaps it was better not to examine that.

He went next door, splashed his face, brushed his teeth. Casey was waiting in the hall when he stepped out again. Flynn nodded curtly. Casey nodded curtly back.

Flynn went back to his room, turned on the fan, turned out the lamp, lay down on the bed. He stared up at the shadowy recesses of the ceiling.

He remembered Julian's face when he'd told him, *I'm not interested in you. I don't even like you.*

Flynn closed his eyes. He didn't want to think about that. When had he grown so cruel? After Paul had died, he supposed. But a lot of people had lost someone they loved during the war. *Most* people had lost someone they loved. What gave him the right to…to close off the way he had? Yes, that was the truth of it. After Paul's death he'd turned off something inside himself.

Anyway, what was so different between Julian and him? Or Julian and Casey? Julian might be a nut but he was honest about what he wanted. And, face it, his instincts were pretty sharp.

Flynn listened to the muted voices down below on the breezeway. Mrs. Hoyt had gone up before Casey and him. It wasn't long before the rest of them went inside. He listened to the rattle and gulps of the old plumbing, and then the sounds of the house settling down for the night. The squeak of floorboards, pops and cracks of timber and rafters.

And then a complete silence.

And yet…there was something alert in the silence. He could feel it. Feel an…intelligence awake and listening. Flynn listened too.

He waited.

And waited.

The ripe lemon moon shone brightly through the window, making it difficult to sleep. He sat up, considered pulling down the window shade, but that was liable to cut off what breeze there was. Even with the fan circulating, the room felt stifling.

Flynn swung his legs over the side of the bed. Maybe he should get dressed and go for a walk. Lying here staring at the ceiling was accomplishing nothing.

The door swung open soundlessly; Flynn felt the disturbance in the air. He stared at the doorway and the tall, pale form standing motionless. Flynn straightened. The hair rose on the back of his neck, and for one hazy moment he wondered if he was staring at a ghost.

"David?" The whisper was so soft it could have belonged to anyone, but Flynn knew.

He whispered back, "It's all right. Come in and shut the door."

The white shadow slipped inside the room and closed the door. Julian came over to the bed and sat next to Flynn. The mattress springs squeaked. "I'm sorry," he said breathlessly. "I know what you told me, but I can't be alone tonight. Do you…" He swallowed the rest of his sentence. He sounded unsure, frightened to death, in fact, and Flynn reached to cover his hand. He found it ice cold.

"What's the matter?" Instinctively he took the chill hand—both hands—in his, chafing them.

"I can't." Julian stopped and tried again. "Do you ever—?"

"Sure. Everyone does," Flynn said easily. He had the strangest sense that he understood everything Julian was not saying. Julian's trembling fingers clutched his as though Flynn were leading him back through the Underworld.

"What happened tonight?"

"Did you hear about that?"

Flynn nodded, realized Julian might not be able to see him, and said, "Yes. They're saying you predicted another murder."

"I didn't predict it. She's already..." He stopped and then gulped out, "And then this house tonight."

"What's wrong with the house?"

He saw the glimmering outline of Julian's face turning to him, but he didn't say anything. Flynn's scalp prickled. "What's wrong with the house tonight?"

Julian's whisper was so faint he had to bend closer to make out the words. "Can I stay with you till morning? I won't be a nuisance. I want to sleep here, that's all. I'll sleep in the window seat if you like."

Flynn absorbed this quietly. "Sure," he said. "But the bed's big enough for both of us if you don't kick too much."

There was a pause. "Are you sure?"

"Yeah." Flynn stood. "Go on. Lie down."

Julian slipped out of his dressing gown. It pooled to the floorboards in a silken sigh, and he crawled onto the bed. Back to Flynn, he lay on his side in a neat, self-contained line, illuminated by the moonlight. Flynn stretched out beside him. There was only about a hands-length between them. Julian's scent was light and clean, like summer wind and spiced oranges. Fine tremors ran through his body. Flynn touched his arm.

"How can you be cold on a hot night like this?"

Julian moved his head in denial. "I'm all right."

Flynn reached for him, and Julian turned, biddable as a babe, wrapping his arms tightly around Flynn. Flynn was thinking...but no. Julian was completely unaroused. He was seeking comfort, that was all, and Flynn responded instinctively, wondering at himself. When was the last time he had lain with another man for any purpose but sex?

Paul.

Paul was the last time. Strangely, tonight the thought of Paul brought no pain.

Flynn stroked Julian's back. His skin was smooth and unblemished as a child's. His hair was fine as silk. As he grew warm, his body relaxed, went boneless, and soon he was breathing in the soft, deep pattern of sleep. Flynn's arms grew tired, but he continued to cradle the other man until he too dropped into sleep.

A mouth brushed his own, light as a spring breeze, the kiss working itself into his dreams.

Flynn smiled and woke. The room was growing light. He had the impression that the bedroom door had just closed. He was alone, but the pillow next to his was indented with the shape of a head, the sheets still warm.

Not a dream. At least, not entirely a dream. His lips still tingled with that kiss, real or imagined.

He was surprised at how well he had slept, how relaxed he felt. He rolled onto his side, stretching comfortably, closed his eyes and fell back asleep.

The next time he woke it was to the muffled sounds of disturbance. The sound of crying filtered through the floorboards. Footsteps were moving rapidly up and down the stairs. He could hear voices; muted, but the tone was clear enough: trouble. Serious trouble.

He rolled out of bed and dressed hastily, hurrying downstairs.

Amy met him in the main hall. Her plain face was worried and weary. "I'm sorry. There's no breakfast ready. The house is in a bit of a commotion. Mrs. Hoyt passed during the night."

"She's *dead*?"

Amy nodded.

"How?"

"Doc Pearson says stroke. He thinks it must have happened soon after she left us last evening. Joan's mighty upset."

"I bet."

"Doc Pearson has her sedated, poor kid. Anyway, can you manage for yourself this morning?"

"Of course."

Amy patted his arm and turned away. Flynn said on impulse, "Amy, is there more I can do?"

She looked at him with surprise. "Why, no. Not just now, David. Thank you for asking."

Dr. Pearson poked his head out of one of the rooms down the hall and called to Amy. She excused herself and hurried away.

Flynn went back upstairs and waited for the bathroom to be free. Casey stepped out and Flynn explained to him what had happened.

"Can't say I'm surprised," Casey said. "She was a prime candidate. Had all the symptoms."

Flynn raised his brows. "Are you a doctor?"

"Er, no. But we're taught the basics." Casey gave Flynn a sideways look and asked, "Feel like going to grab some breakfast? I have time before I have to start on my rounds."

"Sure." It was not so much that Flynn wanted to have breakfast with Casey as he wanted out of that house. What he really hoped was to see Julian that morning, but there was no sign of him so far, and he had no idea which of the rooms down the hall belonged to whom. Walking in on *Grand-père* Devereux would not be good. "I'll get my hat."

They walked down to a small diner and ordered eggs, hotcakes, ham and coffee for thirty-five cents.

They didn't talk much. Flynn was preoccupied with thoughts of Julian and the night before. Had Julian sensed Mrs. Hoyt's death? Flynn didn't, in theory, believe in that kind of thing, although he couldn't deny odd occurrences during the war; men who had sensed that they or other men would die the following day. "The sight," his dear old superstitious Irish granny had called it. Some folks had it; you could only chalk so much up to coincidence.

"How long are you staying at Mrs. Gulling's?" Casey asked. "I'm here for the week."

"I'm staying a few more days."

"Maybe we could get a drink tonight?" Casey's green eyes were bright and alert. His smile was wide and warm.

Flynn smiled back, but he felt disinclined to take him up on his offer. Casey was nothing like Paul after all. He said noncommittally, "We'll have to see how things are at the house this evening."

"Nothing to do with us, is it?"

Us.

No, it was nothing to do with them. Since the war Flynn had made a point of not getting involved in things that weren't his business. At least… to avoid personal involvement. He wrote about the injustices he saw, but he didn't take them personally. He didn't look for trouble and he didn't make trouble his own business. As much as he had admired Gus, the way Gus had thrown himself heart and soul into the causes he'd covered in his stories, the war had convinced Flynn that a man, especially a writer, could do more good by keeping a certain distance, a certain detachment. Like a surgeon.

Perhaps that detachment had spilled over into his personal life. Without Paul…

But he didn't want to keep dragging up Paul's memory. It was beginning to feel uncomfortably like he'd been hiding behind Paul's ghost. Using the memory of Paul as an excuse for, well, not participating in his own life.

He opened his mouth to say…something, but the waitress came to their table, cheeks flushed, eyes bright. "Did you hear? There's been another murder over Carbondale way. A girl named Theresa Martin. They found her by Crab Orchard Creek and they say it's exactly like the others."

"What's like the others?" Flynn asked.

The waitress lowered her voice to a stage whisper. "What it was he did to her."

She bustled away and Casey reached for his coffee cup, saying grimly, "Damned ghouls."

Flynn was inclined to agree, but maybe it was reassuring that even in a place like this people were still shocked by such violence. Wouldn't it be a bad sign if they took it for granted?

After breakfast he and Casey walked back to the boarding house. A black hearse was pulling away as they arrived. A police car was parked in the front.

"Swell," Casey said. "The cops are going to be crawling all over this place thanks to that escapee from a freak show."

Flynn stared at him, at the unexpected venom in Casey's voice.

A sheriff deputy stood outside the front door, and they had to identify themselves to get inside.

Amy met them in the front hall. "What's going on?" Flynn asked, removing his hat.

"The sheriff is questioning Julian."

"Why?"

But he knew why even before Amy said, "Because of the things he said during his show last night. I think they must believe he knows about the murders."

Flynn could hear the murmur of voices from the front parlor. "I thought they were in Cairo last week. Didn't the old man show them his train tickets?"

"He went down to the train depot this morning and I haven't seen him since," Amy said. "I've had my hands full this morning." She hesitated. "That boy isn't… He's not equipped to… Do you think you could…?"

From the parlor he heard a voice say, "You're some kind of colored, aren't you?" This, followed by Julian's murmured answer.

Flynn nodded grimly to Amy and went into the parlor. There was a deputy standing inside the doorway, but Flynn said, "I'm representing Mr. Devereux."

"Are you a lawyer?"

Julian was seated on the sofa. He had not even had time to shave before being rousted out of bed. His hair was uncombed. He wore gray flannels and a white T-shirt. He looked thoroughly disreputable as he glanced up hopelessly at Flynn's entrance. His somber eyes lightened, but he bit his lip and said nothing.

"Who are you?" the sheriff asked, taking a cigar from his mouth. He was a short man with a big belly, a bushy mustache and mud-brown eyes.

"David Flynn. I'm a reporter for *The Atlantic Monthly*."

"A reporter! That's what we don't need around here."

"But that's what you've got," Flynn said. "I'm here to make sure this kid's not being railroaded."

"Railroaded! What the hell do you mean railroaded? We're just asking this young man a few simple questions about how he knows things he's got no business knowing."

Julian leaned forward, elbows on his thighs, head in hands. "I don't know anything," he groaned. "I keep telling you."

"You got up in front of three hundred people and told them where Theresa Martin's body was lying."

Julian shook his head without looking up.

"I take it you're not a believer, Sheriff…? Sorry, I didn't catch your name."

"McFadden. No, I'm not a-a *believer*. I'm a Baptist, for chrissake."

"Is that McFadden with an 'Mc' or 'Mac'? We like to spell names right in *The Atlantic Monthly*."

McFadden's gaze—reminiscent of a bear's small, suspicious eyes—flickered. "I don't see much of a story here, Flynn. We're only asking—"

"Mr. Devereux's cooperation? As Mr. Edgar Cayce has helped the police on occasion with their most difficult cases?"

"He has?" McFadden looked plainly taken aback. "He did?"

Flynn nodded. He had no idea if it was true or not.

Julian raised his head. "You don't understand. I can't…control it. It just happens."

Flynn gave him a warning look and he fell silent, his mouth not steady, eyes sullen.

"Sure, and I can see why you would think that way because it's a great story and it would get you great coverage in the papers. And nothing else makes sense because the Devereuxs were in Cairo when these first murders happened."

"So we've all heard a couple a times, but can he prove that?"

Flynn and McFadden turned to Julian. Julian sounded frightened as he said, "I gave shows Tuesday through Saturday at the Gem Theater on Eighth Street. And there will be the train ticket stubs. *Grand-père* will have those."

"Grand-père," the sheriff said disgustedly.

"The Devereuxs are from New Orleans," Flynn said. This area had been settled by French and German and English and Irish settlers, so he wouldn't expect to see the same prejudice that Italians or colored found.

"I know French!" The sheriff had his dander up. "I do find it convenient his grandfather is absent this morning."

"The Devereuxs could hardly be performing in Cairo and committing murder two counties away. Unless you think young Mr. Devereux really is a sorcerer?"

"I don't believe in that hocus-pocus hooey," the sheriff snarled.

"Then there's your answer."

McFadden stared at him. "And you don't believe in that mumbo-jumbo either."

"That's not the point," Flynn said. "The point is, without magical powers, Devereux couldn't be in two places at one time."

The sheriff continued to eye him grimly, only partly convinced.

"Think what a fine story it would make," Flynn suggested. "This young man using his talents to help the police in their investigation. Why, the public loves this kind of thing. It would be nice to appear in a national paper for something other than the massacre, don't you think?"

The sheriff stuck his cigar back in his mouth and chewed on it thoughtfully. "Meybee so," he said reluctantly. "Meybee so."

CHAPTER SIX

"*I* never know when it's going to happen," Julian said, staring at his hands.

"Speak up," McFadden ordered.

Julian's throat moved and he said more loudly, "Before I turned sixteen, the voices—the spirits—came to me all the time. But then when I turned sixteen, I-I became ill. The spirits only come once in a while now."

"Come every night you've got a show, don't they?" McFadden asked. He added sarcastically, "Or are you charging folks a pretty penny on the outside chance the Count of Monte Crisco is going to show up?"

Monte Crisco. Well, that was appropriate from this pigheaded fool. Flynn was careful not to let what he thought show on his face. He said calmly, "You're doing fine. Just tell the truth."

Julian swallowed hard. He didn't look up. "Last night, during the performance, I heard a woman talking to me. A spirit. At first I was confused. Unsure of why she had come to me. She didn't understand." He looked up, but he was talking to Flynn not McFadden.

"What didn't she understand?" Flynn asked.

Julian closed his eyes. "She didn't understand she was dead."

McFadden turned to Flynn and Flynn shrugged.

"What happened?" McFadden questioned.

Julian drew a deep breath and opened his eyes. "It's difficult when they don't know yet. She didn't come to me willingly. She came because she was lost and heard my voice. She's trapped on this side. They all are."

McFadden asked, "Who?"

"The murdered girls." Julian said carefully, "It happens sometimes with a-a violent death. They don't have time to…to transition. And he's done something to them."

McFadden's voice was dangerous as he demanded, "Who has? What's he done?"

"He…cut them up." Julian put his long, slim hands over his face. His voice was muffled and shaking. "He's cast some spell on them. An ancient spell. They're held here, prisoner—"

"Horseshit!" McFadden jumped up, looking as though he wanted to strike Julian. Flynn rose too, watching him, ready to intervene. Whatever McFadden read on Flynn's face stayed his hand, but he said in a trembling, deep voice, "You're a goddamned liar."

Julian lowered his hands. He looked terrified. "I'm not lying. Why would I lie? I don't want it to be true—"

"What's the name of this murderer then? She must know it, this spirit gal. What's the name of the man who killed those girls?"

"I don't know."

"Because you're a liar. A goddamned liar and a-a mountebank."

Flynn cut across the sheriff, his voice calm, although listening to himself he thought he must sound as loony as Julian. "Did you ask Theresa who killed her?"

Julian shook his head, his shoulders hunched defensively. "I had to tell her she had…crossed over. It was a shock to her and she fled. They do sometimes." His wide dark eyes were absolutely sincere as they met Flynn's. He might be a mountebank or he might be mad—or both. He believed what he was saying.

"All right then," Flynn said. "You could summon her and ask, couldn't you? You could hold a…whatchamacallit? A séance."

"You're as crazy as he is," McFadden exclaimed.

At the same time Julian said with great definitiveness, "No."

Flynn ignored McFadden. "Why not?" he asked Julian.

"I told you I can't control it."

It was the first thing he'd said that Flynn suspected was a lie. "You could still try. You said she's trapped on this side. She came to you once. She might come to you again." He heard himself but dismissed the thought of what he must sound like. Maybe it *was* crazy, but it was logical too, wasn't it? "You could summon her and you could ask her about the last thing she remembers."

Julian was shaking his head with that exasperating, scared stubbornness.

McFadden looked from Flynn to the younger man and said, "You know what I think? I think it was a lucky guess. I think he knew eventually there was going to be another murder. That's what everyone's been saying. His kind like to shock and frighten folks. He said it to get a bigger audience. It just happened to be true."

"He knew the dead girl's name," Flynn pointed out.

"Who says? Today everyone knows her name, so they're saying he knew it last night. There's no proof that he did."

Flynn opened his mouth to argue the obvious, but McFadden said, "Either he's a fake or he's a killer, but I don't believe in magic and I don't believe in ghosts or spirits talking to the living. You want to turn this huckster into a big story for your newspaper like that sacrilegious conman Edgar Cayce, you go right ahead, but you're not making a laughingstock out of me and my boys."

"What's going on here?" Julian's grandfather stood in the doorway, glowering at them all. "What is this? What has he done now?"

The sheriff turned to him with something like relief. "I understand you have in your possession ticket stubs that will prove you and your grandson were in the town of Cairo last week."

"Yes?" Mr. Devereux's eyes moved uneasily from Julian to Flynn. "What of it? Why are you interrogating him?"

"I need to see those tickets."

"Very well." Devereux's suspicious gaze rested on Julian's pale face. He turned away reluctantly.

The sheriff followed him. He stopped in the doorway and threw back to Flynn, "If you do learn something in this séance of yours, you let me know."

When their footsteps had died away, Flynn seated himself facing the sofa and Julian. He wanted to sit next to Julian, put his arm around him—Julian looked sorely in need of comfort—but that was, of course, out of the question.

He said, "What happened last night?"

Julian's face worked. "David, I've told you everything."

"What about Mrs. Hoyt?"

Julian's mouth opened. No sound came out.

"You knew she was dead, didn't you?"

He closed his mouth and shuddered. He nodded.

Flynn stared at him for a long time. "So it's true," he said at last. "The dead speak to you."

"Through me. I'm only the messenger." He tried to smile, but it was a sad, unsteady effort. "And not a very good messenger. It's true what I said. When I turned sixteen it stopped. And I was glad. But *Grand-père...*"

"What?"

Julian shook his head.

Flynn said shrewdly, "The show must go on—and you're the meal ticket. This is the family stock and trade." He considered this. "But now the phone line to the spirit world is working again and you're starting to get calls."

Julian said nothing. He looked all at once much older, older than his age. He met Flynn's gaze and said quietly, "Please. I can't bear it from you."

"Can't bear what?"

"Don't…ask."

"What?" But Flynn already knew what he was going to hear. Yet the idea had not occurred to him until the second Julian spoke, so how could Julian—

"You want me to contact Paul for you."

It took him a second to command his voice. "You could do it?"

"I don't know." He sounded anguished. "Perhaps."

"Well?"

Julian shook his head.

"Why not?" And even Flynn was surprised by the anger in his voice.

Julian studied him and the wounded expression in those doe-like eyes troubled Flynn, disturbed him. "Do you never think of anyone but your-self, David?"

"Me?" Flynn was astonished. "What do you think I came in here for a few minutes ago if it wasn't to help you?"

Julian's eyes glittered with quick, angry tears. "I think you thought it would make a good story to write about a medium working with the police to capture a killer."

"You're wrong."

"I wish that was true." Julian wiped hastily at the tears. His smile was bitter. He rose and left the room before Flynn could decide on an answer.

Listening to the fading footsteps, Flynn realized that Julian *was* wrong—although not entirely.

*A*my was in the kitchen when he wandered in a short while later. Water boiled on the stovetop. She was greasing a heavy skillet. Death or disaster, people still had to eat.

"There's cold buttermilk in the icebox," she told Flynn, looking up at his entrance. Her smile was tired.

Flynn got a glass and the bottle of milk out. "How's Joan doing?"

"That little girl is heartbroken."

Flynn couldn't think of anything to say. Mrs. Hoyt had seemed a foolish and tiresome woman who would probably become more so the longer you knew her, but even newspapermen tried not to speak ill of the dead.

"How's the story coming?" Amy asked and he realized he'd barely had a chance to talk to her since he'd arrived. Or had he arranged it that way?

The buttermilk was refreshing. As he drank, he considered her question. She would be viewing this situation from whatever angle Gus had, and Gus had always been pro-Labor and pro-Union and pro-miners. But how would a man as conscientious and civilized as Gus have viewed a massacre?

"I don't know," he answered. "For all the complaining folks are doing about lawlessness and godlessness, I can't find anyone who thinks Lester didn't deserve what he got or who wants to see those miners prosecuted."

Amy didn't answer for so long he thought she wasn't going to. "It's a mighty shocking thing. I think most people still…"

She didn't complete the thought. Flynn gave a short laugh. "I guess so."

She looked up then and there was an odd glint in her green-blue eyes. "I'll tell you this, no charge. W.J. Lester was and is a fool. An arrogant, greedy, college-educated fool."

As fond as he was of her, Flynn couldn't let that pass. "Amy, my God. They murdered those men. They tortured them and then they murdered them—after promising them safe passage."

Her face tightened. "I don't have to tell you I don't approve of murder. I know that's what it was. Everyone knows that's what it was, plain and simple. People are angry and ashamed and frightened. Frightened about what they learned was inside them." She folded her lips and stared down at the pan on the stove. After a brief struggle, she said, "But you want to hear the truth? The truth is that bunch of thugs Lester imported from

Chicago had already stirred up enough hate to get someone killed before the massacre. They'd been harassing farm people and berry pickers for using roads they'd been using for fifty years. Pushing them around, cursing them, shoving guns in their ribs, even robbing a few of them—and threatening to kill them if they went to the sheriff."

She added shortly, "Not that the sheriff cared to get mixed up in it."

"I've heard a few of them were thugs and gangsters. But that mob killed twenty men that day. And even if every single one of them was—"

"You killed men in the war, didn't you? It was them or you, wasn't it?"

Flynn stared at her. "Is that what Gus thought?"

Her face quivered. She turned back to the stove. "No." He could hear that she was close to tears. It seemed to be his day for making people cry. "Gus said 'Each man's death diminishes me, for I am involved in mankind. Therefore, send not to know for whom the bell tolls, it tolls for thee.'"

Hearing Amy quote John Donne in that flat, plain, unvarnished way struck Flynn absolutely silent.

Maybe it was as he'd said to Casey Lee the night before. Maybe the war *did* have to do with it. A few of those miners had been in France the same time he had, and had seen and done the things he had. If they were like Flynn, they'd come back changed men. Harder and rougher than when they waved farewell to peacetime.

He'd been so sure of the answers when he had arrived on Wednesday morning. He'd planned to write a simple article about the aftermath of violence. He'd wanted to set it straight in his own mind, see it in black and white, saints and sinners, but the reality was many shades of gray. It wasn't anything that was going to be fixed anytime soon and writing more about it wouldn't change that. Plenty of people were already writing and speech-making about it.

Flynn found himself wanting to do something. Something…

"Where's Julian?" he asked.

"Out. He don't like funerals," Amy said cryptically.

*F*lynn walked down to the courthouse to poke around, but he'd already lost whatever enthusiasm for the story on the massacre that he had started out with. The truth was, he was looking for Julian. He told himself that he wanted to take another shot at convincing him to try a séance; that this would make a better story than his original idea of writing about the massacre. Instead, he would write about these murders—and Julian.

But if he was honest, he wanted to find Julian.

He wasn't sure how or why his feelings had changed, but he felt a singular mix of pity and fascination for that strange young man. And, well, a certain amount of lust.

So he walked along the streets, nodding politely to folks, lost in his own thoughts.

It was hot, but there were lots of cloth awnings and shady roofs along the storefronts so it wasn't bad that time of day. He passed the corner park where he and Casey had stopped the evening before. It seemed so long ago.

In front of the courthouse, the old timers were enjoying the latest gossip over their cigars and chewing tobacco, probably exactly what they'd been doing since the Civil War.

He paused for a shine at the old shoe-shine stand. The grizzled old colored man made pleasant conversation while he swiftly polished Flynn's shoes till they shone like glass.

He went into Skeltcher's and had a "root beer" and then walked back to the boarding house. He was walking up the sunny street when he spotted Julian coming from the opposite direction. He raised his hand in greeting, and Julian paused at the house walkway, waiting for him.

"What time is your show tonight?" Flynn asked.

"There's no show tonight." Julian looked weary. "And before you ask again, no, I won't hold a séance for the police."

"It's clear you're not a mind reader," Flynn remarked. "I wasn't going to ask you to give a séance. I was thinking you might like to drive out and have supper at a roadhouse this evening."

Julian's astonishment was almost comical. "Why?"

"Wouldn't you like to?"

"Yes."

The naked—though fleeting—vulnerability of the other man's face made Flynn's chest hurt. What the hell was Julian's life like that the idea of dinner with a friendly stranger should mean so much? But then he probably didn't have friends. He had that crazy old coot of a grandfather driving him from town to town like a gypsy with his dancing bear.

"All right then," he said gruffly. "We'll tell them we're going out to the roadhouse dance."

Julian said hesitantly, "There'll be a viewing for Mrs. Hoyt, won't there?"

"You don't want to have anything to do with that, do you?"

He shook his head, but his eyes were unhappy. "It might seem disrespectful, though."

"I didn't realize you were so worried about appearances."

The slender brown column of Julian's throat moved as he swallowed. "My grandfather isn't…very happy with me."

He hadn't sounded particularly concerned about what the old man had thought the night before. Flynn wondered what had changed. "It's moot in any case. The viewing is tomorrow night at the funeral parlor. You'll have a show to perform."

He knew he didn't misread the relief on Julian's face. Yes, getting Julian out of that house tonight was a good idea for everyone. And there was no denying how much Flynn liked the idea.

Much more, as it turned out, than old man Devereux did. He could hear them down the hall when he went to use the washroom after he and Julian went upstairs. He couldn't make out the words—the Devereuxs were used to conducting their quarrels under other people's roofs—but the tone was most definitely unhappy on the part of both parties.

He was heading back to his own bedroom when he heard Julian say clearly, "I'm neither a child nor a half-wit however much you wish it might be true."

The old man's response was muffled, but the tone was venomous, and Flynn felt a stab of alarm for Julian. That was not a tone to use on someone you loved, and he had an idea that Julian had fewer defenses than some.

When they met downstairs twenty minutes later, Julian was neatly, even dapperly dressed, hat, coat and tie all present and correct. His eyes were shining and he was so obviously happy that Flynn couldn't help an inward flinch at the responsibility.

Mr. Devereux was downstairs as well.

"Going to a dance, eh?" he inquired acidly, his midnight eyes raking Flynn up and down. "Planning to meet a couple of gals and Charleston the night away?"

It was instantly clear to Flynn that the old man knew about his grandson's proclivities—which meant he now knew about Flynn. He said evenly, "That's right."

Devereux opened his mouth, but closed it as Amy came into sight.

"Now don't go picking up any flappers," she warned them as she went around picking up stray items in the hall and parlor. She was holding one of Joan's books on Cleopatra and crocheting that had belonged to Mrs. Hoyt.

"You're the only gal for me, Mrs. Gulling," Julian said charmingly, and Amy laughed.

They met Casey on their way out the door, and he looked plainly taken aback to see Flynn and Julian together. The surprise on his face gave way to an unfriendly expression, but Flynn tipped his hat and kept Julian moving with an unobtrusive hand on his back.

The sun was setting as they backed the old Model T out of the garage and were on their way at last. Flynn glanced over at Julian and said, "I don't think Grandpapa likes me."

"No." Julian was smiling a lazy smile, and Flynn wondered if part of his attraction for the other man was tied up in that fact. He was surprised to find he didn't like that idea.

"Where's the rest of your folks?"

"Dead."

"*All* of them?"

"The ones I know about. My father was killed in a train wreck. My mother predicted it."

"So you mentioned once before. Count Amadeus, that would be?"

"Yes. He was a magician." Julian smiled faintly. "My mother was Zaliki the Seer. She was a fortune-teller by trade, though she was also clairvoyant."

"Like you?"

"Yes. But she preferred telling fortunes." Julian's smile faded and he stared ahead through the windshield.

Prophesying is for...for lowlifes and scallywags.

"What happened to your mother?"

"She killed herself."

Flynn's hands tightened on the steering wheel. He consciously relaxed them. "Why?"

"She missed my father, I expect. *Grand-père* says she went mad. Perhaps she did." He sounded peculiarly disinterested.

"*Can* you tell the future?"

Julian was studying him again, mouth curved in a sly smile. "Sometimes. Sometimes it's not hard to know what's going to happen."

Flynn's face warmed.

They passed scattered houses, gardens, fields and big green lawns that were actually nicely mown weeds. The woods were deep on the edge of town. They passed through them and then the woods thinned to a couple of miles of cornfields, and Julian leaned forward, pointing and saying eagerly, "There it is."

The Dance and Dine Inn was a big, white, two-story house set back away from the road, welcoming lights gleaming from every window. There were lots of cars and a couple of buggies in the front yard, and several shining roadsters parked on white gravel in the mown field next door, expensive ones, lined up all in a row and watched over by two tough characters in straw hats sitting in chairs by the gate.

Flynn pulled up not far from the side-door entrance. They got out and walked across more white gravel and up the big wooden steps of the long front porch. A tall, very black Negro in a white mess jacket greeted them with a big smile and a suave, "Welcome to the Dance and Dine Inn, folks."

As they stepped inside, Flynn took note of two large gentlemen sitting watchfully in a small alcove to one side.

A pretty colored girl in a French maid's outfit led them to a table near a window.

The best tables, the tables on the screened-in porch, were already filled, but it was nice in the main dining room too, and they got one of the last tables by the windows on the far side of the room. The walls were papered in flocked dull red. Alphonse Mucha posters of women in nimbuses and flowered headdresses decorated the walls. Ceiling fans turned slowly overhead stirring the warm air, and small polished brass lamps shone gaily on every linen-covered table.

Flynn studied the menu. There was no booze listed of course, only "soft drinks," ciders, and a beverage called "Grape Drink Français."

He mentioned it to Julian whose mouth curved in that habitual sarcastic smile. He nodded approval to the grape drink and went back to gazing out the window at the moon-shadowed yard.

"Do you know what you're having?" Flynn inquired. Julian hadn't looked at the menu.

"I'll have what you're having."

"You don't know what I'm having," Flynn pointed out.

"It doesn't matter." At Flynn's expression, Julian made a face and said, "Oh well. Have it your way. I can't read."

"You mean there's something wrong with your eyes?" Was this the mysterious illness both Julian and the old man had referred to?

"No." Julian seemed amused. "I never learned how. My grandfather didn't think it was important. For me."

This offended Flynn on so many levels that he spluttered before he finally got out an outraged, "Didn't think it was important? *He* reads. He writes articles and essays for those damned spiritualist magazines."

"That's true." Julian said it placatingly. "I believe he thought it was for the best. That there would be less chance of people claiming I was a fraud if it could be proved that I couldn't read or write."

"Jesus. You can't read *or* write?"

Julian reddened. "You don't have to shout it to the world."

"Sorry." Flynn was still fuming though. He stared down at the menu. When he had himself under control again, he asked, "What do you like to eat?"

"Ice cream."

"Ice cream?"

"Lots of things," Julian amended in an apparent desire to please.

"I'm going to have T-bone steak."

"All right."

Flynn scanned the menu. "They have breast of chicken à la rose and crown roast of lamb and roast duck."

Julian gave this due consideration. "T-bone steak, I think."

Flynn was still trying to come to terms with the notion that Julian couldn't read. Not that plenty of people couldn't read, but Julian's grandfather was a literate man, so to deliberately leave Julian ignorant and uneducated horrified him. Not that Julian *appeared* ignorant or uneducated, but clearly there were considerable gaps.

Untroubled, the object of all this worry studied the crowded room with the same innocent pleasure of someone watching a play. "There's Sheriff McFadden," he murmured, and Flynn, following his gaze, saw that he was correct. The portly sheriff was dining at the roadhouse with an equally portly woman in a puce-colored silk dress. Julian pointed out two policemen, a judge, and a couple of well-to-do Herrin merchants. He was sharp-eyed as any reporter, but that was a necessity in his line of work.

"The law-and-order crowd," Flynn commented.

Julian said sardonically, "Prohibition means bootleggers are running this place instead of honest businessmen."

Their waiter, younger than Julian, arrived, uncorking the bottle of grape drink as he would have decanted a bottle of wine in the good old days. He poured it into Flynn's glass. Flynn sampled it. It was wine all right. Good wine. It might even have been imported.

Flynn nodded, and the waiter filled Julian's glass and departed.

Julian sipped his wine. Meeting Flynn's gaze, he smiled, seemingly relaxed and happy.

"Your grandfather seems to know...certain things," Flynn said neutrally.

"Well, he could hardly miss them," Julian pointed out.

Flynn was still trying to work through that when Julian added, "Why don't we talk about you for a change? I feel like you're interviewing me for a newspaper article."

"What would you like to know?"

"Everything."

Julian gazed at him with such unabashed and unfeigned interest that Flynn felt himself coloring.

"I guess my life is about as different from yours as it could be."

"Not in all ways," Julian said serenely.

"Oh. No. Not in all ways. I was born in Portland, Maine. I graduated from the Fryeburg Academy like my brothers before me. I went to Brown

University—that's where I met Gus, Amy's husband. I got a job at *The Daily News*, but the war was on and I enlisted."

"And that's where you met Paul?"

"That's where I found him again. We'd known each other at Brown." He fell silent, gauging the extent of pain within himself. It was…tolerable, surprisingly so. He said calmly, "After the war I got a job as a contributor to *The Atlantic Monthly.*"

"But you live in New York?"

Flynn nodded. New York and his tidy, quiet brownstone seemed a lifetime away.

"What's that like?"

"Very different." Flynn thought it over. "I guess…things were too easy for me growing up. It leaves you unprepared for the bad times that come."

"I don't know. Maybe it gives a kind of foundation. Having an education. Knowing that you're loved." Julian said it simply, seriously, and for some reason Flynn's throat closed tight. Too tight to say a word. What Julian said was true. Those things should have supplied Flynn the bedrock of philosophical and spiritual certainty. Why hadn't they? A lot of people had suffered through the war and the terrible influenza epidemic that followed, and they hadn't closed themselves off from life and love.

Here was Julian who hadn't had half the advantages of Flynn, was about as isolated and lonely a man as Flynn had ever known, and yet he possessed a calm confidence and an almost childish optimism.

"If you could do anything you wanted in the world, what would it be?" he asked Julian.

Julian's eyes widened as though Flynn were really offering this, as though he had the power to give him whatever he would like. "I'd like to own a café."

"A *café*?"

"Like in France before the war."

"Were you in France before the war?"

"A couple of times. When I was a child. I loved it." He smiled, remembering. "They have these little cafés. Bistros, the Russians call them. I'd like to open one. Omelets stuffed with mushrooms and cheese, *coq au vin*, mussels in cream sauce. And I'd like to sing there in the evenings."

"Sing?"

Julian nodded. His eyes were bright and mischievous. "Yes."

"*Can* you sing?"

"Er, a bit." He was still smiling, and studying him; it occurred to Flynn that it wouldn't matter if he could sing or not. People would love him. In Greenwich? They would adore him.

He put that thought away, and said, "Well, why don't you? You can't do this forever, surely?"

"It seems you can." Julian's smile had faded. He sounded bitter.

"You could surely stop if you didn't want to do it any longer? You're free, white and over twenty-one."

"And what would I live on?"

"What happens with all this money you earn?"

"*Grand-père* controls the purse strings." He was staring out the large window again, his profile hard.

"Don't you get a say in how the money you earn is spent?"

A second or two passed and he thought he wouldn't get an answer, but then Julian turned back to him and he was smiling again. "Anyway, it's a nice dream. Did you get to try much French food when you were over there?"

"We were a trifle busy," Flynn pointed out.

"But you went on leave, right? Once in a while?"

Yes, once in a while they'd had leave. And he and Paul had enjoyed themselves very much. It gave happiness a special shine knowing it could end any time.

Their meals came then, and that line of conversation died a natural death. Along with the T-bone steak were Potatoes à la Hollandaise and Asparagus Tips au Gratin. The kind of food you'd expect to find at the Waldorf Astoria, not in a hick roadhouse in the middle of nowhere.

They ate their food and talked and drank more of the Grape Drink Français. It was far different than the evening he'd spent with Casey. The funny thing was that while Flynn had pegged Casey as more his type, he'd never have considered spending an evening like this with him—well, not after the first couple of drinks at Hotel Lafayette. In fact, he was enjoying himself more than he could remember in years. Julian might be illiterate and more than a bit odd, but he was handsome and witty and very charming when he put his mind to it. Flynn found himself laughing at Julian's sly observations and comments more than he had laughed in a very long time.

"Would you like dessert?" he asked, not wanting the meal to end.

Julian's wide mouth curved. "Yes."

They had a dish of Venetian Ice Cream each.

Finally Flynn paid for the meal and they exited the rear side door, watched over by another dark, smiling gentleman in a white dinner jacket.

In a companionable silence they followed slightly tipsy couples through the warm moonlit night and down a hedge-boarded walkway to the big barn where buttery light streamed into the summer evening, and a jazz band could be heard tentatively warming up.

A couple of St. Louis-style bruisers sized them up inside the entrance, looking them over for flasks or pistol bulges.

Inside the barn, the floor had been polished like black glass. The walls were dark paneled and the lights mellow. A few ceiling fans moved the air languidly overhead.

They got a table away from the dance floor but with a good view of the band. A big-bosomed hostess left them a small paper list of soft drinks.

Flynn studied the list. "What do you want?"

"I prefer gin. Did you ever have a New Orleans Fizz?"

Flynn shook his head. "I don't think they have anything like that here."

"No. Prohibition's spoiled everything."

When the waitress came back, Flynn ordered two Juniper Jennies, which were gin and tonics by any other name.

Flynn watched the small back door of the bar and noticed a tall, short-skirted lady open a door in the partitioned area and smile over her shoulder at the young man who followed her in and closed the door behind. He didn't doubt stairs in there led up to the former hayloft. They were making hay all right, though it was doubtful any bales remained.

The thought of sex with Julian caused heat to pool in his belly, made his groin ache.

He looked across the table and Julian was watching him steadily with those dark and knowing eyes.

Julian smiled and turned his gaze back to the dance band.

Their drinks arrived and they sipped them, Flynn with uncharacteristic self-consciousness.

It was increasingly warm inside the barn as people got up to dance. Half the men were in their shirtsleeves by now, and Flynn loosened his tie and slipped out of his jacket, hanging it on the back of his chair.

Julian raised eyebrows at this lack of decorum.

"Half the fellas in this place have their jackets off," Flynn observed.

The people around them seemed like a cross-section—although there were no old people—an even mix of middle-aged couples and bright-eyed kids. Some of them, especially the girls, looked way too young to have been served hooch in a saloon, but nobody was asking questions at the Dance and Dine Inn.

Scattered here and there were a few single guys hoping to meet the girl of their dreams or getting up the nerve to shell out cash to the ladies of the evening casually strolling about or demurely seated by twos and threes near the edge of the room.

Flynn could easily pass for such young men. Julian… Flynn glanced across the table. Julian was staring alertly at the crowded dance floor as though these were the fascinating customs of South Sea Islanders.

Flynn felt an odd surge of emotion. Amusement? Affection? He wasn't sure.

A muted cornet sang out over the chattering crowd, and a good imitation of Paul Whiteman's version of "If I Could Be with You" rang off the rafters of the old barn.

The drinks were strong and the music was good but Flynn was wondering what the hell they were doing there.

Julian sipped his drink. His lashes lifted and he gave Flynn such a direct, naked look that Flynn's heart seemed to leap and then seize.

A scream—more of a squeal—broke the spell. Flynn spotted two young men at the edge of the dance floor flailing away at each other. Close by was a would-be vamp in a red dress wringing her hands and yelling at them.

Before the knights errant could do much damage, two rough-looking country boys in their first ties and jackets came sailing across the empty dance floor and yanked the combatants apart.

One of the portly Saint Louis-type gangsters, cigar clamped tightly between his teeth, joined them, and it was clear even from across the tables what was happening.

Flynn opened his mouth and Julian said, "Yes. Let's go."

Flynn shrugged back into his jacket, and they made their way through the crowded tables.

The tenor on the bandstand started a song made familiar to Flynn from the war. A few of the boys at the tables began to sing. That impromptu male chorus sent a funny chill down his spine as he and Julian strolled out through the wide doorway into the warm moonlight. The voices faded behind them.

> *There's a long, long trail a-winding*
> *Into the land of my dreams,*

Where the nightingale is singing
And the pale moon beams.
There's a long, long night of waiting
Until my dreams all come true,
Till the day when I'll be going down
That long, long trail with you.

CHAPTER SEVEN

The Model T jogged and bounced across the mowed field, past the hoods in the straw hats, down the gravel drive, and then they were on the main highway headed back for Herrin. Julian scooted over in the seat next to Flynn. The wind whipped his hair back from his forehead. He was smiling that private smile.

Despite the ripe golden moon hanging low in the sky, it was dark and the road was mostly deserted. Flynn took a chance, pulled Julian closer and put his arm around him. Julian snuggled nearer, the heat of his body warming Flynn all down his side.

"I like this." Julian's warm breath against his ear sent shivers across Flynn's scalp. "I like flying through the darkness like an arrow in the night."

"Do you know how to drive?"

Julian shook his head.

"I'll teach you," Flynn said recklessly. "It's not hard."

There was a funny pause and Julian faced forward in his seat again. After a moment, he said, "I don't expect we'll be here long enough for that."

It caught Flynn off guard. He should have expected it; of course The Magnificent Belloc would not be staying long in any one place. That wouldn't be lucrative. Or wise. He was only here for a short while himself.

"When are you leaving?"

"Monday morning."

Flynn nodded. He didn't know what to say.

The bobbing headlights stabbed into the pitch-black night, and the breeze felt good against his face as they sped along. The wall of woods flashed by, tree trunks white in the headlights.

By the time they crossed the bridge over Crab Orchard Creek, Julian was back to business, his nimble fingers caressing Flynn's crotch, making it difficult to keep an eye out for deer or other wildlife.

He risked a glance at Julian's bent profile. Even in that poor light he could see Julian was smiling.

Julian's lashes lifted. He murmured, "Flynn, stop the car."

As though he'd been waiting for that signal, Flynn yanked the wheel and the Model T bounded to a rough idling halt on the dirt turnoff. He switched off the engine, the lights winking out. It was only the two of them sitting in the dark, listening to the breeze whispering in the leaves of the wall of trees a yard or so away. In the distance a fox was barking.

"Come on." Julian vaulted out of the automobile, waiting till Flynn followed. Frogs croaked accompaniment to the crunch of their footsteps as they crossed the clearing to the shelter of the trees.

Flynn glanced uneasily over his shoulder at the car sitting in the moonlight. The road was dark and empty both ways for as far as he could see. He ducked under the low branches.

Julian had found a soft place beneath the trees and ferns. They undressed and lay down in the cool grass and wild mint. The pleasure of coming together, naked and unfettered, was almost unbearably sweet. They held each close and kissed without haste or fear.

"Let's try it this way," Julian said, sitting up.

"What?" But Flynn followed Julian's silent command. They stretched out alongside each other, cock to mouth, mouth to cock. It was far too dark to see anything beyond the pale outline of the other, so they were reduced to a kind of night writing, a sensual brailing as they touched and tasted, fingertips tracing, lips exploring the textures of silky hair and smooth skin, of bones and muscles, teeth and fingernails, nipples, eyelashes, balls…everything seemed fantastic and unknown in the Delphian shadows scented of sex and damp earth and decaying leaves.

At last they settled down to it, hot, wet mouths closing over each other's rigid hardness. It was unreasonably difficult to concentrate on anything but the intense pleasure building in his groin and swelling cock, but Flynn tried. He tried to give as good as he was getting—what he was getting was very good indeed. Julian used everything from his warm breath to the slick tip of his tongue. He sucked hard and fiercely and then so soft and sweetly…

It was torture and delight to have this done to him at the same time he was trying to return the favor, growing hot inside and out, skin glazing with honey dew. Flynn buried his face in Julian's crotch and breathed in the damp, musky male scent. He traced his tongue around Julian's balls, and they were tender as sweetmeats, sweet as cherry cordials, those sweet intoxicating sacs…

Julian made a strangled sound but kept pulling and sucking like a trooper, and the great, rolling wave far out in the distance built speed, growing in height, a wall of pleasured release sweeping inland, knocking down all restraint, all thought, all considerations. That tidal wave of wild delight crashed into Flynn, washed him along in its powerful current. There was nothing like it, flooding him from the ends of his hair to the soles of his feet.

And at the same time he became aware that he had burst the cherry, a wet, salty-sweet rush filled his mouth, like tears of laughter or life-bringing primordial tide. He sucked and gasped for breath and sucked some more.

Later they lay entwined, hearts calming, breath evening, and watched the fireflies flickering overhead and heat lightning flashing along the distant ivory clouds to the south. The only sounds were the crickets and the katydids and the faint splash of the river far behind the trees.

The river's keening song reminded Flynn that a madman was prowling only a few miles away, and that it might not be wise to linger. He kissed Julian's warm, salty mouth. "We ought to think about getting along home."

"I wish we could stay here all night," Julian murmured.

"Be more comfortable in my bedroom."

Julian shook his head. "Not tonight. *Grand-père* will be watching."

"How can you live like that?"

Julian said calmly, "People live however they must."

"Why don't you tell him you don't want to perform anymore? Take your money and go open your café."

He was shaking his head.

"Why not?"

"It's not that simple."

"Why shouldn't it be?"

Julian said irritably, "In case you haven't noticed, I don't actually *know* how to run a café. I can't read or write or cook. I know how to do one thing."

"Con people?" Flynn hadn't meant to say that, it slipped out.

Julian pulled out of his arms and sat up. He said in a silky tone that raised the hair on the back of Flynn's neck, "Oh, it's not all a con. I could tell you things if I wanted to."

"What things?" Flynn was sitting too, reaching automatically for his trousers.

Julian didn't answer, and he repeated harshly, "What things?"

Julian was on his feet now, dressing quickly, ignoring Flynn. He said finally, "I know you don't think so, but it helps people to say farewell to their loved ones."

"But they're not saying farewell to their loved ones. You're making it all up. You're pretending you're hearing voices."

"Sometimes I am hearing the voices."

"But most of the time you're not, you admitted it today to the sheriff. Most of the time you're lying to them."

Julian made a small sound of contempt. "Oh, you're so smart, Mr. Big City Newspaper Man, and yet you don't understand the simplest thing. Didn't you ever notice funerals aren't for the dead? They're for the *living*."

He slipped his shoes on and started back for the flivver.

Flynn caught him up in a few steps, fingers sinking into Julian's arm. "What do you mean, you could tell me things if you wanted to?"

Julian stared at him. In the weird moonlight his eyes looked like the black holes in a skull. Flynn dropped his arm.

Julian said in a low, spiteful tone, "Do you really want me to contact Paul for you? Are you *sure* you want to know what he would say?"

"You *sonofabitch*." Flynn leaped forward, fist raised, and Julian stepped warily back. Flynn grabbed him by his shirt collar, but at the last minute he shoved him down rather than punching him in the face.

Julian sprawled on the ground. Half propped on an elbow, he stared up at Flynn. He said mockingly, "That's what I thought."

"I should let you walk back to town." Flynn turned away. He crossed the clearing in long, angry strides to where the Model T sat outlined in silver moonlight. Behind the trees, the night sky flashed with lightning, like an electrical short behind a purple-black curtain.

Climbing inside, he slammed the door and waited. Julian joined him a few seconds later, brushing his clothes down.

Flynn cupped the crank handle, started the engine. Neither spoke on the rest of the drive back to Herrin.

* * * * *

It was late when Flynn woke on Saturday morning. He had a bad headache and his body ached as though he'd been rolling around on pebbles all night. For a time he lay there wincing as he thought over the events at the shank of the evening.

The fan on the dresser was still droning. A light rain had left the morning cool and fresh. His anger seemed a distant, vague thing now. He was ashamed of having shoved Julian.

He washed his hands and face and followed the smell of coffee down the hallway to the kitchen where Amy was sitting on her own. She looked up and smiled at him.

"How about some flapjacks? I still have batter left."

"Sounds good." Flynn dropped down at the big maple table, avoiding looking directly at the bright sunlight flooding through the open window. How could birds be *so* loud?

"You all didn't drop in on one of those illegal roadhouses last night, by any chance?" Amy inquired, readying the heavy iron skillet.

"Perish the thought."

Amy chuckled sentimentally. "Now if Mrs. Hoyt were still with us, she'd be dishing up the Demon Rum sermon right about now."

"It was more like Demon Gin." Flynn asked belatedly, "How's Joan today?"

"Poor kid." Amy flicked water on the skillet and the beads sizzled. She poured the batter into the pan. "She's taking it hard. She hasn't got anyone here. There's an aunt in Missouri. She'll be coming out for the funeral I guess. She could stay on at the house, of course. Joan, I mean."

Amy went on chattering about Joan and Joan's future. Flynn listened with half an ear. What he really wanted—and dreaded—was to ask about Julian. The words wouldn't come.

He realized that Amy had fallen silent. Her back was to him as she flipped the flapjacks in the hot skillet with brisk efficiency.

Flynn stared at the wide, comfortable outline of her. He said, surprising himself, "I'm sorry I didn't come down after Gus died. I should have been here. To pay my respects."

Amy turned. It was almost as though she had been waiting for this. "That didn't matter. After Gus was gone, it didn't matter. He knew you respected him. He'd have liked to see you, though. I wish you'd come then: when he was still well—after you got out of the army. He used to talk about you a lot." She said it without reproach. She was being honest, and Flynn heard her out without defensiveness.

"I should have. I meant to. I kept thinking there was time for all that. You'd think the war would have taught me that lesson." He'd wasted a lot of time grieving. Not only grieving though, because that was maybe forgivable. He'd also wasted time feeling angry and sorry for himself. He'd hurt other people and it couldn't all be repaired. He could tell Amy that he regretted his action—or lack of action—but it didn't change anything. And he couldn't tell Gus…

Perhaps he understood why Julian thought he was helping people when he let them take those dark farewells of their loved ones.

Amy sighed and said, "I guess it's a lesson we all need to learn a few times before it sticks."

He understood why Gus had loved her despite their many and obvious differences.

Despite the turbulence of his emotions—and his hangover—Flynn's appetite was not affected much, and he kept eating pancakes as fast as Amy kept them coming, buttering them and spilling syrup on their pale faces reminding him of that big golden moon over the trees the night before.

The screen door behind him creaked. He turned, uncomfortably aware that he hoped the newcomer was Julian.

It wasn't. It was Casey.

"Well, you're home early," Amy greeted him.

He nodded and set his sample case on the table, pulling out the chair and sitting down heavily. "I thought maybe I'd take Joan out for a drive today. Get her out of the house."

He met Flynn's surprised gaze pointblank.

"Well, that's a very nice thought," Amy said. "She's down at the funeral parlor right now, but she ought to be back anytime soon."

Casey smiled rather unpleasantly. "The old frog was stocking up on remedies for the kid last night," he informed Flynn.

"What remedies?"

"Bromide salts mostly." He was enjoying himself, clearly. "Tincture of belladonna. He's a very sick boy, your pal."

"What the hell is supposed to be the matter with him?"

"Can't you guess?"

"No." Flynn added shortly, "Should you be discussing this with all of us?"

"Now that you mention it, I guess not." Casey smiled again. Funny how Flynn had first found Casey attractive and his grin engaging. He thought now that though he was handsome enough, his smile had a hint of cruelty.

Casey pushed the chair back, picked up his sample case and left the room.

"Where is Julian?" Flynn asked Amy.

"He went out this morning early."

Gathering information for the evening's show, no doubt.

She said uneasily, "What do you suppose he meant about the boy?"

"I don't know. He seems okay to me." All things being relative.

She had a look on her face as though she were remembering something.

"What?" Flynn questioned.

"Oh, I don't know." She seemed flustered to be caught gossiping. "But the old man was closeted with Dr. Pearson for a time yesterday. I did wonder…"

Flynn wondered too, but he realized he had already said too much about it.

Finishing his breakfast, he asked Amy if he could make a long distance phone call. She assured him anything in the house was his to use. He waited until the coast was clear, then went into the hall and called his editor, Ellery Sedgwick, at *The Atlantic Monthly.* He told Sedgwick the massacre story seemed to be hitting a dead end, but he had a new angle on spiritualism and sleuthing.

"I thought you couldn't wait to get back to New York?"

"I can't. But since I'm here I need to make the trip worth my while. I simply don't think there's much story in the massacre. Nothing that hasn't been covered."

"I tried to tell you that."

"You were right. But this spiritualism angle, well that's new." He told Sedgwick about the murders, and Sedgwick heard him out in thoughtful silence.

"Well, one thing's for sure, you haven't been this excited about a story for a long time. I'll be looking forward to seeing what you come up with. The spiritualism racket is still news."

Flynn was thoughtful when he rang off.

The house was empty and hushed with a funereal silence when Flynn left for the Opera House that evening. The Devereuxs had departed for the theater earlier to prepare for their final performance while the rest of the household was at the funeral parlor viewing for Mrs. Hoyt.

Flynn took the street trolley and arrived at the Opera House in plenty of time—which turned out to have been a wise decision. It was a full house, every one of the nearly five hundred seats filled. News of The Magnificent Belloc's conversation with the latest victim of the "Little Egypt Slayer," as the local papers were now terming the maniac, had spread far and wide.

Flynn listened absently to the discussion floating around him.

The stage had not been broken down from the high school theatrics on Friday evening, and before the stage crew drew the long red curtains, the whispering audience was treated to an inside peek at *A Midsummer Night's Dream* forest fairy kingdom. A golden lantern moon hung in the fanciful swirls and star-swept blue-black night. Shy woodland creatures peeked out behind painted trees and rocks. Glowing fireflies and fairies were strategically placed about the *mise en scène*. Flynn was reminded of the evening before. There had been a kind of magic in that woodland bedchamber.

Eventually the houselights dimmed. From behind the curtains a Victrola offered a scratchy rendition of "Angel Friends." The audience sang along.

> *Floating on the breath of evening, breathing in the morning prayer,*
> *Hear I oft the tender voices that once made my world so fair.*
> *I forget while listening to them, all the sorrows I have known,*
> *And upon the troubles present, faith's pure shining light is thrown...*

The spotlights went on, the curtains slid slowly open on the fairy kingdom, far more realistic and beautiful now that the main houselights were dimmed. Julian—The Magnificent Belloc—dressed once more in the finery of a doomed aristocrat, sat in the golden throne. He was smiling remotely as the audience finished.

> *Bless you Angel friends, oh never leave me lonely on the way,*
> *For your gentle teachings ever meekly may I watch and pray,*
> *For your gentle teachings ever meekly may I watch and pray.*

Pretty ghastly stuff in Flynn's opinion. The audience trailed off, and someone killed the magnified rolling gallop of the Victrola.

Belloc rose and strolled to the edge of the stage.

"Good evening."

"Good evening," the crowd answered back like thunder.

Julian smiled one of those practiced, charming smiles. "You will not be surprised to learn a great number of people are still under the impression that clairvoyance is a mysterious art, practiced by peculiar individuals who seem to be invested with singular—even sinister—powers, which they exercise within the confines of a dark and mysterious room. The séance room."

The audience tittered at his friendly mockery.

"These ignorant ones are unaware that many persons of considerable and various abilities have had psychical experiences of a veridical nature, and are familiar with the power of seeing either past or future, or both, as well as events that are happening at a distance."

He strolled casually to the other side of the stage. "Seeing the past and becoming aware of the possibility of witnessing people or happenings at a distance that cannot be perceived by the physical sight alone should bring us nearer to a comforting realization of the unity of all life and the existence of other spheres, of hitherto unexplored conditions in which dwell those whom we have known and loved in their earth lives, and later have mourned, because the physical process called death has removed them from the limitations of our physical sight and hearing."

The hall was silent, only the occasional cough or throat clearing interrupting the solemn hush.

"This is reassuring, is it not?"

"Yes," thundered back the audience.

"You have all heard of the well-authenticated and numerous cases which have been recorded. It becomes evident that this faculty of clairvoyance is a natural one, and can be used under natural conditions by perfectly natural people. The séance room is merely a laboratory, a quiet place where suitable and harmonious conditions can be assured, unhampered by the noise and distractions of the outer world."

He paused as though giving the opportunity to object. A pin would have sounded like an anvil hitting the floor in that silence.

"Tonight, this hall will serve as our séance room as we attempt to contact those who have gone before us."

Belloc returned to the golden throne and threw himself into it with careless grace.

"We will now summon my guide in the spiritual realm, le Comte de Mirabeau. He is your true host this evening."

Closing his eyes, Belloc bent his head, fist against his lips as though he were deep in thought. For a long time no one spoke, no one said anything. Then he lifted his head and murmured in French. There were rustles and whispers in the theater. Flynn smiled cynically, and yet he couldn't deny that he was engrossed along with the rest of the audience.

Belloc's eyelids fluttered, he straightened and opened his eyes. He had a distinctly French inflection as he said, "This one has been waiting, hanging back. He does not wish to grieve you, *monsieur*, but you must relinquish hope." His bright gaze stared past the footlights. "He was a soldier. His name was Christopher, *oui*? Lt. Christopher Thompson. Reported missing in battle." Julian shook his head regretfully, and a collective sigh seemed to escape the audience. "Who is here for Christopher?"

An elderly gentleman rose and stood erect as possible as he gripped his cane.

"He died bravely, *monsieur*. He wishes you to know that. And he wishes you to know that he is...how you say? Adjusting well to the...er... rules. In fact, he says there are far fewer rules on the other side. Love abounds. Heaven is and will be perfect love and harmony."

The elderly man nodded curtly. He seemed to struggle to speak, but in the end he lowered himself slowly and painfully once more. Belloc withdrew and closed his eyes again. More mumbling in French.

"Ah, Grand-mère. Helen. Qui est ici pour Helen?"

Sighs and rustlings.

"She died during the beginning of the influenza epidemic."

More whisperings.

No one laid claim to Helen, and Belloc shrugged and went on. "She wishes you all to know that the dead do not sleep. They are alive, as you are alive. Do not forget. Do not forget them."

Belloc subsided once more. On this evening the spirits seemed to be mostly those of soldiers and people who died in the Spanish Flu epidemic. Belloc was sincere and fluent, but something seemed off to Flynn. Slowly it dawned on him that whatever Belloc's attitude, Julian was nervous.

He wasn't sure how he knew, but he knew it.

"Maggie, Cyrus says that you must take the old tonic. The pink-colored one you were accustomed to take. It is better for you. Thomas, your dog is at Harrison Farm. Patrick says that he is happy and well again and free from pain. Martin is watching over you and the children, Louise."

Julian caught his breath. He clutched the arms of the throne and his knuckles turned white. "David, Paul says you…Paul says there is nothing to forgive."

Flynn heard this with a shock of disbelief. He sat very still, barely breathing.

Belloc opened his eyes and stared blindly at the wall of audience. "The quarrel meant nothing, would have been forgotten but for a German bullet. You know it is true."

People looked around, but Flynn didn't move, didn't breathe.

Belloc exhaled a long ragged breath and went on, sending messages to the mothers and wives of dead soldiers and sailors. Flynn continued to sit deaf and unseeing. A sob tore out of the woman next to him. A middle-aged man took out a handkerchief and blew his nose.

What was Belloc saying now?

Flynn forced himself to listen again. Shook off his numb preoccupation. But there was nothing to hear or see. Belloc was leaning back in his gold throne, exhausted. His face was white and strained, harsh breaths seemed to reverberate in the elegant Opera House. He rolled his head from side to side as though in a fever.

"No."

He sat up and glared stage left. *"No."*

Mesmerized, the audience watched as he jumped up, putting the throne between himself and another invisible presence.

"What do you want?" Monsieur le Comte seemed to have departed in a rush, taking Belloc with him. There remained a tense, angry young man speaking to what appeared to be…a ghost.

There was a long silence. People looked at each other, moved restively in their seats.

Julian said, "You must go. I can't do anything more for you."

A nervous ripple of laughter flowed up and down the aisles of the darkened theater. The audience began to whisper and talk amongst themselves. Julian glanced at them, glanced back at whatever was on the stage with him—or whatever he was pretending was on the stage. But, no, Flynn didn't believe that. As difficult, as bizarre as it was to conceive of, there did seem to be some…presence on the stage, hiding in the painted woodland.

Julian made an anguished sound. To the audience, he said, "Theresa is here again tonight. She says she can't rest—none of them can rest—until this murderer, this madman, is caught."

He stopped, biting his lip. The words seemed torn from him. "He is among you even now. You must *trust no one.*"

There were gasps and cries of horror and then, terrifyingly, every light in the theater went out.

An absolute pitch black descended on the Opera Hall.

There was an instant of frozen horror and then pandemonium. The audience rose in a surge, shoved their way down the rows of seats, crowding into the aisles in panic, pushing their way toward the doors. Voices cried out for calm, for order.

Flynn rose, also calling for reason, for quiet. People continued to try and push past to get to the jammed aisles.

The overhead lights went on.

People stopped their hysterical shoving and pushing and looked around, blinking, as though woken from a nightmare. Flynn looked back at the stage. It was empty.

CHAPTER EIGHT

$\mathcal{T}$he house was dark when Flynn let himself inside.

He made his way to the front parlor, turned on a lamp and sat down, resting his head in his hands. If what he had witnessed that night at the Opera House was legitimate, it was the most amazing proof of psychic ability or perhaps supernatural power that he had heard of. And if it was faked, both Julian and Old Man Devereux deserved to be locked up and have the key thrown away. People could have died in that theater tonight. If the lights had not come back on when they had, people probably would have. As it was, three ladies had fainted and had to be carried from the theater.

Flynn did not believe in spiritualists or ghosts or any of that mumbo-jumbo, but he couldn't argue that Julian Devereux had seemed on several occasions to tap into the uncanny. It was possible he had guessed from comments Amy had made and his own psychological insights that Flynn had not been back to Herrin to see Gus for years. It was possible he had guessed from Flynn's behavior that Paul and Flynn had argued the night before Paul died.

He was shrewd and he was clever. It was even possible he had heard rumors of a missing girl named Theresa Martin and taken a gamble that she was the murderer's latest victim.

But it was not probable.

Which meant what? That Julian did indeed have contact with the spirit of this murdered girl? That here was an as-yet-unused tool for finding the killer who had so far eluded the sheriffs? What use were either of those things if Julian refused to utilize this mysterious power he possessed?

Flynn scrubbed his face and sat up. He needed to talk to Julian alone, but there was no telling how long it might be before he and the old man showed up. He switched off the lamp and went upstairs.

In his own room, he turned on the lamp and the fan and sat on the side of the bed to take his shoes off. He noticed that a book lay on the bedside table. *The Encyclopedia Americana.* There was an envelope inserted between the pages as though to mark the reader's place. Curiously, he opened the encyclopedia and began to read.

> *It has to be born in mind that the disease is a progressive, degenerative malady, and that the object of treatment does not lie only in an attempt to combat convulsions by sedative medicinal remedies, but to prevent by every possible means the tendency to mental deterioration which is so important a clinical feature of the disease as shown in the impairment of intellect and memory, by impulsiveness, mental irritability, loss of moral sense and partial or complete loss of productiveness. Male patients are often given over to perverted sexual behavior, a condition that is probably part of the co-existent mental infirmity. It is also accompanied by periodic disturbances, transitory attacks of anger, dream-states or automatic phenomena.*

Flynn's heart pounded very hard with a mix of anger and horror. He wanted to throw the book away, but he couldn't help continuing to read.

> *Hallucinations are infrequent, illusions are common during an attack or following a grand mal seizure, and delusions are transitory, being found usually only in the dream-states. Morbid and sudden impulses are quite frequent, sometimes approaching distinct nerve-storms, during which suicidal and homicidal attacks may occur. Not infrequently the afflicted may set fire to their beds or furniture, commit theft, assaults, homicides, expose their persons and otherwise conduct themselves in an irrelevant and insane manner. Treatment should be commenced at the earliest possible time, after the onset of convulsive seizures, and should be continued for long periods, extending for at least two years*

even in the most satisfactory cases. For this reason treat-ment is best conducted in institutions, asylums or under skilled supervision, by which means the mental and bodily functions can be regulated and submitted to suitable forms of work, exercise and dietary restriction.

He slapped the book shut, then opened it and read the bookplate on the inside cover: *Casey Lee.*

At first he was too angry, too appalled, to think clearly. The message here was stark in its ugliness as a famine victim, and the target only too vulnerable. A wave of grief for Julian overtook him.

The grief was followed by another wave of angry outrage. The book had been left here in warning, and he did not believe it was kindly meant. Flynn didn't know much about medicine or this particular illness, but he knew none of this described Julian.

It could not be true.

But he remembered Casey saying the old man had bought bromides and belladonna. He remembered Amy saying the doctor had been closeted with the elder Devereux. He remembered Julian's veiled references to his "illness".

Was the book meant to frighten him off?

He considered it objectively. It was possible that Casey's ego had been pricked by the realization that Flynn had chosen Julian's company over his own the night before. But what if it was more sinister? This passage was meant to discredit Julian, even perhaps throw suspicion on him.

Why?

Was Julian somehow a threat to Casey? Why should he be?

Flynn did not yet dare to truly consider the personal implications of what he'd read. The main thing that Casey would know about Julian was that Julian had supposedly made contact with the spirit of one of the girls murdered in Jackson County—the neighboring county where Casey had been selling his wares during the period of the murders.

A light seemed to go on inside Flynn's mind. Casey was a traveling salesman. He moved all around the countryside, all around the state, and the nature of his business—cosmetics and medical supplies—made women his first and best customers. That sample case of his was as good as a pass key to most of the homes he visited. And that sample case itself was a clue. *Queen of Egypt Medical Supply Company.* Hadn't the women been mutilated in a grisly imitation of Egyptian burial practices? That was certainly the rumor. And Casey said he'd received medical training, which probably meant he knew enough rudimentary biology to carve the organs out of his victims.

Yes, it all made terrible sense.

Casey had sat out on the breezeway and listened to the others talk about Julian's performance and the contact with the spirit of Theresa Martin. If he was guilty, wouldn't he hear that news with alarm? Wouldn't he wonder whether it was true? What if the spirit of the dead girl *could* tell The Magnificent Belloc who her killer was? Didn't it give Casey the strongest incentive to discredit Julian as quickly and thoroughly as possible?

Of course it did.

And if it was true about Julian's illness? Flynn swallowed hard. There was no pretending that he wasn't stricken at this news. "The Falling Sickness," the ancients had called it. Flynn had witnessed a couple of convulsions. Not a pretty sight. Not something he wanted to think of afflicting someone he…cared about.

And if it was true, if Julian had the disease, was his supposed clairvoyance simply a manifestation of his illness? He opened the book and read again.

> *Hallucinations are infrequent, illusions are common during*
> *an attack or following a grand mal seizure, and delusions*
> *are transitory, being found usually only in the dream-states.*

He forced himself to consider the statement objectively.

Could Julian's psychic abilities be the sad proof of his deteriorating mental condition?

But he had been right about Gus, Paul and Theresa. If he was simply mad—granted there was always the possibility that he was mad *and* clairvoyant.

Flynn raised his head as he heard footsteps down the hallway. Muffled voices. Doors opening and closing. The Devereuxs had returned to the boarding house, and judging by the brevity of the muted exchange, not in great sympathy with each other.

He listened to the washroom plumbing rattle into life. He looked down again at the book he held. Whether Julian was ill or not, it didn't change the fact that Casey had deliberately sought to discredit him, and there had to be a purpose behind that. In Flynn's opinion it gave credence to Julian's clairvoyant declarations if only because Casey was so determined that they not be taken seriously.

And that, in Flynn's opinion, was because there was a very good chance that Casey himself was the murderer.

But how to prove it?

He was now determined to prove it. He couldn't help Julian, but he could pay Casey back for this, for trying to discredit the younger man, for destroying the delicate connection blossoming between them. He forgot completely his own earlier anger with Julian—he had mostly been over it by the morning, if he was honest. Now Casey had effectively wrenched that tentative emotion out by the roots.

Flynn looked down at the tiny print on the page and his anger rose again.

> *Male patients are often given over to perverted sexual behavior, a condition that is probably part of the co-existent mental infirmity.*

No question what that referred to, and Flynn didn't happen to believe it was true. Didn't believe the love of man for man was perverted or mental infirmity. Society and doctors were wrong about a lot of things. Why not this?

The washroom door opened, closed, opened again, and the erratic plumbing rumbled into action.

After a suitable interval, the washroom door opened and closed once more. The house fell at long last into silence.

Flynn closed the book, set it aside and turned out the lamp. He undressed in the darkness and lay down on the bed. The curtains gusted in and out and there was a not-too-distant grumble of thunder.

He rose, went to the window, lowering it halfway. He turned off the fan.

The bedroom door opened a silent foot, and Julian's tall, pale form slipped inside the room. A flash of lightning illuminated him briefly, highlighting his wide eyes, the elegant, exotic planes of his face, his mouth which whispered, "I'm sorry. I had to see you."

"It's all right," David said automatically.

Without turning, Julian locked the door. Flynn met him in two steps, pulled him into his arms, his lips finding that sweet, eager mouth in a long, hungry kiss.

Julian clung to him and whispered, "I missed you so."

I missed you too.

Flynn didn't say it, but it was true. Already, in these few days—four days—Julian had become important to him. More important now that he knew that anything between them, any real relationship, was impossible.

Because it was, wasn't it? If it was true that Julian had that dreadful malady?

Flynn buried his face in the silk of Julian's hair and skin. His own heart was pounding as hard as Julian's.

"I'm sorry for what I said last night," Julian breathed. "I regretted it all day, but—"

"It's all right."

"And then tonight at the Opera House. The message from Paul. It should have been in private. I swear I didn't know it was going to happen."

Julian's arms tightened around Flynn's neck, he leaned his head back and gazed searchingly at Flynn's face. Flynn kissed his yielding mouth softly.

"I believe you."

"I wouldn't hurt you for the world, David." He seemed almost desperate that Flynn should believe him.

Flynn nodded. "I know. I feel the same. I tried to find you today to tell you."

Something about Julian made it easy to let go of his anger, to say he was sorry. Paul had been too much like himself, apologies difficult for both of them. Julian…there was a gentleness there, the kind of sweetness that was unique to the genuinely strong.

Flynn guided them both to the bed. They lay down, freezing at the ping and squeak of old springs and bedframe. Flynn said, "We've got to be careful. The washroom is between my room and your grandfather's, but even so."

Julian nodded.

They fell asleep to the music of thunderclaps shaking the old house to its foundations and the lightning flashes turning the room electric white.

"David."

He could hear the sound of dripping. Flynn opened his eyes. It was daylight; a silvery, cool daylight. Glistening rain was still falling from the eaves. He turned his head. Julian was lying next to him, his gaze fastened on Flynn's.

Flynn blinked a couple of times, cleared his throat. "Hm?"

Julian's mouth covered his. When he broke the kiss, he whispered, "I've got to go."

"Go where?"

"I don't want to be in this house today. After the funeral they'll come back here and it'll be better if I'm not here. Better for me. Better for them."

He was probably right about that, but Flynn didn't want him to slip away. Their remaining time was brief as it was. "Where will you go?"

"I'll find a place to spend the afternoon. I'll be back this evening." He added regretfully, "I'll have to come back."

"I'll go with you," Flynn said on impulse.

Julian shook his head. "It'll cause comment. Better to avoid that now."

"I'll go with you," Flynn repeated. All at once it was very clear in his mind all the disastrous misadventures that might befall someone with Julian's affliction. But even more strongly it came to him that he wanted to spend this final day with Julian. Tomorrow the Devereuxs would be off to Murphysboro and the Liberty Theater. And after that? Another stop in an endless string of Midwestern towns. It was more than likely Flynn would never see Julian again after tonight.

He said stubbornly, "I want to spend today with you."

Julian's winged brows arched.

"I do," Flynn reiterated, and realized how much he meant it. Wanted it. Needed it. He covered Julian's mouth in warm insistence, and he felt the other man's opposition fade.

At last they broke the kiss. Julian sat up, raking his hair out of his eyes. "If you're coming, hurry up then."

He scooped his dressing gown off the floor, pried open the door and peered into the hallway. He was gone a second later, closing the door soundlessly behind him.

Flynn rolled out of bed and headed for the washroom where he washed hastily and shaved. He dressed and was downstairs waiting when Julian arrived a few seconds later.

Julian was smiling and that smile seemed to strike Flynn right in the solar plexus. How the hell was he going to let Julian go?

They let themselves out of the house and walked down to the diner where Flynn had breakfasted with Casey a day earlier. He'd forgotten that nothing would be open on a Sunday morning, and they were greeted by a large unfriendly CLOSED sign in the window. Instead they caught the streetcar and traveled out to Ozark's Park. They managed to get cinnamon walnut rolls and hot coffee from a street stand, and they ate contentedly on a bench in the deserted six acres of well-tended lawns and flowerbeds surrounding a luxury hotel and dance pavilion.

Though they talked, it was about nothing in particular. Just easy and comfortable conversation, and they smiled often at each other.

The storm had left the morning damp and muggy as it warmed up. There was an electrical hum in the air, and Flynn could feel an echo of that buzz every time Julian's gaze lingered on his.

When they grew bored with sitting, they walked down to the lake and skipped stones across the blue surface. Julian turned out to be unexpectedly adept at this crucial skill, and they made a friendly wager as to who would buy lunch. Flynn won by a skip, eleven to ten.

At lunchtime they bought a big striped watermelon and split it in half, sitting in the deep, cool shade. Flynn found himself struggling to stop staring at Julian as he ate the ripe, red melon, wiping occasionally at the juice running down his chin, spitting the seeds into the grass with the insouciance of a Huck Finn.

"These murders…" Flynn said tentatively.

Julian sighed and spit a couple of seeds at a rose, knocking the petals from its yellow head.

"I'm not asking you to check with your contacts in the spirit world," Flynn said. "But…what do you think? As a…a citizen?"

Julian lowered his lashes, considering. He lifted a dismissing shoulder. "It could be someone like you."

"*Me?*"

He grinned at Flynn's consternation. "Someone these women wish to talk to, despite the fact that he's a stranger to them. People talk to reporters. They like to see their name in print."

"What if he's not a stranger to the victims?"

"You mean the slayer could be known to the women?"

Flynn nodded. "Someone they've known for years maybe. Someone they trust *because* they've known him for years. Someone who's been a regular part of the community."

"Like a sheriff or a priest."

"Er...yes. Or a peddler or a trader."

Julian gazed at him with fresh alertness. "Like a traveling salesman?"

"Yeah."

He considered it with evident surprise. "You think Casey Lee is a murderer?"

"Do you?"

"Do *I*?" Julian's eyes widened. "What does it have to do with me?"

"I don't know. I thought perhaps your ability might give you insight into people. A feel for them?" He felt silly even saying it, but there was no denying Julian had a preternatural talent for knowing things no one could reasonably know.

Julian shook his head. "I don't think so," he said with shattering honesty. "I'm no good judging him. I'm jealous because you like him so much."

Into that naked revelation, Flynn said awkwardly, "I don't like him so much."

"You did." Julian grimaced. "Much more than you liked me. You wanted me, but you didn't like me." His smile was self-mocking. "I make you nervous."

Flynn said quietly, "You don't make me nervous any more except, I guess, in a good way." He smiled at Julian's uncertainty. "And I do like you. I wouldn't be here with you now, ants crawling in my pants, if I didn't."

Julian's laugh was lazy. "I guess that's true. And I did try to keep you from coming with me. Do you think Casey Lee is the Little Egypt Slayer?"

It felt so strange to discuss it calmly in broad daylight. Flynn said, "Well, there's a lot of circumstantial evidence. He was in Murphysboro or at least nearby in Jackson County at the time of some of the murders. And he's a person the women might let into their homes without question. He sells medical supplies."

Julian seemed very involved in finding the right blade of grass to make a whistle. "Queen of Egypt Medical Company, yes."

"And he's got medical training. Those women were pretty cut up from what I read."

"He cast a spell on them, I believe. I couldn't quite understand what I was hearing during the performance last night. I don't think the women knew who killed them. He must have drugged them first." Julian added, still not looking at Flynn, "I don't think it was cruelty, you know. I think the man who killed those women is mad. Mad as a hatter. Lee has a cruel streak, but I don't think he's mad."

"Has he done something cruel to you?" Flynn asked, and he was startled at how instantly angry he was at the notion.

Julian looked startled too. "No. I can see the way he looks at Joan, though, the way he talks to her. He's going to marry her if he can. It's not right."

Flynn stared. Was that true? He thought of the small attentions Casey offered Joan. And he thought of Joan's eagerness, her obvious loneliness. Yes, he could see all that now that Julian pointed it out.

Julian said slowly, thoughtfully, "Maybe you're right at that. Maybe the slayer is someone the women have known for years and trusted. They can't see that he's going slowly insane—and neither can he." He swallowed. "Madness can creep up on you."

Flynn thought of the book that had been left in his room. There had been several pages about the likelihood of patients afflicted with that particular disease going mad. Not everyone, true, but the author had been far more interested in discussing the gruesome probabilities.

He opened his mouth to tell Julian about the book, to ask him about this mysterious illness, but Julian jumped up and said, "I need to stretch my legs. Let's walk back down to the lake."

As he spent the day with Julian talking and walking, Flynn felt more and more convinced that Casey Lee was simply trying to discredit the younger man. There was nothing wrong with Julian. He was smart and funny and jolly company as he described the astonishing and silly things that had happened during performances through the years. He laughed at his own mistakes with the same good humor that he laughed at the follies of his fellow performers.

Flynn stared at Julian stretched comfortably on the green velvet lawn. He was smiling faintly, face tilted to the sky, and Flynn's throat tightened painfully. If only this day would never end. He wanted to lean over and kiss Julian's beautiful, mocking mouth. Impossible of course. Even to take his hand and hold it was forbidden for two men. They had been born several centuries too late.

The day flew and soon it was evening and the acetylene gas lamps were coming on all around them, families and couples leaving the park. Flynn and Julian rose and followed them out through the gates.

They caught the streetcar back to the Gulling Boarding House, reaching the house to find it unexpectedly quiet.

They exchanged puzzled glances. But when they looked in the front parlor they found nearly the entire household there, speaking quietly. Not surprisingly, the mood was subdued after the day's funeral.

"There's plenty of food in the kitchen," Amy told them by way of greeting. There was a curious expression in her eyes.

In fact, the entire household seemed to watch them very carefully. *Grand-père* had been glowering from the moment they appeared together in the doorway. Casey Lee sat in a chair near the cold fireplace. A strange middle-aged lady sat on the sofa next to Joan who was dressed in sobering black. The middle-aged lady, also dressed in black, bore a remarkable resemblance to Mrs. Hoyt minus a few years and pounds.

Joan introduced her aunt, Mrs. Packard, and Flynn nodded a polite hello. Julian stumbled through an awkward apology for missing Mrs. Hoyt's funeral. Joan was quick to make his excuses for him on the grounds of his extreme sensitivity to spirits. This brought a politely skeptical nod from Mrs. Packard and a faint, derisive smile from Casey Lee as he met Flynn's gaze.

Flynn, remembering again the book that had been left in his room, met that green gaze with his own stony one and saw Casey's eyes narrow.

Joan, having finished describing the hymns and flowers of Mrs. Hoyt's ever-so-lovely funeral, was saying in her pleasant way, "Julian, I know it's a terrible imposition, but it would mean so much if you would only consider..."

"Consider?" Julian asked warily.

"Holding a séance so that I might talk to Mama."

Julian's recoil was unmistakable. "I'm... I don't think..."

Tears filled Joan's eyes, she clasped her hands together as though in prayer—much to the obvious discomfort of her aunt and Casey—and pleaded, "You're not giving a performance tonight. You could do it right here in the house. I've already spoken to Mrs. Gulling and she's given permission if you would agree."

Flynn glanced around but Amy had slipped out of the room. Not that he blamed her.

"It would just be us." Joan looked around the room with a supplicant's gaze. "Our family here. You do it for strangers. It's not fair that you won't do it for people you know."

"Assuming you do it for real," Casey drawled.

Julian threw him a look of dislike. He stared at Joan. "It's not...that simple."

He looked to his grandfather, who said tersely, "Julian must have time to rally his energies. He's given four performances this week. The toll on his psychic stamina is considerable. He must have time to rest and recover."

"Plus he wouldn't be paid for this," Casey said.

Julian's mouth opened, but he swallowed his angry words as Joan said, "Please, Julian." Tears spilled from her eyes. "I never got the chance to tell Mama good-bye."

There was a strange silence. Flynn became aware of a sense of foreboding. *Refuse,* he thought. *Tell them no.*

Julian sighed. "All right."

Hearing this, Flynn felt oddly weary, almost let down. Yet the day before hadn't he been hoping for this very thing? He himself had suggested a séance to the police. Now he wondered what he'd been thinking.

Joan was still thanking Julian as Flynn turned and went down the hall toward the stairs. Passing the study, he saw Dr. Pearson reading at the long table. He was so engrossed in his book that he was unaware when Flynn stepped inside the room.

"Dr. Pearson?"

Dr. Pearson looked up and stared at him with an unfocused look. He looked like a man who had received unexpected bad news.

"May I talk to you?"

Pearson seemed to shake off his preoccupation. He closed the book and folded his hands on its blue-and-gold cover.

"Sorry, young man. I was miles away. You wished to speak to me?"

"Professionally. Consult you, I suppose I mean."

The doctor's silver brows rose. "I see."

"Yes. Except it's not for myself. I wanted to ask you about…a friend."

"Ah." Clearly Dr. Pearson had heard that one many a time. His expression became one of resigned patience.

Flynn came the rest of the way into the room and sat down at the polished table. He lowered his voice as he said, "This friend is subject to convulsions. Seizures. He's—" Flynn took a deep breath. "I believe he's an epileptic."

"Ah." The doctor's tone was quite different. Could a greater tragedy befall anyone? Beside the grim physical and mental prognosis, there was

the social stigma. No wonder the idea of marriage for epileptics was so frowned on; the notion of delivering children to a similar catastrophic fate would make any sane person quail.

When Flynn didn't continue, the doctor said with brisk kindness, "Poor fellow. I'm sorry to hear that. What is it you think I can do for you— er, your friend?"

Flynn said carefully, "My question is…does the disease always follow the same course? What I mean is, is there any chance of…of recovery?"

Flynn was so sure of the answer he was taken aback when the old man said calmly, "Occasionally. It depends on a variety of factors. Some patients do achieve remission even after many years of seizures. Occasionally the illness can be controlled through treatment. When did your friend first begin to exhibit signs of the malady?"

"I believe he was sixteen."

"That is more favorable than someone who develops the illness earlier in life."

"Is he likely to die from the seizures?"

"Probably not from the seizures themselves. Are the convulsions frequent?"

"I-I'm not sure. I don't believe so. I don't really know."

Pearson considered this, and then light seemed to dawn. He eyed Flynn with mounting hostility. "Does the patient or the patient's guardian know that you're asking for this medical advice?"

Flynn felt his face heat. "No."

"I see."

Flynn gathered his courage. "It's not what you think, sir. I'm asking out of friendship only."

Dr. Pearson continued to inspect him dubiously.

"May I ask you one more thing? Must the illness always end in… mental deterioration and madness?"

"Of course not." Testily, Dr. Pearson rose from the table and went to the tall bookshelves lining the far end of the room. He put away the book he had been reading, scanned the shelf and pulled another. He flipped through it, muttered to himself, and then silently read for a few seconds. His mouth tightened. He replaced the book on the shelf.

"On second thought, never mind. There is a modern tendency to believe the best course of treatment is to lock these unfortunates away as soon as possible in one of the asylums popping up all across the country such as the Craig Colony in Sonyea, New York."

"I've heard of it."

"I'm sure you have." Pearson came back to the table. "If you want the opinion of an old country horse doctor, those well-meaning monsters are responsible for the destruction of far more lives than the wretched disease itself. In fifty years of medical practice it has been my observation that what the epileptic patient most requires is a reasonable routine of rest and activity, interesting occupation for their minds, affection of friends and family, and a diet rich in protein and low in carbohydrate. Mild bromide is useful if the attacks are frequent and severe."

"Is that true?"

"I've no reason to lie to you, young man," Pearson said irascibly.

Flynn thanked him and went upstairs.

Supper was deep-fried catfish, tangy coleslaw, chilled beets, fresh, crusty Italian bread with plenty of butter. Good simple food, and all of it, with the exception of the catfish, left over from the funeral reception.

There was no sign of Julian at the evening meal. The other guests were subdued although Casey Lee did his best to cheer Joan up.

Joan's aunt, Mrs. Packard, eyed Casey tolerantly and asked what she clearly imagined to be shrewd questions about his marital status and income.

After the meal, the household, with the exception of Dr. Pearson who said he didn't hold with such out-and-out superstitious nonsense, retired to the formal dining room. The large, polished oval table sat with a brass candelabrum burning brightly in its center. Julian stood behind the chair at the head of the table. He was dressed in ordinary trousers and a white shirt rather than the rich costume he wore for his stage performances.

His gaze met Flynn's. There seemed to be a message in his eyes, but Flynn was uncertain of the meaning. He moved to take the seat to Julian's left.

"I was expecting something quite different," Mrs. Packard announced, settling herself on a spindly chair which creaked ominously beneath her weight. Whether she was pleased or disappointed was unclear.

"Isn't the Comte de Mirabeau going to join us?" Joan asked uncertainly.

Julian gave her an odd look. "No. Not tonight."

The Comte's night off apparently.

"I still don't feel this is a wise idea," the elder Devereux complained, taking the chair at the end of the table. "Julian is not strong."

"Or perhaps you don't feel he should be doing this for free?" Casey Lee said, making sure he was seated next to Joan who was on the right side of Julian.

The old man said querulously, "I didn't say that."

Julian glanced at Flynn, who offered him what he hoped was a reassuring smile. Julian's smile flickered in return.

Flynn pulled his chair out and sat down with the others. They quickly settled, obeying Julian's instructions to rest their fingertips lightly on the glassy surface. Julian looked grimly around the assembly and requested Joan to say *The Lord's Prayer*, which she did in her soft, grave voice.

Casey Lee squeezed her hand reassuringly, and she gave him a shy smile.

Julian eyed them unsmilingly before offering up a brief petition that the spiritual assembly might enable those humble seekers gathered to receive a fuller measure of celestial knowledge to ease their grieving hearts and seeking minds.

There was silence. The candle flame on the tabletop seemed to brighten.

Julian said abruptly, "Make your presence known."

Silence.

Joan gasped, looking around. Flynn heard it too. They all heard it: a sound like the rustling of large wings. Not the flapping of flight, but a gentle quivering, a trembling beat.

"It's a trick," Casey Lee said shortly, and he reached across the table. Joan murmured protest at the same time Flynn's hand shot out to intercept him. The two men locked gazes. Flynn dug his fingers in hard, and Casey Lee opened his mouth in protest.

Julian said in a flat, cold voice, "You must neither speak nor touch me."

Flynn released Casey, and the other man sat back in his seat, rubbing his wrist.

They rested their fingertips on the table edge once more.

All was still.

The table suddenly rocked beneath their hands. The shadow of candle flame danced crazily against the wall as the candelabrum slid forward a few inches. The elder Devereux snatched it up and placed it safely on the sideboard.

There were gasps and murmurs. Julian said, "Please join your hands together so that all may know that no one is moving the table."

They clasped hands hastily. Flynn's hand closed warmly about Julian's long, cold fingers. He tightened his hold reassuringly and Julian squeezed back.

Amy was seated on Flynn's other side. Her work-roughened hand was comfortingly vigorous. Her profile looked stern.

The table continued to rock and then it slowed and stopped.

Julian asked in a low, almost sleepy voice, "Who are you?"

Silence.

"What was your name on the mortal plane?"

Silence.

"Did you go by the name of Alicia Hoyt?"

Silence.

"Is the woman known as Alicia Hoyt among you?"

Silence.

Mrs. Hoyt's sister sighed restively. Mr. Devereux threw her a warning look.

Joan cried out, "Mama!" She was looking past Julian's shoulder.

Flynn glanced over his shoulder as the others looked up. There did seem to be a pale, glimmering outline of a form, but it did not look precisely human, let alone female. Everyone stared, spellbound.

"Are you Alicia Hoyt?" Julian persisted. He did not look behind. His eyes were closed, his lashes black crescents on his cheeks.

Silence.

"Do you have a message for your daughter, Joan?"

There was a gasp from around the table. A single word appeared in letters of light on the wall behind Julian.

"What does it say?" Joan asked, looking from one to the other of them.

Flynn had to narrow his eyes to make out the small word. "Beware," he read slowly.

There were several intakes of breath. Amy's hand clenched his tightly. Julian's remained cool and lax in Flynn's grasp.

A sound like the rustlings of tree branches—marked from the earlier fluttering of bird wings—filled the room, followed by the sensation of wet leaves or wet…something falling upon their hair and skin. Beads of water seemed to rain from the ceiling and splash on the table. They glittered in the candlelight like raindrops or drops of blood.

There was a distinct sound of someone inhaling and then a fiercely exhaled breath. The candles on the sideboard went dark.

CHAPTER NINE

"Death shall shine in your starless night." The voice came from Julian, but it was several octaves higher than his normal tone and it had an eerie, dreamy quality.

"Who said that?" Mrs. Packard's voice sounded frightened. "What does that mean?"

"Julian?" Flynn asked quietly.

"Don't wake him," Mr. Devereux whispered urgently from down the table. "He's entered into a trance state. It's most dangerous to wake a medium."

"What do we do?" Amy asked. She sounded calm but ready for action.

Mr. Devereux hissed, "We mustn't break the circle of our hands or do anything to shatter the trance."

"But what's the point of it?" Casey asked impatiently.

"Can't you all stop talking?" Joan cried.

A sharp, surprised silence followed her words.

"Julian," she said softly through the pitch darkness that blanketed the room.

"There is no Julian," the queer flat voice coming from Julian said. "There is only Millicent."

"W-who?" Joan quavered.

"Millie Hesse?" Flynn cut across quickly, softly.

"Millie Hesse," agreed the voice.

"Who's Millie Hesse?" Mrs. Packard demanded. "Where's Alicia?"

"Millie Hesse was the first," Casey said in a thick voice.

"No," Amy said. "The third."

The voice that came from Julian said dreamily, "Millie Hesse is the last. The others have gone now, crossed the great river."

"What river?"

"The Mississippi?"

"What the hell is he talking about?"

"Iteru," Julian said in that same vague voice. "First Theresa went, then Anna, then Maria. There's only me now…"

Flynn ignored the nervous babble of voices. He stroked Julian's icy knuckles with his thumb. "What do you want, Millie?"

"Justice for the dead."

"When did you die?"

"The nineteenth of July, 1923. It was a hot, sunny morning when he came to the house."

"Who came to the house?"

Silence.

"Who came to the house?" Flynn repeated.

The voice said serenely, "The sun was shining on the water like silver dust and the leaves in the trees whispered like a hundred tongues. I can't say his name."

"Why can't you say his name?"

"He cut our tongues out in the way of the ancient sorcerers so we couldn't speak his name. I can't go forward. I can't go back. The others have gone. Only I remain. Only I wait for justice."

"This is lunacy," Casey cried. "Ancient *sorcerers*? Devereux is insane. He's a charlatan—or he's insane."

"Shut up," Flynn told him fiercely. "Shut up or I'll shut you up."

"Try it!"

"Don't break the circle," Mr. Devereux entreated from the far end of the table.

Flynn felt the tension go through the circle as though someone had tried to pull free but the others held fast. He urged, "Millie, can you write the word on the wall like you…like Julian did before?"

Silence.

"Millie, someone—you or another spirit—wrote a word with letters of light on the wall. Can you do that? Can you write the name of your murderer—?"

"You're *crazy*!" Casey roared. "You're a goddamned bunch of lunatics!"

A flash of light was followed by great upheaval in the darkness.

"Casey!" Joan cried out in distress.

Mr. Devereux exclaimed, "He's broken the chain of hands."

Amy let go of Flynn's hand. On the other side of Flynn, Julian's hand tightened on his own with near crushing force. A strange drumming sound issued from beneath the table and the chair at the head crashed over, Julian nearly pulling Flynn and his chair over too.

"Turn the lights on!" Flynn yelled.

"What has happened to Julian?" shouted Mr. Devereux.

Pandemonium reigned. The floor was vibrating beneath that queer rapid pounding sound. What was it? Flynn felt his way in the dark and found the rigid mound of Julian's tumbled form. He could hear an alarming choked whistling as though air were being pressed from a bellows, feel the severe muscle contractions of the body convulsing beneath his hands. A flailing arm grazed his jaw.

It was all the worse for being in the dark.

"Get Dr. Pearson," Flynn ordered. He reached out, trying to protect Julian's thrashing head from the forest of table and chair legs.

On the other side of the table Joan was screaming over and over in a complete hysterical fit. There was much stumbling around and cursing in the dark.

"What in tarnation is going on in here?" Dr. Pearson's voice demanded above the mayhem.

Julian's fit seemed to be lessening as the lamp at the sideboard against the wall was lit at last.

Mrs. Packard made her way to Joan and slapped her. Joan collapsed in Casey Lee's arms, sobbing. The others stood bewilderedly gazing down at Flynn and Julian.

Julian lay trembling and pale in the aftermath of his convulsion. His dazed eyes moved unseeing from Flynn's face to the ceiling to the table.

Mrs. Packard and Amy attempted to soothe Joan, who continued to weep on Casey's shoulder. He swept her up in his arms and bore her from the room, the worried women on his heels.

"Well, well. What have we here?" Dr. Pearson lowered himself painfully on one knee and examined Julian curiously but not unkindly. He took his pulse, checked his pupils. "You're all right now, aren't you?"

Julian didn't answer. Did not seem aware of his surroundings yet. He kept licking his lips and blinking.

"Let's get him to bed. The worst of the attack is over. He'll sleep now."

"He should have been dosed properly. You shouldn't have discouraged me," Devereux said to the doctor. He stroked his grandson's damp hair with a shaking hand and whispered in French.

"If he's having these fits more frequently, then yes, we'll have to dose him with the bromides. You said the fits were rare."

"This is your fault!" Mr. Devereux charged, and Flynn gazed up at him stupidly.

"How is it my fault?"

"You know what you've done. Overexciting him, overtaxing his strength, encouraging him to-to unspeakable—"

Flynn waited in horror for the old man to say it. Rescue came from an unexpected source.

"Gentlemen, gentlemen," Dr. Pearson broke in impatiently. "This isn't doing the young man any good. What he needs now is absolute rest and quiet. Save your dispute for later and help me. Between the three of us we should be able to get him upstairs to his room."

"I'll take him," Flynn said roughly. He bent, gathering Julian carefully in his arms. In fact, Julian, for all his willowy height, was no featherweight, and Flynn did require the assistance of the older men to gain his feet.

He needed their help up the staircase as well, but at last they got the sufferer to his own room, undressed and tucked comfortably inside his bed. By then Julian seemed to be coming back to himself. He clutched Flynn's hand.

"David…"

"Shhh."

Devereux senior moved between them, breaking Julian's hold, and there was nothing Flynn could do or say to stop it. He had no rights here despite the way Julian's tired, dazed eyes sought him out.

He turned around as Amy appeared at the bedroom door. "Dr. Pearson, you've got another patient downstairs. Joan took a fit right after the séance."

Dr. Pearson, taking Julian's pulse once more, looked confounded. "Very well." To Flynn he said, "He's all right now. I expect he'll sleep all night and most of tomorrow. Someone should sit with him, though."

"I'll sit with him," Mr. Devereux said with a fierce look at Flynn.

"David," Julian murmured.

"What are you thinking? Mr. Flynn can't stay," Devereux said sternly. The ready tears of the invalid filled Julian's eyes.

Flynn opened his mouth in protest, but what could he say?

He threw one final look at Julian who was wiping shakily at his tears.

Dr. Pearson had already followed Amy out of the room and down the hallway. Their footsteps rapidly disappeared as the elder Devereux said grimly, "A word, Mr. Flynn."

Flynn nodded reluctantly and Devereux followed him over to his own room.

"If you come near my grandson again, I'll go to the sheriff. Julian is not responsible for the things he does. He's ill. You see that. And you know only a man as ill as Julian would let you do those foul, perverse things to him."

"Julian might be epileptic, but he's not a child and he's not insane."

"That's where you're wrong," Devereux said with bitter triumph. "This filthy disease has eaten away his mind and his will. He's like a child, and for your information, the law recognizes that fact and has placed him in my guardianship."

"He's twenty-six years old."

"He is epileptic. Already he shows the signs of moral insanity." He glared at Flynn. "I've told him and now I'll tell you, if he doesn't obey me in every respect, I'll have him committed for his own damned good."

"You won't have him committed," Flynn said quietly. "That would be the end of the golden goose."

Devereux said equally low voiced, "But if the golden goose is going to run away with you, Mr. Flynn, then I will have no choice but to have him committed in the hopes the doctors can help him. Or at least keep him from harming himself."

"Run away with me?" Flynn repeated, stunned.

The old man stared at him suspiciously, then said slowly, "You don't know? You didn't offer to take him away...?" He laughed an acrid laugh. "There. You see now? You see what that poor, sick, young madman made of your using him? You should be ashamed, sir. And if you approach my grandson again, I'll see that you're shamed before all the decent world."

He left Flynn's room, closing the door silently behind him.

For a long time Flynn stood motionless, unable to think past Devereux's words. Distantly he could hear the house still in commotion. He thought that across the hall Julian was crying. His heart squeezed, but he continued to think hard.

There was no way around it, was there?

He couldn't risk exposure. New York might be more sophisticated in its tastes than Herrin, but it wasn't *that* sophisticated. Nowhere on the planet was *that* sophisticated. Oh, they could easily manage it if *Grand-père* wasn't bound and determined to keep his meal ticket. Julian would be safe enough in Greenwich. Flynn could say that he was his distant cousin or some such thing. He would be safe and he would thrive there, and Flynn could make sure he got the care and attention Dr. Pearson had spoken of, particularly the affection and love.

But not if M. Devereux was going to come after them.

He needed to put the thought out of his mind and go to sleep. But sleep wouldn't come—even after the house settled into a heavy, portentous silence. Flynn lay fully dressed, hands behind his head on his bed, staring out the window at the old, tarnished moon.

It wasn't possible, was it?

The old man had already had Julian placed in his wardship. He was two steps ahead of them all the way. They couldn't run away like children or hobos. Start a new life without money or friends?

Perhaps he was the insane one to lie here contemplating such a thing.

And yet…and yet Julian had told the old man they were going away together. Julian *wanted* to go with him.

Sleep was impossible. He felt uneasy, restless. He needed to speak to Julian.

After a time he rose and went down the hall to Julian's room. He eased open the door. The lamp on the dresser was down low. An ominous-looking bottle and a glass with a spoon in it stood next to the bed. Mr.

Devereux sat in a chair near the window, dozing. Julian was lying in bed gazing up at the ceiling.

As the door swung open, he stared at it, stared at Flynn without expression. Flynn came to stand at the end of the bed. "Hello."

Julian nodded politely.

"How do you feel?"

He curled his lip contemptuously, but said nothing. Flynn shot a quick glance at the old man, gently snoring, and sat on the edge of the bed. He took Julian's hand. Julian did not resist, but he didn't respond either. Not even when Flynn leaned forward and kissed him.

His lips were feverish and dry and there was the taste of bitter—medicine or bromide, no doubt—on them.

When Flynn withdrew, Julian gave a long, weary sigh. "Now you know."

"I already knew. I knew the day before yesterday."

Julian's brows drew together. "You did? How?"

"It doesn't matter how." Flynn said, "You could have told me. It doesn't make a difference." And he realized as he said it that it didn't. As frightening as the convulsions were, the fear that the disease might—probably would—grow worse, something about Julian made him feel alive and happy in a way he hadn't in too many years. And if the war had taught him one thing, it was that happiness was fleeting and fragile. You had to grab on to it and hold tight for as long as it lasted.

"Oh, it matters," Julian said bitterly. He glanced at the old man in the chair. "You asked about why I can't take the money I earn and go do as I like? Because he's my legal guardian. And if I don't do exactly as he likes, he can have me shut up in an insane asylum or an epileptic colony like the one in New York."

"He can't do it simply on his say so."

"Oh, David." Julian sounded both miserable and impatient. "You still don't understand. This affliction is…it's a curse. And people blame you as though you had control of it. There are plenty of folks who think I'm crazy for seeing spirits. Let alone if they saw me having fits. Any doctor would have me committed if he told them even half of it and let them examine me. Let alone if they knew…" He gave Flynn a despairing look.

"There's a way around it."

Julian's eyes widened. "What are you saying?"

Flynn threw a quick look at the sleeping man. "Did you tell him you would go away with me if I asked you?"

Julian's mouth trembled. "I shouldn't have, I know it. I know you didn't ask, didn't plan on asking. But I-I wanted it to be true."

"And if it was true?"

Julian swallowed hard. "You know the answer. You know how I felt from the first minute I saw you. But it's no use."

"How brave are you?"

"I don't know." Julian's eyes were puzzled.

"I've got friends and I've got family and they're a hell of a lot more powerful than anybody on the side of your loony *grand-père*. But it would be a fight and it wouldn't be a pretty one. Do you have the nerve for it?"

Julian's riveted gaze held his, so Flynn saw each emotion flash past: joy, doubt, fear, stubbornness, despair. "For myself, yes," he whispered. "But I couldn't do that to you. You'd be ruined. You don't know what it would be like."

"Neither do you."

"It would be bad."

"Yes. Probably. He's a stubborn old coot. But then it would be good. That's what I believe."

"I…wish I could believe too…" Julian closed his eyes. Wet glittered beneath his lashes. "Sorry, David. I…can't talk anymore. I want to sleep now."

"All right." David squeezed his hand and rose. "I'll come and see you in the morning."

Tears trickled down Julian's cheeks. He ignored them stoically and said, his voice nearly steady, "We're leaving on the morning train."

"Not now, surely? Not while you're ill?"

"Oh yes. I'll be well enough tomorrow. He'll want me away from here—and you—as soon as possible."

Flynn stared down at his lover—yes, he acknowledged, his lover—and squatted down beside the bed so that his face was level with Julian's.

"Julian?"

Julian's eyes opened, red-rimmed and overbright.

"We'll see it through together, I promise you. I won't abandon you. I have resources and contacts your grandfather doesn't. Maybe he can paint you—and me—in an unflattering light, but when I'm done I'll have him tarred and feathered and run out of town."

"Don't, David." Julian reached out a quick hand. "He's not evil. He thinks he's protecting me."

"Maybe. But he's using you too." Flynn covered his hand, brought it to his mouth and kissed it. "Rest. I promise it'll be okay."

Julian's eyelids were already fluttering shut.

Flynn watched him and in a few seconds he could see that Julian was sleeping again. He looked with far less affection at the old man, starting to snort as he woke himself with his snoring.

Flynn hesitated. He was ready to do battle now, but clearly Julian was not. It would have to wait, but in one thing he was determined. Julian was not going to be dragged off to another performance in Murphysboro tomorrow morning.

He left the sickroom and stood undecided in the hall.

If he was going to do battle, it would be wise to be as well-prepared as possible. He thought of the medical book that Dr. Pearson had started to hand him and then thought better of. He might as well know now what he was committing to, but either way he was committed. Hope for the best and prepare for the worst, that would be his motto from now on.

Flynn went downstairs. The house was in darkness. The silence seemed complete and absolute. There was a single band of light down the hallway beneath a door. Joan's room he guessed. The other sickroom.

He went into the study and turned on the light. Going to the tall bookshelf, he scanned the green, red, blue bindings for the medical book Dr. Pearson had pulled from the shelf. A gold embossed title caught his eye. *The Burial Customs of Ancient Egypt as Illustrated by the Tombs of the Middle Kingdom.*

For an instant Flynn could not seem to process the information. He recalled his conversation with Julian about the Little Egypt Slayer. That the slayer would be someone his victims knew and trusted, someone with medical knowledge and tools, someone who frequently traveled the countryside, someone so well known and liked that his eccentricities might be taken for granted.

He took the book down from the shelf and it fell open with the loose-leafed familiarity of an oft-read section.

> *A priest then cut an opening in the abdominal cavity. The internal organs were removed in ritual fashion leaving only the heart. The ancient sons of the Nile believed that the heart contained the individual's essence and was the centre of intelligence...*

Flynn closed the book and shoved it back on the shelf, his mind racing to the events of the séance. To those final minutes after Julian had seemed to make contact with Millie Hesse and Flynn had asked the spirit whether she could write the name of her killer on the wall in the letters of light.

He left the study and strode down the silent hall to the dining room. He found the lamp on the sideboard and turned it on. The chairs still lay fallen on the floor, the table had moved two feet to the left. The candelabrum was on the floor. Flynn stared at the wall behind where Julian had sat.

It was simply a blank white wall with two prints of optimistically European landscape. No place on Earth that Flynn recognized. He walked up to the wall and peered closely. There was a small black smudge in the center. He remembered leaning out of his chair to see, but the letters were so small he was unsure how he could have made them out. He bent close and saw the letters, perfectly formed, as though branded in the plaster: *Beware*.

That was the word offered at the first part of the séance. Had Millie Hesse left a second part of the message? Flynn examined the wall with meticulous care. He found another smudge half hidden beneath the bottom frame of the unrecognizable European castle.

He squinted, leaned in closer still. He could barely make out the small scripted letters burnt into the plaster: *Pearson*.

From beyond the grave: *Beware Pearson*.

Flynn turned and ran down the hall to Joan's room. He was distantly aware that Mr. Devereux was coming down the stairs. The old man hissed, "I told you what would happen if you came near my grandson again, Flynn!"

Flynn ignored him. He ran to Joan's door and yanked it open.

The gentle lamplight revealed Joan, naked and still on the sheets. On every flat table and dresser surface of the room stood mason jars of various sizes glinting in the glow of the lamps. An array of surgeon's instruments were arranged on a white towel at the foot of the mattress. Dr. Pearson stood beside the bed calmly, placidly unrolling bandages. Behind him, the full moon seemed to loom outside the window like a great golden eye staring into the room.

As the door swung open, however, Pearson's head jerked up and he gazed in instant affront at Flynn. Though it was the same man whom Flynn had spoken to a few hours earlier, it was the face of a stranger. He rattled out a string of nonsensical syllables—was it supposed to be Egyptian? Perhaps it really was.

"Stop," Flynn ordered.

The maniacal stranger who wore Pearson's body snatched up a scalpel and flew across the room at Flynn.

Flynn caught the doctor by his wrists, and as fragile as they felt, the man had an unexpected and terrifying strength. *The strength of a madman,* Flynn thought dimly, wrestling for possession of the scalpel.

He pulled the scalpel away and hurled it outside the room.

"What the devil do you think you're doing?" Mr. Devereux cried, reaching the doorway.

Flynn threw Dr. Pearson back. He bounced off the bed and fell to his knees, an old man again, broken and bowed. Flynn went to Joan, turning her face to see if she was breathing. To his relief he could see the faint rise and fall of her bony chest, feel her exhalations against his hand.

"Go get Amy and Casey Lee," he told Mr. Devereux, throwing the quilt on the chest at the foot of the bed over Joan. "At least, try to wake them. I'm guessing they're all drugged."

"Drugged?"

"He wouldn't want them interrupting."

Devereux stared at him as though it were Flynn speaking in Egyptian. His mouth moved as he stared back at Joan, at the monstrous array of shining jars and gleaming tools in shocked disbelief.

"Interrupting?" he parroted.

"What do you think he's doing in here? Surgery?" Flynn snapped. "This is the Little Egypt Slayer."

"Y-you're mad."

"No, *he's* mad. Stark, staring mad. It was right there in front of us all the time. Who has a better excuse for traveling the countryside with bloody clothes and bloody instruments? Look, we can talk it out later. Go get Amy or Casey Lee. Or phone the damned sheriff." Flynn lightly slapped Joan's face, calling her name.

Still looking dazed, moving like a sleepwalker, Devereux turned to leave the room.

Dr. Pearson uttered a blood-curdling shriek, launched himself from the floor and grasped another of his razor-sharp instruments from the white cloth on the foot of the bed. He darted across the room, plunging it into the throat of the horror-stricken Mr. Devereux.

Mr. Devereux began to make ghastly choking noises, clawing feebly at the silver blade wedged in his gullet. He slumped to his knees as Flynn grabbed Dr. Pearson and slammed him against the wall. Hard. Pearson's head hit the wall with a crack. He went limp and collapsed on the floor.

Flynn dropped on his knees beside Mr. Devereux. Already the old man's eyes were glazing as he struggled for his final wet gasps. Seeing Flynn, a spark of alertness came into his face. His bloody lips moved, he tried to raise his hand.

Flynn took his hand. "Can you hear me? I promise you I'll take care of him. I love him."

He couldn't tell if the old man heard him or not. Perhaps it was the last thing he wanted to hear. It was certainly the last thing he heard.

For a few stunned seconds Flynn knelt, his mind reeling. Behind him he could hear Dr. Pearson's stentorian breaths. He turned and was struck motionless by the unearthly aspect of the moon, so beautiful, so ancient, so indifferent to all that happened beneath her golden eye.

Unbidden, the words of a poem he'd learned back in his school days returned to haunt him.

Ere for eternity thy wings were spread

Alone I listen'd to thy dark farewell.

In two steps he was back at Dr. Pearson's side. He slammed his head into the wooden floor once more for good measure, and ran shouting to wake the household.

This Rough Magic

SAN FRANCISCO, 1935

To the dread rattling thunder
Have I given fire, and rifted Jove's stout oak
With his own bolt: the strong-bas'd promontory
Have I made shake; and by the spurs pluck'd up
The pine and cedar: graves, at my command,
Have wak'd their sleepers; op'd, and let them forth
By my so potent art. But this rough magic
I here abjure...
~ *The Tempest*, William Shakespeare

Chapter One

It was always a dame, wasn't it? In the dime novels, it was always a dame.

A smart and sassy society dame smelling of gardenias, with a fox stole thrown over her bony shoulders, and a mouth that would make a French maid blink. In real life, the dames Rafferty met were of a different breed. They wore Vogue pattern #7313 and lines of worry in their tired faces. They came to him in the hope that he could locate a missing son or daughter—or straying husband.

There had been one society dame. Rafferty had helped her get back some letters, and her marriage to a Texas oil tycoon had gone right ahead as scheduled. Every now and then she threw some business his way. He could only think that Mrs. Charles Constable was somehow to blame for the very handsome and very nervous young man currently perched on the uncomfortable chair in front of Rafferty's desk.

The chair squeaked as Brett Sheridan, of the Nob Hill Sheridans, gave another of those infinitesimal shifts like a bird on a cracking tree limb. Sheridan's eyes—wide and green as the water in San Francisco Bay—met Rafferty's and flicked away.

Yes, a very handsome young man. From that raven's wing of soft dark hair that kept falling in his wide, long-lashed eyes to the obstinate jut of his chiseled chin.

Not so young, but not so old either. Twenty-six? Twenty-seven maybe? Sheltered, most certainly. The Brett Sheridans of the world were always sheltered. Right up to the moment the world decided to puncture their bicycle tires. Still, a nice ride while it lasted.

Rafferty said, "And you think your sister took this, what'd you call it, folio?"

Sheridan had a nice voice too. Low and a little husky, not too affected, though he'd obviously spent time at a fancy New England boarding school. "Not Kitty. The thug she's running around with."

"Harry Sader."

"Right. Do you know him?"

Rafferty's mouth quirked. He reined himself in ruthlessly. "Despite how it looks, I'm not on nodding acquaintance with every bum in town."

"No. Quite." Sheridan's color rose. Rafferty tried to recall what the story was on him. There was some story. That much he did remember. "I just thought that in your line of work you might have crossed paths before."

"I've heard of him. He runs with Kip Mullens's gang." He could have told Sheridan a story or two about those boys that would have curled his hair, but scaring the client was rarely good business. "Explain to me again what this folio is?"

"It's a book or a pamphlet. In this case, it's a book of Shakespeare's play *The Tempest*." Sheridan bit his lip rather boyishly. "I suppose, technically, it's a quarto, but I admit I don't fully understand the difference. The only thing I know for certain is it's the earliest printed version of the play. It was printed in the sixteenth century, nearly a decade before the First Folio."

Rafferty opened his mouth and then closed it. It probably didn't matter, right?

"And this folio that is or isn't the First Folio is worth a bundle?"

"It's not the First Folio. That was printed in 1623. It contains thirty-six of Shakespeare's plays, nineteen of which previously appeared in separate, individual editions. All the separate editions are quartos except for one octavo. But Mr. Lennox refers to it as a folio. *The Tempest*, that is."

Rafferty could feel his eyes starting to spin. He resisted the temptation to hang on to his desk. "This *thing* is worth a bundle?"

"It's priceless."

"Sure, but I bet the insurance company tagged it with a dollar amount."

"Mr. Lennox is very wealthy. The insurance money means nothing to him. He wants the folio back."

"The quarto."

"Correct. He wants it back at any cost."

"Ah. He'd pay a king's ransom?"

Sheridan nodded unhappily.

"And the last time anyone saw the-folio-that's-really-a-quarto was the night of your engagement party?"

"Last night. Correct. Mr. Lennox hosted a garden party for us—Juliet and me—at his home in Pacific Heights."

"And you immediately jumped to the conclusion that your sister's beau was responsible?"

"There isn't anyone else possible."

Rafferty dropped his pencil and pushed back in his chair. "That so? All swell society folk with arm-long pedigrees, were they?"

There was that wash of color again. Not exactly what you expected from hale and healthy young Harvard bucks. Not unless they were given to unwholesome activities like painting watercolors or writing feverish poetry. Or worse. Rafferty was pretty sure *worse* was not the rumor he'd heard. He'd likely have remembered that.

"No. That is… Yes."

"Which is it? No or yes?"

"It wasn't my immediate thought, no," Sheridan said stiffly. "But Kitty was acting so…so oddly. And the more I thought about it, the more I realized what must have happened. Sader took the folio, and Kitty knows about it."

"You mean she was his accomplice?"

Sheridan's mouth thinned down to a line. His jaw lived up to the promise of that obstinate chin. "Maybe."

"And you want me to find this folio and return it to its proper owner, your fiancée's father?"

"Yes. That's part of it. Mr. Lennox has given the culprit three days to return the folio. After that, he's going to the police."

"Why the stall? Why didn't he ring for the cops last night?"

"Because…because it's obvious to everyone that the crime was what you'd call an inside job."

"Well, that's one thing I might call it."

"Perpetrated by one of the Lennoxes' guests. Lennox is trying to save…someone from social ruin."

"Not to mention prison."

Sheridan paled. "Yes."

"Okay. Three days to find this book or whatever it is and return it to Old Man Lennox. What's the rest of it?"

"I want you to convince Sader to keep his mouth shut about Kitty's involvement—if any—and to get him to agree to stay away from her."

"That's a tall order. Doesn't Kitty have a say in all this?"

Sheridan's throat moved as he swallowed. "No."

"And how am I supposed to convince Sir Lancelot to give up the Lady of the Loot?"

Sheridan's chin lifted. He said with unconscious arrogance, "I understood from Pat that you're reasonably inventive."

"Pat?"

"Pat Constable. She's the one who referred me to you. You to me. Anyway, I should think that the threat of jail would be sufficient to steer Sader away from Kitty."

Rafferty's brows rose. "You want me to blackmail him?"

"I don't want to know anything about it. I just want Kitty out of his cl—free of him."

Rafferty managed not to laugh. The Brett Sheridans of the world did not like to be laughed at, even when they were talking what they would probably refer to as poppycock. Rafferty would have referred to it as something else, but not in polite company, and this company was about as polite as it got—requests for blackmail and intimidation notwithstanding.

"All right," he said.

Sheridan's eyes widened. "You'll do it?"

"Wasn't that the idea?"

"Yes. I just wasn't sure—didn't think it would be this simple."

"Yeah, well, it sounds straightforward enough. Right up my alley." Rafferty tried to look suitably disreputable. He didn't have to try hard these days.

"There's a time element to all this—"

"Three days. I didn't miss it. And it'll cost you more." Rafferty named a figure that should have made the sensitive Mr. Sheridan blanch. He didn't bat an eye as he reached inside his Scotch wool topcoat and withdrew a leather wallet. He briskly counted out the crisp notes.

"You always carry this much cash?" Rafferty inquired, taking the bills, folding them, and tucking them into the breast pocket of his suit.

"Pat told me you weren't cheap."

Rafferty snorted. "I've been called many things, but never cheap."

Sheridan's lashes flicked up, and he gave Rafferty a long, direct look. So direct a look, in fact, that Rafferty wasn't quite sure he was reading it correctly.

"What will your first move be?"

Rafferty blinked. "Huh?"

"How will you proceed with the case?"

"Are you sure you want to know? It'll probably be necessary to, er, bend the rules a little..."

Sheridan drew back as though from a flame. "No. You're right. It's better if I don't know. But you'll…keep me posted on your progress? There's so little time."

Rafferty rose from behind his desk, and Sheridan rose too, automatically. "The minute I find anything out, you'll be the first to know."

"Right. Of course," Sheridan said doubtfully. "Thank you."

"No, no," Rafferty replied urbanely. He was starting to enjoy himself. "Thank *you*."

"*Gee*." Linda's tone was wistful. "He even smells beautiful."

"That's Lenthéric aftershave, sugar." Rafferty turned from the grimy window as Brett Sheridan's tan V-8 convertible sedan sped away down California Street. "He fills the suit out all right, but if he's got the brains of a Pekingese, I'll eat my hat."

Linda laughed. She was a blonde bit of a girl, barely five feet in her socks. Not that Rafferty had seen her in her socks—or anything but those prim little numbers she wore on the Saturdays, Mondays, and Wednesdays she manned his front office. He'd met her—rescued her, if you took her word for it—the morning she'd escaped with hours-old Baby William from the Drake Home for Unwed Mothers in Sausalito.

"Do we have a case?"

Rafferty reached into his pocket and showed her the wad of bank notes.

Linda gasped. "Who do you have to kill?"

"This is honest dough for honest labor. I may have to rough Harry Sader up a little."

Linda's big brown eyes went saucerlike. "Harry Sader?"

"He's managed to get his claws into Little Lord Fauntleroy's big sister. I'm going to encourage him to let go—among other things."

"What other things?"

"Our client thinks Harry stole a book."

"I didn't know Harry could read."

"I guess it's a very valuable book, and it would keep Harry in gin and greyhounds for the foreseeable future."

"Harry Sader is trouble."

Rafferty flashed her a grin. "Trouble is my business." He reached for his hat.

* * * * *

Central Station was a quaint little cottage tucked in between Chinatown and North Beach, a cozy home away from home for the bulls, and a place of refuge for the rummies, grifters, and quiffs who regularly graced its halls and cells. As usual they were doing a brisk business when Rafferty stepped inside, letting the door swing shut on the clinging, clammy, June fog.

"You know your way," growled the sergeant at the desk, barely looking up.

Rafferty did know his way, and in a few minutes he was sharing a smoke and a lousy cup of coffee with his oldest friend.

"We never heard anything about it," McNulty said, tamping the tobacco in his pipe. He was a slim, dark man. Dapper for a copper. Dapper for anyone who wasn't a cardsharp or Nob Hill scion. Once upon a time, he and Rafferty had pounded a beat together, but Rafferty had made the mistake of belting the son-in-law of the assistant chief right in the kisser. Fastest way to make detective, he always assured anyone who asked.

He told McNulty now, "That's because Old Man Lennox is keeping the lid on to give the owl a chance to put the book back."

"Never figured Old Man Lennox for a member of the Optimist's Club."

Rafferty shrugged. "What can you tell me about the Sheridans?"

McNulty sucked on his pipe for a few seconds. "For starters, they're broke. Linus Sheridan lost just about everything in the crash."

Rafferty paused midlighting his cigarette. "Is that so?" He shook the match out.

"Yep. There was money on the wife's side, but she flew the coop when the kids were still in school. Ran off with a count or something and died on the Continent."

"I think I maybe saw the movie."

McNulty chuckled. "One of our fine old San Francisco families. They've been limping along for the last few years waiting for a bail out. The eldest girl, Katherine, was engaged to Robbie Covington, but that fell through when he broke his neck falling off his polo pony. Her standards must have dropped a few flights if she's running with Harry Sader. The youngest girl, Sophie, is supposed to be some kind of musical prodigy."

"An expensive hobby."

McNulty nodded. "There's an expensive second wife too. Sheridan's former secretary. So it looks like it's up to young Brett to save the family fortune. He was engaged to Frances Westhook, but that fell through. Then it was Mavis Kearny-Ross. That fell through too. But Juliet Lennox stuck, and it looks like she'll go on sticking right up to the altar."

"What's the story on young Sheridan?"

McNulty shook his head. "No story that I know of. Spends most of his time in the society pages squiring beautiful women around."

Rafferty grunted. "Ambitious."

"There was some kind of crack-up during college. Over study or over athletics or maybe both, I don't know. He was training to be a lawyer, but nothing ever came of it. Nothing ever comes of anything with that one, but if he does manage to marry Juliet Lennox, she'll make a man of him. That dame could make a man out of King Kong."

Rafferty grinned lazily. "I don't know the lady."

"That's because you don't read the society pages."

"I can't say that I do. Not many of my clients reside in Pacific Heights."

"No, I guess not. That may change if you find this book or pamphlet or whatever it is."

"I don't know that I want it to change."

McNulty shot him a keen look. "No. Well, maybe not. So you took the case?"

"I guess it won't hurt to poke around a little. See what there is to see. Sheridan may be broke, but he handed over twice my usual fee without batting an eyelash."

"He must have borrowed it."

"Lennox is one of these self-made men, as I recall. Oil, wasn't it?"

"Cattle. Meatpacking, to be accurate. He's Powell Packing Company nowadays."

Rafferty whistled. "What happened to Powell?"

"Lennox ran him out. He's not a man to cross, I can tell you that. If Sheridan's sister did have something to do with lifting that book, it could be the biggest mistake of her life."

"Next to getting involved with Harry Sader."

McNulty drew on his pipe. "Next to that."

The phone jangled on McNulty's desk.

Rafferty pushed up out of his chair. "Okay. Thanks for your help, pal. I guess I'll mosey on out to the old homestead. Put my ear to the ground."

"See you, Neil." McNulty reached for the phone. "Homicide Squad." He held the handset down and called to Rafferty, "Watch out for bushwhackers."

CHAPTER TWO

"*O*h darling, you *didn't*." Juliet's expression was both amused and vexed. "A private detective?"

"If you had a better idea—" Brett drained his martini glass and set it on the table a little harder than necessary.

They were lunching at the Golden Pheasant, one of Juliet's favorite watering holes. As usual, the place was packed. Brett would have preferred someplace quiet where they could have actually talked without being overheard. Juliet wanted the baked stuffed squab chicken under glass.

"No, of course not. But a-a private eye is going to make us look ridiculous. And it's so unnecessary."

"Unnecessary? In three days your father is going to turn the matter over to the police."

"But so what?" She smiled at him, though her blue eyes were puzzled. He was seeing that puzzled look more and more these days. He needed to make more of an effort. They were so close now. The wedding was less than a month away.

"We don't need that kind of scandal right before the—our—wedding. That's all."

She studied him and then smiled, resting her hand over his clenched one. "You're fearfully nervous about this, aren't you, Sherry? Are you not sleeping again?"

"Of course I'm—I'm sleeping perfectly well. You must realize how very bad this kind of thing looks, Julie. Until it's cleared up, suspicion lies on every one of us."

"Not on *us*, silly." She was laughing at him openly now. And with good reason. His behavior must seem peculiar at the least. "Anyway, I think Father's got it all wrong. It's obvious that it had to be one of the servants who took the folio." Brett stared at her with such disbelief that she made a little face. "It's no good looking at me like that. I don't have your pedigree, darling. I'm just a poor little daughter of the nouveau riche. I think mysteries are terribly exciting, if you want the truth. I adore Mr. Hammett's stories. It isn't as though the scandal has to do with *us*."

He could have put his head in his hands and howled.

The waiter came with another tray of martinis. Brett ordered the squab with rice valencia for Juliet and the eastern choice top sirloin for himself.

"Very good, sir." The waiter took the menus.

Brett picked up his drink and swallowed half of it in a gulp. Dear God it was noisy. The babble of voices seemed to ricochet off the amber wood of the tables and chairs and ceiling. He was getting a headache.

Juliet sipped her martini. "What's the name of this shamus that you've hired?"

"Rafferty. Neil Patrick Rafferty."

"Oh. Very Irish. I suppose he's going to stick his nose in everywhere and ask all our friends a lot of annoying and embarrassing questions?"

"That shouldn't bother you, since you *adore* Mr. Hammett's stories so much."

It was sharper than he'd intended. Her face looked hurt for an instant. He really had to get control of himself. She was right. His nerves were shot to pieces, and he wasn't sleeping. Hadn't slept well for longer than he could remember. Once they were married it would be all right. Everything would be all right then.

He said reassuringly, "Mr. Rafferty came highly recommended. From Pat Constable, in fact."

"Pat Constable? What on earth would she have needed a private eye for?"

"I've no idea," he lied. "I just recalled that she once mentioned using one and that he was efficient and discreet."

Juliet took another sip of her martini and made a little face. She didn't really like martinis, but that was what everyone in their crowd drank. Brett stared up at the stained glass window panels of yellow and blue pheasants. Pretty birds. Not very smart. Good eating.

"I can't wait to see Daddy's face." Juliet relaxed, whether due to the alcohol or his words. "Oh well, then. If Pat Constable says he's okay, I'm sure he's wonderful." She took another sip and giggled. "What's he like, your shamus?"

Your shamus.

Brett had a sudden, shocking mental image of himself in Neil Patrick Rafferty's brawny arms, Neil Patrick Rafferty's hard mouth pressing his own. He felt the blood rush to his head. His heart began to pound with something close to panic. He reached for his glass and finished his drink.

He put the glass down and said indifferently, "He looks like a prize fighter. He's got a scar on one cheek, and his nose has been broken a couple of times, I should think. And he has the palest, coldest, bluest eyes I've ever seen."

"But you liked him?"

"I…didn't think about it one way or the other. He looks like he'll get the job done. In fact, I feel sorry for anyone who gets in his way."

She smiled, at least partly humoring him now. "When will I get to meet him?"

Brett shook his head. "I don't know. He wasn't forthcoming about his methods."

"That's all right. I love surprises." She was teasing. One thing he was not was surprising.

Their lunches arrived then, and she began to talk about hand-blocked wallpapers, Sanvale fabrics for drapery sets, and sterling silver coffee sets.

His mind wandered. Through the windows, he watched people hurrying along Geary Street. Watched the automobiles flashing by. The fog had lifted, and it was turning into a bright, sunny day. Still cold for June. Juliet worried a lot about the weather, theirs being a June wedding.

"Sherry, darling, I don't think you're listening," Juliet said.

He quoted back, "'The Nukraft feature of the Sealy Airlite mattress is made of patented hair and latex cushioning that prevents bunching and promotes circulation of air.'"

The thought of that mattress made his mouth dry. But it would be all right. For all her frank ways, Juliet was essentially naïve.

Juliet smiled affectionately. "I'm going to make you a wonderful wife, darling. You'll see."

"I know, darling," Brett replied.

* * * * *

Sophie was practicing when Munson opened the front door of Sheridan House to Brett. The notes of William Alwyn's Piano Concerto No.1 went skipping madly down the mosaic-lined entry hall and played hide-and-seek among the ten Corinthian marble columns of the two-story rotunda that formed the centerpiece of the mansion.

"Is Kitty at home?" Brett asked as Munson took his hat, coat, and silk scarf.

"No, sir. Miss Katherine is at an afternoon tea for friends of Mrs. Norbert Walters."

Mrs. Norbert Walters was a stickler for the proprieties, which meant Harry Sader would be persona non grata at any social gathering of hers. Brett was relieved to know that Kitty would be out of Sader's company for the afternoon, at least. He was increasingly afraid she was going to do something really stupid. Something there would be no going back from. But perhaps she'd already done that, if she'd helped Sader steal the *Tempest* folio.

Munson said, "Mr. Sheridan wished to see you as soon as you came in, sir."

Brett nodded. Forewarned was forearmed, and if he was lucky, he'd manage to avoid the old man until dinner.

He went slowly, feet nearly dragging with weariness, up the grand staircase with its Tiffany glass panels and Etruscan statuary on the newel posts. The puckish flats and sharps of the concerto nipped at his heels. If he could sleep for a little while—just a short nap—he'd be better able to think what needed to be done.

He was starting to wonder if he hadn't jumped the gun in hiring a PI. Juliet was right. It was probably an extreme measure to take. If he could talk to Kitty, talk to her like they'd used to talk to one another, maybe disaster could be averted without having to involve an outsider.

Halfway up the staircase, he met Justine on her way down. She was dressed to go out. Overdressed, in fact, but that was usual. Having made the mistake of marrying for money where there was none, Justine dealt with the problem by simply ignoring it. Beneath the silver fox coat, she was wearing a black evening gown with a great deal of sparkly bits. There were more sparkly bits in her hair, like crumbled stars.

"There you are, Sherry. Linus was looking for you." She paused, her black eyes looking him up and down. She was tall for a woman. Tall and tawny, with straight, sleek dark hair and large, exotic eyes. Brett always suspected it was her faintly unconventional looks that had won his father over. Having squandered much of the family fortune on Etruscan art and statuary before the crash, it was only to be expected he'd be a pushover if a reasonable facsimile strolled into his life after the dough ran out.

"Was he?"

"He's going over his catalogs again. You know what that means." Her smile was maliciously sympathetic. "Poor boy. You do look half dead.

Little Juliet has you jumping through those hoops of fire, doesn't she?" She continued down the stairs, laughing lightly.

He wasn't sure why he bothered, but he asked anyway. "Where are you going?"

Justine called airily back, "Least said, soonest mended. There's Shakespeare for you."

He'd always thought it was the Bible. He continued down the corridor. There were no longer fleets of servants to maintain the stately halls of Sheridan House, but the Munsons had insisted on acting the part of loyal family retainers, and the place could still pass muster if no one looked too closely. Roses and gladiola fresh from the garden filled tall crystal vases, and some very nice oil paintings in the Romantic tradition adorned the walls.

The thick carpet stifled his footsteps, but even so, as he passed the library Aunt Lenora looked up from where she sat in a pool of lamplight.

"Sherry! Dear boy! Look. Look what I have." She beckoned to him.

Reluctantly, Brett entered the room and approached the desk.

Aunt Lenora pushed the untidy tendrils of white hair from her eyes and turned the stamp book his way. "What do you think of that!"

The stamp read *India Four Annas*. The blue head of a woman floated upside down in a red frame.

"It's new." It was the best he could do, and he hoped he was wrong. He knew a few things about stamp collecting—no one could live in the house and not know a few things about stamp collecting—but though he thought many of them pretty, he found it impossible to keep them all straight. The prettiest ones always seemed to be the most ferociously expensive.

"Of course it's new. It's an inverted India Four Annas, silly. I'd hardly keep *that* a secret."

That was debatable. This was a house of many secrets.

Brett ventured cautiously, "Inverted. So…rare?"

She was poring over the book again, her spectacles sliding to the tip of her small, pointed nose as she peered at the pages. "Hmm? Oh very rare, dearest. Very rare."

"How did you get the money for it?" His voice sounded unfamiliar even to himself.

Aunt Lenora looked up in surprise. "I asked Mr. Weiss to keep an eye out for me. Of course I never dreamed he'd really find one. They really are *quite* unique."

"But how did you pay for it?"

Her eyes narrowed. "What an odd question. I'm not sure what you mean, dearest?"

"I mean, this is a very expensive stamp."

"I have my little rainy day fund, you know that. I've been saving up."

Rainy day fund? Surely it would have to be a torrential downpour fund to pay for a stamp that rare? The monthly allowance from her trust fund was no more than pin money. And she spent every cent of it each month.

Brett was thinking this over, trying to decide how best to approach the delicate subject of her finances, when she said brightly, "What a lovely party that was last night."

He stared at her dubiously. "Was it?" All he remembered of the party was the end when his father-in-law-to-be had discovered the missing folio and threatened them all with arrest.

She beamed back at him. "Dear little Juliet does think the world of you."

"Yes. I'm a lucky man."

"Oh yes." She looked back at the stamp book, murmuring vaguely, "Even if the Lennoxes aren't *quite* our sort of people."

* * * * *

By dinnertime the nagging ache behind Brett's eyes had turned into an enthusiastic whaling away that rivaled Gene Krupa on his drum kit, complete with cymbals. The pulse of pain that filled his ears was unfortunately not quite enough to drown out the conversation of his nearest and dearest.

"After all, Livy wrote his famous account of the origins of Rome toward the end of the first century BC. He repeatedly mentions Fanum and stresses its importance." Linus Sheridan reached for his glass, washing down the wilted dandelion greens and browned parsnips with which Mrs. Munson had stretched their evening meal. A dab hand with vegetables, their cook, and a woman who understood economics better than most in the house.

"Kitty should have been home by now," fretted Aunt Lenora, helping herself to another pork chop from the plate Munson held for her. "She never used to be so inconsiderate."

No one commented on Justine's absence from the table. By now, it was her rare appearances that were noteworthy.

"And I *know* I would be accepted if we could simply afford the tuition," Sophie was saying at the same instant. That, Brett realized, was directed at him.

"We can't. Afford it, I mean."

"But we can once you marry Juliet." Sophie's green eyes met his. She was not the beauty Katherine was. She was not even pretty, really. But did that matter with a talent like hers? Maybe it did to girls, but Sophie never gave any indication that she cared about anything but her music. Which was a great pity, because if she'd marry some nice, rich, indulgent young fellow, her worries would be over.

As it was…she was pinning a great deal of hope on William Lennox's generosity. Granted, Lennox did, clearly, look at this marriage as a way of purchasing his entrée into high society. Which underlined how little he knew about high society.

Brett said mildly, "She doesn't come with a dowry, you know."

"Of course she does. Or you wouldn't be marrying her."

Their father was now illustrating his point—infallibly something to do with Etruscan archeology—with a speared bite of cheese soufflé. The green-speckled yellow wedge wobbled on the tip of his fork. "But he failed to mention where Fanum was situated, and after the fall of Rome, all memory of its exact location was lost to time."

"There's no point studying music in this country," Aunt Lenora commented. "Sophie should go to Paris. You must go to Europe, dear, for the best teachers."

And so it went. So it always went. The thought of setting up his own household on the other side of the city was one of the greatest incentives for a quick and speedy marriage. Of course the family was distressed at the idea that Brett would not be bringing Juliet home to the Castle of Otranto, but Juliet had stuck to her guns on that point. It made things blessedly simple for Brett, who was quite a skilled diplomat when he had to be. He'd had a lot of practice.

Munson appeared at his elbow with the plate of chops, but Brett passed. Someone had to pass if Aunt Lenora was to have her two helpings. All Brett had to do was remember that missing folio, and his appetite faded away to nothing.

He sat through dinner listening with half an ear, wondering where the hell Kitty was, wondering whether Rafferty had begun his investigation, wondering whether hiring a private eye was an even bigger mistake than trying to resolve this thing on his own.

It was a relief to escape at last to his rooms. Juliet was attending the opera, and he was off the hook for the evening. Thank God for that, because opera might have proved to be the sticking point.

Brett dug out *Bertram Cope's Year* from its hiding place at the bottom of his desk and read for a time. The novel had been recommended by Pat Constable. He found it amusing and clever and rather disquieting. One of the most disquieting things was that Pat should recommend the book to him, but that was silly. Every now and then he actually managed to forget that anyone knew the truth about him, but that was him merely kidding himself. No one who knew was likely to forget.

Amy Munson brought him his usual nightcap. He drank it and turned more pages of the book. Somewhere in the back of his mind he heard the familiar sounds of the household settling down to sleep.

He continued to read.

The wedding took place during the latter half of April, as demanded by the enterprising wooer. Then there would be a rapid ten-day wedding-journey, followed by a prompt, business-like occupancy of the new apartment on the first of May exactly.

He began to get that queasy feeling again as though he'd eaten an enormous greasy dinner.

The house was quite silent now.

At last he heard the familiar stealthy squeak of the floorboard outside his door. Brett rose, threw on his silk brocade dressing gown, and yanked open the door to his room.

Kitty, a few feet past his door, halted, then walked back to him. "Sherry." She pushed her hair back and summoned a weary smile. "Can't sleep?"

"I was waiting up for you."

She held on to her smile, but her eyes grew guarded. "Oh?"

She wore a pale green tea gown that matched her eyes. Not new, but she carried it off as though it was straight from Bergdorf Goodman's spring collection. Kitty had all the looks in their family. She was held to be one of the great beauties of the day by the people who kept track of such things. She was two years older than Brett, but those who didn't know them often thought they were twins.

Brett pushed wide the door to his room. "There's still a fire in my room."

"Can it wait? I'm dead, darling."

"We've got to talk, Kitty."

If it was an effort to keep smiling, she hid it. "About what?"

He forced himself to go on with it. "About last night. About Harry Sader."

Her face hardened. "Mind your own business, Sherry. I don't give you a hard time over the *burgomeister's* daughter, do I?"

"That's a cheap crack."

"Cheap is what it isn't. She's paying top dollar for you, little brother."

He answered without thinking. "And what's Harry Sader paying for you?"

She slapped him. She'd always had one hell of a golf swing, and the crack of palm meeting cheek seemed to echo down the silent hallway.

Neither of them moved a muscle.

"Feel better now?" he asked at last.

She was shaking, her eyes glittering with something like tears, though she never cried. Hadn't cried even when Robbie died. She looked and sounded like a stranger as she said, "If you know what's good for you, you'll stay out of my affairs."

"He's a crook, Kitty. How can you be involved with someone like that?"

Her rage spilled over, though she kept her voice low. "And we're supposed to be better than that? Don't give me that holier-than-thou routine. Have you taken a good look at the family you're marrying into? Why, William Lennox probably stole that damned folio himself for the insurance money."

"You know he didn't."

"I don't know anything of the kind, and neither do you." The tension drained from her, leaving her pale and oddly muted. "Brett, let's not quarrel. At least...if we're going to quarrel, let's do it tomorrow when we've both had some sleep."

"Three days, Kitty. That's all we've got. In fact, it's down to two now. If Lennox goes to the police—"

"Harry had nothing to do with it. I was with him the whole time."

"You're lying."

"I'm *not* lying."

His eyes narrowed. "What are you afraid of?"

Kitty glared at him and then looked away. She looked as exhausted and drained as he felt. "Brett, I don't tell you how to live. Mind your own business."

"This *is* my business." A hint of pleading crept into his voice. "You're my sister, for God's sake."

She shook her head, turning away. "Do what you want. I can't stop you from meddling. But don't say I didn't warn you."

Chapter Three

 $\mathcal{T}$ hough the rest of San Francisco lay beneath a white layer of fog, the sun was shining in Pacific Heights. The swells that lived in that neighborhood probably paid extra for the privilege. They could afford to.

Rafferty parked his gray Buick sedan on Washington Street in front of the block-long limestone French baroque château owned by William Lennox. He went through a wooden door in a tall white brick wall, crossed the long paved courtyard, and walked right up to the imposing front entrance beneath an ornate porte-cochère and tall square columns. He wouldn't have been surprised if a division of household guards had rushed to intercept, but no one did. No one seemed to notice. He rang the bell.

After a calculated interval, a butler who looked like a close relative of Bela Lugosi came to the door and inquired, in a high-hat British accent, what Rafferty required. Rafferty required an audience with that man of affairs, William Lennox.

Dracula regretted that Mr. Lennox was not available.

"What about Miss Juliet Lennox?" inquired Rafferty. "Is she home?"

"I do not believe so, sir," Dracula drawled in a manner clearly designed to discourage tradesmen and others whose names were not found in the pages of the *Social Register.*

But you didn't get anywhere in the private investigator business if you took no for an answer. "Ask her if she'll see me. Tell her Mr. Brett Sheridan asked me to pay her a call."

Dracula could not be said to unbend, exactly, but he allowed Rafferty to step into an entryway that resembled nothing so much as a giant marble crypt. Left to his own devices, Rafferty resisted the temptation to take his hat off out of respect for the deceased. He strolled over to a gigantic window overlooking a formal baroque garden cascading down the hillside. Beyond was the green-blue glitter of San Francisco Bay.

He didn't know much about flowers, but he imagined it took a chain gang worth of gardeners to keep that jungle of roses and hydrangea and vines and ornamental grasses from swallowing the house whole.

The majordomo returned at last and indicated Rafferty should fall in. Rafferty followed him down a long corridor running east to west. Opening off the corridor were a lot of opulently and overfurnished rooms. The furniture looked like the kind of thing that would have had even old George V ringing for a cushion.

They trekked outside, hiking down a series of granite terraces. Bees hummed in drunken ecstasy, and a few birds warbled insults to the other tenants. It was about as tough a neighborhood as you could find in Pacific Heights.

Through the curtain of trees and shrubbery, Rafferty heard the flat rhythmic smack of a tennis ball and a girl swearing.

As they drew near, he saw his client and his client's fiancée in sparkling tennis whites playing on a clay court surrounded by a tall fence. The match appeared to be a fierce one. Dracula forbore to interrupt, and for a few minutes they watched the young lovers at play.

Even with her hair in her eyes and her face shining, Juliet Lennox was a very pretty girl. She was blonde, medium height, and curvy in all the right places. She had the wholesome good looks of a girl raised on raw foods and fresh milk. She also had the look of a girl who liked to win.

Brett Sheridan looked like an advertisement out of *Esquire* magazine.

They seemed evenly matched, though somehow Sheridan managed to hit the ball each and every time so that, while Juliet had to work for it, she was able to return all his shots. He was either an indifferent player or he was a *very* good player. After a couple of minutes, Rafferty figured Sheridan was a very good player.

And maybe a pretty good judge of character—or at least of his fiancée.

The play ended. Sheridan won game, set, and match, but all by only the smallest possible margin. Juliet was flushed and pretty in defeat—her obvious chagrin tempered by her admiration for Sheridan.

Sheridan, as usual, gave about as much away as one of those J.C. Leyendecker illustrations. He really was a disconcertingly beautiful young man.

Arms loosely linked about each other's waists, they came to the fence, where Rafferty waited. Dracula, Rafferty only noticed then, had silently retreated from the field of battle.

"Hello," Juliet greeted him. "Are you Sherry's shamus?"

"That's right," Rafferty said. "I'm the shamus."

She threw a playful look at her betrothed. "Sherry didn't mention how handsome you were!"

Rafferty's eyes met Sheridan's, and Rafferty thought that the younger man's gaze seemed to pick up the green glints of the surrounding woodland. For an instant there was something intriguingly faunish in that wide, tilted regard. Then Sheridan was opening the fence gate, holding it for Juliet, saying with faultless courtesy, "Miss Lennox, may I present Mr. Rafferty?"

Juliet offered her hand, and Rafferty shook it. She had a firm grip. "Sherry said you're going to find my father's folio."

"That's right."

She tilted her head. "You sound sure of yourself."

"Mr. Sheridan assures me there's a short list of suspects," Rafferty said blandly.

She laughed. "Are you going to interrogate *me*?"

"Juliet is a great admirer of the work of Dashiell Hammett." Sheridan's tone was dry.

"Oh yeah?" Rafferty eyed her with new interest. "*The Maltese Falcon*, huh?"

"That's right. And *The Thin Man*." She smiled affectionately at Sheridan, perhaps picturing them as Nick and Nora Charles quaffing cocktails and trading quips as they solved murders in the smart set. If so, she had a more powerful imagination than Rafferty and Mr. Hammett combined.

"Juliet and I were together all evening," Sheridan said.

No sense of fun, apparently. Juliet pouted at him briefly. "Perhaps I had an accomplice."

Sheridan sighed.

Rafferty's mouth twitched. He repressed it determinedly. "When was the theft of the folio discovered?"

"Just after midnight." That was Sheridan again. Clearly hoping to get this over with. Rafferty didn't entirely blame him. Now that he knew more about Brett Sheridan, he could understand why he didn't want people sniffing around his affairs too closely.

Juliet said, "It could have been taken at any point during the evening. It was a garden party, but you know how that goes."

Rafferty could say with certainty he'd never been to a garden party. He didn't. "How many people knew about this folio?"

"Everyone." Juliet sounded certain of that.

"*Everyone?* That's a lot of people."

"Mr. Lennox is very proud of his collection," Sheridan said.

Juliet frowned at him. "Why don't you call him *Daddy*?"

The beautiful blank face went blanker still. "He's not my daddy."

"He's going to be."

"I don't call my own daddy Daddy." Sheridan's gaze slanted Rafferty's way. "Mr. Lennox has been collecting Shakespearean rarities for the past two decades."

"But the *Tempest* was the jewel in his crown. He's very fond of telling people how he outbid some English lord for it. Daddy's very proud of beating out one of those damned foreigners."

Rafferty happened to be looking right at Sheridan, so he saw the tiny ironic smile that crossed his face—before being instantly smoothed away.

"Daddy tells everyone that story," Juliet was saying. "And he shows everyone the folio."

"So everyone at this party knew about the folio. Did they know where the folio was kept?"

"Sure they did! Come on," Juliet said, linking her arm through Rafferty's and reaching to Sheridan. "You'll want to see the scene of the crime."

They marched arm in arm back up the steps to the house. Though Juliet was clinging to his arm, it was Brett Sheridan that Rafferty was conscious of. Pretty strange, considering Juliet was walking between them, but over her light flowery scent, he could pick up a hint of Lenthéric aftershave and clean masculine sweat. He could hear Sheridan's light easy breaths over the quick, uneven breathing of the girl.

"Are you a fan of William Shakespeare, Mr. Rafferty?"

Rafferty quoted, "What light through yonder window breaks? It is the dawn and Juliet."

"Close enough!" Juliet was amused. "You should get on well with Daddy."

Over the top of her head, Rafferty met Sheridan's eyes.

Juliet never stopped chattering, so it was no surprise she was breathless by the time they reached the top of the hill. Most of the gab had to do with her wedding to Sheridan, which was only a couple of weeks away.

The bridegroom maintained a stoic, manly silence.

They went inside the house, and Juliet led the way up a curving grand staircase. There was a lot of glittering glass and marble and gold leaf and giant oil paintings of European nobility and landscapes that bore no resemblance to any place in America—the castles being the first clue.

"Nice little place you've got here."

Juliet chuckled. "I'll tell Daddy you said so."

Daddy seemed to figure into a lot of her conversation. Rafferty wondered how Sheridan felt about that. But then if anyone knew about cockeyed families, it would be Brett Sheridan.

"This way," Juliet said. "It was a garden party, so no one was supposed to be wandering inside that night, but..." She shrugged slim shoulders.

The library was huge. Rafferty had been in smaller public libraries. The walls were of the palest green. The forest green draperies were held back by gold tasseled ropes. The furniture matched the woodwork and was upholstered in green velvet. The thousands of leather-bound books displayed harmoniously coordinated spines of red and gold and green. It was impressive, but it didn't look like a room where people did a lot of reading.

"This is the display case where the *Tempest* was kept." Juliet led the way to what looked like a carved case about the size of a pool table. "Daddy says it's not a very good play."

"I like it," Sheridan said with an unexpected streak of stubbornness.

"You better not admit that! Mr. Rafferty will think you're a suspect." She smiled at Rafferty. "You can see where they broke into the case."

"And they only took the folio?"

"Only the folio." That was Sheridan. "It was the most valuable thing in the case."

The display case was lined with green velvet and littered with a number of objects that Rafferty was sure were also plenty valuable—drawings, maps, prints, books.

"These things all belonged to Shakespeare?"

Juliet laughed. "Oh no. There isn't anything left like that. Daddy would own it if there was. No journals or letters or old manuscripts. But there's an English translation of an Italian story called *Rhomeo and Julietta* which was published in 1567 and there are a couple of volumes of the *Chronicles of England, Scotlande, and Irelande* published in 1587. Everybody thinks that those books shaped *Macbeth* and *King Lear*. See?" She pointed out the items.

"So Shakespeare was lifting his ideas from other writers?"

"He sure was, the old rascal."

"I guess you learn something every day. Can you get me a guest list for the garden party?"

"Of course." She gave the display case a fond pat.

Rafferty was watching Sheridan, who, despite his occasional comments, was busy examining the break in the glass lid of the case. Did he know what he was looking at? Because he was not looking at a break. He was looking at a cut. And not the cut of an experienced cracksman either. That was interesting. An amateur, but an amateur who knew where to get hold of a glass cutter—and had apparently brought it to a garden party.

Perhaps feeling Rafferty's gaze, Sheridan lifted his lashes. He gave Rafferty one of those oddly unguarded glances. Rafferty felt a funny warmth pool in his belly.

"Gosh, I better change out of these things," Juliet exclaimed. "I'll leave you two to it. Don't solve the crime without me."

She was gone, and the room seemed loud with silence.

"Dashiell Hammett, huh?" Rafferty said.

Sheridan smiled faintly, straightening. "The twins are worse."

"Twins?"

"Sebastian and Viola. Juliet's half brother and sister." Sheridan's half smile faded. "I don't understand why you're wasting time on this kind of thing when you know who the thief is."

"Because I don't know who the thief is. I know who you think the thief is, but that's not the same thing. Secondly, if you're right, you want to hide your sister's involvement, isn't that so? Which means I need to throw suspicion around a little. Ask a lot of people a lot of questions, not just talk to your sister and solve the crime."

"Oh. Yes. You're right of course. I'm just worried…"

That went without saying. Was there a more worried fellow in all of society? Granted, not without reason.

"Why is Lennox so sure this had to be an inside job?"

Sheridan's impatience showed again. "Because it was. Sader gained entrance to this house through my sister. When Julie says Lennox tells everyone about his collection, she means he tells people of our—"

He stopped.

Not in time, but he did stop. Rafferty grinned, enjoying his discomfiture. Probably enjoying it too much. *Julie and Sherry.* Wasn't that sweet? And in keeping with the level of naïveté that imagined the underbelly of the city knew only what the upper crust was up to when the upper crust deigned to tell them.

Sheridan said suddenly, "Rafferty, I think I made a mistake."

Rafferty opened his mouth, but they were no longer alone.

"Brett, my boy." William Lennox filled the doorway. Almost literally. He was a big man. Rafferty recognized him from his photographs in the *Chronicle* and the *Examiner*, but the papers didn't do the man justice. It wasn't just his size, though add a bronze coating and he could have doubled for many a park memorial.

"Sir." Sheridan didn't quite click his heels, but only because he was wearing white canvas sneakers.

"Juliet tells me you've hired a private investigator." Lennox's eyes were bright and black as a raven's. They moved from Sheridan to Rafferty and back again.

"Yes. Mr. Lennox, this is Mr. Rafferty." Brett came around the display case to stand beside Rafferty. "I thought it would be the fastest way to wrap this matter up."

"No need to do that." Lennox made no move to shake hands. "The folio will be returned within the allotted time."

"You know that for a fact?" Rafferty asked.

"Yes." Lennox smiled—and Rafferty understood why he generally refrained. "I believe my reputation precedes me."

"Even so," Sheridan said, surprising both Rafferty and Lennox. "It won't hurt to have a little insurance."

Lennox didn't look pleased. "If you've the money to waste, I guess you can do what you like with it."

It was the mannequin immobility of Sheridan's expression that did it, that put Rafferty squarely and unexpectedly on his side. Maybe McNulty was right. Maybe he was too soft-hearted, but he liked a guy with guts, and he began to think Sheridan had one hell of a lot of guts to stick to the course he'd set.

"Cigar?" Lennox had made like a continental plate and shifted into the room. He offered a leather box of cigars. "Brett doesn't indulge." It was clearly a mark against Brett.

Rafferty declined. "Since I'm here, you mind if I ask a couple of questions?"

"Fire away," Lennox said, cutting the torpedo-shaped cigar.

"Mr. Sheridan says you're sure the, er, folio was taken by a guest and not a servant. How can you be so sure?"

"Everyone—and I do mean everyone—in my employ, whether in my home or one of my factories, is subjected to thorough investigation. No one gets close to me or my family that I don't know everything there is to know about them."

Lennox was looking straight at Rafferty, but Rafferty could feel the instant tension in Sheridan's motionless figure.

"Yeah? Sometimes things get overlooked."

Lennox made a dismissing noise. "I doubt that. I hire the Pinkerton Agency to conduct my inquiries. I guess you've heard of them?"

"The name rings a bell." Rafferty glanced back at the display case. "You're probably right. I can't see why a servant would wait till the night of a big party to pull a job like this. It would be smarter to fake an ordinary burglary one night when everyone was out of the house."

"Exactly." Lennox looked almost approving.

"Unless they were hoping to throw suspicion on one of the guests," Sheridan commented.

It wasn't a bad thought, so Rafferty wasn't sure why he drawled, "I guess Miss Lennox isn't the only one who reads Mr. Hammett." He regretted the crack when Lennox laughed. He had a harsh laugh that seemed to take what little humor there was out of the situation.

"I like you, young man. What did you say your name was again?"

"Neil Patrick Rafferty."

"Ah. Irish." Lennox's bushy eyebrows drew together in a forbidding line.

Rafferty smothered the quick flare of irritation. Surely if there was one thing he'd learned at St. Finian's Home for Foundlings it was to let that kind of thing slide like water off a duck's back. "American. Born and raised here."

Lennox considered it and nodded. "Sure. Why not? What else did you want to know?"

"This manuscript—"

"Folio."

"Quarto, isn't it?"

Lennox was taken aback. "Uh, yes. You're quite right. Are you familiar with the works of William Shakespeare?"

"I know how *Romeo and Juliet* ends."

He wasn't being smart, but Lennox seemed to think he was getting at something. He laughed that loud laugh that was like getting smacked between the shoulder blades. "Very good. You hear that, Brett?"

"I heard."

Rafferty pushed on. "Nobody could get rid of that folio through the usual channels. Who would pay—who *could* pay—for an item like that?"

"Another collector," Lennox answered immediately. "Folger's dead now, of course. Cochran and Huntington too. I suppose Emily Folger might take an interest. Lord Horn would probably give his eyeteeth for another shot at it. He's over in England."

"What about in this country? In this state."

Lennox frowned, thinking it over. "Howard Dobson. He's down Los Angeles way."

"And in San Francisco?"

"No one that I know of."

"Okay. Is it possible anyone would have taken the book for another reason?"

"Like what?"

"Spite? Revenge? It's no secret you think pretty highly of this collection. A man like you makes enemies."

"That's true." Lennox looked thoughtful. "I've stepped on a few toes now and then." Stepped on a few necks, more like it, but Rafferty stayed noncommittal as Lennox added, "Nobody like that would have been at my girl's party."

He and young Sheridan had more in common than they knew.

"Sure. I guess that's about everything. Just one more question. You discovered the folio was missing around midnight. You told the remaining guests that you would wait three days before calling in the cops. Why was that?"

Lennox looked at Sheridan. "Maybe I wasn't born into San Francisco's old money, but I know how things are done. My daughter is marrying into the Sheridan family. I don't want any scandal, if I can avoid it. I don't want anything to spoil my little girl's happiness."

Sheridan looked steadily back at his prospective pop-in-law.

"Makes sense to me," Rafferty said easily. "What about the guests that left before the theft was discovered?"

"Eh?"

"A number of people had left the party by then, right? What makes you think the crook wasn't one of them?"

Lennox looked like he still didn't quite understand the question.

"And if it was one of those guests who skipped out early, they're not going to know about the three days' grace period, right?"

"Nor will they care," Sheridan interjected. "Whoever stole that folio doesn't give a damn about the three days' grace period. The thief had to expect his crime to be immediately reported."

Lennox puffed his cigar and looked thoughtfully from one of them to the other.

"Let's not be too hasty," Rafferty said. "Maybe there's a way we can use these three days to our advantage."

"Two days," Lennox said. "That's all that's left now. I'm a man of my word."

"It's possible we can get the thief to cooperate."

Lennox shrugged, unconvinced.

"I'll see you out," Sheridan said.

Rafferty nodded. He nodded good-bye to Lennox as well, but Lennox had already forgotten him. He stood over the damaged display case, smoking his cigar and gazing down at his collection with an expression that did not bode well for the thief.

"Where are you going now?" Sheridan asked as they started down the grand staircase. Below them, a Chinese houseboy carried a silver tray laden with covered dishes toward the tall glass doors opening onto the terrace.

"As soon as I get that guest list from your fiancée, I'll start talking to people."

"You *need* to start with Kitty."

Rafferty threw him an easy glance. "I don't give you advice on how to do your job. I mean, if you had one."

Sheridan's face flushed with irritation. "I've paid you a great deal of money, Rafferty. You're wasting time we don't have to waste. Sader is not going to give that folio back out of the goodness of his heart."

As a matter of fact, Rafferty figured Sheridan was right about that—assuming he was right that Sader had the folio at all. Rare manuscripts were really not much in Harry Sader's line. "What was your sister thinking bringing a guy like Sader here that night?"

"I don't know." There seemed genuine anguish in that. "She seems to have lost all sense of…of propriety." He checked, and so, accordingly, did Rafferty.

A boy and girl in riding habits appeared at the bottom of the staircase, seemingly having wandered in from a Philip Barry play.

"Somebody lose a fox?" Rafferty asked of no one in particular. He could practically see his reflection in their shining black boots.

Sheridan made a sound like a smothered laugh.

"Hello!" The girl called up. She was about fifteen or so, blonde curls and angelic features—nearly as angelic as those of the boy with her. They were fraternal twins, but they could almost pass for identical.

"Hello," Rafferty returned.

"Is your name Rafferty?"

"That's me."

"Are you *really* a detective?"

"That's right."

"This is Fred and Ginger." Sheridan continued down the staircase. "But I'm going to marry their sister anyway."

Rafferty laughed. "Viola and Sebastian, I presume?"

"Hey, he *is* a detective," Sebastian drawled. He laughed and ducked away as the girl swiped at him with her riding crop.

"We're supposed to give you this." Viola trotted up a couple of stairs and handed over a crackling sheet of paper to Rafferty. "It's from Julie. It's the guest list." To Sheridan, she said, "Julie's having brunch on the south terrace."

He acknowledged it.

"Have you figured out who stole Father's folio?" Her eyes were big and blue but not guileless. In fact, she'd be quite a handful before much longer. Rafferty almost felt sorry for Old Man Lennox. This one would more than make up for daddy's girl Juliet.

"You know about that too, huh?"

"Everyone knows about it," Sebastian said.

"We were there," Viola said. "We're witnesses."

"Suspects," objected her brother.

Viola laughed.

"Don't mind them," Sheridan said. "They'll be weaned soon and go to good homes."

Viola stuck her tongue out at him.

Rafferty glanced down at the guest list. There were roughly twenty-five couples. It was going to be a very long day. He'd have to recruit Linda for this one.

"Nice meeting you," he said to the girl, and turned to Sheridan. "I'll talk to you later." He intended it as reassurance, since Sheridan was clearly beginning to doubt the wisdom of his investment.

"I'll walk out with you."

"Wait," Viola said quickly, nimbly retreating as the men advanced down the stairs. "Do you need an assistant? We could be your Watsons, Mr. Rafferty."

"You're late for your riding lessons now," Sheridan said.

Viola ignored him. "Well?" She gazed challengingly up at Rafferty.

"Sorry, kid. I work alone."

"We could be your apprentices."

"Another time."

"Told you. Come on, V. We're late." Sebastian turned away.

Viola pouted briefly. "Have it your way, flatfoot. See if we share any clues with you!" She turned and ran back down the stairs, following her brother down the corridor.

"Delightful," Rafferty remarked. "She handles that whip like she used to work for Pharaoh."

"You should have seen her before charm school."

Rafferty and Sheridan continued out to the marble mausoleum of the front entrance, where the butler returned his hat to Rafferty.

"Look, I've been thinking," Sheridan said as they went out into the spring-scented sunshine. They walked toward the white brick wall and the street beyond. "If you'll give me a chance to drive home and change my clothes, I could go with you when you talk to these people." He nodded at the list Rafferty held.

"Nah. That wasn't just a gag for the kids' benefit. I work alone."

"I wasn't suggesting we go into partnership." Sheridan brushed aside the vines and opened the blue door in the wall for Rafferty. "I simply mean that in this case—and with these people—it might make it easier if I went along and explained your...role."

"My role?"

"In this business."

Rafferty preserved a straight face. "You think they won't talk to me?"

"I wouldn't."

"I can be a very persuasive fellow."

"Can you?" Sheridan sounded weary, weary for such a bright and beautiful morning.

"Sure I can. Buck up. We'll find this folio/quarto/thingamajig."

"When will you talk to Kitty?"

Rafferty thought about it. "If you're that worried about it, I'll start off with her. Do you know where she's lunching?"

Sheridan shook his head. "She was evasive this morning. On Sundays she usually brunches with her friends at Blanco's."

Brunches. "Huh. Is that so?"

It wasn't a question, but Sheridan answered anyway. "Yes. I don't know if she…"

Rafferty leaned against the side of his car and waited, watching Sheridan's handsome, mobile face go through successive, fleeting changes: indecision, worry, self-consciousness, resolution.

"You don't know if she…"

"I started to tell you earlier. I think I…made a mistake. Last night."

"I've made a few in my time. One of them cost me the price of a Florence Reichman hat." He didn't bother to explain the hat had been for his elderly landlady.

"Not that kind of mistake." Sheridan bit his lip. "I accused Kitty of being involved in the theft of the folio."

"You're right. That was a mistake."

Sheridan's gaze met Rafferty's—and fell. "I know that. But I thought that if I could convince her to talk to me, to tell me what happened, I might be able to resolve this without—"

"My help?"

"Without scandal."

"That's what you're paying me for, remember?"

"Yes." Sheridan continued to stare down the street. A yellow-and-red cable car was chugging slowly up the hillside.

"Will she tell Sader?"

"I don't know. She might. She probably will."

"You're probably right."

Sheridan's expression was wry as he met Rafferty's eyes again. "I know it was stupid. You don't have to say anything. In fact, I'd regard it as a favor if you didn't."

Rafferty laughed, amused in spite of himself. "All right. It could be worse. Sader knows he's bound to be the first person people suspect. Even if he was innocent. Your suspicions won't come as any surprise to him."

"You think I'm a snob."

"Sure." Rafferty shrugged. "It's only natural."

Sheridan offered that odd little twist of a smile. "I might surprise you, Mr. Rafferty."

Rafferty watched him disappear through the door in the brick wall.

"You might at that," he muttered.

CHAPTER FOUR

$\mathcal{T}$he idea came to Brett over cocktails at Herbert's Grill.

He was having a drink—several drinks, if someone wanted to get specific—with Clive Day and Max Keene. Clive was always good company, and Max was one of Brett's oldest friends. One of the few people who knew the truth about the thing with Emmett and did not think any the worse of Brett.

The club was for men only, which was perfect since Brett had all he wanted of petticoats for the time being, and it wasn't particularly busy on a late Sunday evening. The barman was reading the paper, and at a table in the corner, a group of men was getting even drunker than Brett and his pals.

Brett sipped his whisky highball and absently listened to Clive and Max talk polo and politics.

"I heard the Ashton brothers will be playing for Britain in next year's Westchester Cup," Max said.

"Where did you hear that?" Clive asked. "That's not what I heard. I heard it'll be Guinness, Roark, Hesketh Hughes, and some other chap."

Brett responded automatically, but all the while his mind was on Rafferty and what he might have discovered that day. He *had* to have discovered something. There was so little time left.

"Your round, Sherry." Clive interrupted his thoughts.

Brett shook off his preoccupation and ordered the next round of whisky highballs. The talk returned to polo.

He had been home twice during the afternoon, but there had been no word from Rafferty since they'd parted company that morning, and Brett was increasingly anxious. Only one day left. After that, Lennox would bring in the police, and it would surely be only a matter of time before Sader came under suspicion—and with him, Kitty.

"Why so glum, chum?" Max asked, jogging his arm.

"I can answer that," Clive said. "His heart is broken. He's sold that little Argentinean gray to Anderson."

"Not the little mare!"

"Yes, why not?" Brett said. "Juliet's not keen on polo. I'll probably end up selling the whole string."

At the rate things were going, he'd probably have to sell off his stable long before the marriage.

"I'll believe it when I see it," Max said. "Even Flash Gordon plays polo!"

They went on in that vein. Brett answered during the pauses and laughed at all the right places. He could keep up that kind of thing for hours, and sometimes it felt like he did.

"How's Katherine?" Max asked casually. "We don't see enough of her these days."

"Not since poor old Robbie," agreed Clive. "Can't say that I blame her. Awful shock for a girl."

"Yes," Brett agreed. "She's all right."

Clive said, "Thought for a while last weekend you were going to follow in Robbie's hoofsteps. You were riding like a madman, Sherry." He delivered a friendly punch to Brett's shoulder.

Brett laughed it off. Not that he didn't occasionally think it would simplify things if he could arrange to conveniently break his neck one sunny afternoon…

Like hounds after a hare, his thoughts circled back to his most pressing worry.

There had been little time to find a buyer for the folio. It was too unusual an item. Paintings, Ming vases, those things were much easier to move. And it was unlikely someone like Sader would already have a buyer lined up, even if the theft had been planned. And it had been. Even Brett could tell that much. That lopsided hole in the glass top of the display case hadn't come from someone punching through the glass. Someone had carried a glass cutter of some kind right into the party. Unbelievable.

Clive was saying, "D'you you hear the Mongols used to play polo with two teams of riders and a dead goat?"

"Sounds like a very slow game," Max replied. "Should have at least one dead goat for each team."

Clive knocked Brett's elbow again. "Come on, old man. You have to admit that was funny."

Brett obligingly elbowed him back and laughed.

He was reminded that, according to Sophie, Kitty and Sader had plans for the evening. Drinks and dancing at the Elbo Room. He really should let Rafferty know—assuming he hadn't found out for himself. Given what he was paying the fellow, he shouldn't have to do his job for him. He winced inwardly. He was starting to sound like his father. It wouldn't be long before he'd be damning the younger generation.

Of course, Sophie might have got that wrong. She was a much better musician than listener. But Kitty and Sader *were* out most evenings.

Which meant…

Which meant Sader would not be home.

Which meant if someone were to visit his rooms, they might be able to find the folio, wherever he'd hidden it.

Brett pushed back his chair. Clive and Max blinked up at him.

"Something we said?" Max inquired.

"No. Got to see a man about a horse." They were laughing as Brett added, "I'll see you idiots later."

They raised their glasses in a toast.

* * * * *

It was no trouble to grab a streetcar from Powell Street. Over the treetops and eaves of the old houses, he could see the pagoda-style roofs of Chinatown. Brett jumped off the trolley on the corner of Powell and Pine and walked along the moonlit sidewalk till he came to an old Victorian with a sign out front reading ROOMS TO LET.

He went up the front steps and knocked on the door. A small, spry woman with hennaed hair came to answer it. "Yes? What did you want?"

"Are you—"

"I'm Mrs. Dumbrille. I'm the owner of this establishment."

"How nice to meet you. Is Harry in?"

Mrs. Dumbrille eyed Brett with deep suspicion. "Who wants to know?"

"Er...Bertram Cope."

Not unreasonably, this did nothing to reassure her. "Never heard of you."

"Harry has."

"Mr. Sader ain't in."

"That's odd. He told me to meet him here. Is it... I suppose it's all right if I wait?"

"I don't know about that. Mr. Sader's particular about such things."

Brett reached slowly for his billfold. "Harry and I are practically family."

She watched him with bright, unblinking eyes, but made no move to take the money.

Worse luck.

"What do you want him for? You're no sharper and you're no cop." The last was said tentatively, as though, evidence to the contrary, she couldn't quite think of any other reason someone would be paying a call on Harry Sader.

"A cop?" Brett laughed. "Lord no. As a matter of fact, I owe Harry money." He offered her a rueful face. "Gambling debt. I thought I'd better pay up while I have the cash."

"You don't say!"

"Not very often."

Mrs. Dumbrille chortled at that one, opened the screen door with its gingerbread trim, and reached for his money. He was startled to see she had a hook for a left hand.

"I guess Harry wouldn't be any too happy if I let you escape. You can wait for him upstairs." She nodded for Brett to come inside.

He followed her down a short hall, the focal point of which was an enormous chandelier that threw eerie green and red specks of light across the dark paneling.

"You looking for a place?" Mrs. Dumbrille inquired over her shoulder. "I got a nice corner room available."

"Not at the moment, no."

They went up a narrow staircase and down a dimly lit hall papered in gray with the faded red flowers and leaves of another era. Behind a door came the sound of a radio and Bing Crosby singing "It's Easy to Remember." Mrs. Dumbrille walked all the way to the end of the hall. A dirty window looked over rooftops and open windows and dusty treetops.

She unlocked a scratched door. "If you *are* ever looking for a place to stay, I run a quiet, respectable house. Reasonable rates. Ask Harry."

"Sure," Brett replied. "You never know."

"That you don't, dearie!" She went away down the hall, brisk as the breeze across the bay. When she turned the corner, Brett opened the door and stepped inside the room. It smelled of cigarettes and cheap aftershave. The moon hung outside the window like a ripe peach dangling from one of the low-hanging branches.

Brett felt for a light switch. A tired illumination washed the room and its meager furnishings: a battered highboy dresser, an iron bed—

unmade—an enormous scratched and peeling wardrobe. The wardrobe looked like it might have been part of the house's original furnishings and was simply too big and too awkward to move through all its renovations.

Right next to a bottle of scented hair oil on the highboy was a framed photograph of Kitty. It was a picture taken before Robbie's death. She looked happy and healthy, and Brett felt faintly queasy seeing her image in these squalid surroundings, as though she were really in the room with him.

He felt queasier when he opened Sader's top drawer and found a pistol lying there with his Jockeys.

On the other hand, maybe it was a good sign that the pistol was in his drawer and not on his person, but what in God's name was Kitty *thinking* getting involved with someone like Harry Sader after such a fine chap like Robbie?

Brett rifled quickly through the undergarments, searching for the folio. It would be impossible to mistake that fragile browned pamphlet with the copper-engraved image of Shakespeare for anything like a pulp magazine, but there were no pulp magazines either. There was nothing remotely resembling a book or reading material.

He went quickly through the other drawers, sliding them quietly in and out.

Nothing of interest in any of them.

He moved on to the bed, checking hurriedly beneath the mattress.

Nothing.

That left the wardrobe. He opened the heavy, carved doors. Sader's shoes were lined in a gleaming row beneath his suits and trousers. His clothes were stylish but cheap. To give him credit, everything was clean and well cared for. Sader took great pride in his appearance. Too much pride, in Brett's opinion.

There was no accounting for what appealed to women. Brett's taste ran to something more…honest. Something rugged and real. Hard muscles beneath smooth skin that smelled like soap not scent. Something—

But he was getting distracted. Badly distracted.

Brett pushed aside garments to check the back of the wardrobe. There was a metal bank in the shape of a spaniel. It clinked dully, stuffed with loose change. There was a red, flat, metal box for a boy's Erector Set. Brett opened the box, and it was full of letters. Letters bound in silk ribbons. The handwriting was feminine, but it wasn't Kitty's.

Either way, he didn't see how he could read another man's personal letters. But what if Sader was already married? What if he was black-mailing some woman?

He was debating with himself over this ethical quandary when he heard footsteps coming down the hall.

He jumped over the bed in a bound and switched out the light, waiting tensely.

The footsteps grew louder. Someone was coming.

He looked around the moonlit room. He had three options. The window—and a fifteen-feet drop—the bed, or the wardrobe.

He went for the wardrobe, diving back over the bed and cramming into the crowded cedar-scented space, crouching behind the row of clothing. He left the door slightly ajar, exactly as he had found it. Or at least as he hoped he had found it. It was hard to remember now.

His heart thundered in his ears so that it took several long seconds before he registered that the scratching at the door was not the sound of a key turning the lock.

It was someone picking the lock.

That was so astonishing that he forgot everything else, watching intently through the cracked door.

The door to the room swung open, and two burly shadows entered.

Now what the hell did he do?

Brett ducked back, thinking. He could hear them moving around the room. They did not speak. They were very quiet. Quieter than he had been, which ought to be a lesson to him on how these things were done.

Could they be the police?

No. If they had been police, Mrs. Dumbrille would have unlocked the door for them. And police would turn the lights on to make their job easier.

No, whoever these bruisers were, they were not police—which meant that Brett did not want to confront them. Not that he wanted to confront the police either, but he had the honest citizen's trust in law and order—and the men who enforced it.

A small circle of light swung past the opening of the wardrobe. He leaned cautiously forward, once more putting his eye to the narrow opening between hinge and frame. Yes, there were two of them with flashlights, two bulky figures searching through the drawers he had gone through himself just a few minutes earlier.

Were they searching for the folio?

It seemed hard to believe someone like Sader would have anything else of value. If he did, Brett hadn't discovered it.

Unless it was these letters that he was now sitting on.

CHAPTER FIVE

$\mathcal{T}$he Sheridans were all nuts.

Any one of them was capable of having stolen the *Tempest* folio from William Lennox. From batty Aunt Lenora with her stamp collecting mania and her forgetfulness regarding debts incurred playing bridge, to little sister Sophie, who would probably sell her soul for a music scholarship to Juilliard. Hell, even Munson the butler had horse-racing gambling debts. Granted, the butler hadn't been at the Lennox garden party. But then maybe neither had the thief.

Rafferty had learned a great deal about the Sheridans over the past couple of days. He knew about Katherine's breakdown and Brett's breakdown and little Sophie's habit of taking things that didn't belong to her from stores that enjoyed the patronage of one of San Francisco's oldest families too much to report her to the police. He knew about Linus Sheridan's mania for all things Etruscan. (Although a number of people thought it was Egyptian.) He knew about the wife who didn't stay home many nights—and the wife who had run off with an English lord. And who the hell could blame either of them?

He knew just about everything there was to know about the Sheridans. He probably knew more than Brett Sheridan knew, which was why he wasn't totally convinced Katherine Sheridan had anything to do with that missing folio. They had all been at the garden party that night. Even the current Mrs. Sheridan.

Rafferty had his eye on the current Mrs. Sheridan. The word around town was she had married Sheridan for his money, but in Rafferty's opinion that did Justine an injustice. She was far too smart a lady not to have known exactly what Sheridan's financial situation was. No, she'd married him for his social standing—which remained considerable. Even in times of financial hardship, a family like the Sheridans could get a lot of mileage from their name alone. Most merchants wouldn't cut them off for some time—maybe years, if the ailing family bank account continued to be plumped up by the occasional infusion of the cash that came from selling off a few valuable family heirlooms.

Nor, thanks to the excellent replicas with which those heirlooms were replaced, were the other Sheridans likely even aware of what Brett and Katherine were up to. Except Justine. Justine was too sharp not to notice the efforts of the two eldest Sheridan children to save the family fortune.

Or what remained of it—which by now was probably not much.

Maybe that was why Brett had determined to sell the one thing left of value in Off Ye Olde Rocker Manor—himself.

Katherine, his longtime partner in crime, had seemingly lost all interest in the proceedings after the death of her fiancé on the polo field. That didn't mean she didn't have the know-how or contacts to dispose of the folio—just that she didn't give much indication of caring enough one way or the other to bother. And running around town with Harry Sader didn't change that. Not in Rafferty's opinion.

Opinions. Who was it who said, "don't judge a man by his opinions but what his opinions have made of him"? It was a screwy thing, no doubt, but Rafferty's opinion of Brett Sheridan had changed considerably from the minute he'd discovered Brett was secretly selling off his birthright so that the nuts he shared a name with might continue to live in blissful, self-centered comfort.

*W*hen Rafferty finally got back to the office late on Sunday afternoon, Linda was restlessly waiting to report. He tried to avoid asking her to work Sundays, but there hadn't been any choice this time. He couldn't follow four people on his own, and this job was too delicate to hire out.

Linda took out a small pad and began to read. "Eight o'clock a.m., Lenora and Sophie Sheridan attended church services at Grace Cathedral."

"Who drove them?"

Linda looked up briefly. "Sophie drove. They returned home immediately following. At ten thirty, Sophie left again for piano lessons at one Henry Cowell's. She drove herself and arrived at eleven o'clock. She spent most of the afternoon practicing her scales or whatever they do in that house." Linda looked disapproving as she flipped the pad page.

"Something up there?"

She shook her head, but said, "I don't know, but I wouldn't send my kid to take lessons from a guy like that."

"He's supposed to be a genius."

"Maybe he is; maybe he isn't. I've heard some stories."

Rafferty smiled faintly but let it go. He was very fond of Linda, but aside from the one slip that had resulted in Baby William, she was about as straitlaced an Effie as a gumshoe could hope to find.

"Sophie left Cowell's at two o'clock and went shopping at I. Magnin's on Geary Street. She didn't buy anything."

"Did she glaum anything?"

"Not that I could tell. She was trying on fancy dresses. The kind of thing you'd wear to a piano recital—if you were the one playing the piano. When she finished torturing salesgirls, she headed home. She didn't leave again, unless it was after I signed off."

Rafferty thought it over. It seemed to confirm what he'd heard previously about the youngest Sheridan. "So no men friends?"

"No friends at all, as far as I could tell. At least, I haven't seen any sign for two days."

"I think she's our least likely candidate. Not that she wouldn't be above a little grand larceny—we know she's light-fingered—but I don't think she'd have any idea of where to find a fence. Hell, I doubt if she was even aware the folio existed—although I bet she could tell you where each and every piano is in the Lennox house, and whether it's in tune or not."

Linda chuckled. "I think you're right about that. You want me to keep on her tomorrow?"

Rafferty shook his head. "Nah. Tomorrow you'll focus your attention on Katherine."

"Oh ho! How do I rate the prime suspect?"

Rafferty grimaced. "She made me."

Linda burst out laughing. "She made you? She *is* good."

"Or I'm getting sloppy in my old age."

"You don't blend in with a crowd, that's your problem."

"It depends on the crowd."

"True." She was smiling at Rafferty affectionately. Once upon a time, she'd entertained a girlish dream or two about him, but she'd eventually accepted he wasn't that kind of boy, and they'd settled down to a real friendship. "What about Aunt Lenora? She cheats at cards and she's a welsher."

"She's another one I think we can write off. I just don't see Aunt Lenora carrying a glass cutter in her reticule. Or being able to wield it with any efficiency, do you?"

Linda chewed her lip. "No."

"Plus, she doesn't drive. She'd need to enlist someone to take her to her fence."

"It looks like Mr. Sheridan was right. Although his old man is kind of a suspicious character, from what I hear."

"Too suspicious. He's an out-and-out nut. The psychology is all wrong. If Lennox was missing an Etruscan gimcrack, Linus Sheridan would be our first suspect. When it comes to his collection, anything goes. All's fair in love and war. But ordinary thieving? No. He thinks he's above anything like that."

Linda snorted. "Okay. I'll take Katherine tomorrow. Does that mean you're taking Justine?"

Rafferty nodded.

"What happened last night?"

"Nothing out of the ordinary for her. She went to dinner with a gentleman friend, a Mr. Daniel Shaw of 31 Presidio Terrace. They dined at Palais Royal on O'Farrell Street, and then the lady returned to the gentleman's apartment, where she spent most of the evening before returning home to her kith and kin."

Linda described Justine with an impolite but probably accurate word.

"Justine is smart, capable, strong, and likes nice things. I don't have any reason yet to believe she's resorted to stealing in order to have them, but of anyone in that family, she seems to me the candidate with the most staying power."

Linda nodded and glanced at the clock over the battered filing cabinets.

"You better run along home, sugar. Baby William is going to start objecting to these hours."

"Sure. You're going to miss your date with the lady of the manor if you don't get moving. Where's she taking you tonight?"

"Hopefully not to Mr. Shaw's again. Not that I don't enjoy catching up on my studies of local architecture."

She was laughing as she grabbed her hat.

Rafferty used the washroom at the end of the hall to shave. He changed into the clean spare shirt he kept in the little cloak closet.

Mr. Scheiner, the actuary next door, was unlocking his office door as Rafferty headed for the elevator. It was very rare for Scheiner to work a Sunday, let alone a Sunday night. They nodded politely in passing, but

Rafferty said nothing. In six years, they'd never exchanged more than nods and a few polite words.

"Big evening, Mr. Rafferty?" the elevator operator asked as the dented grill slammed shut.

"Bible study," Rafferty remarked, and the kid laughed more loudly than the joke deserved. That was what he got for playing to the peanut gallery.

He walked around the corner to the garage where he kept his car, climbed in, and started the engine. He turned down California Street as the white globes of the street lamps were winking, blinking, and nodding on.

* * * * *

Shanghai Low read the long red-and-white neon sign. *Chow Mein.* And on the red awning: *Luncheon, Dinner, Cocktails.* Even on a Sunday night, the Shanghai Low was hopping. Justine Sheridan slithered out of her taxi and disappeared inside the gray brick building.

Chinatown's restaurants catered largely to Occidental tastes. The nightclubs were plush and roomy with large dance floors and orchestras to play exotic versions of popular tunes. A lot of the clubs featured floor shows offering everything from acrobats to scantily clad chorus lines. According to Shanghai Low's menu, the secret to their considerable popularity was the "successful combination of the age-old cuisine of China with the sanitary methods of the present progressive age."

Rafferty amused himself by ordering a Shanghai Red Angel Special and the chop suey while he watched Justine talking earnestly to a tall, thin man who looked a lot like Sigmund Freud. Not that Rafferty had met Freud, but he liked to read, and sometimes he read science fiction.

The dancing stopped, and the floor show started. Young Oriental girls in silver lotus blossoms and not a hell of a lot else pranced out swinging miniature Chinese lanterns. They did a cute little routine that involved a lot of high kicks. They were followed by a traditional lion dance. Two men inside a giant gold-and-brown lion costume weaved and ducked while the orchestra beat an assortment of drums and cymbals and gongs.

Rafferty ate his chop suey, drank his fancy drink, and kept one eye on his quarry. Justine and Sigmund had their heads bent together, their drinks untouched on the table in front of them, their faces serious.

There was no way to overhear, no way to get any closer to them. The room had been packed even before the dancing girls started their number.

He had no idea who Sigmund was, though he looked like a bookish type. Rafferty was gambling that Harry Sader was eventually going to join the party. Once upon a time, before Justine Shaver was Mrs. Sheridan of the Snob Hill Sheridans, she'd been pals with Harry Sader. Rafferty had a theory about that. Sader lived on Pine Street, which was just around the corner, if you wanted to be generous with the geography.

He found himself wondering what Brett Sheridan was doing on a Sunday night. Presumably something with the well-endowed—in all areas—Miss Lennox. How did that work? He couldn't imagine. Oh, not the physical logistics of it. He was a man of the world and prided himself that he was capable of giving pleasure to female lovers as well as male. That wouldn't be the difficult part. But the rest of it…the part that mattered. How did that work for someone as sensitive and intelligent as Brett?

The waitress came up to take his plate. Rafferty ordered another Shanghai Red Angel Special.

The lion dancers were picking up the pace. The lion was leaping and whirling, twitching its long tail and opening and closing its jaws with its playful pop-up teeth in a silent roar.

Rafferty shifted so that he could just make out the bald top of Sigmund's head. Sigmund had turned and was now watching the floor show too.

A bad feeling started in the pit of Rafferty's stomach. He got up, apologizing to the patrons whose view he temporarily blocked as he angled for a better vantage point. The crowd fluctuated, and he was able to see through the wall of bodies to Justine's booth once more.

Except it was no longer Justine's booth. Two graceful lotus blossom dancers were now sitting with Sigmund.

There was no sign of Justine.

CHAPTER SIX

"Anything?" came a hoarse whisper.

"Nah. You?"

"Nah."

Brett peered out again. He could just discern their features in the reflected light. What he saw was not encouraging. As a matter of fact, they looked rather like a pair of Etruscan demons.

He sank silently back into the cheap suits and did some more reconnoitering. He had already noticed that the two intruders didn't seem concerned with hiding the evidence of their search. As they pawed through Sader's drawers, they dumped the contents on the floor.

"This bird ain't the sentimental type."

"He ain't in a sentimental business."

They moved to the bed. They yanked the bedding and then the mattress off the iron frame. One of the shadows bent down, and Brett heard the sound of cloth ripping.

By now he was quite sober. Sober enough to realize he had been anything but when he had determined to search Sader's room.

He ran through possible alternatives, but none of them was very attractive. He could try to grab the gun from the dresser, but even if he could get to the dresser before they grabbed him, he wasn't sure the gun was loaded. He was familiar with hunting rifles, but gats were an entirely different thing.

He could try to make it to the window, but that left the problem of the fifteen-foot drop, and he preferred not to break his neck tonight if it was at all possible.

He could stay right where he was, but it had already become evident to him that the intruders were going to search every square inch of Sader's quarters. They could hardly miss a giant wardrobe sitting in the middle of the room. Nor could they miss him sitting in the middle of the wardrobe like Miss Muffet on her tuffet.

As it wasn't possible that they would overlook him, he needed to think how to handle their discovery. The only possible advantage he had was surprise.

It wasn't much, but it was all he had.

He decided to play that card while they were engrossed in their stealthy disembowelment of the mattress.

Deciding and doing it were two separate things. Brett ordered himself to act. Yet, the order given, he continued to watch and wait, hoping against hope that some other alternative might arise.

It wasn't until one of the men stepped toward the wardrobe that Brett accepted that time was up. He threw open the cupboard with all his force, knocking the intruder back. An oath escaped the man.

Brett leaped out. He ran for the door.

And he nearly made it. He did certainly catch them off guard, but he was unfamiliar with the room, and his foot caught in the spilled blankets. He careered into the door and scrabbled blindly for the handle.

They had locked it behind them, and by the time he had turned the latch, they were on him. The three of them crashed into the wall, knocking over the small table beside the bed. Brett threw a punch at a looming shadow and had the satisfaction of feeling it connect, the blow shivering up his arm.

The satisfaction was short-lived as the next instant he was doubling over himself from a blow landed beneath his ribs. His breath *oofed.*

He tried to turn his pained momentum into a charge, head-butting his nearer assailant in the guts. The man staggered back, swearing, and pounded Brett's back. It was like having a sledgehammer fall on him, and he barely managed to keep on his feet. He began to swing in earnest.

Brett had boxed in college. He was quite a good boxer, as a matter of fact, but this was no fight like anything he'd known. This was a brawl, brutal and ugly. He was thrown into the chest of drawers, which smashed back into the wall. He went down on all fours, was kicked in the ribs, dragged to his feet again, and hurled into the wall. He managed to land a couple more punches, but against the two of them, it was like a gnat biting an elephant. His arms began to feel weighted, as though he were hitting through water.

A huge hand locked in his hair, and the pain was bright and infuriating. "All right, pally. Now we're going to have a little talk," snarled a voice against his ear.

The door flew open, the lights flared on, and Mrs. Dumbrille shrilled, "What's going on here?"

For a one-handed woman she had one hell of a grip. She hauled off the thug trying to push Brett through the wall and threw him across the bed. When the other came barreling toward her, she tossed him off with such force he nearly went through the window.

She was a ventriloquist too because she did it all while screeching from across the room.

A hand locked on his biceps, and Brett was hauled to his feet. His legs nearly gave way, but he managed to stay upright and focus on his grim-faced rescuer.

"Time to go," Rafferty said.

Brett couldn't remember ever having been quite so surprised—nor happy—to see anyone in his life. He could have hugged Rafferty, but then he'd been feeling that way from the minute he'd first laid eyes on him. Instead he allowed himself to be half guided, half shoved out the door, past Mrs. Dumbrille, who was still demanding to know what was going on.

Brett and Rafferty ran down the stairs, slamming into the wall and banister in their haste. They reached the ground floor and hurtled out through the door into the foggy night, the screen banging forlornly shut behind.

Rafferty said, "This way. I'm parked—" But before they'd reached the pavement, the screen flew open again. The wooden steps pounded beneath the footsteps of the two thugs racing to cut them off.

Rafferty hooked a hand around Brett's arm, and they ran the opposite way, toward Chinatown.

They dived down the first alley they came to, splashing through puddles that were probably not rainwater, backed by tall dark buildings casting strange and fantastic shadows in the moonlight. Rats skittered away. Weird music drifted from shuttered windows, and now and then the smoky scent of exotic flowers seemed to curl out from beneath a bamboo door.

This was not the pretty, charmingly exotic Chinatown Brett knew— the crowded cobbled streets and bazaars full of stalls with flowers and trinkets and mysterious delicacies.

Pain began to make itself felt. Forcibly. He slowed, hand to his side, and then stopped. Rafferty, running slightly ahead, glanced back and stopped too. He walked back.

"What is it?"

Brett's breath began to catch up with his pounding heart.

"Do you know where we are?"

"Sure I do."

"Where are we?"

"Not so far from *Du Baan Gai.* Grant Street to you." Rafferty sounded out of breath too. "What the hell did you think you were doing back there?"

"You're supposed to be a detective. What did it look like to you?" It hurt to talk. Brett put a hand to his mouth. His lip was cut and swollen.

"To me? It looked like another Snob Hill twit digging in where he had no business. But what do I know? Apparently I'm so bad at my job, my clients have to solve my cases for me."

"Oh shut up. I haven't asked for my money back, have I?" Brett took out a handkerchief and dabbed at his lip. "Look. I'd had a few drinks, and I thought—" He winced. He'd lost his hat, and his coat was torn. It was beginning to dawn on him just how lucky he'd been. He might just as easily be standing there with a broken nose and cracked ribs. He wasn't entirely sure he wasn't. "Anyway, it looks like we lost them."

"Yeah, we lost them. Not sure what else we might have lost. If you planned on conducting your own investigation, what did you hire me for?"

Brett lowered the handkerchief and glared at Rafferty. "I might as well conduct my own investigation. Where've you been all day? I told you at the start there was a time element. Tomorrow is day three. If you can't get Sader to give up the folio, we're sunk."

"I know what day it is. I also know better than to—"

"Have you spoken to Kitty? Have you spoken to Sader?"

"No."

"No," Brett said bitterly. He flung away and began to walk, uncaring of the direction.

Rafferty caught up to him in a few feet, catching his arm and bringing him to a halt. "Listen to me; I tried to talk to your sister. I tracked her down to the Palace of Fine Arts—"

"The Palace of Fine Arts?"

"Yeah. But she lost me." It obviously galled him to admit that. "She ducked out the back. She was on to me."

"I don't think she went there to look at the lagoons." Brett's anger drained away. He shivered, now feeling every ache and throb of his battered body. "It's true, then. Kitty *is* involved."

"She's involved in something." Rafferty peered more closely at him. "Come on. You look like you could use a drink."

He turned, and Brett followed him unspeaking as they left the alley and came out on a street with low awnings and sidewalks littered with wooden barrels and rice sacks and baskets full of vegetables, some recognizable and some from another planet. Nightingales hung in bamboo cages. Colored hanging lanterns and banners with Chinese characters rustled in the night breeze.

The few people about paid no particular attention to them.

Rafferty seemed to be searching for something. He glanced back at Brett, gestured, and disappeared inside a dingy hallway.

They climbed the stairs and found a door guarded by an elderly man lolling before it and drawing on a long bamboo pipe.

Rafferty spoke a few words in Chinese to him, the man nodded, and Rafferty opened the door. They brushed into another narrow hallway, this lit by gas jets. At the far end of the hall was yet another door, this one built to last in heavy oak and iron.

"Where the hell are we?" Brett muttered.

Rafferty shook his head.

A small square opening in the door slid back to reveal a pair of dark, wary eyes. A guttural voice made some inquiry. Rafferty responded.

The door swung open.

They were in another short corridor with a third door still barring their way. It wasn't quite as sturdy as the second door, and it had a hole in with a latch string. Rafferty tugged on the latch string, and the door opened.

They entered a large smoky room with a small stage and a long gaming table in the center. On one side of the room was a small band of three musicians; on the other was a perfectly ordinary looking bar. A Chinese torch singer in a clinging red dress warbled "It's Easy to Remember" from the stage. At least, the tune was "It's Easy to Remember." The syllables were as foreign as the songs from the little bird cages on the street below.

Customers lined both sides of the gaming table which was piled with a mound of copper coins with holes in the center.

"What is this place?" Brett asked.

Rafferty gave him a sardonic look. Well, maybe it was a silly question. Brett followed him as Rafferty dived through the crowd. He surfaced at the bar and ordered two cocktails. They appeared almost instantly in gold-rimmed martini glasses.

"Here's mud in your eye," Rafferty said, raising his glass.

Brett sampled a perfectly ordinary orange blossom. Gin and orange juice and ice. Tart and tangy. It stung his lip, but it was worth it. "How did you find me?"

Rafferty's reply was interrupted by a roar from the gaming table. The mound of copper coins was whisked away by a small ivory rake. Rafferty turned back to Brett and said, "I was in the neighborhood."

At Brett's expression, he sighed. "No sense of humor, that's the trouble with the young these days."

"You're not a hell of a lot older than me."

"I'm a lifetime older than you, sonny boy."

Meeting Rafferty's smiling but hard blue gaze, Brett couldn't help but think that was probably true.

"The fact is, I followed your stepmother to Shanghai Low."

"I know it. It's a nightclub on Grant Street."

"That's right. Right around the street from Harry Sader's place."

"Why were you following Justine?"

"Your stepmother introduced your sister to Sader, didn't she?"

"That's right."

"The word around town is she and Sader are still pretty good friends."

Brett shook his head. "Justine dislikes Sader. She's never made any secret of it."

"She may say they're not pals anymore, but everyone I've talked to who knows the pair of them claims they're still thick as thieves. And thieves might be the operating word."

Brett took a swallow. The room was warm, and the alcohol helped numb his aches and pains. So did the way Rafferty kept looking at him with that mix of amused exasperation and something disconcertingly close to liking. "Did Sader show?"

"No. No, but I think your stepmother was waiting for him. Him or someone else who never showed. She left around eight, and I decided to see if I could find Mr. Sader at home and receiving." He added with grim humor, "Instead, I found young Mr. Sheridan at home and receiving on Mr. Sader's behalf."

A tired splutter escaped Brett as he finished the rest of his drink. "Better to give than receive; that's the truth. Do you know who those thugs were at the boarding house?"

"I didn't get a good look, but they reminded me of a pair of bookends that used to work for Kip Mullen."

"Never heard of him."

"I'd be worried if you had." Rafferty signaled for another round.

Brett nodded, but with one day left, it all felt pretty hopeless. "What now?"

"Now I give up being subtle. I find Sader and I make him talk."

Brett raised his head quickly.

"Hey. We're not sunk yet." Rafferty grinned. "It's not that I can't get rough. I just like to take a civilized approach when I can. You can appreciate that."

"I'm sorry. It's not that I don't… You have no idea what it's like…"

He hadn't meant to say even that much. It was a jolt when Rafferty's pale blue eyes looked right into his own. "Maybe I have more of an idea than you think."

Did he mean…? What *did* he mean? He couldn't possibly know, and yet Brett was quite sure as he stared back at that tough, handsome face that somehow Neil Patrick Rafferty did know all about him. All about the unacceptable things he'd done and the unacceptable things he wanted to do—some of them to Rafferty himself.

He swallowed hard.

"Drink your drink," Rafferty advised. "I'll take you home."

Brett heard himself say, "Maybe I should go with you."

Rafferty's mouth quirked. "One of these days, maybe you should. But not tonight. And not to see Harry Sader."

Brett tossed off the rest of his drink, and then he followed Rafferty out a side door and down a couple of hidden stairways until they opened a door and found themselves in an alley. A different alley, undoubtedly, but it still felt like they were going in circles. Across the way, he could see tall dark buildings with ornate lacey balconies.

Rafferty bumped against him. "This way."

Brett stumbled, a tin can bouncing away, and Rafferty reached out to steady him.

Somehow Brett was in Rafferty's arms, and Rafferty was kissing him. The startling reality of it transfixed Brett as though he'd been struck by lightning. Rafferty tasted like orange blossoms and cigarettes. The raw wet heat of that kiss shocked Brett motionless for an instant. He pushed Rafferty away—and then, when Rafferty didn't budge, shoved him again harder.

Rafferty staggered but came right back at him, grabbing Brett's arm, pushing him to the rough brick wall. He leaned in, bringing his mouth down on Brett's fiercely, and the pressure of that hot hungry mouth moving on Brett's blotted out the smells of the alley and the night fog and the strange sounds of nightingales in cages. Blocked out everything but the shared breath and the heated skin and the flutter of eyelids and edge of teeth.

The kiss seemed to go on for uncounted time. Rafferty's mouth was no longer hard and punishing, his lips warm and soft and opening to Brett's searching tongue. Brett wanting more and more—even while a little voice in the back of his mind was telling him to stop. To think what he was doing, what a mistake he was making.

Rafferty's body leaned into his, pushing him back against the wall, and Brett could feel the heat of that taut muscular body through his own clothes.

Their mouths reluctantly drew away, and Brett rested his head on Rafferty's broad shoulder for a brief moment, giving in for just one fleeting second to...this.

Rafferty's hurried breathing was warm against his ear.

Then Brett lifted his head. He pushed Rafferty away—this time without anger, reluctantly even—but when Rafferty's arms closed around him, he didn't struggle nearly as he should have. Couldn't do it, somehow.

Rafferty's hands slipped underneath his clothes, and Brett jumped at the shock of cold hands on his warm skin. Rafferty's touch was gentle. His voice, a quiet, wordless murmur, was gentle. It was the gentleness that undid Brett. It was unknown, unlooked for. He wasn't a novice at anything but the gentleness. Shivering, he let himself go with it, reached for Rafferty once more.

Rafferty's mouth settled on his, Rafferty's warm mouth. Brett felt a desperate yearning diving inside his guts and knew this would not be enough. He needed more. So much more. He surrendered to the kiss, wrapping his arms tightly around Rafferty's lean waist, drawing him closer.

Rafferty's mouth was moving in silent question, and Brett's hands went to his belt. He unbuckled his trousers, he unzipped himself, he pushed his trousers down, starving for touch. He closed his eyes tightly, afraid to watch. Rafferty gave a funny half laugh, said something husky and incoherent; then he sank to his knees in the alley that smelled of the unglamorous Orient, and there, beneath the cold stars and the glowing lanterns, he brought warmth and life to Brett.

Afterward, Rafferty held him until Brett's breathing slowed, evened out, and his shaking legs could hold him.

Rafferty said, "We can't stay here."

Brett opened his eyes. He felt dazed.

"Come on," Rafferty said. "We're taking a chance like this."

Brett nodded. He wanted to ask why Rafferty had done it. He wanted to ask him if he'd consider doing it again sometime. He pulled his trousers up, fastened himself inside with almost steady hands.

Rafferty led the way, hands in his pockets, brisk and sure, hat tilted at a rakish angle. He looked the same, showed no outward signs of what he had done. The incredible thing he'd done. What *they* had done. Maybe it wasn't an unusual occurrence for him. Probably not. There had been more than one reason Pat Constable recommended him.

They walked briskly, and the fog swallowed their footsteps.

Chapter Seven

"You okay?" Rafferty asked as they drew up in front of Sheridan House.

Brett nodded. He hadn't said a word since the alley behind Ah Koon See's gambling house. Not on the long walk back to Rafferty's car and not on the short drive back to the Nob Hill mansion. It went without saying that Brett regretted what had happened.

Rafferty probably ought to regret it too, but he didn't. It had been his pleasure to do that for Brett. His pleasure to give Brett a few sweet minutes with nothing asked in exchange. Why that should be so, he wasn't sure. He wasn't normally so chivalrous. Maybe he just felt sorry for the guy. Brett Sheridan had chosen about the toughest road a man could choose. He was a fool, but he was a brave fool in his way.

"All right if I come in and ask a few questions?"

"I think it's high time," Brett retorted acerbically, reaching for the door handle.

Rafferty sighed and followed the crown prince up the steps to the main entrance, where they apparently had to wait for Jeeves to let them in. Rafferty opened his mouth, got a look at Brett's profile in the porch light, and closed it. Even discounting the alleyway romance, there was a difference between getting chucked off your polo pony and getting worked over by two toughs who knew their business. He could see that by now Brett was stiff and sore and starting to shiver.

And here Rafferty stood with the taste of Brett still a memory on the back of his tongue.

Better not to think of that now.

"You know, you handled yourself okay back there."

Brett looked so astonished and alarmed, Rafferty hastened to add, "At Mother Machree's rooming house."

"Oh." Brett grimaced. "Thanks."

"No. I mean it. The Marquis of Queensberry never got jumped in the dark by two hoodlums. You did all right."

The door swung open, and the butler who liked to play the ponies greeted them. They were ushered inside an enormous entryway lined with mosaics like something out of a museum. Somebody's idea of ancient Rome or, more likely, Tuscany. Beyond tiles of olive trees and grapevines and naked nymphs trying to outrun inebriated satyrs were about a dozen marble columns holding up a two-story rotunda with racy painted panels in the domed ceiling.

Jeeves took their coats and Rafferty's hat. He made no comment on Brett's torn coat or missing chapeau, which was surely the sign of a well-trained minion. Or maybe the high society life was more boisterous than Rafferty figured.

As they reached the grand staircase, he noticed the giant portrait of a stunningly beautiful woman. Eyes like emeralds and hair like a dark cloud. That would be the first Mrs. Sheridan. Rafferty wondered how the second Mrs. Sheridan felt about the life-size portrait in the foyer.

"Mrs. Sheridan has only returned home herself, sir," Munson volunteered to Brett.

"Oh?" Brett said, glancing at Rafferty.

"Yes, sir. The family is gathered in the drawing room."

Rafferty would have figured that was a normal occurrence, but Brett seemed to go pale. "What's happened?"

Munson didn't vouchsafe anything but a prim, "I believe they're waiting for you, sir."

Brett nodded and started upstairs, taking the steps two at a time. He seemed to have forgotten all about Rafferty, which suited Rafferty fine. He was looking forward to seeing the Sheridans in their natural environment.

They reached the second level, which featured a marble fountain, a couple of small trees growing in stone urns, and more statues that probably belonged in museums. The Sheridans were busted flat, but you'd never know it to look at this place.

Brett broke to the left, striding down yet another tunnel, this one carpeted in Persian jewel tones. Rafferty tagged along admiring the artwork, much of which he happened to know were forgeries. Good forgeries, though. The best.

They came at last to the drawing room, where the clan had gathered.

"Why, in my day..." Linus Sheridan actually had an arm up pointing to the ceiling like Mark Antony summoning his friends, Romans, and countrymen. He broke off at the sight of his son and heir. "Brett! Where the devil have you been?"

"Where *have* you been?" asked a young dark-haired woman on the sofa. That would be the musical prodigy, Sophie. "Father's nearly worn a hole through the carpet. And my head."

"What's happened?" Brett asked, looking around the room.

No one answered immediately—or at least not directly.

"Brett, dearest!" Lenora Sheridan smiled tremulously and tucked at a silver tendril of hair. Her gaze flicked to Rafferty. "And Mister...er..."

"Rafferty," Rafferty supplied.

"Mr. Rafferty. I don't believe we've had the pleasure," Justine said from her sofa. She smiled widely. "Not formally, anyway."

Ah. Well, Rafferty had wondered if she'd spotted him. She was a canny lady, the second Mrs. Sheridan, though perhaps *lady* wasn't quite the word.

Brett recollected himself and made the introductions. He managed to leave out all the essentials, barring Rafferty's name, but it was smoothly done. He finished up, "Neil and I went into Chinatown. We had a little trouble." It was said so naturally, Rafferty almost bought the story himself.

"And what were you two gay blades doing in Chinatown?" Justine inquired. She didn't have a voice; she had a purr—like a well-fed tiger.

Brett looked at Rafferty. "The usual thing, Justine. Wine, women, and dim song."

"Dim *sum*." Rafferty picked up his cue. "And you forgot the gambling."

"It only counts if you win."

The girl, Sophie, laughed. The old lady twittered some more. Justine's eyes glinted. "I missed where you said you knew Neil from, Sherry?"

Brett's eyes met Rafferty's. "Neil is a member of my club."

If Rafferty had been a man given to blushing, he'd have blushed then. He couldn't quite get a handle on Brett Sheridan. At times he seemed bolder than brass and at others, as shy as a young girl. Shyer, if the girl was one of his sisters.

"You young wastrel," fumed the old man, breaking up the fun. "How can you think of such things at a time like this?"

"At a time like what?"

Sheridan Senior thrust a letter at Brett. "What do you think of this, eh?"

Brett took the letter and read.

"A member of the Pacific-Union Club?" Justine chuckled and held out her hand to Rafferty. "Are you sure you're not a private dick?"

Rafferty recovered his normal aplomb and took her hand. He winked.

She laughed again. "Leave it to Sherry."

"A policeman?" quavered Aunt Lenora, her hand going to her lace fichu. Her eyes darted in fright from Rafferty to Brett and back to her brother, who was still muttering like a teakettle about to boil.

"No, ma'am," Rafferty reassured her. "Nothing like that."

The girl uncurled from the sofa and approached with wide green eyes. She too reminded Rafferty of a cat. In her case, a small black cat. A very different animal from her step-mama. She was not exactly pretty, but there was something about her that would make her difficult to overlook in any crowd of girls. A certain uneasy intensity—the uneasiness belonging to everyone around her.

"Hiya," Rafferty said.

She tilted her head, considering.

Yep. Nuts. The bunch of them.

Brett looked up from the letter, his face masklike. "Kitty's run off with Sader."

"What?"

Brett handed him the letter. Rafferty scanned it.

Dearest Pater,

Please don't be angry. After much thought, Harry and I have decided to throw in our lot together. We're going to be married in Las Vegas. We're neither of us children, and we don't want any fuss. We simply want to be together.

I'll write when I can. Until then, love to you all.

Your
Katherine

Now this was something Rafferty hadn't seen coming. He should have, and if Katherine Sheridan had been another kind of girl, he probably would have. But that was his biggest mistake, because all girls were the same when it came to the Harry Saders of the world. It was one of the great mysteries.

"It doesn't even sound like her," Brett said.

"Is it her handwriting?"

Brett stared at him as though the question were too complicated. He sat heavily on the arm of a sofa that looked too fragile to take anything more than the weight of a malnourished butterfly. The sofa squeaked but held together.

"Why would she do such a thing?" he asked. He still seemed to be talking to Rafferty. Not that Rafferty blamed him.

"Because they're in love," Justine answered. "And I guess she's tired of being treated like a half-witted child." She added, as Sophie started to speak, "*You* are a half-witted child."

"She's ruined," Linus Sheridan moaned. He paced up and down in front of his marble fireplace. "She's ruined herself. Who the devil will have her now?" He wheeled to face Brett. "You've got to go get the little fool. You've got to bring her home before it's too late."

"It's already too late," Justine said. "It was too late the day she met Harry Sader."

"Oh, don't say that!" Aunt Lenora cried. "Brett, your father's right. You *must* bring your sister home."

Brett rubbed his forehead wearily.

"Uh…" Rafferty began. But no one was listening to him. Linus and Lenora continued to exhort Brett to ride to the rescue. The girl examined her fingernails.

"You'll just make bigger fools of yourselves," Justine observed. She lit a cigarette and placed it in a long ivory holder. "Not that that should worry anyone."

Rafferty gazed at the crowd of them with disgust. Certifiable. Every one of them. How long had they been sitting here lamenting the elopement? Since teatime? Had they been crying into their cucumber sandwiches all afternoon? Why didn't Pater get off his duff and fetch his wayward daughter home?

"When did she leave?" he asked.

A lot of blank faces looked at each other and came up empty.

Rafferty snorted.

"All right. I'll go after her." Brett stood up. He moved like he hurt, and no doubt by then he probably did. It had been a long night. A long night for

Rafferty too, but no one had worked him over. "Have Munson bring my car..." Brett trailed off. "Oh hell."

$\mathcal{T}$he others looked taken aback.

Brett turned to Rafferty. "Can you give me a lift?"

"To Las Vegas?"

"To Herbert's Grill on Powell Street. I left my car there."

Rafferty consulted his inner oracle. "Come to think of it, why not make it Las Vegas? I needed to talk to Sader myself, remember?"

Brett hesitated. "Is that on the level?"

"Sure. I've been thinking I'd like to get away for a few days. And if Sader cuts up rough, it won't hurt to have someone to hold your coat, right?"

The relief in Brett's strained gaze did something unfamiliar and unwelcome to Rafferty's heart. *No.* No, he definitely did not want to start feeling like that about Brett Sheridan. That was begging for grief.

"Katherine is hardly a child," Justine objected. "If she chooses to—"

"Be quiet!" Linus Sheridan snarled. "What do you know of these things? You grew up on a chicken farm in the Sunset District."

Justine's eyes narrowed, but she continued to puff serenely on her cigarette holder. "Suit yourself, my dear. You always do. Fortunately you don't care what your friends think of you."

Sheridan turned puce. Before he could express himself, Brett headed for the door. "Let me throw some things in a bag, and we can be on our way," he told Rafferty.

He was gone, and Rafferty faced a battery of curious eyes.

"I think yours is a very good idea," Aunt Lenora said. "That Harry Sader is a nasty piece of work. I can't imagine *what* Kitty is thinking."

"Animal magnetism," Justine said. She reached for the highball glass on the table next to the sofa. "There's a lot to be said for it."

"Where did you say you know my son from?" Sheridan elder asked, eyeing Rafferty with sudden suspicion.

"We know some of the same people. So you were all at this garden party on Friday night?"

"That's right." Justine sipped her drink, watching him over the glass rim. "Why?"

The girl, Sophie, had returned to her corner of the other sofa. She watched Rafferty with that steady, unblinking gaze.

"Brett was telling me a valuable manuscript went missing."

Aunt Lenora made a fluttery gesture with her hands and then sat very still, like a sparrow hoping to evade the notice of a hawk.

"What of it?" the old man barked out.

Rafferty shrugged. "Must have been exciting."

Justine laughed. "Have you ever been to one of the Lennoxes' parties? It would take armed robbery. Possibly murder."

Sheridan threw her a quick, bleak look.

"Sherry thinks one of us took the folio," Sophie observed casually.

"Maybe one of us did."

"Justine, how can you say these things," Aunt Lenora protested.

"Rubbish. Poppycock." Sheridan was quickly turning apoplectic. "No one here reads Shakespeare!"

Justine must have read Rafferty's expression correctly. She laughed. "Now if a pair of Etruscan doors went missing, that would be a different matter. Doors, wasn't it, dearest?" she asked her lord and master. "That you tried to buy from Count Bieda. Or were they windows?"

Sheridan scowled at her. "It was a perfectly legitimate transaction."

"Legitimate but not legal."

They reminded Rafferty of people in a play. A play he would pay money to avoid seeing. To his relief, Brett returned. He had washed up and changed his clothes.

"Ready?" he asked from the doorway, Gladstone in hand. To his father, he said, "I'll call when I know something for sure."

"Nice meeting you all," Rafferty said.

"The pleasure was ours," Justine said into a noticeable silence.

"They won't be headed for Las Vegas," Brett said as they started down the grand staircase.

"No?" Rafferty had doubts about that himself, but he wanted to hear Brett's reasoning. "What makes you think not?"

"There's no reason for them to go to Las Vegas. They can be married just as easily in Reno, and it's only four, maybe five hours away versus twelve or so."

"True."

"Besides, if Kitty really was planning to head for Las Vegas, she'd never volunteer that information. The only reason she added that was to throw us off the track."

"Makes sense to me."

Brett raked that perpetual dark thatch of hair from his eyes. "Not only that, our family owns property near Lake Tahoe. Kitty and Sader could safely hole up there while they decide what to do about the folio."

That made the best sense yet. Especially since Kip Mullens's boys seemed to be hunting for Sader. How Mullen fit into this thing, Rafferty had no idea. Maybe Mullen didn't. Maybe it was a coincidence he wanted to pull Sader in, but Rafferty didn't like coincidences.

"Reno it is."

Brett threw him a hard-to-read look. "I know this is beyond the call of duty. I'll pay for your expenses. Don't worry about that."

"Sure. Thanks." Knowing the state of Brett's finances, Rafferty was curious how he intended to make good on that promise. He appreciated the thought, though.

* * * * *

They were in the car and turning right onto the Embarcadero through the maze of cable car tracks and just past Davis Street when Brett said, "Do you think those goons will go after them?"

"I don't know. I've been trying to figure that one out myself." Rafferty wasn't going to lie. "It depends on why they were looking for Sader."

"And whether they know about Kitty?"

"I doubt if he kept her secret. She's too big a catch. Sorry, but that's the truth. It looks like he planned on marrying her from the start."

"Financed by the sale of the folio." Brett's voice was bitter.

"We still don't know that for a fact."

"You don't think this proves it? He's marrying her so she can't testify against him."

"I'm sure Sader could find another reason for marrying your sister. She's a beautiful girl. Good family. I bet a lot of guys have wanted to marry her."

Brett glanced at him but said nothing.

"It is just possible somebody else took that folio, you know."

"I wish that were true."

"That's not reassurance. The *somebody else* could still be one of your kinfolk. They've all got motive, if you want to look at this thing like a cop."

Brett didn't pick up the challenge. He said thoughtfully, "Pat said you used to be a cop."

"That's right. I walked a beat about a hundred years ago."

"Why did you leave the force?"

"The force left me."

It was meant to be a joke, a brush-off. Brett didn't laugh.

Rafferty found himself reluctantly explaining. "The truth? I smacked the son-in-law of the assistant chief right in his big, fat mouth."

"You don't say."

"That's what I said to him." Rafferty's smile was grim. "I don't have any regrets. I'd probably still be walking a beat. I like being my own boss."

Neither said anything for a time.

Brett asked all at once, harshly, "Why did you do it?"

"Huh?"

"What you did tonight."

Oh that. Rafferty was wondering whether Brett was going to turn into one of those hysterical queers who blamed other men for "turning" them, but then Brett added, very quietly, "What you did for me."

For me.

It softened him in a way Rafferty found alarming. He made himself say with casual indifference, "I don't know. I guess I wanted to."

Brett was silent again. They turned right onto Harrison.

"Did you know about me? Before Chinatown, I mean."

"Not for sure," Rafferty lied.

"You took a hell of a chance."

"I'm a guy who takes chances."

Brett thought it over. "You must have been pretty sure. What did Pat tell you?"

"Nothing." That, at least, was the truth. "But I knew…that is, I figured if Pat sent you, there was a possibility…"

Brett stared out the passenger door window.

Rafferty was startled to hear himself breaking one of his cardinal rules. The rule about discretion. "Did Pat ever tell you what I did for her?"

Brett turned back to him. "Retrieved some of her letters from a blackmailer."

"Did she tell you who the blackmailer was?"

"An ex-lover."

If Pat had shared that much, his instinct was right about Brett. "That's right. A woman by the name of Maida Grail."

Brett said neutrally, after a pause, "Pat's a big believer in the sanctuary of marriage."

Sanctuary, not sanctity. Was it unconscious? "Yep. It seems to work for her."

"It works for most people like us."

There was no reason that should hurt, but it did, somehow. Rafferty said calmly, "I wouldn't know."

CHAPTER EIGHT

$\mathcal{B}$rett's lashes quivered. He opened his eyes to…pink. It took a few seconds to separate the first rays of rose-gold dawn from the frothy pink plumes of gnarled and crooked smoke trees lining the highway.

He had fallen asleep.

The surprise of it held him silent for a few seconds, and another mile of pale pink clouds rolled by.

He slept so rarely these days—and rarely deeply—that the moment almost seemed magical.

As did the landscape. Where on God's pink earth were they? He sat up from his awkward slump against the door, yelping as his bruised and stiffened muscles protested.

"Cock-a-doodle-doo to you too." Rafferty spared him a glance.

Brett cautiously eased over and upright. A plaid car rug had been thrown over him. He automatically clutched at it as it slipped away. "Where are we?" He peered at his watch.

"At a guess? About twenty miles from the middle of nowhere."

Brett's yawn turned into a laugh. He rubbed the corners of his eyes. "It looks like it. You've been driving nearly three hours. You want me to take over?"

"Nope." Rafferty threw him a friendly look. "Anyway, I stopped an hour or so back to stretch my legs and get a cup of coffee at a roadhouse. I'd have woken you, but you were dead to the world."

"Maybe this is the secret to my sleepless nights."

"You have a lot of sleepless nights?"

"A few." Brett joked, "My bad conscience."

"I doubt that. We're coming up on Auburn. We'll stop for breakfast the next likely looking place."

The next likely looking place was the Apple Blossom Inn in Auburn. It was a pink stucco Spanish style café, open but empty at five in the morning.

Brett headed straight for the pink and gray tiled washroom, which was scrupulously clean and smelled strongly of bleach. He splashed cold water on his face and studied his dripping reflection in the mirror. He needed a shave. There was a faint bruise on his cheekbone, but the swelling of his lip was already going down. He remembered the alleyway in Chinatown the night before and watched his face turn a painful red. The color receded nearly as quickly. He must have been out of his goddamned mind.

He bent over the basin and splashed more cold water until he was in danger of drowning. With a fistful of paper towels, he dried his face and hair and damp shirt and then went to rejoin Rafferty.

Rafferty didn't look up from the red menu in front of him. "If the food is as good as the coffee, we're in luck."

Brett slid into the booth and tried the coffee. Rafferty was right. The coffee was a miracle. He swallowed gratefully.

The waitress came and took their orders. Rafferty ordered steak and eggs, Brett a stack of buttermilk pancakes.

In the bright light of day, he felt constrained in a way he hadn't in the safe darkness of the speeding automobile. He felt the need for conversation. Any conversation on any topic, provided it had nothing to do with what they'd done in the alien-scented darkness of the back alleys of Chinatown.

"Did you grow up in San Francisco?"

"Yep." Rafferty smiled faintly, studying Brett. "How about you?"

Brett said wryly, "Don't tell me you didn't check up on me along with every other member of my family."

Rafferty shrugged and ticked off the itinerary of Brett's life. "Phillips Exeter Academy, then Harvard, where you studied prelaw until your junior year when you fell ill and returned home."

Brett buried himself in his coffee cup. "That's about the size of it."

"You didn't go back and finish?" The answer was sitting right in front of him, of course.

"No."

To Brett's relief, Rafferty let it go. Their breakfasts came, and they devoted themselves to the very good food before them. Brett's bacon was done to a crisp, and the buttermilk pancakes were golden and fluffy, drenched in pale syrup that tasted like sweet distilled sunshine. He was hungrier than he'd realized, and he ate every bite.

Through the window he could see the Sierra Nevada Mountains, snow-topped even in June. It looked like it was going to be a beautiful day. He glanced at Rafferty, who was eating at a more civilized pace, pausing to breathe and even take occasional sips of coffee.

"How are we going to find Sader and my sister once we get to Reno?"

Rafferty swallowed a mouthful. "I know a guy who'll be able to steer us in the right direction."

"They're probably married by now." Brett pushed his plate away.

Rafferty glanced at the clock next to the Coca-Cola sign with the slogan DON'T WEAR A TIRED THIRSTY FACE. "Not necessarily. They wouldn't have arrived before midnight, and most of those chapels don't open before noon. Anyway, marriage is better than the alternative, right?"

Brett nodded gloomily.

"What happened? Her fiancé was killed?"

"A week before their wedding. Robbie Covington. Swell guy. The three of us grew up together. I don't think Kitty ever got over it. Although that still doesn't explain what the hell she's doing with a bum like Harry Sader." Nothing *could*, in Brett's opinion.

"It's a mystery to me, but she's not the first. Women seem to find Sader attractive. Maybe it *is* animal magnetism."

They shared a wry look before the waitress arrived, coffeepot in hand, to top their cups up. Rafferty returned his attention to his meal.

He was a funny guy. Brett hadn't missed how he'd avoided answering anything about his own background. He'd have liked to have pushed, liked to have known a little bit more about Rafferty, but something about the other man discouraged prying. Which was kind of ironic given his profession. Or maybe not.

Even with as short an acquaintance as theirs, Brett had come to like Rafferty. He liked his toughness, his competence, his good humor. As Pat had said, he was a good man to have on your side. A good man to have as a friend.

Brett hoped they would become friends. It was probably too soon to know for sure. The impression he had was that he mostly amused Rafferty, but that had been a…lovely thing Rafferty did for him. The loveliest thing anyone had done for him in a very long time. And nothing asked in return. That was the bit he couldn't get over. He'd paid people to do that for him, but he'd never had anyone do it simply because they wanted to.

Rafferty spoke, jarring him out of his thoughts. "So where would someone unload an item like this folio?"

Brett frowned. "You're asking *me*?"

"I am."

"Do I look like someone who would know where to fence stolen goods?"

"No," Rafferty admitted. "You don't." His eyes met Brett's, and there seemed to be a smile lurking in the back of them. "But yet you are."

Brett froze midmotion of bringing his coffee cup to his lips. It was so fleeting—barely a waver and even less an actual pause—that he told himself Rafferty wouldn't notice.

"I don't follow you." He replaced his cup neatly in its saucer.

"Sure you do." Rafferty was still smiling, still easy. "Give me a little credit. I wouldn't say it if I didn't have my facts straight. For the past three years, you and your sister Katherine have sold off nearly ninety family heirlooms, including a Renoir painting, a couple of eighteenth century Kashan carpets, and a slew of Ming porcelain. You've replaced them with painstaking replicas that would fool anybody who didn't know exactly what they were looking for."

Brett said mechanically, "I don't know what you're talking about." He forced himself to meet Rafferty's gaze, his own expression cool and blank.

"Look, don't get me wrong. I work for *you*. And, if you want my opinion, I think you've got brains, imagination, and nerve. I don't think for one second that you took the folio, but I think your shared sideline in saving the family fortunes is one reason you believe your sister did. She would know exactly how and where to dispose of it."

What was the point of denying the obvious? He merely looked like a fool on top of being caught out as a liar and thief. "Yes. But we never took anything that…"

Rafferty finished for him, "That wasn't ultimately supposed to be yours?"

"There isn't anything left. There shouldn't be, anyway. The house should have been sold after the crash. If we could have done that, if we could have sold the house and the junk inside it and agreed to live within our reduced circumstances, we'd be all right now. Instead…"

"Instead you and your sister are secretly siphoning off assets to keep the ship afloat. Except the name of the ship is the *Titanic*."

Brett's laugh was unamused. "I don't blame Kitty for wanting out. I just don't understand why she chose Sader."

"And is marrying Juliet Lennox your way of getting out?"

Something shrank inside Brett. "No. It's not. Shouldn't we get on the road again?"

Rafferty's brows rose. "I guess we should." He nodded to the waitress, who was dusting a glass-covered dish of pastries.

She brought over their check. Brett moved to pick it up, but Rafferty was faster. "I'll get this one. You can get the next." He smiled faintly at Brett's expression. "Don't look so worried." He was whistling as he led the way out to the car. "It's going to be a warm one today."

The air felt dry, and the cooking scents of the café mingled with the cedar and fresh mountain air.

"You want me to take a turn behind the wheel?" Brett asked.

Rafferty shook his head. "I like to drive." Rafferty got behind the wheel again, and Brett went around to the passenger side.

They continued up Highway 40, through rolling green foothills of oak and cedar. Rafferty tried the radio, but after a blast of fuzzy music, there was nothing but static. Nothing to do but talk, and Brett wasn't sure he had the nerve for any more of Rafferty's revelations.

"Light me a cigarette," Rafferty asked after a time.

Brett complied, taking out the gold cigarette case Juliet had given him for his last birthday. He drew out two cigarettes, stuck them into his mouth, and lit them. He handed one to Rafferty, drew on the other himself.

"How did you get into the PI business?" he asked after an interval.

Rafferty tapped the gray tip of his cigarette into the car's ashtray. "I guess I was just a naturally curious fellow."

"Do you handle a lot of murder cases?"

Rafferty smiled faintly. "Like Sam Spade? No. Not a one. Not so far. I'm in the lost-and-found business, mostly. And mostly what people lose are other people."

"And do you always find them?"

"No. And sometimes when I find them, the people who hire me wish I hadn't."

That was a depressing notion. Brett blew out a thoughtful stream of smoke and gazed unseeingly at a distant deer leaping away into the pine trees.

"Did you know more deer attack humans than bears?" Rafferty asked.

"No."

"Appearances are deceiving. It's true."

Brett laughed. "How do you know that?"

Rafferty shrugged. He tipped more ash in the tray. "I like to read. Like I said, I'm a naturally curious fellow."

"How's curiosity pay?"

"It pays all right."

The Buick began to wind higher into the trees and rocks of the Sierra Nevadas.

"You said your family owns property in Reno?"

"Near Lake Tahoe. The estate belonged to my mother's family. I've seen pictures of the house, but I've never been there. Not that I remember. Kitty has. She won't have forgotten."

Rafferty didn't respond, his eyes on the rearview mirror.

Brett started to turn but thought better of it. "Something wrong?"

"I don't know. I think maybe we're being followed."

"Are you joking?"

Rafferty's smile was hard. "What in our acquaintance thus far would lead you to think I'd joke about that? There was a black Packard 120 with two guys in fedoras behind us when we stopped for breakfast. Thirty minutes later, they're still behind us."

"Are you sure it's the same car?"

"Nope. Not positive. Not to swear to it in a court of law." Rafferty added, "But I sure as hell think so."

"How would they have found us?"

Rafferty didn't answer at first as the winding road took more of his attention. "Maybe they followed us all last night."

Brett's heart stopped.

Into his stricken silence, Rafferty said, "I don't think that's what happened. If they know about your sister—and there's plenty of reason to think they do—they'd know enough to watch your house."

"Then they're going to track us all the way to Reno?"

"Maybe..." Rafferty's gaze was in the rearview mirror again. "The thing is..." He sounded like he was thinking aloud.

"The thing is what?" Brett ventured the question.

"They're not bothering to hide from us anymore."

What did that mean? Did it mean what it sounded like? Because what it sounded like was not very reassuring.

Brett risked a look back himself. The black Packard was several twists of the road behind them, but it was coming up fast with a reckless disregard for both safety and concealment.

"There are only so many places we could be headed on this road. I'm guessing they know we're not planning on a week in Truckee."

"I'm guessing you're right." Rafferty had both hands on the wheel now, and the cigarette dangled from his lips. He looked uncompromising and as flinty as they came as he accelerated out of the last curve and the car leaped ahead.

They flew up the snaking road, flying in and out of shadow, and all the while the powerful Packard drew ever closer.

Rafferty's face grew grimmer as he coaxed every bit of speed from the Buick. They gained a little on a downhill stretch, due to his skillful driving, but lost it again on the uphill lug.

They crested the top of yet another ridge, and the black wolf behind them lunged forward and slammed into their bumper.

White-knuckled, Rafferty fought for control and kept the fishtailing Buick from plunging off the mountainside drop on the far side of the road.

The Packard fell back but zoomed up again. Rafferty floored the accelerator, and the Buick jumped ahead.

They tore down the narrow, curving ribbon of road. Brett hung on to the door frame with one hand. With his other, he gripped the back of his seat and watched the Packard gain on them once more.

"They're going to ram us again!"

Rafferty's jaw tightened. "No they're fucking not." As the driver of the Packard made his move, Rafferty wrenched the wheel to the right. The Buick swung onto the shoulder as the Packard sliced forward, fender scraping along the Buick's left side. There was a horrendous grating of metal, and the Buick crashed over the berm and slammed down in a small stony clearing, rocking onto its side and then landing heavily.

The Packard roared past, brakes squealing as it went into the next turn too fast. The driver fought for control, and the black car managed to stay on the road. They disappeared around the next bend.

Chapter Nine

"*Jesus Christ*." Brett looked more mad than scared, which was good, because Rafferty was scared plenty for both of them.

He was angry too, that went without saying, but the idea that he might have been responsible for getting someone killed—getting Brett Sheridan killed—shook him more than he'd have expected.

He inspected the damage to the Buick—scraped paint, two flat tires, and a bent axel—as Brett walked back to the road to watch the black Packard, now well down the mountain as it whipped through the next series of curves.

Brett swore with elegant economy, finishing up with, "Where the hell are we?"

Rafferty glanced up as Brett trudged back to the Buick, his shoes sliding on pine needles. "Right where we were before the car went off the road."

Brett gave him what the romance novels called *a withering glance.* "That helps."

"You know as much as I do. We're somewhere between Camp Spaulding and Soda Springs."

"Swell. Do we go forward or back?"

"You want to toss for it?" Rafferty pulled out his lucky coin, a doubloon he'd won in a card game from an old sea dog who swore up and down the gold piece was part of the treasure of the sunken *San Augustin* in Drakes Bay. "Call it."

"Heads means we head back."

Rafferty nodded and tossed the coin. It flashed, spinning in the clear mountain air.

"Wait." Brett turned and ran back up the berm. Sure enough, a blue Ford pickup with white-walled tires and a bed with three large pigs came chugging around the bend.

Brett flagged the truck down. It pulled to the side, and the driver got out. He inspected Rafferty's disabled car and agreed to give them a lift into Norden.

Into Norden turned out to be an exaggeration. Norden, once an old mining town, mostly amounted to a handful of falling-down buildings from the 1800s. There was a general store, a gas station, and a café called the Alpine House.

The café had a public phone, and from there Rafferty was able to summon a tow truck from Truckee.

They smoked a couple of cigarettes and watched chickens pecking at gravel outside the little café while they waited for the truck to arrive. At last it rumbled up, and they set off to retrieve Rafferty's Buick.

By the time the Buick had been chained and towed into the town of Truckee, it was midafternoon, and it was clear they would be spending the night in the mountains. The town's only mechanic promised it would be unlikely to take longer than that to repair the Buick, which was fortunate since Rafferty thought Brett was about to have a stroke as it was.

"But there must be another way to get to Reno tonight, surely?"

The grizzled mechanic pushed his cap back and studied Brett as though he were some unexpected natural phenomenon. A two-headed calf, maybe. "No can do, sonny. I'm the town's only mechanic, and I've got a line of machines needing fixing. I already spent half the day digging you fellers out."

"But we could pay you to—"

"Okay. Thanks, mac." Rafferty fastened his hand on Brett's arm in warning.

Brett started to speak again, but Rafferty steered him into the bright thin mountain sunshine. "Let it go."

Brett freed himself. "What do you mean, *let it go?* We don't have time to let it go. We need to get into Reno."

"In case you've lost your hearing, we're not going anywhere. So let's make the best of it."

"To hell with making the best of it. There's got to be another way. Somebody else in this place owns a car!"

"Look around you." Rafferty gestured impatiently at the towering pines and a main road that looked like it was straight out of a Tom Mix movie. There were even a couple of horses tethered at the end of the street in front of the general store. "Nobody here gives a damn about your sister or a missing folio or William Shakespeare or any of the rest of it. They've got their own problems and their own lives. And believe it or not, your money and your name don't mean a whole hell of a lot out here."

Brett opened his mouth.

Rafferty overrode him ruthlessly. "Not to mention the fact that you don't have money to be throwing around."

Brett drew himself up straight. "I can get the money."

"Really? Without revealing what you need it for?"

Brett started to speak but stopped.

"For God's sake," Rafferty said impatiently. "You didn't honestly think you were going to stop her marriage?"

"Why not?"

"Come on, you're not that naïve."

"Go to hell."

"Brett." Rafferty grabbed his arm again, forgetting that they were on the street—such as it was—in broad daylight. "You can't stop her from marrying Sader if she wants to marry him. She's free, white, and twenty-one."

"She's making a mistake."

"And you never made one, is that it?"

Brett's lips parted. He stared into Rafferty's eyes, and the turmoil in those green depths got to Rafferty like an arrow to the heart.

"Brett," Rafferty said softly.

Brett's eyes widened with fear. He made an aborted move to pull free, then stood motionless, listening.

Rafferty's grip tightened. "Listen, as far as I'm concerned, we're after the folio. That's it. Your sister…is a big girl. If she asks for our help, that's one thing. But I don't get the feeling she's asking for anyone's help."

Brett flung away from him and strode quickly up the wooden side-walk. A couple of yards away, he turned around and walked back. "Look, I know what you think, but this doesn't have anything to do with my sister marrying beneath her station or any of that rot."

"I don't think—"

"Yes, you do. You think we're all a bunch of snobs and phonies. But those hoods would have shoved us off that mountainside if you'd let them. I don't know what they want Sader for, but something tells me they're not going to consult Sir Walter Raleigh before they deal with my sister."

"Huh?"

"You know. The cloak over the mud puddle."

"Uh…right. Look, I understand you're worried. I think Sader and your sis are on the run, and I don't think they're running from us. So maybe Mullens's goons are looking for them. That doesn't mean they'll be easy to find."

"That's one consideration. The other is that this is the third day."

"I know."

"After today Lennox will report the robbery to the police."

"I know."

"Seeing that you know such a hell of a lot, what's your solution?"

"I don't have a solution. Lennox is going to report the robbery. Sader will come under suspicion."

"And my sister with him."

"Maybe. Maybe not. But there isn't any point in wearing yourself out over what can't be changed."

After a long moment, Brett sighed. "Isn't there?"

"No."

Brett finally relaxed a fraction. "All right. What next?"

"Let's find a hotel or inn or stable or someplace we can spend the night."

What they found was the Riverside, a four-story hotel originally built in 1873. Though the Riverside did a brisk business during the ski season, there were plenty of rooms available in the summer months, and they were able to secure two neighboring rooms with private baths.

Rafferty's room offered an old brass bed, antique dresser and side table, a wash basin with a small mirror, and a picturesque view of the surrounding mountains. He washed up at the basin, accepted the fact that he was going to have to buy a change of clothes before much longer, and went downstairs to join Brett for lunch at a nearby café.

They had the small patio out back to themselves. An arbor covered by grapevines threw a tired fountain into deep shade. From inside, a radio played "Puttin' on the Ritz." They drank coffee and ate BLTs.

Rafferty, being a pragmatist, had already resigned himself to their plight. It was his considered opinion as plights went, they could have been much worse off. Brett had also resigned himself, but in his case, he had worn himself to a frazzle reaching the inevitable conclusion. That was the problem with these guys who lived on their nerves.

Rafferty ate his sandwich and considered the problem of Brett Sheridan. Unaware that he was under observation, Brett ate his sandwich and stared moodily at the mountains.

The sooty length of his eyelashes fascinated Rafferty. They were longer than any he'd seen—real or artificial—on a girl. And the line of his mouth. No man should have a mouth that beautiful.

"So tell me about Juliet," Rafferty invited when his observations began to get uncomfortable.

The long lashes lifted. The sensitive mouth firmed. "She's a great girl."

"I figured."

"I met her last year at a black-and-white ball held at the Palace of Fine Arts. We hit it off." Brett shrugged.

"You've been engaged before."

It was the wrong thing to say, it seemed. Brett's face turned into a stark mask of bones and hollows. "That's right. So what?"

Clearly there was something here, but what? "So nothing."

"You must have had some reason for bringing it up. What have you heard?"

"Nothing. Sorry. Force of habit, that's all."

Brett said mockingly, "Nothing? Oh, I'm sure you must have heard *something*."

Rafferty shook his head. "I guess if I'd asked questions, I'd have heard something. Someone always has to say something about broken engagements, don't they? But I didn't ask. I don't care."

Brett stared at him, and then his mouth curved bitterly. "You're too soft-hearted to be a private dick, Rafferty."

"That's the first time I ever heard that."

"I bet it's not." Brett drank the rest of his coffee and pushed his chair back. "Since we're stuck here, I'm going to have a bath and a nap."

Rafferty watched him disappear inside. He finished his lunch and wandered down to the few shops on the main street and bought himself a toothbrush, a razor, a pair of pajamas, a change of underwear, and a new shirt.

When he got back to his room, he bundled his dirty clothes and handed them over to the laundry service. Then he had a nice long soak himself in the claw-footed tub in his private bath.

The hotel parlor on the second floor offered several bookshelves mostly crammed with titles popular a few years earlier. There was *A Girl of the Limberlost* and *How to Win Friends and Influence People* (which Rafferty had already read), but there were also novels by Hemingway, Fitzgerald, and Dos Passos. Rafferty had read some of that stuff too, but he found it depressing and not very realistic. Clever stories about book people. That was his opinion. He spotted *The Thin Man*, grinned to himself, and pulled it from the shelf.

> *I was leaning against the bar in a speakeasy on Fifty-second Street, waiting for Nora to finish her Christmas shopping, when a girl got up from the table where she had been sitting with three other people and came over to me.*

He passed Brett's room on the way back to his own, but there was no sound from inside.

* * * * *

At dinner, which they ate at a small Italian restaurant only a yard or so from the hotel, Brett seemed like his usual self. Not that Rafferty really knew what Brett's usual self was. More accurately, Brett put himself out to be charming, something he did well and without really trying.

He ordered an extra bottle of wine and told several amusing—and probably wickedly inaccurate—stories about people who frequently appeared in the society pages. Rafferty had no problem with that. He had no problem with any of it, but as he drank the wine and listened to the stories and watched Brett's face, he wished that he'd relax as he had a few times during their acquaintance. His guard had been up ever since Rafferty's unfortunate reminder of his engagement.

Juliet Lennox seemed like a nice kid, but the more Rafferty saw of Brett, the more he didn't want to think of Brett married to her. That was stupid. Brett was going to marry that girl if it killed him. And maybe it would.

But that wasn't Rafferty's problem.

It wasn't even his business. Still, he watched Brett's face in the candlelight and his heart ached in some indefinable way. Maybe he *was* getting soft.

"How come you change the subject any time I ask about you?" Brett asked over the Italian cream cake he'd ordered for their dessert.

"Who, me? My life's an open book."

"Yeah, the *Book of Secrets*. You change the subject. You *fence*." Brett was speaking very precisely, very carefully in the way of the experienced inebriate. You'd have to know him to know he was getting drunk, and what did it say that Rafferty already felt he knew Brett well enough to recognize the signs? Subtle as they were. It wasn't just the way Brett spoke; it also had to do with those bright, incalculable looks he cast from beneath those ridiculous eyelashes.

"Touché," Rafferty said lightly. "What did you want to know?"

"Everything. Anything."

Jesus. How much *had* he had to drink?

"Ask me something."

"How old are you?"

"Thirty-four."

"Where were you born?"

"I don't know."

A flash of irritation crossed Brett's face. Amused, Rafferty said, "I *don't* know. I was a foundling. I was left on the steps of St. Finian's Home for Foundlings with a letter stating my name pinned to my blanket by a St. Jude's medal."

"You're a foundling?"

"I was. Technically, I think I'm too old now days."

Brett's eyes narrowed. "Where did you go to school?"

Rafferty grinned. "San Francisco State University."

Brett began to splutter. "Why do you pretend…?"

"What? I don't pretend a damn thing. If people want to think I never passed the fourth grade, how is that my problem? Anyway, if it makes you feel better, I never graduated."

"You quit to become a cop?"

"That's right. To become a detective. Only it didn't work out that way."

"Because you belted the assistant chief's son-in-law in the mouth?"

"Fastest way to make detective."

"What did he say to annoy you so?"

Rafferty considered it over his last mouthful of wine. He said finally, "Maybe one day I'll tell you."

Brett considered this, but by then the waiters were hovering. He confiscated the bill, paid the damages, and they wandered back up the moonlit walkway to their hotel.

Rafferty had run out of things to say. Or rather, he knew better than to say the things he wanted to say, and he was out of small talk.

They went up to their rooms on the second floor.

"You think the car will be ready in the morning?" Brett asked at his door.

"I think so. It didn't look like there was a very long line ahead of us. I think he just wanted to make a point."

Brett considered this, nodded. "Good night."

"Night," Rafferty replied, still unable to think of anything better.

Brett opened the door to his room and went inside. The door closed firmly behind him.

Rafferty sighed and went on to his own room.

$\mathcal{I}$t was the moon that woke him. That bright bold silver face staring in

through the hotel window, hanging in the night sky like a Chinese lantern.

For a few seconds, he lay unmoving in the wide brass bed with its sheets scented faintly of juniper and mountain air and considered the silence. When he heard the balcony outside his window creak, he rose and went to stare out.

Down the walkway, he could see the small orange dot of someone smoking in one of the wooden rockers that faced the empty street below.

He stood there watching that slow arc of the cigarette in the darkness. June or not, it was cold in the mountains at night. Too cold to stand here and sure as hell too cold to go outside. He should go back to bed. That was what a smart guy would do.

"Oh to hell with it." Rafferty growled, and he left his room to light-foot it down the hallway and slip out the door leading onto the balcony.

He wasn't trying to sneak up, but quiet was second nature to him, and he had reached the man in the rocker before he was noticed. That was obvious, because when he asked quietly, "You all right?" Brett dropped his cigarette and jumped to his feet like someone struck by lightning. His hand even went to his chest like he thought his heart was going to leap out of his throat.

"Sorry. I'm sorry," Rafferty said quickly. "I didn't mean to startle you." That fear was too real, too genuine to ignore. It was painful in some inexplicable but physical way. How the hell long could anyone live like that before they snapped once and for all?

Brett leaned back against the railing. "Not at all," he said politely, faintly. He was still dressed, and the faint, faint scent of Lenthéric mingled with tobacco and the faraway spicy scent of the pine trees. It felt as if they stood on the edge of the world. That everything familiar lay behind them now and only uncharted wilderness ahead.

"What are you doing out here?"

"That should be obvious," Brett replied with a shade of his occasional irascibility. "I was having a smoke." He bent, found the smoldering cigarette butt, and stubbed it out on the railing before straightening again.

"At three o'clock in the morning?"

"I don't sleep much."

Rafferty found himself drawn forward. "Why's that?"

Brett shrugged. "Don't know. I just...don't." His eyes shone in the darkness.

They were nearly touching now, practically chest to chest. Brett's interest in the proceedings was unmistakable. It would have been the easiest thing in the world for Rafferty to put his arms around him, but he didn't forget that three o'clock in the morning or not, they were, to all intents and purposes, standing on a stage facing downtown Truckee.

Neither one of them spoke.

"It's a long day ahead tomorrow," Rafferty observed at last.

Brett said nothing. After a second or two, Rafferty realized he was shivering. He could just make out that almost imperceptible vibration.

He said brilliantly, "You're cold."

"Yes."

"Come inside." And, despite the fact that it was unwise, he took Brett's hand, lacing fingers, as he led him down the walkway and back inside the building.

By common if unspoken consent, they went to Rafferty's room. He locked the door behind them.

They shucked their garments. Brett sat on the edge of the bed. He was still shaking as Rafferty stretched out beside him, pulling him down. That was probably not the cold. For a few moments, Rafferty just held him quietly. Trying to reassure without words.

Brett's erection had wilted away, but that would come back fast enough, nerves or not. Rafferty's own arousal was almost beyond bearing, but he wasn't going to rush this. There wasn't a lot he could do for Brett, but he could show him how sweet this could be.

Remembering that rushed encounter in the Chinatown alley, he found he wanted to taste Brett's mouth again. Needed to. Entwining his fingers in soft, ruffled hair, he leaned down and parted Brett's moist lips with his tongue.

He felt Brett's cock stir back to life.

Brett shuddered and then seemed to relax, sucked tentatively on Rafferty's tongue. He gasped, groaned deep within his throat and came, wet hot and sticky all over Rafferty's front.

Rafferty stilled in surprise, and then held him, stroking his back. He was oddly moved by that boyish lack of control. His own near-painful arousal subsided a little.

"God. Sorry," Brett muttered into his neck.

Rafferty gave a quiet laugh. "Now that we got *that* out of the way…"

Brett shook his head in disgust at himself, still not facing Rafferty.

"Nah. It's okay." Rafferty nuzzled the hollow before his ear. "It happens to everybody."

Brett pulled away, rolled onto his back. "Does it?"

Rafferty didn't like that thread of acid beneath the flat words.

He drew him back, and Brett didn't resist. "Yeah, it does. Of course. Just relax."

After a tense moment, Brett did, his long, thin body going boneless and quiet in Rafferty's grip. Rafferty stroked him, kissed him, whispered an encouraging word or two.

Brett said finally, "You're not like I thought you'd be at first."

You neither. Rafferty said, "No? What did you think I'd be like?"

"Not like me."

"Queer, you mean?"

Brett tensed again, but then he sighed. "Are you? Do you let guys do that to you? Fuck you?"

"Sure."

Brett raised his head as though trying to read Rafferty's shadowed face.

"Sure," Rafferty said. "I'll let you do it, if you like."

He could feel Brett's astonishment, and he could feel the tiny twitch his cock gave. He smiled inwardly.

He kissed and cuddled Brett some more. It had been a long time since he'd done that with anyone. Since he'd felt like lowering his own guard. Something about Brett brought out funny feelings, things like…protectiveness, tenderness.

Brett grew drowsy and pliable beneath his attentions. "Why don't we sleep for a while?" Rafferty murmured, though sleep was the last thing on his mind.

It was the wrong thing to say. Instantly Brett was rigid with alarm. "We can't take the chance of oversleeping. If we were found together—"

"Relax. *Relax.*" Rafferty had to restrain him with an arm around his waist to keep Brett from leaping from the bed. "I don't oversleep."

Brett made a disbelieving sound.

"I mean it. Just what I said. It's like I've got a built-in clock here." Rafferty touched his own forehead. "I always know what time it is. And if I tell myself I want to sleep for five minutes, fifteen minutes, three hours, it doesn't matter. I wake up right on the dot."

Brett had stopped pulling away, but he wasn't lying down again either. "If we got caught—"

"Shhh. We're not going to get caught. Come here." Rafferty tugged him back down. "Jesus, you're wound tighter than a Swiss watch. Close your eyes and rest a little. It's nice being with someone like this."

The gleam of Brett's eyes seemed to go wider in the gloom.

"What?" Rafferty asked.

"I just…didn't think you'd see this…that way."

"What way?" When there was no answer forthcoming, Rafferty considered. He said with grim amusement, "You think I don't get lonely?"

"Lonely?" Brett repeated it like it was a foreign word. An alien concept. And yet Brett Sheridan was probably the loneliest man Rafferty had ever known—whether Brett knew it or not.

"Sure. I don't get this very often either, you know. Not like this. Not with someone…"

The steady shine of Brett's eyes never swerved. "Someone?"

"I…like. Someone it feels good to be with. Like this but also to have a meal with. To talk to."

Brett's eyes closed. "You shouldn't say stuff like that, Neil."

"Why not?" Rafferty said boldly, "I mean it."

Brett said with soft finality, "That's why you shouldn't say it."

Chapter Ten

*W*arm, breathing pillow beneath his cheek…

He had slept deeply, soundly. It was getting to be a habit with him. Opening his eyes, Brett took quiet stock of Neil's sinewy arm around him, Neil's breath stirring his hair, Neil's cock poking him in the hip. And his own bumping right back.

Neil.

It was not a good idea to start thinking of Rafferty as Neil. Nor was that small glow of contentment at either name a good idea. In fact, it was a bad idea. A lousy idea to start thinking that here was someone who understood. Who even maybe belonged to him in a funny sort of way.

It would be a funny way indeed if Neil belonged to him. And if anyone ought to understand that, it was Neil. But maybe the rules were different in Neil's world. Maybe Neil didn't worry about what people thought. If he didn't like what they thought, maybe he just punched them in the mouth like that son-in-law of an assistant chief.

Brett didn't have that luxury. He couldn't afford to start feeling…well, anything, really.

But he wished he had—was dismayed to realize that for the second time he'd accepted pleasure from Neil and done not a damn thing to reciprocate.

"Nah, I'm awake." Neil's raspy voice startled him. Neil's eyes opened. He gave a half smile, sleepy, friendly. "See. Plenty of time."

Brett swallowed. "For what?"

"For whatever you want."

All Brett's careful reasoning flew out the window and flapped its wings as it headed south. He finally managed, "What do *you* want?"

Neil's eyebrows rose. "Is it my turn?"

The implication that there would be other times and other turns was almost too precious to examine. Because it wasn't possible. Whatever was happening between them, no matter how astonishing and gratifying, was a temporary, makeshift sort of magic. It wouldn't last—couldn't last— beyond this adventure.

Neil had to know that as well as he did.

But whether he did or didn't, this was something Brett could do for him. Something Brett had learned to do rather well at his fancy prep school, where such things were merely rites of passage and not the keys to the citadel.

"It's about time, don't you think?"

"I don't keep track." Neil smoothed back Brett's hair and kissed his forehead. Once again Brett was nearly undone by the casual tenderness.

He pushed up and crawled between Neil's long, muscular legs. Neil shifted obligingly, watching him curiously over the naked thrust of his cock.

Brett bent and took Neil into his mouth, and the strangest thing was that every nerve in his body seemed to tingle in instinctive, blind reaction to everything he did to Neil. The taste of Neil, the scent of Neil, and oh, the *feel* of Neil. And Neil, so generous in his responses, gasping and moaning softly and shuddering as Brett worked tongue and lips and even teeth with the greatest possible skill. Now and then he'd lift a feeble hand to stroke Brett before dropping back into shivering sensation.

It was just them, the world narrowed down to this—the two of them together, giving and receiving pleasure and comfort. He licked and suckled and nibbled and kissed, and his reward came at last, sweetly, violently, an explosion of creamy, salty fluid that would have to be dealt with but seemed funny.

"Jesus Christ…" Neil sounded very Irish all at once. "You've a mouth like an angel."

Brett snorted. That was some religion the Catholics had. He mopped at himself with the sheet. Not at the traces of Neil's deliverance. He had come again himself. No surprise there. He had all the self-control of a flash fire.

Neil reached for him, pulled him down, hand curving around the nape of Brett's neck. His mouth was warm and sleepy, rousing little shivers in Brett. It was all so strange, especially being kissed by another man. Neil's mouth was so soft, so gentle. It seemed to stop Brett's heart in his chest.

He wanted to lay his head on Neil's shoulder and sleep in his arms for a little while longer, but his worry of being found together was stronger. It was dawn. Even in a mostly empty hotel, people would be up soon, moving around, paying attention.

It was difficult to fight the lethargy that gripped his mind as well as his limbs, but he drew away.

"We should get moving."

Neil blinked at him, heavy-eyed and flushed. "What's the rush?"

Brett shook his head, kept on shaking it. He scooped his clothes up and moved silently to the door. He had to look back, though. Neil was watching him, his eyes dark and moody.

He said nothing.

Brett let himself out and slipped into his own room, leaning back against the door, his heart thundering in his chest as though he'd just escaped some fearful danger. The taste of Neil was still on his lips, and his skin seemed to feel the pleasurable imprint of Neil's hands.

He sat on the side of his bed, his legs too weak to hold him.

He couldn't go through this again. He thought of Emmett, and his heart stopped in something close to horror. What was he doing? Had he blithely forgotten the terrible lessons of his Harvard years? It wasn't that he even blamed Emmett. It had been bound to end the way it had from the start. But if he had known then what he knew now? He'd never have started.

And this time…he did know.

The Truckee hotel served a cold breakfast of baked goods, fruit, and cereals. Brett had his pastry and coffee waiting for Neil, who seemed to be taking his time. When at last he showed up, bathed and shaved, wearing his freshly laundered white shirt, Brett's heart did another of those infuriating jumps.

What was the matter with him?

What was the matter with Neil, who apparently thought they had all the time in the world, settling down to his coffee and cereal with every appearance of pleasure, though Brett wouldn't have figured he would be much for continental breakfast.

"Something wrong?" Neil asked as Brett wandered over to the window.

"No."

"Have another cup of coffee. You're making me nervous."

That would make two of them, if it was true, but Neil didn't have a nervous bone in his body.

He stared down at the street below and saw that their car was being delivered. The mechanic got out and went inside the hotel. Brett went downstairs and met him.

The money he'd got from the sale of his gray polo pony was going fast. He hadn't planned for cross-country junkets or he'd have sold her little brother as well, much as he hated losing either of them. But the fact was, Juliet hated polo—was convinced he was going to break his neck as

Robbie had—and if he didn't marry Juliet, he wouldn't be able to continue to afford polo anyway, so either way, the ponies would have to go.

He heard the echo of his thoughts with surprise. *If he didn't marry Juliet?* There was no question of that. None.

He paid for the car repairs, took the keys, and went up to where Neil was finishing his coffee.

"Where'd you duck off to? Somebody tailing you?"

His easy good humor further aggravated Brett. Obviously what they had done was nothing to Neil, already dismissed. That was the right attitude—the very attitude Brett wanted to cultivate—but he found it irritating in Neil.

"I thought *we* were tailing somebody," he said tartly.

"There's my cue." Neil wiped his mouth and dropped his napkin over his plate.

They went downstairs. Brett tossed the car key to Neil and told him that the rooms were taken care of.

"You're very efficient this morning."

Brett didn't bother to answer, leading the way outside.

Soon they were on their way again, leaving the old-fashioned town of Truckee in the golden dust that fell like powdery rain behind their tires.

"You want to tell me what's on your mind?" Neil asked as they began to wind through the pines and oaks once more.

"Nothing to tell." Brett said it with the right amount of distant surprise at the question, and Neil dropped the subject, as Brett had known he would.

* * * * *

RENO THE BIGGEST LITTLE CITY IN THE WORLD read the arched sign over downtown Reno.

"Where do we start?" Brett asked. He'd never been to Reno, and he was dismayed at the size of it. Not the physical size of it but the number of people wandering the streets. Were they *all* there for divorces?

"North Virginia Street," Neil told him. "I know a guy at Harold's Club."

Harold's Club offered two slot machines and a large roulette wheel called a flasher suspended from the ceiling with a huge mirror so players could see the action and make bets on their own layouts. "The guy" Neil knew turned out to be a bouncer, a big, burly guy with red slicked-back hair and a face like a jackhammer. He declined to speak in front of Brett, so Brett took a hint and wandered off to play one of the slot machines.

He was scooping up his winnings, about ten dollars' worth of silver, when Neil rejoined him.

"Cookie says he hasn't seen Sader since last summer." Neil's brows shot up at the silver, but he refrained from comment.

"That's it? That's all he had to say?"

"Pretty much."

Brett's eyes narrowed. "What aren't you telling me?"

"Kip Mullens's boys have already been here asking around."

"We've got to find them first, Neil."

"We will."

But they didn't. They tried wedding chapels, and when they had no luck, they tried the casinos and hotels. They didn't hit every place in town, but they must have come close. They prowled from the largest casino, which was the Bank Club, to the smallest, which was called simply Roy's. They visited the Cedars, Club Reno, Crystal Bay Club, the Country Club, the Dog House, the Fortune Club, the Golden Bank Club, the Golden Phoenix Hotel, the Grand Sierra Resort, the Great Provider, Lawton Springs, the Owl Club and finally the Ship and Bottle.

No one in all the town of Reno had seen Harry Sader.

The bartender at the Ship and Bottle said, "Harry Sader? He's a popular guy these days."

"Meaning?" Neil asked.

"Meaning a couple of birds was here earlier asking about him. And havin' the same luck."

Brett and Neil exchanged looks. "That's the good news," Neil told Brett on their way back out to the street. "They're not having any more luck than we are."

"I've had better news." If Brett never saw the inside of another casino, it would be too soon. His head ached from the smoke and flashing lights and noise. His feet ached from trudging miles of boardwalk.

"Sure, but you have to admit it's a relief to know your big sis isn't playing patty-cake with Kip Mullens's boys."

Brett nodded. The daylight was fading, and the neon lights were coming on all around them, offering keno and taxis and buffets.

"You said your family owned a house here?"

"A château near Lake Tahoe. It's called Chambord. My grandfather purchased two hundred acres of land up here in 1903 and built a small version of a famous French castle. I've never been there. To the French castle, I mean."

Neil nodded.

"No one has since my mother... Anyway, according to the terms of my mother's will, the place can't be sold. It can only be donated to the state as a park, and so it's remained in our family. There's a caretaker who lives on the premises. That's all I know."

"Will there be any problem with putting us up for the night?"

"I don't know why there would be. The place belongs to us. It's kept up out of my mother's estate."

"Mais oui." Neil unlocked the Buick. "Let's grab some grub and go find this French château of yours. We'll have another look for your sister first thing in the morning." At Brett's expression, he said, "If she's here, we'll find her."

Newly hopeful, Brett said, "Maybe Kitty did take Sader to Chambord. They could hole up there safely and no one the wiser."

"Maybe." Neil was noncommittal. "If they weren't fussy about getting married first."

Brett swallowed hard.

* * * * *

The lavender twilight had paled to shell pink over the silver blue lake when they reached the tall iron gates of Château Chambord. Tall trees of alder, aspen, cedar, and pine surrounded the estate. Beyond the lacey gates, they could see the graceful towers on either side of the mansard roof. The building was made of a soft cloud-colored stone, like the castle in a fairy tale.

A very old man in a cowboy hat and boots, accompanied by a young springer spaniel, came to the gate to greet them.

It took a fair bit of explaining before he would let them inside the grounds. Even after he understood who Brett was and what he wanted, he seemed reluctant to let them past the gate.

"Is my sister here?" Brett demanded at last.

That confused the old man even more. "We haven't seen any of you since…longer than I can remember. Not since her ladyship brought you here that last time. Never once."

"Has she called? Is she expected?"

"No." Russell, the caretaker, looked beyond Brett to Neil, who was watching the proceedings without comment.

"Then I don't understand the problem."

"No problem. No problem at all." Russell unlocked the gate and moved aside. As the car drew slowly through the gates, he called, "You'll find Dorothy up at the house."

"Who's Dorothy?" Brett muttered as they continued up the drive.

"The housekeeper?"

"It's an empty house. Why would there be a housekeeper?"

"Who pays the staff here?"

"It's complicated. It comes out of a special fund."

Neil grunted.

He turned out to be right. Dorothy was the housekeeper. She greeted them at the door, as flustered as Russell had been to find the family attempting to take residence. She showed them quickly around the château with its large timber ceilings and stone fireplaces.

"Do you live here?" Brett asked.

"No. No. I live down the road a piece." Dorothy looked uneasily from Brett to Neil. Clearly these people had been left on their own and unsupervised for too long. "Well, I'll get the beds made up and be on my way. The kitchen is completely stocked, if you're hungry."

She left them in the large downstairs living room.

"Is it my imagination or did she seem scared to death?" Brett took off his hat and absently smoothed his hair.

"Maybe not scared. Worried?" suggested Neil.

Brett shook his head. He went to the large bay of windows facing the lake. The blue water had turned red in the sunset. The tall trees cast attenuated black shadows across the green lawns.

"Back in the old days, my mother's family used to stay here for two months out of every summer. They'd have a full staff. Chauffeurs, maids, cooks, laundry workers. Even a boatman."

"Are they all gone on your mother's side?"

"She was the last. Sometimes I think it would be..." Brett stopped.

Neil eyed him curiously.

"Oh well. Things are what they are."

Neil said, "Sometimes they're what you make of them."

It was too hard to look him in the eyes. "I should see if there's a telephone."

"I'll see if I can get a fire started," Neil said easily. "I think we're in for rain tonight."

To Brett's surprise, there was a telephone, one of the new round-base rotary dial monophones that had only become available the previous year. He was still puzzling over that when his call finally went through the seemingly endless relay of operators and exchanges until at last Hardwin, the Lennoxes' butler, was speaking. After that it was only a minute or so before Juliet herself came on the line.

"*Sherry*? Sherry is that you, darling? Where on earth *are* you?"

"I'm in Lake Tahoe, darling." He was conscious of his voice carrying down the short hall to the room where Neil was.

"What are you doing in Lake Tahoe, for goodness sake?"

"Kitty…eloped last night."

"She *didn't*! Not with That Man?" Juliet sounded deliciously horrified.

"She did. Anyway, the reason I called is I wanted to sp—"

"Did you catch them? Were you able to stop her?"

"No. Look, Julie, may I speak to your father?"

"Daddy?"

"That's the one. Big chap. Eyes like a blue ribbon hog at the State Fair."

Juliet gurgled a laugh. "Sherry. You're very *bad*. Daddy's not here."

"Where is he? I need to talk to him."

"I don't know where he is."

"Listen, Julie darling, this is very important. I want him to postpone going to the police about the theft. If you could—"

"Oh, but he already went to the police."

The floor seemed to shift beneath Brett's feet. *"What?"*

"Daddy went to the police yesterday."

"But he said he wouldn't. He said he would give the thief three days. It's not the end of the third day yet."

"But it has been three days. Four days, really. As good as."

"But he can't count Saturday. And anyway, it's only six o'clock. He should have at least waited until midnight."

"Darling, what *are* you talking about? It's been four days. Anyway, it's not as though he stipulated an exact time."

"But the theft occurred after midnight, so—"

Juliet's faraway voice said patiently, "Yes, but yesterday morning, he said he'd given the thief long enough and why should he give him any more time to escape with the jewel of his crown. Meaning the folio."

"Yesterday morning? So he *didn't* wait three days!"

"He changed his mind. Daddy does that."

For a few vital seconds, Brett couldn't seem to think past this calamity. "He's already spoken to them? It's already done?"

"Yes, silly. I keep telling you. Darling, what *were* you up to that you forgot what day it was? We've had the police here and everything. They found the glass cutter in the hydrangeas."

There was a rush-bottomed chair next to the table with the phone. Brett sat down on the chair. Juliet was still buzzing away in his ear like a cheerful mosquito.

He said finally, foolishly, "But he gave his word."

"It wasn't his *word*," Juliet objected. "He just said that was what he was going to do. Anyway, Daddy said that he'd only delayed because of how snooty your family is about scandal, but then you'd gone and brought in a private detective, so it was all beside the point. Which is true."

Brett opened his mouth to argue this, but what was the use? It was done. The bastard had gone to the police after all. Of course, it was what he should have done in the beginning, but having waited so long, would it have killed him to give Brett a few more hours?

Not that a few more hours would have made a difference. Brett considered this fact dully. The truth was, he had wasted three—no, four—days and spent one hell of a lot of money for absolutely nothing. Worse than nothing, because on top of everything else, these past days had awoken feelings he'd believed were safely buried. Or at least controlled.

"Sherry, are you there?" Juliet was repeating plaintively.

"I'm sorry. What did you say?"

"When are you coming home?"

"I… Tomorrow, I suppose."

"Oh that's good. We're supposed to go to the theater, remember?"

It seemed like another lifetime ago. "Yes," he replied politely. "If I'm home in time."

"You have to be," she said simply. "I'll see you then, shall I?"

"Yes."

"I love you. Oh! And give my love to Kitty."

He opened his mouth, but she was gone. The line began to click and buzz. He replaced the handset in its cradle. It occurred to him that more than anything he wanted to talk to Neil—and that was the worst news of all.

Chapter Eleven

"What's the matter?" Rafferty rose as Brett returned white-faced to the living room and sank down on the sofa.

He was thinking death or, at the very least, several broken bones, so it was a great relief when Brett said, "Lennox went to the police."

Rafferty just managed to bite back, *Is that all?* Clearly it was no small matter to Brett, who was sitting there like a marble effigy in search of a tomb. He said neutrally, "Well, it *has* been four days."

"It *hasn't* been four days," Brett snapped. "It won't be four days until after midnight. And anyway, he went to the police around lunchtime yesterday, so he didn't even give it three days."

"Ah."

He managed not to let even a quiver of a laugh into his voice, but Brett still glared at him as though it were somehow Rafferty's fault. Maybe he felt it *was* Rafferty's fault. After all, Rafferty had promised to find the folio and break off the sister's romance with a ne'er-do-well, and so far he was batting zero. And the reason for that spectacular failure was at this very instant gazing at him with wide, stricken eyes. It was no use pretending that he didn't find Brett Sheridan a distraction.

Even coming along on this wild-goose chase—there had been no excuse for that. It had made no sense whatsoever that Sader would bring the folio to Reno. Rafferty should have stayed in San Francisco and kept hunting for the book, but he hadn't wanted Brett to confront Sader on his own.

In the end, Brett hadn't had to confront Sader at all, because Sader wasn't in Reno. And neither was the erring sister.

Nice going, Rafferty.

"All right, so he's gone to the police. That was bound to happen sooner or later. You know that as well as I do."

Brett's eyes narrowed in that way he had, reminding Rafferty of a bad-tempered mink.

"We haven't had luck connecting Sader to the theft, so the police aren't going to waltz in and slap the bracelets on him either. I'm sorry we weren't able to wrap this up before Lennox went to the cops, but the case isn't closed. Not by a long shot."

Astonishingly, Brett said, "I'm not blaming *you*."

Rafferty felt his face redden. "Maybe not. Maybe I'm blaming myself."

Brett shook his head. "Don't. You're right. Three days wasn't enough time."

It should have been. That was the thing. It wasn't a complicated case. The crime itself was about as unsophisticated as it got. Maybe that was the problem. Rafferty kept looking for subtlety where there was none. He kept rejecting the obvious solution as too easy, but maybe it *was* that easy. Maybe the solution was hiding right there in plain sight.

"The fact is, if we do find out that your sister is involved, it's possible you can convince Lennox to hush it up. He wants this marriage."

Brett looked away. Then he faced Rafferty with an odd smile. "The old man hates me."

Rafferty was taken aback, and it must have showed. Brett chuckled. "I'm the means to an end, that's all. And once that end is served, he'd like nothing better than for me to break my neck on the polo field so his little angel can marry some red-blooded gorilla like himself."

It was tempting to follow that line of discussion, but Rafferty resisted. "So have his little angel ask for clemency—assuming Katherine's involved. We haven't found proof of that yet."

Brett sighed and rubbed his face. It had been a long, long day. They were both dead tired.

Rafferty said slowly, "Or..."

"Or what?" Brett lowered his hand, watching Rafferty alertly.

"If we do find a connection between your sister and the theft, it's possible we can...cover it up."

A log shifted in the fireplace.

"You would do that?" Brett spoke without inflection.

"Yes."

"Why?"

Because there's nothing I won't do for you. The thought came unbidden, a paralyzing revelation. When had it happened? *How* had it happened? It terrified him. Irish or not, he had never gone in for lost causes. There was no cause more lost than this one.

"Why?" Brett repeated, watching intently.

Rafferty shrugged. "She's a good girl from a good family. Anyway, it's what you hired me for, right? To get her out of it, if she's in it."

"Yes."

"Well, then?" Rafferty shrugged.

Something changed in Brett's face. He reached out, brushing fingertips across the scar on Rafferty's cheekbone. Rafferty realized that he was kneeling in front of him, in front of the sofa. He didn't recall getting on his knees like a Victorian suitor—or a penitent—but there he was, kneeling close enough to lean in for a kiss.

"How'd you get this?"

Rafferty's skin tingled beneath that feather-light touch. "Disagreement over a bar tab."

"Who won?"

"The guy with the broken whisky bottle."

Brett's mouth quirked in commiseration. "Sorry."

"Not at all. I was the guy with the broken whisky bottle."

Brett laughed and sat back into the cushions, his hand falling away.

After a second or two, Rafferty rose and went to tend the fire in the grate. His skin still carried the feel of Brett's fingertips.

"The police found the glass cutter in the hydrangeas," Brett said at a seeming tangent.

"Did they?"

"Yes. There's a problem with that, though."

Rafferty glanced around. "What's that?"

"After the theft was discovered, some of us searched the grounds. There was no glass cutter in the hydrangeas. I searched them myself."

"You know what you need?" Rafferty asked.

Brett raised his head. He had been staring moodily up at the dark beams. He raised his brows in inquiry.

"A stiff drink and a hot meal."

"At this point, I'll take a hot meal and a drunk stiff."

Rafferty laughed. "Come on. I'll feed you."

"And he can cook too," Brett marveled, following him into the kitchen.

The windows were dark, and far away, the blue-black distance was split by the occasional fork of lightning. A summer storm was rolling in. They were common in this area.

Rafferty opened the refrigerator—all the modern conveniences in Château Chambord—and studied the contents. "How about an omelet?"

"All this food," Brett said uneasily, looking over Rafferty's shoulder at the well-stocked icebox. "Why so much food?"

Rafferty chose not to answer that. He gathered eggs, butter, and cream. "Check the larder for onions, will you? And potatoes, if they have them."

Brett nodded like a man accepting a dangerous mission. He was back in a short time with potatoes, onions, and parsley.

"There's an herb garden out back." He watched Rafferty assemble his ingredients. "Where did you learn to cook?"

"This isn't cooking." Rafferty was amused. "No, you've got to scrub those vegetables first."

Brett looked doubtfully at the pile of produce before him.

Rafferty shook his head. "I take it you've never peeled a potato in your life?"

"Er, no. But how hard can it be?"

"How about this? You handle the cocktails, and I'll take care of the meal."

"Done." Brett vanished but returned a short time later with a cocktail shaker and glasses.

Rafferty sipped his martini and added the onions and diced potatoes to the butter sizzling in the pan. He glanced at Brett, who had fallen silent.

"Something wrong?"

Brett looked at him as though he'd forgotten he wasn't alone. "What?"

"Something the matter? You look like you swallowed a squirrel."

Brett recollected himself and poured his own martini. "I'm just thinking. Look at this place."

Rafferty had looked plenty already. He said mildly, "Someone forget to dust the whatnots?"

"No, that's just it. Everything is in readiness. There are no dustsheets. There is no dust."

Rafferty began to see.

"Maybe your sister called ahead and had them prepare the place."

"It didn't seem like it."

"No. The caretaker was expecting someone, but it wasn't you, and it isn't your sister."

"Then who?"

Rafferty wasn't about to touch that. The only reason Brett hadn't figured it out already was because he didn't want to know. Presumably he was tougher than he'd been in college, but Rafferty wasn't forgetting that mysterious crack-up nobody had been willing to talk about.

Brett didn't wait for an answer. "So what's our next move? Do we head back to Reno and start all over again tomorrow?"

"It's your dime."

"What if they did go to Las Vegas?"

"Nah. I think you were right about that. I don't see your sister volunteering any information that would help anyone looking for them. The problem is, just because they didn't head for Vegas doesn't necessarily mean they came here."

"But it makes perfect sense. If they're going to be married…" Brett's voice trailed and died.

Rafferty could read his thoughts as though they were posted in neon lights. The biggest little worry in the world.

"Listen, don't borrow trouble. You've got no reason to think she lied about that. No reason to think she wouldn't insist on marriage. For that matter, as I keep pointing out, we don't know that she had anything to do with the theft of the folio. We don't know that Sader had anything to do with the theft of the folio."

"If they didn't come to Reno, why were those goons headed this way?"

"I think they started out following us, believing we would lead them to Sader, but once they figured out where we were headed, they didn't need us anymore. In fact, it was to their advantage to have us out of the way."

"Sure. Or maybe it was sheer coincidence that we got in the way of them speeding to spend their paychecks at the casinos."

Rafferty laughed.

Brett sipped his martini. He asked offhandedly, "Did you ever think of taking on a partner?"

"Nah. Unless you count Linda."

"Linda? The little blonde girl who answers your phone?"

"That's the one. Anyway, we're not usually so busy that there's work for another operative."

"You could be busier, though. Pat said you're choosy about the cases you take."

"I'm in a business where being choosy can keep you out of jail—not to mention alive." Rafferty covered the frying pan. "We'll let those cook about ten minutes, till the potatoes are tender and brown underneath."

"What if you had someone sending jobs your way?"

"Like a referral agent?"

"Right."

It wasn't easy, but Rafferty made himself say it. "I like things the way they are."

Brett's face closed. He said instantly, "Of course."

Rafferty cracked the five eggs into a small mixing bowl, beat them lightly with a fork, added the cream, salt, and pepper. "When is this wedding of yours?"

"Two weeks from Saturday."

"I guess you'll be going on one of those long continental honeymoons?"

"Not so long as that." Brett's laugh was humorless. "I can't afford anything too extravagant."

"Paris? Some place like that?"

"You seem very interested in my honeymoon plans." There was an edge to Brett's voice.

Rafferty poured the egg mixture over the browned potatoes and covered the pan. He reached for his cocktail, aware of Brett's cool gaze.

"All right," Brett said drily. "I'm getting married, and you don't need a partner. No need to get in an uproar. I get the message." He topped his cocktail glass again.

"It's just easier. For both of us."

"Sure. I said I got the message." Brett moved away to the table and sat, stretching his long legs out. "Now I know why they call you guys flatfoots. If you weren't before this job, you would be after."

His tone was easy and natural. Rafferty liked him all the better for it. And he liked Brett plenty already.

He checked the pan and found that the egg was starting to solidify on the bottom. He used the spatula to push the outsides of the omelet toward the inside, lifting up a corner and tipping the pan slightly to the lifted corner. When the edges were starting to crisp, he lifted the edge of the omelet to make sure the egg wasn't sticking, then picked up the pan's handle and, in one quick movement, tossed the omelet so it flipped over and landed facedown in the pan.

Brett laughed. "Now you're showing off."

He was, of course. "Are you impressed?"

Brett looked up, and just for an instant, his face was soft and unguarded. "From the minute I saw you."

CHAPTER TWELVE

$\mathcal{B}$rett watched the shadow of pine trees sway against the ceiling, ebony

needles painting moonlight across the knotty walls and plank floors.

He had closed the window as the temperature dropped. He could still hear the night sounds through the glass. The mournful sough of the wind, the faraway yip-yip-yipping of coyotes, the scratching of branches against the side of the house.

It was another sound he listened for, though.

But perhaps he was wrong. Perhaps Neil wouldn't come.

Why should he, after all? It wasn't as though Brett could offer him anything.

But he wanted Neil all the same. Wanted him tonight more than he could remember wanting almost anything in his life. In fact, tonight it seemed as though all his life had been spent leading to this moment. Leading to moonlight and shadow and waiting for the door to open.

Waiting for Neil.

The night ticked by on the brass alarm clock next to the bed.

He didn't hear the door open, but he felt the breeze of its closing, and then a tiger-striped shadow passed before the window. Brett pushed up on one elbow. He pulled back the blankets in welcome.

The bed dipped, and Neil slid in beside him. They reached for each other. Neil wore only boxer shorts, but his skin was warm and his arms were strong and already familiar as they wrapped around Brett.

"I was afraid you weren't coming."

By way of answer, Neil pushed his fingers into the hair at Brett's nape, drew him close, and kissed him until neither could breathe.

Brett moaned and opened to the hot, erotic push of Neil's tongue. He reached out blindly, hand clenching on Neil's hard thigh while Neil deftly, swiftly unfastened the buttons of his pajama top. Laying the shirt open, he stroked Brett's bare chest, thumbs brushing nipples that contracted painfully tight to the touch.

"Wait!" Brett gasped. "If you do that—"

"So what?" Neil whispered back. There was a smile in his voice, and there was gentleness too. "We've got all night. I remember how it was when I was your age."

That easy, amused acceptance was nearly his undoing. Brett arched up, bit back the pleasured noises threatening to tear out of him, and Neil gathered him closer still, half laughing, half warning. He stroked Brett's hair back and then drew him close for another kiss.

There was a rumble of thunder in the blue-black distance. Brett tried to concentrate on it, tried to think about anything besides the wonderful things Neil's hands and mouth were doing to him. It felt so good. There wasn't a word for how good this felt. But it frightened him to have so little control.

"Slow down," he pleaded.

And wonder of wonders, Neil did. His touch changed, and the almost unbearable stimulation eased up, gave Brett a chance to catch his breath, to experience something beyond going up like a rocket.

Neil went back to kissing him, and Brett's eyes stung with relief. He hated being so out of control, so helpless. It was embarrassing on top of everything else—though even that was different with Neil. Different because Neil seemed to take it in stride, treat it as something endearing as opposed to the failure it was.

But this was failure, wasn't it? This predicament of his—his inability to satisfy a woman, to feel anything at all unless a man was doing it to him.

"Where've you gone?" Neil asked softly. He was stroking Brett's softening cock.

"Sorry."

"*Sorry?* What are you sorry about?"

"I'm such a…"

"You're such a what?" There it was again, that unexpected and somehow terrifying gentleness. So much better, so much easier, if Neil had simply been the hard-boiled tough he'd seemed at first glance, because *this*… He could see himself starting to need this, to trust it, to depend on it.

"I can't do it, Neil." He half sat up.

"No?" Neil was still fondling him, still amused and tolerant, and even as Brett was making his excuses, his willful body was responding again to that experienced handling.

"I'm getting married in a couple of weeks." He sounded anything but confident—clutching at the recollection of his engagement like a life preserver bobbing on a high sea.

"I know."

Yes, Neil knew. Neil was the one who kept reminding him of that wormwood truth. Yet here Neil was with his hand wrapped around Brett's cock, his breath warm on Brett's groin. "I can't…give you anything."

"Have I asked you for anything? What is it you think I want?" Neil sounded a little cooler now, and though he was still stroking and petting, the gentleness had gone. Now he was handling Brett's penis and balls with deliberate and knowing expertise. He was bringing Brett to climax in a couple of swift, sure strokes. "I know what *you* want."

Brett whimpered—and came. That hot, sticky gush splashing over his own belly—and Neil. It was a relief, but it was humiliating too.

"Sorry," Neil said after a bit—and he did sound genuinely sorry. "That wasn't fair." He stroked Brett's thigh in apology.

Brett shook his head, putting his arm across his face. But his body was already recovering, already hoping for more. What did that say about him?

Neil said with an earnestness that surprised even him, "Brett, you're going to wind up in a loony bin if you keep pushing yourself to be something you're not."

The unfairness of it roused him to protest. "I can't be *this*."

"You *are* this."

Brett shook his head.

Neil swore and sat up. "Take a look at yourself and tell me you're not just like me."

Brett didn't have to take a look at himself. He already knew the worst, sprawled in his sheets, mouth swollen with Neil's kisses, legs splayed, his cock standing up erect like a flagpole, already hopeful that there would be more. Much more.

"I'm *not* like you." Not that he didn't share Neil's appetites, but he didn't have Neil's courage, Neil's ability to punch the world in the mouth and go his own way.

But, oh, how he wished he was.

"People are depending on me." Sometimes it seemed to Brett like the whole fucking world was depending on him. Leaning on a reed.

Maybe Neil caught some of the angry desperation beneath the rejection. His eyes glinted, seeming to see Brett even in the dark, and that electricity was still alive and crackling between them—or maybe it was the storm moving in from over the mountains—but they were drawn together again.

"Sweetheart," Neil murmured, moving closer. He kissed Brett's naked shoulder, his collarbone, his throat, his cheek, parted Brett's lips with his own warm mouth. Pushed his tongue inside. Brett closed his eyes, his tongue tangling with Neil's, that terrifying excitement churning within him.

He sighed in pleasure as Neil's mouth broke away to kiss his nipples, his chest, his belly, and he began to moan softly. And when Neil's tongue lapped delicately at the base of his cock and then moved still lower, deeper, Brett experienced a tremulous, peculiar thrilling unlike anything he'd ever known.

"Please…please…" Perhaps at some point he would be ashamed to remember his hoarse, frantic voice begging for more, but not tonight.

For a few seconds before the world splintered apart in the wake of the wildest magic of all, he wondered what it would be like to be together, to lie down together at night and wake in each other's arms. Was there anywhere in the world that safe? Anywhere people minded their own business and let a man live his life in peace and privacy?

Nowhere that he knew of.

*H*e woke to the dazzling sunshine of a mountain morning after a storm.

Neil was snoring softly against his shoulder, one leg thrown possessively over Brett's.

He could hear the faint buzz of music beneath the floorboards, a radio playing and a woman singing quietly along. A contented sound.

He eased away from Neil, grimly amused at Neil's delusion that he could wake at will. Or maybe Neil didn't recognize the danger in this house, believing them to be entirely alone.

Brett found his robe and shrugged into it, looking out the window. Someone was fishing down by the dock near the boathouse.

Too hard to be sure at this distance, but he didn't think it was the old caretaker. But if it wasn't Russell, who was it?

He glanced back at the bed. Neil continued to sleep. He had rolled onto his side and had one arm looped over a pillow. It was tempting to climb back in there with him, but Brett didn't want to take a chance on frightening Dorothy.

He tied the tasseled belt around his waist and left the room, shutting the door soundlessly behind him.

As he went down the main staircase, the delicious aroma of frying fish reached him, and his stomach turned hungrily. Last night's omelet had been tasty but not really substantial. Dorothy's voice, backed by the radio, grew louder as he approached the kitchen. Her low, clear tones sent a peculiar prickling over his scalp. There was something familiar there, something beyond the words of a popular song…

> *Each little moment*
> *Is clear before me*
> *And though it brings me regret*
> *It's easy to remember*
> *But so hard to forget.*

He walked through the door into the kitchen.

A tall, lean woman stood by the stove panfrying fish. Not Dorothy. He saw that at once. She was too tall, too thin, too young. She wore khaki trousers and a flannel shirt, and her dark hair was pulled back in a ponytail, careless as a young girl. But she was not a girl.

She turned, and eyes the same green shade as his own widened as they met his gaze. Her face was the mirror image of Kitty's—only years from now, matured and slightly softened. The feminine version of his own.

Brett's mouth opened, but no words came to him. No nothing. If the words had been there, they would have been a protest.

"Good morning, Brett," his dead mother said.

*A*n annoying breeze wafted against his face. Brett's nose twitched. He fought the desire to sneeze.

Beneath his ear echoed a steady, fast *thump...thump...thump*. Hard arms held him in a grip that was as much comfort as support.

"You couldn't think of a better way to break it to him?" He knew that voice, though this was the first time he'd heard Neil Patrick Rafferty really angry.

"I didn't realize it would be such a shock," a second voice protested. A woman's voice. A voice that, despite time and lack of continuity, was still so appallingly familiar his eyes stung. "I had no idea he still thought—"

"Never mind all that. Get some brandy," Neil snapped.

The annoying breeze dissipated along with rapidly disappearing footsteps.

"Sweetheart," Neil murmured. He had called Brett that last night too, but now he sounded so genuinely worried that Brett knew he couldn't hide any longer.

He lifted his lashes and was surprised by an expression on Neil's face that he knew Neil would not want him to see. He closed his eyes again, giving Neil time to rearrange his features into the usual rock formation.

Neil said in ordinary tones, "Jesus, Sheridan. You scared the hell out of me."

Brett opened his eyes. "I thought she was dead." He made an effort and managed to sit up. His head swam and then cleared.

Had he really fainted? This truly was beyond embarrassing—and he'd already had a few moments with Neil he'd have as soon forgotten. He was never going to live this down.

Not that Neil was likely to tease him. He still gripped Brett's shoulder and arm as though he thought Brett might swoon away again. He didn't have to worry. It had been a shock, no denying that, but Brett was recovering fast.

In fact, as he put the puzzle pieces together—including the sky-colored giveaway lack of any surprise on Neil's part—he was getting angry.

He pulled away. "You already knew, didn't you?" Narrow-eyed, he watched Neil. Watched Neil, for the first time in their entire acquaintanceship, try to avoid his gaze.

Neil didn't have a chance to answer—not that he needed to. *She* was back.

Arabella Sheridan. No. Not Sheridan. But his mother, all the same.

She knelt, handing him a snifter of honey-colored liquid. Brett took the glass, tossing the brandy back in one gulp. He pushed to his feet, ignoring the helping hand Neil provided.

The brandy helped. He staggered over to the kitchen table and dropped down in one of the hard-backed chairs, glaring at both of them.

Arabella rose, unreasonably and annoyingly poised. "I'm sorry, Brett. I didn't realize your father had persisted with that stupid piece of fiction all these years."

He was going to have to deal with it, of course, but oddly enough, it was the other betrayal that hurt more.

He looked at Neil, and Neil, understanding him perfectly, said, "It wasn't my place to tell you."

"Really? What the hell am I paying you for?"

"To find a missing folio."

"I see. My mistake. I imagined the terms of our agreement had… altered."

He had the satisfaction of seeing that hit home, but it was small satisfaction given the circumstances. Warning flared in Neil's eyes, but it was unnecessary. Brett had said all he was going to. It wasn't as though *he* ever forgot how careful he had to be. He was grateful now that he hadn't made the mistake of trusting Neil any further than he had.

Which was, admittedly, way too far.

He turned to his mother.

"Why did you let us think you were dead all this time?"

Her long, slender throat moved. "That was your father's wish." His silence forced her to further explanation. "It seemed only fair. The scandal was…harrowing as it was. Your father always had a horror of scandal." She added drily, "At least in those days."

But she was above and beyond scandal? It angered him further. "And that was all right with you? To let your children believe you had *died*?"

"Of course it wasn't all right! But what choice did I have? It wasn't as though I would ever be allowed to see you. Your father made that clear from the start. It seemed kinder to close that door."

"Kinder to whom? You?"

"Perhaps." Her expression was rueful. "Oh Brett, I know you're angry and shocked. I was forced to make a choice that no one should have to make."

Angry and shocked, yes. Certainly…bewildered. He couldn't shake the conviction that he was dreaming. It was just…impossible that he should be sitting in this kitchen, speaking with his mother.

Anything he said now would be a mistake. He couldn't begin to sort out his feelings. More than anything, he wanted to escape this…whatever it was. Reunion? Revelation? He wasn't ready or equipped to deal with it.

He stood, relieved that his equilibrium was back to normal, that he was perfectly steady. Physically steady, at least. He said, "It's no… There's no point to this. I'm never going to understand what you did."

"If you would just give me a chance—"

He shook his head, risking a look at Neil. "We need to be on our way."

Neil's eyes were dark with things unsaid, but they would have to stay unsaid. Brett didn't want to hear it from him either.

"Brett." Arabella reached for his arm. He stood motionless. "Your father was supposed to tell you the truth when you came of age. That was part of our agreement."

"I can't blame him for not wanting to rip old wounds open." His own capacity for cruelty surprised him as he added, "It's not as though it makes any difference now."

She blinked but took it on the chin.

"Are you coming?" Brett asked Neil. He didn't have to say the rest of it aloud—that he was leaving with or without him.

Neil rose too. He nodded.

CHAPTER THIRTEEN

*H*e was in love with Brett Sheridan.

That was the bad news. There was no good news.

Rafferty wasn't sure, but he suspected he might have started falling for Brett that very first morning when he'd sat there, hollow-eyed and white as a ghost, calmly relating the insane notion that his sister had stolen a priceless antique during his engagement party. Any doubts he'd had had been resolved when he walked into the kitchen to see Brett lying like a corpse next to the kitchen table while his disgraced mama fanned him frantically with yesterday's paper.

Now he watched Brett shoving things—and who brought yellow silk pajamas on a safari like this?—into his Gladstone. Brett looked around for something else he could cram into the bag.

Rafferty said, "Do I get to say something, or are you never going to understand what I did either?"

"Nothing to explain." Brett spotted his toiletry kit and dumped that into the holdall too. "You're right. You were paid to do a job. No reason for you to involve yourself in my family's messy affairs." He directed a look—no doubt intended to be cool but, in fact, blazing—at Rafferty.

Rafferty reached behind and slammed shut the bedroom door.

Brett squared his shoulders, watching him warily.

Rafferty said, "I didn't tell you because you were already under a strain—and your sister's elopement didn't help. If it had seemed important or relevant, maybe I'd have said something. I'm not sure. If I'd realized her ladyship was showing up here any time soon, I'd have certainly said something before letting you walk in on her."

Brett frowned at the emphasized ladyship. That had gone right over his head at the time, but Rafferty could see him making the connection now. "You didn't say anything because, as you point out, that's not what I hired you for. You didn't say anything because it's messy and complicated, and you don't like messy, complicated things. You didn't say anything because you didn't want the responsibility of breaking it to me and having to deal with the consequences."

That was all perfectly true—as far as it went. Rafferty wanted… needed Brett to understand the rest of it.

He opened his mouth, but Brett said, "Save it. The only thing I care about now is finding Kitty and that goddamned folio."

If there had been one chink in his armor, Rafferty would have persisted, but there wasn't. Brett was calm, even cold, and all business. And just because Rafferty's feelings had changed didn't mean a damn thing had changed for Brett. In fact, he'd gone out of his way the night before to remind Rafferty that nothing *had* changed. So no point in making heavy weather of it.

"Right. Then what do you want to do next?"

Brett buckled his Gladstone. "We may as well head back to San Francisco."

It was the last thing Rafferty expected. "You're kidding."

Brett shook his head.

"You want to give up?"

"It doesn't matter what I want. We're not going to find them. We may as well head home."

"We've barely started looking for them."

"We're wasting our time."

Rafferty said slowly, "You're running away."

That got to him. "The hell I am!" Brett's face flushed. "There's no point hanging around here."

"Maybe there is."

Brett's face was disbelieving, but the nebulous idea in the back of Rafferty's mind took form.

"Hear me out."

"Go on."

"If your sister and her beau did take that folio, they've got to unload it somewhere, right?"

Brett's nod was terse.

"Your… Lennox said they'd need to try to sell it to another collector."

"So? We're not going to find another collector in Reno."

"That's where you're wrong. Well, maybe not in Reno, but in Tahoe."

"What are you talking about?"

"That English lord your mother ran off with. What was his name?"

Brett stared. Rafferty could see him thinking rapidly. "Horn," he said at last.

"Lord Horn."

Brett nodded.

"Does that mean anything to you?"

"No."

"Who did Lennox say might be willing and able to purchase that folio?"

Brett scowled. He said slowly, "Lord Horn."

"Bingo." He could see Brett was struck by the coincidence too. "Maybe your sister knew something you didn't. Maybe one of the reasons she headed for Reno and not Las Vegas was because she knew your mother and her husband were returning to the States for a visit. Maybe one reason your mother and her husband are visiting the States is because the folio Lord Horn would give his eyeteeth for is available again?"

Brett let go of the Gladstone. It dropped to the floor with a little *thud*. He sat on the bed. "Is that what you think is going on?"

"It's a possibility. It didn't occur to me until a little while ago, but it is a possibility."

Brett said nothing.

"It wouldn't hurt to ask, right?"

Brett snorted. "You think we'd get an honest answer out of any of them?"

"I think," Rafferty said carefully, "your mother will tell you anything you want to know. Your…opinion carries considerable stock with her right now."

"You want me to use that?"

Brett was staring at him with something close to dislike. Rafferty bore up under it. "That's up to you. Last night you were hinting around at having an interest in my game. Well, my game is about finding out the truth; however you have to go about it."

"And that means using people?"

"I've done a hell of a lot worse things than, as you quaintly put it, *use* people."

Brett said nothing.

"Suit yourself," Rafferty told him. He opened the bedroom door.

"Wait a minute."

Rafferty waited.

"All right. I'll ask her. I doubt if she'll tell me the truth, but why not? Maybe Kitty and Sader are planning to show up here today." He unbuckled his bag, pointedly turning his shoulder on Rafferty.

Okay. He was mad, and he'd gotten his feelings hurt. Well, that made two of them. The one thing Rafferty could do for him was get this mess with the folio sorted out, and that was what he planned on doing.

"I'll see you downstairs."

Brett nodded curtly.

Rafferty went to his own barely used room and treated himself to a shower in his private bathroom. The shower tiles featured art deco pink wisteria winding up a blue-green trellis, and in the distance was a green knoll with a small château. The shower and sink fixtures were all gold plated.

Must be nice, he thought grimly, scraping the whiskers and shaving soap from his jaw and staring at his hard-eyed reflection in the steamy mirror. No wonder Brett couldn't contemplate—

No.

To put that thought into words was to acknowledge a wish—a hope—that he refused to recognize.

He wiped his face, changed into his fresh shirt, and went downstairs again.

Lady Horn, formerly Arabella Sheridan, was sitting at the table, talking quietly to a tall, lean, sun-browned man in his early sixties. The man was dressed in well-worn corduroys, a battered hunting jacket, and a green felt hat, but he was no hobo, even if he dressed like one.

Arabella looked up and hastily rose. That quick nervous grace reminded Rafferty of Brett.

"Mr....Rafferty was it? How is...my..." Her voice faltered, and unexpectedly, he felt sorry for her. Hell, if he'd been married to Linus Sheridan and his Etruscan doodads, he'd probably have run off with the first bloke in a green felt hat who asked too.

"He's okay. You threw him a little, popping up like this. He had you neatly dead and buried."

Lord Horn was standing too, and Arabella made quick, almost absent, introductions, clearly wanting only to hear about Brett. Her gaze was fastened on Rafferty with painful intensity.

"Good to meet you," Horn said briskly. It was hard to picture anyone less like Linus Sheridan than Lord Horn, but that was probably the idea.

He wasn't handsome, strictly speaking, but he had a general oddball attractiveness.

"I had no idea Brett still thought…" She managed a smile. "All these years, I imagined he simply didn't want to have anything to do with me."

Well, he *didn't*, but it wouldn't be useful to say so. Rafferty made a noncommittal noise.

"Do my other children also believe I'm dead?"

Maybe it was going to be easier than Rafferty had thought. "I thought your daughter Katherine was in contact with you."

Arabella and Horn exchanged surprised looks. "Why would you think that?"

Rafferty was saved having to explain by the arrival of Brett. He had washed and shaved and looked unreasonably well groomed given that he didn't have any more of a change of wardrobe than Rafferty.

"Brett." Arabella's tone was almost right, the emphasis almost as casual as she must hope. The problem was she didn't seem to know what to say next.

Rescue came from Horn. "Delighted you've decided to look us up at last," he said, moving to shake hands. "Couldn't be a better welcome-home present."

Arabella picked up her cue. "Why don't we have breakfast in the dining room? Cecil and I usually don't bother most of the time when we're here, but this is a special occasion."

Rafferty looked at Brett, but Brett didn't meet his gaze. He had closed off the easy natural line of communication between them that Rafferty had come to take for granted.

Horn was still nattering—as he put it—filling up the threatening silences with explanations no one was requiring. They heard how he had been fishing since early that morning, with considerable success, and that he and Arabella had arrived very late during the night.

Their arrival had been neatly covered by the thunderstorm—or perhaps the fact that Brett and Rafferty had been otherwise occupied. Either way, they'd all had a narrow escape.

"Just before dusk is the best time for brown trout. You find them in the shallow areas along piers and rocky bottoms. But there are plenty of golden trout at this end of the lake. Do you fish?" Horn took off his coat and hat, looking from Rafferty to Brett.

"It's been a few years," Rafferty answered. He was trying to eavesdrop on Arabella's conversation with Brett. Not that it was much of a conversation. If Brett had said three sentences, Rafferty hadn't managed to overhear them.

Arabella was running on. "Of course we heard from Russell that you had arrived earlier. You've no idea how difficult it was not to barge right in and wake you up. You can thank Cecil for an undisturbed night's rest."

Rafferty could see Brett struggling with that one. Safe to say, Emily Post didn't cover these contingencies.

He and Lord Horn were sent to set the table in the dining room, so Brett was going to have to do without whatever moral support Rafferty's presence offered—probably minimal.

"One thing I am curious about, old boy," Horn remarked as he handed over fistfuls of hallmarked silver for Rafferty to set the table with. "And don't think we're not overjoyed to have you, but why did you choose *now* to pay us a call? Isn't Brett marrying some heiress or another in a week or two?"

"As a matter of fact, we were looking for Brett's sister. She eloped Sunday night, and Brett thought she might have come here."

"Little Sophie eloped? By gad, but she's only a child, isn't she?"

How time flew when you were estranged from your family. "Not exactly. But I meant the other girl. Katherine."

"Katherine? Engaged to her childhood sweetheart, isn't that so? Not such a crime if they decided to dispense with the big church wedding, eh?" Horn's gray eyes studied Rafferty.

"That's off. The childhood sweetheart broke his neck a few months ago playing polo, and Kitty took up with a small-time crook by the name of Harry Sader."

"Ah…" Horn thought this over. "A Reno wedding. Is that the idea? And you think they'd come here?"

Rafferty shrugged. "It struck us as a possibility."

Horn was now laying out porcelain plates with the speed of an ambitious footman. One thing for sure, he didn't seem like any member of the British nobility that Rafferty had ever seen—not even the ones in the movies.

"It seemed like a possibility. Especially because—"

"Cecil! What do you think?" Arabella rushed into the room, Brett behind her. Brett's harassed gaze found Rafferty's, but Rafferty was unsure of the message there. Help? Fire? Murder?

"What is it, my heart?"

"The *Tempest* folio is on the market again."

"Good gad!" Lord Horn's pleasant gray eyes seemed to ignite with unholy light. "Are you sure?"

"Brett has just informed me it was stolen from Lennox."

Horn exclaimed with unsportsmanlike joy, "By Jove! Can it be true?" He looked from Rafferty to Brett.

"It's true," Rafferty admitted. "In fact, we thought the, er, thieves might have contacted you."

"Contacted *us*?" Clearly Horn was not offended so much as delighted at the idea. "Do you really think so?"

"They think Kitty and her newly wedded husband stole the folio and might bring it to us," Arabella explained.

"But that would make the most sense," Horn said eagerly. "That *is* the obvious solution."

Brett was shaking his head. "Except Kitty doesn't know you're alive," he said to his mother.

"Oh, but she might," protested Horn. "After all, you didn't know Arabella was alive until last night. She might have discovered the truth."

"She'd have told me." To Rafferty, he said, "We're on the wrong track after all."

"Are you sure? This is a pretty big coincidence—"

But Brett was shaking his head. "It's not a coincidence at all, because Kitty never came to Reno."

"What are you talking about?"

"I've been thinking about it. I'm pretty sure Kitty went to Las Vegas."

"But you said—"

"I know. I was wrong. Kitty knows me too well. She knew that I would know she'd never actually include her destination in an elopement letter, so she deliberately included her destination."

Neil said faintly, "Huh?"

"To throw us off the trail."

"How hard did you hit your head when you blacked out?"

Brett said impatiently, "Don't you get it? Kitty said she was going to Las Vegas because she knew that way it would be the last place we'd ever look."

Rafferty put a hand to his head. It was still in place. "So where's the folio?"

"How should I know?"

"I thought maybe you'd figured that out too."

"No."

Rafferty turned to Horn and Arabella, who were struggling with their obvious disappointment. "Has anyone contacted you in regards to this folio?"

Horn shook his head. "No." He brightened a little. "At least, not that I know of. Perhaps they've contacted my solicitor in England."

"So Katherine isn't coming?" Arabella asked with painful disappointment. No one replied.

"We've got to go back," Brett told Rafferty. "We've got it all wrong."

"If someone wanted to sell a Shakespearean rarity like a folio of *The Tempest*, how would they go about it?" Rafferty asked Horn.

"Assuming he understood what it was he had in his possession—"

"I think this person does."

"The obvious thing would be to contact myself or another potential buyer directly. That would guarantee the highest price for the item."

"It carries the greatest risk too, though."

"True."

"If this person chose not to contact a buyer directly?"

"Well, there are people who will broker these kinds of deals. Some less reputable than others."

"Anybody in Chinatown?"

"Chinatown?" Horn looked taken aback. "San Francisco's Chinatown?"

"Right."

"Well..." He looked at his wife. "There was a place in the old days. I don't know if it even exists now."

"Ah Ong's shop," Arabella supplied. "On Jackson Street. Near the Great China Theatre. He used to advertise magical remedies for everything from gout to lovesickness. You know the kind of thing."

"The Great China has been dark for over a year, but I think I know the place you mean," Rafferty said. "Sort of like an old-fashioned chemist's shop?"

"Yes, except with dried seahorses and snake wine and joss-paper prayers."

"That's the place," Horn agreed. "The old man, Ah Ong, is about a thousand years old, and he knows his Shakespeare like an Englishman."

Rafferty looked at Brett. Brett nodded.

"Oh, but surely you'll stay for breakfast at least?" Arabella protested, seeing that exchange of looks.

"I'm afraid we need to start back," Brett said, that stubborn jut to his chin in evidence. For such a sensitive lad, he had a head harder than a mule's.

"But the food's already prepared. The table is set." Arabella swallowed. She didn't look like a woman who shed tears easily, but they were looming now.

Rafferty couldn't help it. "Sure," he told her. "At this point, a couple of hours won't matter." He ignored the warning look Brett gave him.

"That's settled, then," Horn said briskly with a quick, grateful glance. He pulled out a chair for his wife. "I'll get the food, my heart. You sit here and chat with young Brett."

Young Brett was speaking daggers with his eyes, but Rafferty just gave him a pleasant smile like he didn't understand the problem. They had to eat breakfast somewhere. Right?

Yeah, he was probably a sap, but Rafferty felt sorry for Arabella, and the fact that Brett so desperately wanted to avoid spending time with her was all the more reason he probably needed to.

And if Rafferty was wrong? Well, he'd been wrong before.

CHAPTER FOURTEEN

$\mathcal{N}$eil pulled neatly beside Brett's tan Ford V-8 in the parking garage on Powell Street. He said with what sounded like forced cheerfulness, "There you go. All's well that ends well, as jolly old Shakespeare would say."

It was the first comment either of them had made in hours. Not since they stopped for lunch, and the conversation then had been strictly of the weather variety. Brett had been preoccupied with the shock of finding his mother alive and well—and apparently still living in sin. He wasn't sure about the last part, since their reunion hadn't stretched as far as shared confidences.

There had been a final moment before their departure when, either by accident or design, both Horn and Neil had abandoned him with Arabella. Brett had asked bluntly—more bluntly than he'd meant to, but he was still struggling with a deluge of disbelief and anger—"Do you have any regrets?"

"Do I have any regrets?" Her smile had been strange. "My decision cost me my children. I have *many* regrets. But if what you're really asking is would I do it all differently if I had it to do again? The answer is no. No."

It hadn't done a whole hell of a lot to diffuse his anger. A fair bit of that anger had slopped over onto his feelings for Neil. The fact that Neil had kept the truth from him about his mother had hurt ridiculously. What else had he kept from Brett?

His feelings for Neil were already confused enough. The fact that Neil apparently condoned a woman abandoning all her responsibilities and commitments in order to satisfy her own selfish desires… What did that say about Neil?

What did that say about Neil's friendship with Brett?

Although, in fairness, Neil had been the one who seemed to make it clear the night before that there wouldn't *be* any particular friendship in the future. Not once Brett was married. That was the only possible course open to them, and it was—should be—a huge relief that despite the things they had done together on this wild-goose chase of theirs, Neil wasn't going to press Brett for more.

Yes, a huge relief.

And it made him all the more angry with Neil.

"You don't have to worry about anything," Neil was saying. "I think I've got a pretty good handle on the case now. There are still a few things to check up, but as soon as I know for sure what happened to the folio, I'll give you a full report."

Neil sounded businesslike but reassuring, very much on his professional manner. Even in the gloom of the garage, Brett could see that he was in a hurry for Brett to get out and go.

Maybe he was afraid Brett was going to be difficult. He'd mentioned Brett's crack-up a couple of times. He probably knew all about what had happened with Emmett, and he was probably uneasy in case Brett had formed another one of his unsuitable attachments. He didn't have to worry. Brett had understood how the world worked for a long time now.

He gave Neil a cynical smile and reached for the door handle. It surprised him when Neil caught his arm. Neil let go instantly, but he said, sounding strained, "Are you okay?"

"Of course. Why shouldn't I be?"

Neil gave a funny laugh. "Right. Well, if you need to…" In the face of Brett's silence, he didn't finish it.

"Thanks. I'll keep that in mind." Brett's tone was ironic. He got out of the Buick and walked across to his own car.

Neil continued to sit, idling the engine. What was he waiting for? Brett lifted a hand in brief dismissal, and Neil finally took the hint and threw the Buick into reverse.

Brett sat unmoving, watching in his rearview mirror as Neil pulled out of the garage and turned right on Powell Street.

* * * * *

"Welcome home, sir," Munson said, taking Brett's hat, coat, and bag. He sounded as though Brett had merely stepped out for lunch, whereas Brett felt as though he'd been gone for years. It was almost unsettling to see how little had changed.

His glance fell on the giant portrait of his mother near the staircase, and he nearly missed Munson's colorless, "Miss Katherine and her husband are in the drawing room with the rest of the family."

"What?"

Munson forgot himself so far as to say, "Yes. They arrived an hour or so ago. At least, Miss Katherine did. Mr. Sader had to leave but has since returned." He caught himself immediately.

"Thank you. I'll go up and add my congratulations."

"Very good, sir."

Brett went quickly up the staircase, imagining the conversation in the Munsons' quarters that evening. As he reached the drawing room, he heard Harry Sader's quick laugh, followed by Aunt Lenora's "It will be so… lovely to have a young married couple in the house."

Poor Aunt Lenora. And she'd thought the Lennoxes weren't "quite our sort." How about tussling over the pork chops with a cheap four-flusher like Harry Sader?

Justine drawled, "Isn't that nice. We're not losing a daughter; we're gaining a son-in-law." She smiled lazily at Brett's entrance. "Well, well. The prodigal returns."

"Where the devil have you been?" his father demanded in his usual greeting.

"Oh, Sherry," quavered Aunt Lenora, her gracious mask slipping for an instant. "Kitty has married Mr. Sader."

Brett went straight to Kitty, meeting her defiant eyes and kissing her flushed cheek. "Wish me happy?" she inquired.

"You know I do." He turned as she blinked fiercely at the unexpected emotion filling her eyes, offering his hand to Sader. "Harry. Congratulations."

"Thank you, little brother," joked Harry. He was as tall as Brett, very fair and quite handsome, if you liked the type. Brett didn't.

"Well, I think it's too bad you had to elope," Sophie said. "Nothing ever happens in this house."

"I thought you'd be relieved not having to dress up as a flower girl," Kitty retorted.

"Flower girl!"

Justine laughed. Brett glanced at her as a thought occurred. If his parents had *not* divorced, Justine's marriage to his father was invalid. Was his father so obsessed with his own preoccupations that he'd forgotten his first wife was still alive? Or had he deliberately…?

He stared at his father, barely registering his, "Why didn't you phone or send a telegram or find a way to get a message to us? Where have you been this whole time? How can you be so irresponsible?"

"Yes, where have you been?" Kitty asked mockingly. "I was half expecting you to show up at my wedding." Harry laughed and gave her a little squeeze. "Did you ever find that item you were looking for?"

"No."

"What were you looking for?" Sophie asked interestedly. "Justine's been looking for something too."

"Isn't it past your bedtime?" Justine inquired.

Sophie snorted dismissingly.

"There's some delicious chocolate sponge cake here." Aunt Lenora moved to slice a piece of cake. "Did you have a nice trip at least?" She offered the plate to him.

"It was…interesting." Brett met his father's gaze. His father continued to glare at him. What exactly was it that he blamed Brett for? Had he really imagined Brett would be able to stop Kitty's marriage? Had Brett really imagined he could? For the first time he began to consider his family in the context of the outside world. Was it possible that they were more than a little off-kilter? Rafferty thought so, no question of that.

"What happened to your friend, Mr. Rafferty?" Justine spoke up, uncannily seeming to read his mind. "Did he actually go to Reno with you?"

"Are you getting divorced already?" Kitty teased.

Everyone laughed nervously. Brett joined in obligingly, and then choked down his piece of cake, drank the tea Justine poured, and listened without hearing more than one word in ten to the plans of the newlyweds. The gist seemed to be that Harry would be moving into Sheridan House with his new bride as soon as possible.

The more the merrier, right? And he certainly couldn't—and didn't want to—picture Kitty living at Mrs. Dumbrille's.

"I ran into a couple of friends of yours in Reno," he said, cutting across Harry's opinions of the ideal car for a pair of newlyweds—just in case anyone wanted to buy them a wedding gift.

Harry's expression smoothed out to one of polite interrogation. "Pals of mine? I can't think of any pals of mine who would hang around *that* town."

Even Kitty had to roll her eyes at that one.

"I think so," Brett insisted mildly. "Everywhere we went, they had already been there asking after you."

After a pause, Harry said, "Maybe they had me confused with someone else."

"Maybe they did."

Harry's expression altered to one of blinding revelation. "*Oh.* I bet I know what it was. There was a little…miscommunication between my former employer and me. A little misunderstanding." He smiled reassuringly at Kitty. "We got it worked out."

"What happened?" she asked.

"It's nothing. Really, angel."

Harry didn't know Kitty if he thought she'd be fobbed off with a pat on the head. She continued to frown at him, and Harry said with elaborate nonchalance, "There was this mix-up about a…a bank deposit. See, I was the only one with the deposit slip. But we got it all worked out."

"Is that where you rushed off to when we arrived home?"

"That's it." He kissed her forehead. "Everything's fixed now."

"What is it you do, Harry?" Aunt Lenora ventured.

"Yes, do tell us, Harry," Justine drawled.

"Well, ladies, I'm afraid I'm currently between positions," Harry admitted.

Brett could think of a position he'd enjoy seeing Harry in. He turned as Munson appeared at his elbow.

"Miss Juliet Lennox is on the phone for you, sir."

Until then, he'd completely forgotten that Juliet had wanted him to take her to the theater.

In fact, he had very nearly forgotten Juliet.

"Brett, where on earth *are* you?" she said, sounding less good humored than usual when he finally picked up the phone.

"Darling, I'm sorry. I just got in."

"Well, how soon can you be here? We're going to miss the first act."

The wave of weariness that swept over him nearly had him folding up on the marble steps of the staircase.

"Julie, I don't think..." He stopped in the face of that formidable silence. Occasionally she reminded him very strongly of her father.

Brett looked at his watch. Seven thirty. "It's going to take me at least an hour to bathe and change. I've been traveling all day."

She sighed. "Brett."

"I am sorry, darling." *Please, please, darling. Let me off the hook this once...*

Juliet huffed another of those much-tried sighs. "All right. Apology accepted. *If* we can get there by intermission. That way the evening won't be a complete loss."

The receiver clicked off. Brett replaced the handset slowly. He turned and jumped as Aunt Lenora appeared before him.

"Auntie. I didn't see you there."

She threw a furtive look over her shoulder and handed him a small black book. He took it automatically. It looked like an address book.

Aunt Lenora hissed, "This is what Justine has been looking for. I stole it from her room."

Brett opened his mouth, but no gumball of wisdom dropped out.

Seeing that his thinking apparatus was stuck, Aunt Lenora shook his arm lightly. "She's up to something, Brett. Beside every name in that book is a dollar amount. She's *charging* people for...something."

He swallowed. But the words that came out weren't the ones he intended. "Aunt Lenora, did you know my mother was alive?"

It was Aunt Lenora's turn to jump. She gulped. "W-why would you say that?"

"I saw her. I spoke to her."

"You never went to that house?"

"Of course I went to the house. We were looking for Kitty. We thought she might have gone there."

"You shouldn't have done that! The house is *hers.*"

"You *did* know." He couldn't believe it. All this time. All the lies. He was beginning to go numb.

Aunt Lenora was blinking in evident fright. He remembered sobbing his heart out in her lap when they'd told him his mother wasn't coming back, that she was dead. They hadn't been allowed to cry in front of their father—nor even speak their mother's name.

"Brett, you were too young to understand. The truth was…too terrible. It was easier this way."

"Easier?"

"You'll understand one day." She patted his arm, looked nervously over her shoulder. "Hold on to that book. We're going to get rid of her one way or the other."

She bustled away down the hall.

* * * * *

He half killed himself getting to the Lennox mansion on time, and then in the end, Brett still had to wait for Juliet while she changed her dress yet again.

Viola and Sebastian kept him company. If you could call being circled by sharks "keeping company." He watched them with the distant feeling of an explorer observing a newly discovered tribe of Pygmies. He was going to be marrying into this family. They too were going to be partly his responsibility soon.

It felt increasingly unbelievable, but that was the way one always felt after a long trip. The normal world felt strange and out of focus, while the illusionary world of one's holiday world seemed sharply, vividly real.

"We used to have a brother named Hamlet. Did you know that?" Viola inquired. She and her twin had been playing cards, but she had obligingly laid them aside when Brett had been ushered into the sitting room.

"Yes."

Sebastian prodded for the third time, "Your turn, V."

"We're not playing now, Seb. We're amusing Brett."

"Mostly," Brett agreed.

Seb yawned and threw down his cards. "He was Juliet's twin. He died of typhoid fever."

"I know. What brought this on?"

"I don't know," Viola said vaguely. "Just…life's awfully brief, don't you think?"

"'Out, out, brief candle!'" Sebastian quoted.

Brett knew they had been smoking before he walked in, despite the swift concealment of evidence. Now he began to suspect the glasses on the table did not contain apple juice.

"You're just starting out. You've got plenty of time."

Sebastian's laugh was oddly adult. Viola kicked her brother without heat. To Brett, she inquired politely, "Did your detective ever solve the case of the tempest in a teapot?"

"You'd know if he had." There was a stack of colored travel brochures on the table next to them. Brett picked them up, his heart sinking at the sight of the Riviera, Biarritz, Monte Carlo, *L'hiver à la Côte d'Azur*. He'd told Juliet several times he couldn't afford anything like this.

"No, we wouldn't," Viola said. "Everyone treats us like children."

He grinned. "You *are* children."

She stuck her tongue out at him.

Juliet arrived then, looking lovely in a blue silk gown that perfectly matched her eyes. It was also the dress she'd been wearing when he arrived, but Brett refrained from pointing it out.

"What are you two doing down here drinking and smoking when you're supposed to be doing your homework?" she scolded as Brett draped her fur coat over her shoulders.

"You'd better watch it if you don't want us telling Father what time you get home," Viola sweetly shot back.

"*Of* course what they really need is to be sent away to school," Juliet said as Brett drove away from the house. "But Daddy won't hear of it."

Brett nodded absently. "Julie, darling, you do remember what we talked about before?"

"What's that, Sherry?"

"About our honeymoon."

She giggled. "Are you worrying about that, silly? That's the problem with stuffy old prep schools. Daddy's right." She rested her hand lightly on his thigh and squeezed.

Brett nearly swerved into oncoming traffic, but managed to regain control of the car. Juliet was still laughing at him.

"That's not what I meant," he practically stuttered. "I meant our wedding trip."

"Oh. *That.* Yes?"

"I told you before"—he heard the note of irritation in his voice and worked to cover it—"that I can't afford anything extravagant. My family isn't as wealthy as yours."

"I know." She sounded bored as she stared out the side window. "I'm not marrying you for your mother."

"What?"

She threw him an impatient look. "I *said* I'm not marrying you for your money."

Was he starting to crack? He thought she'd said—

But no. Of course not. He really was overtired and overstrained.

"I can't afford anything like Monte Carlo or Biarritz or any of those places. I know it's not what you'd choose, but we'll be staying with family friends in their country home outside Paris."

"I know that, Sherry. You've told me about a million times already."

Come to think of it, why was she marrying him?

"But those travel brochures—"

"What travel bro—Oh!" Juliet laughed. "You silly. Those aren't mine. Those are Sebastian's."

CHAPTER FIFTEEN

A very small sign in the corner of the shop window read in English CHINESE MAGICAL MEDICINE.

Rafferty stepped back and had another look at the shop. It was just as Brett's mother and Lord Horn had described it: a small building tucked out of the way on Jackson Street, not far from the now closed grand old Great China Theatre with its graceful crimson curved eaves.

Despite its prosaic name, Jackson Street could have been an avenue in the Far East. Long banners with Chinese characters hung from ornate balconies. Tall, pagoda-style lamps decorated with golden dragons and tiny bells glowed cheerfully from each street corner.

The street was crowded even late on a Wednesday evening, but it looked deserted inside the shop as Rafferty peered through the window. He tried the door, found it unlocked, and pushed it open.

Inside the shop, it smelled of queer and mysterious things. The shelves were lined with rows of red lacquer boxes with brass handles. Teakwood chairs were ranged against the walls, botanical watercolors hanging above them.

It was not completely deserted. The proprietor was not the reported thousand-year-old man in a plum-colored quilted silk jacket and apple-green silk trousers, however, but a much younger fellow in an Arrow shirt. He was about Brett's age and he stood behind a fully modern teakwood counter. He was tossing peanuts to a small brown-and-black monkey.

At the graceful tinkle of temple bells, he smiled widely.

"Good evening, sir. What may I interest you in this fine evening?"

"What do you have?"

The young man considered him, a pucker between his thread-thin brows. "Something for the digestive system, perhaps?"

Rafferty grinned broadly, continuing to browse the tall shelves. "Nah. I eat like a horse." There were several scrolls but no books and certainly nothing by William Shakespeare or any Western author.

"Man is not a horse," the young man informed him loftily, tossing another peanut to the monkey. "The principal teaching of Chinese medicine is achieving the delicate balance of yin and yang. This is the internal harmony which connects all things of the mind, body, and spirit."

"Right. You have anything for a young man who suffers from, uh, early whatchamacallit…seminal emissions?" Rafferty was unsure what made him ask, but the shopkeeper's startled and then sly half smile made him regret the impulse.

"Yes. Indeed! Your unfortunate situation is not so rare as you might imagine, sir."

"It's not for me," Rafferty was irritated to hear himself say. "It's for my…brother."

"Ah." A pitying—and disbelieving—look. "The undue loss of the seminal secretion in a natural way, that is, from too frequent intercourse with the other sex, is unwise and evil, but when resulting from self-pollution, no language can describe the nature of those sufferings which violated nature is compelled to endure."

"It's nothing like that." Rafferty dearly wished he'd kept his mouth shut. After all, it wasn't as though he and Brett were going to… Anyway, he wished he'd kept his mouth shut, that was all. "Another time, maybe. I'm not in the market for dried toads right now. Actually, I was looking for the man who used to own this shop. His name was Ah Ong."

The monkey screamed annoyance at the halt in the peanut supply. The young man hushed it absently, his dark eyes suspicious.

"Why are you seeking Ah Ong?"

Rafferty glanced over his shoulder as though he suspected the monkey of trying to horn in on his deal. "As a matter of fact, I heard he was an expert in the work of William Shakespeare. That he was able to occasionally broker deals for wealthy collectors seeking rare volumes."

The man's face was now entirely without expression. "And you are such a collector?"

"I'm looking for a very rare volume; you've got that right."

The young man nodded very slowly. "And how did you hear of Ah Ong, if I might ask?"

Rafferty played his ace. "Lord Horn recommended him to me."

The dark eyes went as wide as almond-shaped eyes could go. "You are Lord Horn's emissary?"

"That's right," Rafferty lied cheerfully.

"But I spoke to Lord Horn only this afternoon. He said he would have to see the item before he could make any decision."

"That's right. He sent me to have a look."

"*You* are an expert in antiquarian books?"

"Sure. Why not? Oh. Don't let this mug fool you. Appearances can be deceiving, friend."

"Yes." The young man reached his arm out, and the monkey jumped onto it. It chattered, scolding Rafferty.

"Cute little trick," Rafferty commented.

"Er, yes." He seemed to consult his ancestors briefly. He smiled fleetingly. "Perhaps you had better speak to my honorable father."

"Who's your father?"

The young man raised his invisible brows in surprise. "I thought you knew. I am the son of Ah Ong." He pushed aside the beaded doorway and beckoned Rafferty to follow him.

Rafferty came around the tall counter and followed the young man into a small back room that smelled of a number of things, some pleasant, some merely weird. The room seemed to be used for keeping extra stock. There were dried toads on wooden sticks, jars of strange mushrooms, bundles of tanned eels, and withered seahorses.

"Do a brisk business in this stuff, do you?"

"We do. Yes."

They went down a narrow passageway and then down a long set of steps not even the width of an arm's length.

"Isn't it a little damp for your elderly father down here?"

Ah Ong Jr. made no reply.

The hair prickled on the back of Rafferty's neck. He surreptitiously loosened his pistol in its holster.

"How did the item happen to come into your possession?" he asked.

The monkey turned around and told him in as plain as English to shut up. Rafferty whistled soundlessly.

They came at last to a heavy brown door clearly meant to withstand assault. Ah Ong Jr. took out a surprisingly modern-looking key ring, unlocked the door, pushed it wide, and called into the dark, "Father? Forgive me for disturbing your sleep. A man has come about the William Shakespeare folio."

He seemed to lean into the doorway to better hear a faint response.

"I think he said 'turn the damn light on,'" Rafferty remarked.

Ah Ong Jr. whipped around, a small deadly-looking derringer in his hand—only to find Rafferty's pistol an inch from his nose. Rafferty cocked the pistol.

The monkey clapped its tiny hands over its eyes. Ah Ong Jr.'s went wide. He stuttered. "W-what is the meaning of this, sir?"

"The meaning is the same as your peashooter, only in English."

The derringer wobbled but did not lower. "I knew it! You have come to rob me."

"It depends on your definition of rob," Rafferty retorted. "I think you have something that doesn't belong to you. Let's leave your ancient, honorable father to get some shut-eye and discuss it upstairs like gentlemen."

The derringer was reluctantly lowered. Rafferty squeezed to the side and gestured for the young man to precede him up the stairs again.

Ah Ong wriggled past, clutching his monkey to him like a baby. He trudged slowly up the stairs, clearly trying with each step to think of some way to outwit his captor.

"Come on, scramble." Rafferty nudged him with his pistol.

"You will be very sorry for this, sir."

"I'm sorry for a lot of things, so put it on my tab."

As they neared the top of the stairs, Rafferty heard a girl saying in English, "There isn't even anyone here!"

This was followed by a familiar voice that made Rafferty's bullet-proof heart go soft as Chinese silk. "He wouldn't leave the shop unlocked and unattended."

"This is the craziest idea. I can't believe you've dragged me here. If Daddy knew— *Sherry*, you can't go back there!"

Juliet gave a little shriek as Rafferty gave Ah Ong Jr. a shove, and he staggered out through the beaded curtain. She relaxed when she saw Rafferty right behind him.

"Mr. Rafferty!"

Rafferty touched the brim of his hat. "Miss Lennox." His gaze tangled with Brett's startled one. "Mr. Sheridan. Fancy meeting you here." He couldn't help the smile that curved his mouth. There was never going to be a time that he wasn't happy to see Brett.

"Is it true?" Juliet was gasping as though she'd been punched. She even put a protective hand to her breast. "Did Viola and Sebastian really steal the folio?"

That was unexpectedly good work on Brett's part. Rafferty threw him an approving look. "What was it tipped you off?" The glass cutter should have done it, it was the tipping point for Rafferty, but at the time he'd thought it flew over Brett's admittedly preoccupied head.

"Travel brochures," Brett said. "They were planning on leaving town. They got the idea from some story in *McClure's* magazine."

"By Willa Cather," Juliet said. "But this is just too ridiculous. To think that my little brother and sister would steal from our father!"

"Somebody in your house did. I don't think your father faked the crime, so unless you're confessing—"

She clutched at Brett's arm. *"Sherry."*

"He's kidding." Brett patted her hand. "Mr. Rafferty's got a peculiar sense of humor."

"Maybe you thought I was kidding when I wasn't," Rafferty said. He was still on the adrenaline high of nearly shooting or being shot, but the murderous look Brett directed his way cooled him off fast.

"I can't believe it," Juliet was saying. It was more of a moan. "Why would they *do* such a thing?"

Brett sighed and kept patting her, so apparently this had been covered at length at some earlier point.

Rafferty said, "Too many issues of *Black Mask*, if you ask me."

"No one is asking you," Juliet snapped. "If the folio is here, where is it?"

Rafferty tilted his head inquiringly. Ah Ong Jr. sealed his lips with a defiant look.

"I don't want to get rough with the monkey," Rafferty warned him.

Ah Ong Jr. unsealed his lips. "It's in the safe."

"Get it. And don't try any funny business."

Maybe the monkey misunderstood and heard *monkey business*. At any rate, it chose that opportunity to jump from his master's shoulder to Juliet's head. She screamed—as did the monkey—and grabbed at it, trying to throw it off. Ah Ong Jr. whirled and tried to grab Rafferty's gun. They struggled, the gun went off, and a bullet shattered the window about half a foot to the left of Brett.

Brett looked in astonishment at the hole in the window. Juliet looked too and stared at Rafferty. "You…nearly…shot…him."

"I…" Rafferty's voice died. He looked in consternation at Brett.

"That was…close," Brett said slowly. He couldn't seem to stop staring at the broken window.

"Jesus Christ." Rafferty wondered if he was going to take a turn at fainting himself.

Brett glanced at him, then looked more closely. He said gruffly, "Neil. You missed by a mile."

Ah Ong Jr., clutching his monkey once more, started to sidle away. Neil shook off his horror and yanked him back into place. "We've all had enough fun and games for one evening. Where's the folio?"

"I accepted this article in good faith. I have done nothing wrong."

"Yeah, yeah. It never occurred to you that a couple of kids might not have come by a priceless antique book honestly?"

The Oriental looked suitably inscrutable.

"Just get the damn book," Rafferty growled.

Ah Ong Jr. tossed the monkey to his shoulder, where it proceeded to tell Rafferty what it thought of him. The man bent down, yanked aside an oriental carpet with dragons chasing each other in an endless circle. A perfectly modern floor safe was revealed.

Junior's nimble fingers turned the dial first one way and then the other. He opened the safe, reached inside, and withdrew a flat, brown-wrapped parcel.

Rafferty set the parcel on the counter and unwrapped it. Within the folds lay a brittle, brown pamphlet. The thin features of William Shakespeare smiled enigmatically up at them.

* * * * *

"If you feed that damn cat, we'll never get rid of it," Rafferty warned Linda.

She straightened. The cat, a particularly mangy-looking yellow specimen, disappeared down the hallway. "Oh, I see. But if you feed him, he won't take it the wrong way?"

Rafferty grimaced. "Nope. We alley cats understand each other." The grimace deepened as he went through the stack of bills on his desk.

The summer breeze, scented by exhaust and cooking lunches from the other offices below them, wafted in his half-open window. From next door came the muffled sound of that damned Bing Crosby song.

"You shouldn't have returned Brett Sheridan's fee," Linda said, coming in to perch on the edge of his desk. "He'll have plenty of dough now." She had that unconscious sympathetic note in her voice again, the one that people used when you were bereaved. Women were too damn intuitive sometimes.

Rafferty looked up and laughed, tossing the last envelope aside. "Isn't it time you were on your way?"

"I don't mind working today if you need me. Mrs. Butler is watching William."

Rafferty shook his head. "Off home wi' ye, me darlin' girrrrl. And enjoy your Saturday."

Linda said with a rare display of stubbornness, "It's your Saturday too. Why don't you…"

That was the question, wasn't it? Why didn't he…do something. Anything.

"Crime waits for no man," he said lightly.

"Then we should have plenty of business these days." She was gathering things, eager to be on her way. Well, it was a beautiful hot day, and she should be spending it having a picnic or a swim with a handsome young man. Even if he was two years old.

*I*t was quiet after she'd gone. The sun continued to shine through the open window. A fly buzzed in, decided it was too hot, and buzzed out again.

Rafferty finally relented and checked his watch. Noon.

So that was that.

Brett was married.

Well, it wasn't as though he'd ever expected anything else, really. Brett had his life planned out from the start, and nothing had happened between them to change that—far from it.

Had he hoped? Maybe. More fool him. When he'd sent the money back and heard nothing, well, that should have told him whatever he still needed to know. And yet, right up until last night, he had hoped. A little.

Last night he'd accepted that Brett was going to go through with it. And knowing that, he had thought perhaps he would see him one last time. One last hurrah. One last…whatever it would have been to Brett.

He knew what it would have been to *him*. Needless to say, it would have meant too much. In that sense, Brett had done him a favor. A kindness, really, to break it off cleanly and coldly.

You don't amputate a limb over a series of days.

Anyway, he'd known that if Brett didn't come to him last night, he wouldn't come at all. Never again.

Too much of a gentleman to leave a lady at the altar.

Too much of a gentleman to continue a liaison that no decent man would have entered into in the first place.

Too much of a gentlemen. Period.

So that was that. No use thinking about it again. Not that it stopped him any.

> *What seest thou else*
>
> *In the dark backward and abysm of time?*

That was a line from *The Tempest*. With all those long nights on his hands, Rafferty had borrowed a copy of the play from the library, reading out of curiosity. He'd found it a surefire means of getting a good night's sleep. It had some good lines, though.

Misery acquaints a man with strange bedfellows, for example. That was a pretty good one.

He sighed and tipped his chair back, staring up at the watermark on the ceiling. It looked a bit like…Africa? Or was it some kind of vegetable?

"I see you're hard at work," a familiar voice said crisply.

Rafferty sat up so quickly his chair nearly overbalanced. Brett stood in the doorway in gray summer flannels that nonetheless clearly spoke—in a British public school accent, no less—of Bond Street. Beneath Rafferty's astonished gaze, he raked his dark hair out of his eyes in that unconscious nervous habit.

"What the hell are you doing here?" Rafferty demanded. His tone was rougher than it had to be, trying to hide—even from himself—that exultant leap his heart gave. "Aren't you supposed to be on your way to Paris?"

"No. That's all over. I told Juliet last night…it wouldn't be fair."

"Just like that, huh?"

"It was a little tougher than that. Tougher on Julie. The old man isn't pleased either."

"Which old man?"

"Take your pick."

"I see."

Brett offered a funny smile. "You don't sound very happy to see me."

"Should I be?"

Brett shrugged. His lashes lowered, concealing his eyes. His mouth took on that pensive line. It just wasn't fair that a guy should look like that. It wasn't fair that with a simple flutter of his eyelashes he could make Rafferty's heart leap and twist like a trout on a line.

"Well?" Rafferty demanded. "To what do I owe this honor?"

Brett frowned and looked at him directly, then. A look as hard and straight as Rafferty's own. "Do you honestly not know?"

For possibly the first time in his life, Rafferty couldn't think of a single thing to say.

Brett entered the room, seemed to waver about where to sit, and headed for the window. He rested his arm on the sash and stood looking down at California Street. The bright sunlight gilded his profile.

Rafferty couldn't seem to tear his gaze away from him. He wondered if he'd fallen asleep. Maybe he was tipped back in his chair right now, snoring to rattle the windows, and any second his chair would crash over, and he'd be back to the reality of never seeing Brett Sheridan again.

Brett said abruptly, "Look…"

Rafferty was already looking. He said, "Well?"

Brett bit his lip, slanted Rafferty a quick glance. "You're not making this easy."

"I don't know how to make it easy for you." It was the simple truth.

Brett stared back out the window. His pretty mouth went bitter for a moment. "But if you knew, you'd do your best, wouldn't you?"

Rafferty nodded. That was the simple truth too. No point pretending otherwise.

Brett seemed to think about it some more. At last he said, "There was someone. Once."

"Sure." How could there have not been?

"You asked about college. About what happened."

The breakdown. That's what he meant. "You don't have to tell me."

"Sure I do." Brett half closed his eyes as though the sun was suddenly too bright. "He was a friend…and I thought more. I thought it was the same for him. He said it was. He swore it was. But it wasn't. He got tired of it. Of me, I guess."

Rafferty's heart was beating in hard, heavy slugs. He didn't want to hear this.

"And…I lost my head completely." Brett gave a faint laugh. "I was so stupid. You wouldn't believe it. Or maybe you would. Having…finally let myself feel that way, I couldn't stop it. And the more I pushed and bullied and begged, the worse it got. Finally Emmett—my friend—went to…" He swallowed on it.

Rafferty realized that what he was feeling was anger. No, he was past anger; he was furious with this long-ago college punk who had hurt Brett so very badly. Nearly finished him.

Brett sighed. "There would have been a-a tremendous scandal, but I cracked up completely. Which was actually fortunate, because everything—my behavior—was put down to working too hard. The old over-study and over-athletics."

Neil rose and went to him. Close enough to touch but not touching. "What do you want? All you have to do is ask."

Brett said finally, "I love you, Neil."

Rafferty's heart seemed to stop. "Yeah?" he managed to say.

"Yeah." Brett was still talking to the window. "I swore I'd never let that happen again, but…it did."

He was so close…but he was so far too, and Rafferty didn't know what to do about it. The wrong move might break the spell. But maybe this spell needed to be broken—no gentle enchantment but the blackest magic?

Brett was saying, "I don't know what that means to people like us. I don't think there's any future in it. But there's no future without you either." He looked at Neil again, his face twisted, but he got control and stared determinedly out the window. "I don't know. I want neither of us to go through another night like last night."

Rafferty drew him away from the window, out of view of any curious gazes, pulling Brett into his arms without haste or roughness. He was rewarded when Brett leaned into him, holding him tightly, resting his forehead against Rafferty's.

"I've known plenty of guys," Rafferty said. "I even loved a couple of them, but I've never felt about anyone the way I feel about you. I never will. Somehow you know when it's the real thing, and this is the real thing for me."

Brett's arms tightened, and Rafferty held him closer still. He said more softly, "I can't change what happened in the past, and I can't predict the future, but I'm here for you now. I won't ever knowingly hurt you, and I'll do my damnedest to never let you down. That's my plan for now and from now on. How does that sound to you?"

Brett raised his head. His eyes were wet. He said, "It sounds like a good place to begin."

Rafferty angled his head, and Brett's warm mouth touched his. The sounds of traffic below and the radio next door and the pigeons on the sill faded away in the shimmering summer light.

Snowball in Hell

Los Angeles, 1943

CHAPTER ONE

"Hell of a thing," Jonesy said for the third time.

Matt agreed. It was a hell of a thing. He turned his gaze from the gaggle of reporters smoking and talking beside the grouping of snarling cement saber-toothed tigers, and returned his attention to the sticky, bedraggled corpse currently watching the birdie for the police photographer.

Whoever had dumped the dead man had counted on the body sinking in the black ooze of the Brea Pits, and in the heat of the summer when the tar heated up and softened…maybe. But it was December, a little more than a week before Christmas, and it had been raining steadily for two days. No chance in hell. The body had rested there, facedown in the rainwater hiding the treacherous crust of tar beneath, until the museum paleontologists excavating the site for fossils had made the grisly early-morning discovery.

"Looks kinda familiar," Jonesy remarked gloomily, as the plastered hair and drowned eyes were briefly illuminated in the white flash of the camera.

Matt bit back a laugh. "Yeah? Must be the fact that he's dead."

Jonesy looked reproachful, although after thirty-three years on the homicide squad, he'd seen more than his share of stiffs. They both had, though Matt had seen more violent death and destruction during his seven months in the Pacific than he had in his eleven years on the force.

"No identification on him at all?"

"Nope. Even the label was cut out of his jacket. No sign of his hat or shoes."

Matt considered this. Soaking in water and tar hadn't done John Doe's clothes much good, and they'd have to wait 'til everything dried before they could hope to get much from an examination. How much they would get then was doubtful, but that suit didn't look particularly old or worn, and the tailoring was the kind that showed its worth even in the worst conditions—which these were.

Laughter drifted from the circle of statues where the reporters and a couple of photographers waited impatiently. Matt knew most of them: Williams from "The Peach," Mackey from the *Times,* Cohen from the *Mirror* and Tara Renee of the *Examiner.* The only one he didn't recognize was the slim man lighting Tara's cigarette. Thin, brown fingers cupped the lighter against the damp breeze; lean, tanned cheek creased in a smile as Tara flirted with him. Tara flirted with everyone, but she was a good little crime hound.

"Who's that?" Matt asked Jonesy, and Jonesy looked up from the meticulous diagrams he was making of the crime scene and followed Matt's stare.

"Doyle. *Tribune-Herald.* Heard he was with the Eighth Army in North Africa 'til he picked up a case of lead poisoning." Jonesy grinned his lop-sided smile. "Got hit by machine-gun fire in Tunisia."

"Yeah, well, there's a lot of that going around." But Matt's interest was unwillingly caught. "So he's English?"

"Nah. Hometown boy, Loot."

"Doc's here, Lieutenant," one of the uniformed officers said as the police ambulance bumped its way over the grassy verge.

Matt nodded and then nodded again toward the reporters. "Tell 'em I want to see Miss Renee and…" He thought it over. "Doyle."

When he glanced back, Jonesy was giving him an old-fashioned look.

"What's that for?" He'd known Jonesy a long time; Jonesy had been Matt's old man's partner. Back then he'd been big and rawboned with a shock of red hair and a face full of freckles. The hair was gray now, and the freckles had faded into a permanently ruddy complexion, but he was still one of the best detectives on the force—sometimes Matt was afraid Jonesy was too good a detective.

"She's a firecracker, that dame. Can't understand why any woman would want the police beat."

"I guess she got tired of garden parties and ladies' fashion." He watched the uni approach the reporters. Heard the protests of the men from the *Daily News,* the *Times* and the *Mirror.* Watched Doyle's surprise at the summons. Doyle looked past the officer and caught Matt's gaze. Matt held it for a moment, then looked away, jotting down a few more crime scene details in his notebook. From the tire tracks, it looked like whoever dumped Mr. Doe into the goo had driven as close as he safely could to the water's edge. Maybe that meant something, maybe not.

Out of the corner of his eye Matt could see Tara and Doyle crossing the soggy grass toward him. Tara's heels sank into the mud, and Doyle cupped a chivalrous hand beneath her elbow, which amused Matt in a sour way. Tara either had designs on Doyle or thought she could get something out of him—anyone else would have been handed his arm back half-chewed.

"Doesn't look like he drowned," Jonesy was saying.

"He didn't drown," Matt replied.

The police ambulance rolled to a stop and parked in the weeds and mud. Across the field and through the trees Matt could see oil derricks slowly bowing and scraping against the leaden sky.

"What a smell!" Matt heard Tara exclaim, and the other reporter, Doyle, said, "Bitumen." He had a quiet voice, and Matt only caught his reply because he was listening for it.

"Hello, Lieutenant," Tara said, and Matt turned to face her. "To what do we owe this honor?" Tara was a very pretty girl with glossy black curls, sparkling dark eyes, rosy cheeks and a little pointed chin that she wagged too much. But somehow Matt didn't like to shut her up. Maybe because she reminded him a little of Rachel.

"Miss Renee," he said gravely. He glanced at her companion. "You're Doyle from the *Tribune-Herald?*"

"That's right." Beneath the khaki trench coat, Doyle was medium height and very thin. His hair, what Matt could see of it beneath his wide-brimmed hat, was very fair—sun bleached. He had the overlay of tan that comes from years spent under a blazing sun, but beneath it he was sallow. His eyes were light, maybe blue, maybe gray—unexpectedly bright in his lean face. He studied Matt curiously.

"We've got a little problem," Matt said to Tara. "I thought you might be able to help." She gave him a pert, inquiring look, and Matt stepped aside so they could get a look at John Doe. "Either of you recognize him?"

He was watching Doyle. Not because he expected Doyle to recognize the dead guy—he didn't figure Doyle had been back in town long enough to be of much use there—he was just giving him a break after Tunisia. Doyle glanced down at the corpse with the weary indifference of a man who's seen too much death—and froze.

There wasn't any mistake. Doyle's blue-gray eyes widened. He went perfectly still, apparently forgetting to breathe.

Next to him, Tara gasped, and Matt automatically turned his attention, thinking a drowned man was too much for her first thing after break-fast. "Phil Arlen," she murmured. She raised her dark eyes. "That's Philip Arlen."

Jonesy gave a low whistle.

Matt asked, "Benedict Arlen's kid?"

"I'm sure of it."

Matt could feel the echo of her words rippling through the ranks of the crime-scene men. Benedict Arlen was old money, oil money.

Matt looked back at Doyle, but Doyle had recovered himself. He met Matt's gaze and agreed evenly, "It's Arlen."

"You knew him?"

"I went to school with Bob. His brother. Robert Arlen."

"The old school tie," Matt said dryly. "Was that high school or college?"

"Loyola High School. Loyola University."

Catholic, Matt thought. Jesuit trained. Not that it mattered to him. He hadn't given a damn before the war, and he sure as hell thought the world should have learned something about hate by now.

The coroner joined their little tableau. Doc Mason was a beanpole of a man in a black raincoat. As usual, he was smoking a pipe, the pleasant homely scent carried on the rainswept breeze helping to mask other, less pleasant, odors. "Okay for me to get to work, Lieutenant?"

"He's all yours," Matt said. "The crime scene was contaminated from the minute the professors pulled him out of the drink."

Doyle was watching him with those light, alert eyes.

"What a scoop!" Tara said. "And here I thought it was a slow week for news."

"When was the last time you saw Phil Arlen?" Matt asked Doyle.

Doyle shrugged. "It's been a while."

"Nathan's only been home a couple of weeks," Tara said. "He was a war correspondent in North Africa. He was wounded at Medenine." She made it sound like Doyle had done something especially clever. Yep, she was interested in Doyle all right.

At the same time Matt could feel Doyle's discomfort, his desire to shut Tara up. Matt could have told him to save his strength.

"Had enough for one war?" he asked, not unsympathetically.

"So they tell me," Doyle said.

"Lieutenant Spain was on Guadalcanal," Tara put in ruthlessly. "He took two bullets in the leg."

"Now I can predict rain." Matt held out his hand as a fat drop hit his nose, and Doyle laughed. He had an easy, rather husky laugh. Matt found himself smiling back, but he wasn't forgetting Doyle's shocked reaction to the body of Phil Arlen. Of course that could have been the jolt of a John Doe turning out to be someone he knew—but if he instantly recognized Phil Arlen waterlogged and streaked in mud and tar, he must have seen him fairly recently. And as far as Matt knew, the closest Arlen had come to the front lines was watching newsreels in the front row of Grauman's.

"Have you found any shells?" Doyle asked, watching the coroner. Tara did a double take.

"You've got sharp eyes," Matt commented. And now Doyle had attracted Jonesy's attention too.

"He was shot?" Tara asked.

"He was shot all right," Doc Mason said, getting to his feet. "Twenty-two caliber maybe, fairly close range. Must have hit the sternum and ricocheted around inside. There's no exit wound." He chewed on his pipe stem. "Something funny here."

Aware of two very quiet and very attentive reporters, Matt said, "Fill me in later."

Doc nodded. "We better get him inside."

The rain began to patter down as a couple of men lifted Arlen's body onto a stretcher and carried him across the grass to the waiting ambulance. The morning smelled of rain and asphalt and pipe tobacco.

A couple of yards away, the other reporters had moved from grumbling to outright sedition.

"Okay, thanks for your help." Matt nodded dismissal to Nathan Doyle and Tara.

"You're not making a statement?" Doyle asked.

"Lieutenant Spain never allows himself to be rushed," Tara informed him, and Matt shook his head a little at her.

His eyes met Doyle's again, and a smile tugged at Doyle's mouth.

"Welcome to the neighborhood, Mr. Doyle," Matt said.

"Thanks." Despite the smile, there was a shadowy look to Doyle's eyes, the kind of fatigue that didn't have anything to do with lack of sleep or months in a hospital. There was no question which beat Doyle would have preferred to be covering.

"Come on," Tara said, and she linked her arm in Doyle's. "The royal audience is at an end."

Sardonically, Matt watched her shepherd Doyle, the two of them hoofing straight for the main gate, skirting their clustered colleagues who threw friendly and not-so-friendly jeers and insults after them. Lights flashing, the coroner's ambulance rumbled past them, splashing through the pools of muddy water as it turned the opposite way, heading for the rear entrance of the park.

"That Doyle's an interesting fella," Jonesy remarked.

Matt said nothing, turning back to face the silvery-black pool.

He and Jonesy just stood there. Matt was thinking about the unpleasant task before him: informing Benedict Arlen that his youngest child was dead. Kind of ironic when everyone knew Arlen had paid a small fortune to keep the kid out of the draft. And now he was dead. Murdered. He might have had a better chance dodging bullets overseas.

As he watched, a giant bubble of methane gas formed on the watery surface of the pit, expanded and dissipated in a silent gooey pop.

"Disrespectful, tossing the Arlen kid in that muck," Jonesy said reflectively.

"Homicide's disrespectful," Matt replied.

*B*enedict Arlen lived in a white stucco Spanish colonial revival-style mansion in Mandeville Canyon. The house was surrounded by twenty acres of palm trees and hedges and flowering Mediterranean plants. Two bison, clearly pets, ambled contently past the large tiled fountains.

A butler who must have been dragged out of retirement—or possibly eternity—when the regular guy enlisted, met them at the carved wooden doors and did his unsteady best to run interference.

Matt left Jonesy to deal with the majordomo, and he proceeded along the tiled hallway lined with paintings of the Old West by Charlie Russell, until he came to a room and heard voices behind a half-open door.

"You're wrong, Nathan," a man was saying in a querulous voice. "I tell you, Philip is perfectly all right."

Matt couldn't hear the answer, just the quiet murmur of words, but he had the disquieted feeling he knew that voice. He pushed open the door onto a room with a Gothic ceiling and leaded windows with iron grilles. There were vibrant Indian rugs on the floor and lots of heavy, dark Spanish furniture. Oil paintings by Frederic Remington decorated the white walls, and bronze sculptures of bronco busters and buffalo hunters topped the tables.

Benedict Arlen sat on a long velvet-covered sofa next to a giant fireplace in natural stone. A captain-of-industry portrait of him hung over the fireplace—he didn't do it justice. He was a frail-looking man in a plum-colored smoking jacket. He had a beaky nose and thin white hair.

Standing in front of the fireplace was Nathan Doyle.

He glanced up as Matt entered the room, and his expression was unreadable. He said coolly, "Lieutenant Spain, isn't it?"

"It was three hours ago. I'd be hurt if you'd forgotten already."

Doyle said, "I haven't forgotten."

"What are you doing here?" Matt figured he knew what Doyle was doing there. He'd known a few news hawks like that, willing to do anything, pushing past the women and children, trampling over flowerbeds and graves to be first with a story, but he hadn't thought Doyle was the type.

Studying him now—slim and self-contained as he warmed himself in front of Benedict Arlen's cavern-sized fireplace—he still didn't seem like the type.

And Matt thought again about Doyle's recoil when he recognized Phil Arlen's body.

Maybe he'd been shocked because he didn't expect to see Arlen's body there because…that wasn't where he'd left it.

When you're a cop you learn to think like that.

Jonesy slipped quietly into the room behind Matt. He took out his pad and pencil. Doyle opened his mouth to respond to Matt's question, but Benedict Arlen beat him to the punch.

"What is the meaning of this?" he demanded, like somebody in a play. He sat bolt upright, staring from Matt to Doyle as though he suspected they might be in this—whatever it was—together. Which was certainly an odd idea.

Matt identified himself with a show of his badge, and Arlen goggled as though he couldn't believe it.

Doyle said, "I thought Mr. Arlen should hear about Phil from someone besides the police. That it would be less of a shock."

"I tell you Philip is perfectly all right," the old man protested, but now he sounded frightened. "We've paid the ransom. There's no reason for them to harm him."

It was obvious from Doyle's expression that this information was news to him. He stared at Arlen, and Matt said, "Sir, are you telling me that your son was kidnapped?"

The old man hesitated, chewing his lip. "We received a call Sunday evening informing us that Philip had been…taken. We were given twenty-four hours to deliver one hundred thousand dollars."

The old man faltered as Jonesy whistled. "We were promised that Philip would be released twenty-four hours after that." At Matt's expression he said defiantly, "We didn't inform the police. We were expressly ordered *not* to inform the police or Philip's life would be forfeit."

Doyle rubbed his forehead and said nothing. He didn't look at Benedict or Matt.

Matt said, "I'm very sorry to inform you, Mr. Benedict, but Phil was found shot to death this morning at Brea Tar Pits."

The old man shook his head stubbornly.

Everyone's initial reaction was denial; Matt had been through this too many times to count. There was nothing for it but the straight truth. He drove on. "His body was recovered by some of the museum staff members working at the dig. Mr. Doyle made the initial identification, but we'll need confirmation."

The door to the room opened and a tall, elegant woman strode into the room. She wore trousers—the kind that only certain rich, fashionable ladies wore—and her dark hair was coiled intricately on her head. "Dad, they're saying on the radio that Phil is *dead*." She stopped short, taking in Doyle's presence. "Nathan…" She looked at Matt. "So it's true."

"Yes," Nathan said. "I'm sorry, Ronnie."

"Lieutenant Spain, Homicide Division," Matt said. "And you are—?"

"Veronica Thompson-Arlen," she said. "I'm married to Robert Arlen, Phil's brother." She glanced at the old man sitting bent forward, head in hands, and she slipped past Matt and sat beside him on the sofa, putting an arm around his shoulder. "Oh, Dad. I don't know what to say."

She looked up at Nathan. "Couldn't there be any mistake?"

Nathan shook his head. "It's Phil."

Matt said, "What do you know about this kidnapping?"

She barely glanced his way. "Not a lot. Bob, my husband, was supposed to deliver the ransom money on Monday night to the Griffith Park Observatory. He did. Everything went according to clockwork on our end." She shook her head. "I can't understand why they would have killed him."

"They?" Nathan asked. He caught Matt's eye and looked momentarily discomfited.

"I—I just assume there would be more than one of them. A gang, perhaps. It was a woman's voice on the telephone both times. But a woman wouldn't have been able to kidnap Phil without help of some kind, surely?"

"Both times?" Matt repeated, with an eye to Doyle.

"A woman called Sunday evening to tell us Phil had been kidnapped and that we had twenty-four hours to gather the ransom money. Then Monday evening she called and told us where to deliver the money. She promised that Phil would be released unharmed Tuesday, this evening—if everything went according to plan."

"And the money was left at the Griffith Park Observatory? Inside or out?"

"Outside. The planetarium is only open in the day now to prevent enemy planes from using its lights to target the city. The money was to be put in a satchel and placed on the east observation terrace in a planter beside a little staircase leading to an arched doorway. Bob was supposed to leave the money and walk away—which he did." She turned back to the old man. "He did everything they wanted, Dad. You know that."

The old man said nothing.

"We'll need to talk to your husband, Mrs. Arlen."

"Thompson-Arlen. Yes, of course. He's at home today. He wanted to be available…in case."

Matt nodded thoughtfully, studying Benedict Arlen. The old man seemed to have retreated into his own dazed thoughts.

He glanced at Doyle. He was watching the old man and the woman without emotion. The fireplace threw shadows across his thin face. Made his eyes glint oddly.

"Again, very sorry for your loss," Matt said formally. "We'll keep you informed as the investigation develops."

Neither the man nor the woman responded. Matt looked at Doyle again, and found him watching him. He said shortly, "Did you want to tag along to Robert Arlen's?"

"Sure." Doyle's surprise was evident.

Matt said, "Come on, then. You can introduce us." He was thinking it might be a good idea to keep an eye on Mr. Doyle of the *Tribune-Herald*.

"Why would they have killed him?" Doyle sounded like he was thinking aloud. Matt glanced his way, and Doyle glanced back. He seemed genuinely puzzled. "If the ransom was paid, why did they kill Phil?"

"I don't know. It's not good business," Matt admitted. He was very conscious of Doyle sitting a few inches from him. Very conscious of his restless energy, of the faint, heathery aftershave he wore, of the fact that Doyle was as physically aware of him as he was of Doyle. He could tell from the way Doyle avoided even the most casual physical contact, and from those flickery sideways looks he was giving him.

"They should have called us at the start," Jonesy said. "They made a big mistake not calling us in."

"It doesn't make sense," Doyle said. "They have to realize that no one else will pay a ransom if there's no chance of getting the kidnap victim back alive."

"They may not be professionals," Matt said. "This may have been a one time only."

Doyle thought this over. "True."

"Hell of a time for this," Jonesy said. "Christmas." He shook his head.

Matt spoke to Doyle. "What were you doing at the Arlen house?"

Doyle turned those cool, lake-water eyes his way. "I told you. I thought the old man should have fair warning before you lot turned up."

"Us lot?" Matt said. Every so often Doyle had—not an accent, exactly, but an English turn of phrase. It sort of irritated Matt—and it sort of amused him. The more he saw of Nathan Doyle, the more interested he was. Mostly it was professional interest. Mostly. He said, "Now why don't I believe that?"

Doyle stared. "I don't know. It's the truth."

And now Matt was convinced it wasn't. Maybe Doyle read that in his expression. He said, "All right, honestly, I'm not sure. I did think the news would come better from someone who wasn't a cop. But...maybe it was also curiosity. Reporter's instinct."

Jonesy met Matt's eyes in the rearview mirror. Matt asked, "Did you know about the kidnapping?"

"No." Doyle was definite, and Matt thought he believed him—on that point.

"What was Philip Arlen like?"

"I didn't know him well."

"Yeah, you said. You're pals with the brother. Robert Arlen."

"We aren't pals," Doyle said. "We travel in different circles, but I knew Bob pretty well when we were at school. Phil was younger than us. I think there were about eight years between him and Bob. To tell the truth, he was a pain in the ass. The old man spoilt him rotten. I don't know how he turned out, but when he was a kid he was a tattletale and a sissy." He met Matt's gaze. "I didn't like him much."

"You're kidding."

Doyle smiled—a quirky smile that creased his lean cheek and tilted his eyes. A very attractive smile. Matt ignored it.

"When was the last time you saw him?" Matt had asked this at the tar pit. He waited to hear what Doyle would say now that he'd had time to think about it.

Doyle said vaguely, "I've seen him a couple of times at the Las Palmas Club. I can't tell you for sure."

"Okay." Doyle was too smart to tell an outright lie, but Matt was beginning to get the picture.

"How did the Brothers Arlen get along?"

Doyle's hesitation was noticeable. "Okay, I think. Phil was always the old man's favorite. I guess Bob had plenty of time to get used to the idea."

They didn't talk much after that, listening to the police radio, and the hiss of tires on wet streets.

Jonesy pulled onto Wilshire Boulevard, and they could see the neon sign of the Bryson Apartment Hotel from blocks away, burning bright in the gloomy late morning. The slick and crowded streets were decked in gaudy garland banners, palm trees twined with Christmas lights, and department store windows decorated with elaborate displays of Santa's villages and winter wonderlands.

Jonesy pulled up in front of the Bryson Apartment Hotel, and they got out, pulling hats down and collars up against the gray rain and ducking between the classical columns with their irritable-looking stone lions balanced aloft.

The Arlens lived in a penthouse on the ninth floor, below the ballroom and the glass-enclosed loggias with their distant view of Catalina Island.

Bob Arlen opened the door, took an awkward step back, steadying himself with a walking stick. He was a tall, well-built man with light brown hair. The left half of his face was badly scarred, twisting into unidentifiable emotion; the right half of his face merely looked surprised.

"Nathan," he said. "I wasn't expecting you."

"Mr. Arlen." Matt showed his badge. "Lieutenant Spain, LAPD Homicide Division. May we come in?"

He gripped his walking stick with both hands, leaning heavily on it. "It's about Phil, isn't it?"

"Yes," Nathan said. "I'm sorry, Bob."

"I read it in this morning's extra." Bob Arlen led them through to a living room with glass doors looking out onto a small balcony. Rain bounced down on large potted plants and metal railings. "I couldn't believe it. I still can't."

"We're very sorry for your loss, Mr. Arlen," Matt said formally. "You didn't go into your office today?"

"I was waiting to hear—I thought there might be news."

And there had been, though maybe not the news Arlen had been waiting for. He looked tired and shocked, but not overcome with grief. Not as far as Matt could tell.

Arlen waved them over to chairs and made his way to a rosewood bar cart laden with crystal bottles and stemware. "Can I offer you gentlemen a drink?"

"No thanks," Matt said.

"Nathan?"

"Yes, thanks, Bob."

Arlen poured two stiff whiskies from a bottle of Lord Calvert with a steady hand, although it was clearly not his first drink. "Ice? Soda?"

"Neat." Nathan took the glass with a murmur of thanks. Matt realized he was far too aware of every move Nathan Doyle made. He wanted to think it was his copper's instinct warning him, but he had the uneasy feeling it was something very different.

Bob Arlen made his way over to a low sofa, managing to juggle both his walking stick and glass with an unbeautiful efficiency that indicated a lot of practice.

"What can you tell us about your brother's kidnapping?"

Arlen sipped his whisky before his measured answer. "The *pater* got the call Sunday evening. A woman said that Phil was being held for one hundred thousand dollars, and that if we didn't come up with the money by five o'clock on Monday evening, he would be killed. She said she would call back on Monday with directions on how the ransom would be delivered."

"Any idea who this woman might have been? Was the voice familiar?"

"No."

"How long had your brother been missing at that point?"

Bob shook his head. "I wouldn't know. I'm not sure Claire would even know. Phil…came and went as he pleased. I think he spent more time at the Las Palmas Club than he did at home."

Matt looked at Nathan who said, "Claire is Phil's wife."

"They've been married just over a year," Bob said. "Claire's a sweet girl. Not really Phil's type. My father pushed for the marriage. I have no idea why."

Matt talked and let Jonesy take the notes; he'd found people talked more easily when they didn't realize they were going on the record. "And this unknown woman called back on Monday evening and told you where to deliver the money?"

"Griffith Park Observatory. It's closed at nights now, and I was supposed to leave the money in a bag in a planter on the east terrace at midnight."

"Were you on time?"

"I was early. I left the money at eleven thirty in one of the cement planters along the wall. When I came back an hour later, it was gone."

"You didn't see who took the bag?"

He shook his head. "I wanted to wait around and see if I could spot the kidnapper, but my father was adamant that we not do anything to endanger getting Phil back safely." He shrugged. "I drove away, walked around the park, looked at the merry-go-round, then went back to make sure the pick-up had been made."

Jonesy said, "Lot of things could go wrong with that plan. The fact is the kidnappers might never have received the money."

"It was their plan," Bob said. "We didn't get a vote. We had to do it their way."

Matt said, "And according to the kidnappers, if things went according to plan, your brother was to be released this evening?"

Bob nodded. "Instead, they killed him, the dirty bastards." He drained his glass, looked to see if Nathan needed a refill. Nathan did not. He was staring out the glass doors at the sparkling chains of rain.

"Did you keep a record of the numbers of the ransom money?" Matt asked.

"I wanted to. My father was against the idea."

Matt repeated patiently, "Did you keep a record?"

"Er...yes."

"Might we see that record?"

Bob left the room. A key turned in the front door lock, the door opened, and Veronica Thompson-Arlen entered. She wore a fur coat that was several years old; her cheeks were pink from the cold. Oddly enough, it seemed to Matt that when she saw them grouped around her living room, she relaxed a little.

Nodding hello, she moved over to the bar cart and poured herself a drink. She offered Nathan another. He declined, seeming to only then recall that he had a drink. He swallowed a mouthful, glanced at Matt, glanced away.

Bob returned with a list of the serial numbers.

Matt thanked him.

"What's that?" Veronica asked, and when Bob explained, she flushed. "Oh, Bob. You shouldn't have! What if the kidnappers somehow got wind of it?"

Jonesy said, "Unless they were morons, the kidnappers would assume that precaution was taken, Mrs. Arlen. Don't think for a minute keeping track of those numbers had anything to do with your brother-in-law's death."

"I hope not. Dad would be…devastated."

Matt said, "Did your brother have any enemies, Mr. Arlen?"

Bob and Veronica exchanged a funny look.

"Not that I'm aware of," Bob said.

"Oh, Bob," Veronica said wearily. "What's the point of lying?" She looked at Matt. "My brother-in-law was a charming boy, but of course he had his enemies. We all have our enemies, don't we?"

It seemed like a stagy thing to say. Matt tried to remember what, if anything, he knew about Veronica Thompson-Arlen. He thought that she had not come from money, but she acted to the manor born, so maybe he was mixing her up with the other one, Phil Arlen's wife—now widow.

"Well," he said, "I have a few, but they're mostly guys I've put behind bars. What kind of enemies did your brother-in-law have?"

"Carl Winters for one," Bob said.

"Oh, Bob!" Veronica protested, just as though she hadn't been saying a minute earlier they needed to come clean.

"Who's Carl Winters?" Once again Matt looked to Nathan Doyle for the answer. And once again Doyle knew the answer. For someone who claimed he hadn't kept in regular touch, he seemed to know a lot about the Arlens. And they seemed to still be on a first-name basis with him. Maybe it was the papal connection. The Catholic community was a tight-knit one, although Doyle didn't look like much of a churchgoer to Matt.

"Claire Arlen's brother," Doyle answered. "Her twin brother, I think. He runs a bookstore on South Grand Avenue. Rare and antiquarian books."

"I think Carl felt bitter about the way Phil treated Claire," Bob said.

"And how was that?" Matt asked.

Bob shrugged uncomfortably.

Veronica said, "Phil was not ideal husband material." She smiled at Bob, and there was no doubt she thought her own husband was a prize worth hanging on to.

"And how did Claire feel about Phil?"

There was a pause, and Veronica answered. "I guess you'd have to ask her, Lieutenant."

"I guess I will," Matt said.

*T*ara Renee stood frowning beneath the striped awning of the Las Palmas Club. She brightened when she spotted Matt and Jonesy. "What'd you do with Nathan?" she asked, trotting to keep up with Matt as he strode toward mahogany doors with stained-glass windows of green palm trees and azure oceans.

"Unhooked him and threw him back." Matt eyed her curiously. "What did you want me to do with him?"

"Artie Cohen said he saw you haul him off in a police car."

"We didn't haul him anywhere," Matt retorted. "We invited him to accompany us to Bob Arlen's since he knows the family. I thought he might be useful to have along."

"Was he?"

"Yep."

"Nice break for Nathan."

Matt stopped and subjected Tara to a narrow-eyed inspection. "Okay, what's on your mind, Miss Renee?"

"*Miss Renee?* You're so formal!" She dimpled at him, but Matt knew her too well to be swayed. "Nothing's on my mind. I'm glad Nathan's getting a few breaks. He deserves them. What'd you think of him?"

"What am I supposed to think of him?" Matt shrugged. "How well do you know him?"

"Are you jealous?"

He sighed.

Tara made a face. "Alright, already! Not a lot. I didn't know Nathan before the war. One thing I do know. He writes beee-ooou-ti-fully. I keep telling him he should write a novel. The kind of thing that gets slapped between embossed leather and sent to the *Saturday Evening Review* boys to chew over. He's too good for this racket."

Matt shook his head and rapped on the doors. "You seem very interested in Nathan Doyle."

"I *am* interested. He's an interesting fellow, unlike the louts I usually meet in my trade." She batted her eyelashes at Matt. "Don't worry, Lieutenant, you'll always come first with me."

"That's what worries me," Matt said, and she laughed. He liked her laugh. That was when she reminded him most of Rachel.

"Jonesy still loves me," she said, with a backward glance for Jonesy.

"You remind me of my granddaughter," Jonesy said. "She needs a good spanking too."

Tara raised her eyebrows.

Matt said, "Anyway, what the hell was he doing with the Eighth Army for how many years?"

She shrugged. "I don't know. He doesn't talk much. He did say he was in Greece in forty-one." She gave Matt a funny grin. "He said he always wanted to see the birthplace of democracy."

"Greece, huh?" He turned as the mahogany doors were unlocked and dragged open. A bald-headed man with a mouthful of gold teeth glowered at him, and Matt showed his badge. The glower didn't go away, but the man stepped back, and Matt and Jonesy stepped inside. A beefy arm barred Tara's passage.

"I'm with them," she protested.

The doorman said, "Pull the other one, sister. You're no cop. Your legs aren't bad enough."

"Nice try, Torchy Blane," Matt said. The heavy doors closed on Tara's protests.

The bruiser led them through a lounge, which opened onto an inside garden with a small waterfall, and then through to another larger lounge with a stage, where a platinum-haired girl was running through some swing versions of Christmas standards while a man at the piano tinkled along.

A man and woman sat amidst the sea of empty tables. They had the easy rapport of an old married couple, but in fact Sid Szabo and Nora Noonan were longtime business partners. The rumor was that they were lovers as well, but observing them together, Matt wasn't sure.

Nora Noonan was not beautiful, but she had a self-contained, intelligent face—like a portrait of the Madonna. Her hair was reddish blond. She wore a well-cut tweed suit. Sid Szabo was one of the handsomest men Matt had ever seen—like a Sunday matinee idol. Dark hair and eyes so blue you could tell it from across the room. He was watching the girl on the stage, but Matt knew he hadn't missed their entrance.

Nora Noonan was smiling her slight, enigmatic smile as Matt and Jonesy approached the table. "Well, Detectives, we heard the news on the radio. I had a feeling you'd be showing up."

"Lieutenant Spain," Matt said, and flashed the tin.

Nora Noonan raised her eyebrows, pretending to be impressed. "May I offer you a drink, Lieutenant Spain?"

"No thanks. What can you tell me about the Arlen kid?"

"Do sit down!" She smiled at Jonesy. "Sergeant? You look like a drinking man."

Jonesy made some uncomfortable assurances to the contrary, and she smiled that smile again. Szabo watched them, unspeaking, his eyes not missing a move—and yet his attention remained with the girl now warbling "I'll Be Home for Christmas."

After they were seated, Nora said, "The truth? I wouldn't shed any tears over Phil Arlen—except for the fact that he owed me forty grand."

Matt whistled. "Is that right? Forty thousand dollars in gambling debts?"

"Gambling is illegal in this state, Lieutenant," Nora said mildly. "This was a personal loan."

"For?"

Nora smiled. "I didn't like to ask. After all, Arlen was a good customer—and he came from a good family. I felt sure he'd make good on his debt."

"He was a weasel," Szabo said.

Nora looked exasperated. "Sid—"

"He was a weasel," Sid repeated. "Why pretend anything else?" His stone-cold eyes studied Matt boldly. "You talk to the wife? She was here Friday night threatening to kill him."

"Sid!" Nora sounded truly put out now.

Szabo turned his profile and stared at the stage and the singer. "Talk to the wife," he said.

"Cherchez la femme," Nora remarked. "Maybe." She shrugged her tweed-clad shoulders. "I guess it makes as much sense as anything these days."

"The fact is, we're investigating Arlen's death as a kidnapping gone wrong," Matt said—and now he had the attention of both.

"A…kidnapping? The radio didn't mention that," Nora said carefully. Sid said nothing.

"That's right. Arlen didn't come home Saturday night. His family received a ransom demand on Sunday. The money was delivered, but Arlen was bumped off anyway."

"My goodness," Nora said faintly. "They paid the ransom?"

"Right."

Nora looked at Sid. Sid looked at Nora.

Nora said finally, "That doesn't make much sense. Killing the victim, I mean, if the ransom was paid on time. Not a sound business practice."

"That's what I say," Matt said. "Anyway, the last time anyone saw the Arlen kid was here on Saturday night."

"I wouldn't know," Nora said. "I wasn't here. I had one of my sick headaches."

She looked at Sid, who said flatly, "He was here. He was always here. We should have charged him rent."

Nora made a pained face—the Madonna putting up with a lousy suggestion from Joseph—and said, "Philip was somewhat enamored of Pearl." She nodded to the girl on the stage. "Pearl Jarvis. She sings here Tuesdays through Thursdays."

On Mondays the club was closed, and on weekends the big names appeared. The Las Palmas Club attracted a lot of big names: Tommy Dorsey, Crosby, Glenn Miller, Benny Goodman. It was one of the city's hot spots, though Matt would have to take the word of others for that. He was not much for nightclubs.

It was Szabo's turn to look irritated. "Pearl put up with the puppy, that's all. She was just being nice to a customer. They're all good girls here."

"Sure," Matt said. "Convent-reared, every one of them. So Philip hung around Pearl, and Philip's wife was jealous?"

Nora laughed a cool little laugh. "Well, I expect she wasn't *pleased* about it, but I don't think Claire Arlen is the type to go around murdering husbands."

"You might be surprised what wives will do," Matt said, holding her gaze.

Nora's dark gaze sharpened. She looked down at her drink. "True," she murmured.

Matt said to Sid, "Do you remember what time Arlen left here on Saturday?"

"I wasn't keeping track of him. He was pretty drunk, that much I do remember."

"When was the last time you remember seeing him?"

"Sometime after midnight."

"Who was he with? Pearl?" Matt glanced at the canary. She looked like a million other girls to him. Nice figure, nice face—nice voice too— but clothes too tight, hair too blond and skin too painted.

Sid smiled sourly. "Nope. They weren't talking that night. He was with a reporter. What's his name from the *Tribune-Herald*. Doyle, that's it. He was with Doyle the last time I saw him."

Chapter Two

CARL WINTERS BOOKSELLER read the black-and-gold script on the sign above the long bow window. And beneath, in smaller letters: The Fine, the Rare, the Antiquarian.

Bombastic, in Nathan's opinion. The man sold words, he didn't write them. Or at least not that Nathan knew of. But then he didn't know a lot about Carl Winters. What he did know wasn't heartwarming.

He pushed through the door and found himself in one of those hushed and rarefied establishments where tomes were sold by the size and matched leather bindings—and cracking a book's spine was a hanging offense. Plush maroon carpet deadened his footsteps as he made his way through Ming vases, Chippendale chairs and a few strategically placed bookshelves to the front desk. This long black wood construction could never be called a *counter,* and nothing so plebian as a cash register sat there. A cool and elegant blonde wearing a pair of horn-rim spectacles that had to be for show observed his approach.

"May I help you?"

"I'd like to speak to Mr. Winters."

She didn't quite allow herself a smirk, but her "Did you have an appointment?" was clearly rhetorical.

"No. I'm Nathan Doyle." He showed her his press pass.

Her pointy little nose twitched. "Mr. Winters is not speaking to the press."

There was an answer to that, but Nathan bit the inside of his cheek. She didn't look like she had much sense of humor. "Okay. Well, could you remind him we met Saturday night at the Las Palmas Club?"

She tipped her head, studying him over the top of her glasses, then, reluctantly, she abandoned her front desk post and sashayed through a pair of oversized carved doors, vanishing into a discreet back room.

Nathan leaned back against the front desk and studied the very nice watercolors on the wall. England probably. A very different England than the last time he'd been there. He supposed you could still find places like that, rural pockets mostly untouched by the war. He hadn't seen any. Not in England. Not in North Africa.

Outside the shop windows, holiday shoppers in raincoats, umbrellas tilted against the rain, bustled along the wet street, laden with parcels and shopping bags. Funny, that. Come wind or rain or sleet or world wars, people still celebrated the holidays. Maybe it said something about the human spirit. Or maybe it said something about the strength of habit.

"Mr. Doyle?"

He turned as Carl Winters approached. He was alone. There was no sign of the Dresden-figurine salesgirl. That alone assured Nathan he was on the right track.

Winters was a trim and dapper midforties. He wore a pale yellow carnation in his lapel and Nathan could just about see his reflection in the gleam off Winters' hand-stained antique copper brogues. His lustrous hair was prematurely white, but the face beneath was tanned and youthful. Though he was smiling, his eyes were wary, and Nathan understood why.

They shook hands briefly, and Winters said—heading Nathan off, it seemed—"Is this a sympathy call or a request for an interview?"

Nathan studied his face. "I can't say I'm particularly sorry about Phil," he said. "Are you supposed to be?"

"He was a lowlife. A creep. That's off the record *and* on."

Nathan smiled.

"But I didn't kill him," Winters added.

"Sure. Any ideas about who might have?"

"Anyone who had the displeasure of his acquaintance."

"Including your sister?"

"Leave Claire out of this."

"She brought herself into it by showing up at the Las Palmas Club on Saturday night."

"That was…nothing," Winters said curtly.

"It was *something*." Nathan was gentle but definite. "The police are liable to think so, anyway."

Winters' face changed, grew ugly. "I see. This is a—a shakedown, is that it?"

Nathan shook his head. "I couldn't keep it quiet if I wanted to. Too many people saw your sister threaten Phil. Too many people saw all three of us at the club on Saturday."

"That's right," Winters said. "But Phil was still alive and kicking when Claire and I pulled out. We left him to *your* tender mercies."

Nathan shrugged. "Phil was alive when I left him." He considered Winters levelly. "The story is he was grabbed by kidnappers. But I guess you would have heard that from your sister."

Winters didn't so much as blink.

Nathan nodded thoughtfully. "You don't buy the kidnapping story either."

"I buy it. I'm just waiting for you to accuse me of kidnapping and murder."

"Times are tough," Nathan said. "Not many people have leisure or luxury to read these days." He glanced at a copy of William Blake's *Songs of Innocence* under glass on the ebony counter. "Not at these prices."

"I do very well," Winters said. "It's not a crime. Even in wartime."

Nathan just studied him, and Winters said edgily, "I don't know what you think you've heard…"

"We both know what Arlen was," Nathan said coolly. "I heard enough on Saturday to figure out that he was putting the screws on you. I can make an educated case as to what he had on you."

"What he *thought* he had on me," Winters corrected.

"If you were paying him to keep his mouth shut—and apparently you were—"

"That doesn't mean anything. I paid him because scandal can ruin a man in my position. It doesn't matter if it's true or not, just the hint of it's all it takes. That's the way the world turns."

"Maybe so." Nathan was thinking that if Winters had nothing to fear he would have told his brother-in-law to go to hell. He hadn't because he didn't want Arlen planting that seed of doubt in anyone's minds. It was liable to start people looking, and Winters couldn't afford that. Nathan understood that line of reasoning because he couldn't afford people to start looking either. He added, "I guess you weren't happy about the way he was treating your little sister."

"No, I wasn't happy," Winters said. "But, believe it or not, Claire loved that little rat. She wouldn't have thanked me for removing him from this mortal coil." He swallowed hard. "This is liable to kill her."

"She seemed healthy enough to me on Saturday," Nathan replied. "Healthy pair of lungs on her."

Winters' face darkened again. "She didn't kill him. And I didn't kill him. And as far as paying Phil hush money, what were *you* paying him for?"

Nathan's smile was wry. "I didn't pay him. I couldn't afford to."

Winters stared at him. "Then it seems to me," he said, "you've got as good a motive for murder as anyone."

"It does seem that way," Nathan agreed.

*P*hilip and Claire Arlen lived up the road a bit from the Robert Arlens, in a fashionable five-story Spanish-Italian apartment hotel called the Los Altos. The hand-tinted postcards sold in the lobby said the Los Altos "Catered to a Particular Clientele," which always amused the hell out of Nathan.

He ran through the stone courtyard, fountains gurgling with rain and water, and ducked under the ornate stone entrance. The lobby was carpeted in red, the walls creamy, and the light muted. A large flocked Christmas tree stood at one end, a spill of gaily wrapped, for-display-only "presents" beneath its feathery limbs. Nathan went up a couple of flights of stairs, down a hall with intricately carved wooden panels, and rang the buzzer of Philip Arlen's apartment. Veronica Thompson-Arlen opened the door.

"Oh," she said, surprised. She did not seem like a woman frequently caught off guard. She had been a navy nurse, Nathan remembered, Bob's nurse after he cracked up his B-25 Mitchell during a failed bombing run over Japan. Love among the bedpans. Bob hadn't come out of it too badly. A game leg, a scarred face, a beautiful young wife and a nice cushy job waiting for him. A lot of guys had it a lot worse.

It made sense that Veronica would be there to comfort her sister-in-law. Nathan said, "Hi, Ronnie. Is Claire home?"

"She's resting. Why?" She glanced over her shoulder into the silent interior of the apartment. The drapes were drawn, blinds closed. "Nathan, she's not well enough to speak to anyone. Phil's death has devastated her."

"I'll be careful with her."

"But why can't it wait?"

Good question. He said, "You'll have to take my word that it can't."

Veronica studied him. "I don't know you that well." Then she shrugged. "Bob says you're a straight shooter. I'll ask Claire if she feels up to talking to you." She hesitated as though there were something more she needed to say then seemed to change her mind. She turned and walked into the other room.

Nathan looked around himself. The word was that old man Arlen had cut the purse strings to young Philip in an effort to bring him into line. The way Nathan heard it, the old man wanted Philip to enter the family business—take his birthright corner office at Arlen Petroleum—and to spend a few more nights at home. It was no secret that Phil had declined. But it didn't look like he and the missus were suffering unduly. The apartment was very nice—they were all very nice apartments at the Los Altos—although it didn't come with the finger bowls and champagne glasses doled out to occupants of the Bryson. Still, it didn't look like baby brother was exactly strapped for cash. Claire's bloodline was impeccable, but the Winterses had been at financial low tide for decades, ever since the big crash in '29, so the funding wasn't coming from her side of the family.

Veronica appeared in the doorway and beckoned Nathan in.

The living room was dark; it smelled of pine trees and Elizabeth Arden. A five-foot evergreen stood unadorned in one corner, and various scattered ornaments winked and glinted in the dim light. He could just make out the woman sitting on the sofa near the French doors. Claire Arlen's hair appeared to be the exact shade of the pale carnation her brother wore in his lapel. She was fair and small and built. She wore some kind of frothy negligee set, and she looked as fragile as the Christmas tree angel sitting on the table beside her elbow.

Nathan glanced around and Veronica had disappeared.

Claire said in a dull voice, "Carl called to tell me you'd probably turn up. I didn't kill Phil."

Nathan took off his hat and sat down on the ottoman. "You were pretty upset with him on Saturday night."

"Not with Phil. With *her*. That woman."

"Pearl Jarvis?"

Claire nodded. "The torcher. 'I'm Getting Sentimental Over You.'" She laughed a bitter little laugh and covered her eyes with her hand. "I used to like that song!"

"Was Phil having an affair with her?"

"I don't know." She wiped her eyes. "I didn't think so, but then…" She shook her head. "There was something between them."

"It seemed like you thought so on Saturday night."

She took her hand down and glared at him.

He made sure his voice stayed low and soothing. "Did you ever try to talk to Pearl?"

"Her?" She sounded indignant. "That tramp?"

He smiled apologetically. "I know wives sometimes do—try to talk to other women."

Something in his smile seemed to disarm her instinctive affront. "Are you married?" she asked.

"No."

"Got a sweetheart?"

He shook his head. "I've been overseas."

Claire shook her head like he couldn't possibly understand. "I did try to talk to her once. She just laughed at me. Told me Phil was free, white and twenty-one. When Phil found out I'd been to see her, he slapped me. Carl told him if he ever laid a hand on me again—" She broke off.

"He'd kill him?" Nathan finished.

She didn't reply.

"I guess I'd feel the same," Nathan said. "If someone treated my sister that way."

"Do you have a sister?"

"No."

"Then what do you know about it?" She turned a mutinous profile and stared unseeingly at the row of photos on the credenza. "Anyway, it was only the one time. Carl didn't kill Phil. He was killed by the kidnappers."

"Why do you think they did that? After the ransom was paid?"

"How should I know? Maybe…Phil saw one of them. Maybe he saw or heard something and they couldn't afford to let him go. Maybe…there was a problem with the money. Maybe they didn't receive the ransom payment."

"Do you think there *was* a ransom payment?"

That brought her face forward in a hurry. "What are you suggesting?"

"Yes, what *are* you suggesting?"

That was Veronica, standing in the doorway behind him. He hadn't heard her, and he wondered how long she had been standing there.

He said simply, "Nothing the police won't think of on their own."

"Listen," Veronica said. "Regardless of what Bob thought of Phil and the way Phil conducted his affairs—sorry, Claire, honey—he wouldn't do anything to jeopardize his safety. That's not brotherly love, it's the kind of man Bob is—and you ought to know it. Bob delivered that money exactly per the kidnapper's instructions."

"I believe you," Nathan said.

"I don't care if you believe me or not. You've outstayed your welcome, Mr. Doyle."

Nathan glanced at Claire, but she seemed to have tuned out again. She was staring at the grouping of photos, her hand resting lightly on her midriff as though she felt ill—and he couldn't blame her for that. He rose and followed Veronica into the outer hallway with the Italian carvings. He put his hat on, and she said abruptly, "You're getting the wrong idea about Phil. Mostly he was just young. If Benedict had let him enlist like he wanted to, he'd have been all right. The irony is Benedict wanted to keep him safe at home."

"Just boyish high spirits, is that the story?" Nathan inquired.

She met his gaze levelly. "We all have our stories, Mr. Doyle. Don't we?"

Nathan had lunch—a drink and a smoke—at the High Hat, where most of the reporters from the larger papers hung out. It was a nice little place with decent food and strong drinks. There was a piano bar in the evenings, and out back was a red-carpeted patio with several tables beneath green umbrellas. Because of the rain, everyone was inside and the bar was noisy and blue with smoke. Most of the noise centered on the Arlen story, and Nathan took a fair amount of razzing about being picked up by the police.

He grinned, easily deflected the questions and listened closely. Everyone seemed to be running with the same angle: a kidnapping gone wrong. He hoped that meant the police were investigating it the same way. He wasn't convinced though. Lieutenant Spain seemed the thorough kind.

For a moment he let himself dwell on the thought of Lieutenant Spain. Alert, aggressive—probably an ex-marine. They were all tough bastards. But Spain had that boy-next-door quality too. And that infrequent and devastating smile—and eyes just the color of a Scottish loch at sunset, sort of green-gold, like summer bracken or polished cairngorm.

And the fact that Nathan was thinking like this about *a cop* indicated just how bad things had gotten. Maybe he really was losing his mind.

It was after two o'clock by the time Nathan caught the Yellow Car for Wilshire Boulevard and the Las Palmas Club. By then he was feeling the cumulative effect of too many drinks and too many sleepless nights. He was still a long way from being fit—there were days when he wondered if he would ever feel truly fit again. And the worst part was he didn't really care either way.

Like all such places, the Las Palmas Club seemed smaller in the daylight. Rain sheeted off its striped awning and gargled down the gutters of Wilshire.

He expected to have trouble getting into the club but, in fact, he had very little. An ugly, bald-headed bruiser let him inside and, after a brief wait in the foyer, he was shown into a leather-lined office. As he entered the room, Nora Noonan and Sid Szabo broke off what appeared to be an intense discussion. Sid swung away and went to glare out the rain-streaked window.

Nora rose from a Queen Anne chair behind an equally magnificent desk. "Mr. Doyle, you're becoming a regular."

Nathan smiled and shook hands. "I'm afraid I'm here in my official capacity."

"And what's that? Snoop?" That came from Sid, his back to the room.

"The Arlens are news in this town," Nathan said mildly.

"Of course they are." Nora shot Sid's back an exasperated look and then smiled again at Nathan. "We always like to cooperate with the press, but I'm not sure how much help we'll be. Frankly, it's not the best publicity for us, Phil Arlen getting kidnapped off our doorstep."

"Was he kidnapped?"

"The police seem to think so."

"What do you think?"

She directed another one of those looks at Sid's unresponsive broad shoulders, waiting in vain, it seemed, for him to chime in. "It seems likely. The last time anyone seems to have seen him was here."

"With you," Sid said.

Nathan turned his way. "That's right. Phil and I walked out together. We said good night. He went his way and I went mine."

"So you say."

"Sid!" That time Nora couldn't contain her impatience. The smile she turned on Nathan was apologetic and charming. "There's no reason we can't be civilized. Would you like a drink, Mr. Doyle?"

Nathan thought about it. He couldn't remember if he had eaten at all that morning. He suspected breakfast had consisted of a nip from the flask belonging to Fred Williams of the *Daily News*. And there had been several drinks after that, but the alcohol was helping him get through this—and there was still a long way to go—so he said, "Sure."

Nora poured him a generous two fingers from a bottle of Four Roses. "Sid?" she inquired.

"You know I don't drink during the day," Sid returned.

Nora winked at Nathan and took a dainty sip. She reminded Nathan of a nun with the high white collar of her blouse and her plain, intelligent face—although he'd never seen a nun taking a nip.

He said, directing the question to either of them, "What can you tell me about the relationship between Pearl Jarvis and Phil Arlen?"

"Why are you trying to start something? There was no relationship," Sid said, turning to face the room—to face Nathan. "The little weasel had a crush on Pearl. Lots of guys do."

"Mrs. Arlen seemed to think it was a little more than that."

Nora sighed. "Perhaps it was. What can it matter now? Arlen's dead."

"Yeah," Nathan said. "Supposedly his kidnappers bumped him off after they picked up the ransom money. Any idea why that would be?"

"Maybe he got on their nerves," Szabo said. "It's been known to happen."

"Maybe," Nathan agreed. "How much was Arlen into you for?"

"Forty big ones," Szabo said. "So if you're thinking Nora and I have a new sideline—"

"If you have, you came out sixty grand ahead on the deal."

Nora laughed. "We're gamblers. We're not crazy."

"I agree," Nathan said. "For that kind of risk it would have to be worth a lot more to you than sixty—or even a hundred grand." When neither of them responded, he asked, "Would it be okay if I talked to Pearl?"

"Why?" Szabo asked.

As though he hadn't spoken, Nora said, "That's up to Pearl. She's not here right now. You can probably catch her after her show this evening."

"Do you have an address for her?"

"No," Szabo said.

Nora looked regretful. "We don't give that kind of information out, Mr. Doyle. But come back this evening. We'll see you get the best seat in the house. Nothing's too good for the gentlemen of the press." She smiled a secret sort of smile.

Nathan looked at Szabo. "Any reason you don't want me to talk to Pearl?"

"Why should there be?"

Nathan shrugged. "Every time her name comes up you get a little testy. You have a lot of problems with her?"

"We don't have any problems with her."

"She's very good," Nora said. "Very talented. Have you ever heard her sing 'I'm Getting Sentimental Over You'?"

"Once or twice. She knows how to sell a song." Nathan said to Szabo, "Maybe you did like her. Maybe you liked her too much."

Szabo stared long and unblinkingly at Nathan.

Nora said, "I guess you haven't heard the rumors about Sid and me, Mr. Doyle."

Nathan smiled. "I guess I might have—but I don't believe everything I hear."

*H*e was not going to be very popular with Whitey Whitlock, his editor. At the rate he was going, the *Tribune-Herald* was going to be the only paper in town that didn't have a major story filed on the Arlen murder. That in itself was liable to look suspicious.

He couldn't help it. He didn't have a lot of time. Every time he thought of a particular police lieutenant with a pair of shrewd hazel eyes, Nathan could hear a clock ticking. It wasn't going to take Lieutenant Spain long to put two and two together because—unless Nathan was very wrong— Lieutenant Spain already had an inkling or two.

Of course he could be letting his imagination—and guilty conscience—run away with him. He thought back to what he'd read in Spain's eyes. The look he'd first seen across the sand and weeds and grass that morning—a very different look from the one he'd seen by the time they parted ways after leaving Bob Arlen's apartment. Had he interpreted that look correctly? Or was he seeing what he wanted to see? It was hard to know sometimes.

Either way it was moot now. Spain had picked up the scent, and Nathan recognized, without knowing almost anything about the man, that Spain was a very good tracker.

There was still a chance, if he acted quickly, and that's what he had spent the morning doing.

He needed to find Pearl Jarvis. Needed to hear her story, find out what she had to say, but if she wasn't deliberately lying low, she was sure giving a good impression of it.

Having struck out at the club, he wasted another hour hunting down her last known address. But Pearl no longer resided at the rooming house in Echo Park, and Nathan got an earful from her former roommate about owed rents and a missing Bonwit Teller evening coat.

From Echo Park he trailed the elusive Miss Jarvis back to an apartment on Highland Avenue, but it was the same story—or at least a similar one—there. Miss Jarvis had vacated owing a month's rent and claiming loudly that she knew nothing about a misplaced cultured pearl choker.

Pearl was clearly a girl who moved around a lot even in Los Angeles's wartime housing shortage. But maybe she had good reason. It seemed that way to Nathan. From Highland Avenue he finally tracked her down at a rooming house on Hill Street.

But although Pearl technically still lived at Mrs. Malloy's, she was not at home.

"When do you expect her back?" he asked.

Mrs. Malloy was vague. "Not 'til after the last show tonight." Her face took on a suspicious look. "No gentlemen visitors after seven o'clock."

"I wouldn't dream of it," Nathan said, and that was true.

It looked like he was going to have to settle for talking to Pearl after the last show at the Las Palmas Club.

He caught a streetcar back to Broadway and Third, pushing through the arched entrance of the Tribune-Herald Building, making his way through the inside courtyard, looking up to see rain washing across the skylight. Taking the caged elevators up, he mentally hammered out his story. He didn't have anything. He was trusting that no one else did either, but he didn't know. He hadn't noticed any extras showing up on the street, but he'd been so preoccupied, somebody could have pushed a paper into his hand and he wouldn't have noticed.

Had the cops managed to talk to Pearl? Something Szabo had said before Nathan left the Las Palmas Club made him think not. Not then, anyway. But even if the cops talked to Pearl, they might not know which questions to ask. In fact, Nathan was trusting that they didn't, that they were still investigating Arlen's murder as a kidnapping gone wrong.

Whitey Whitlock greeted him with the usual inquiry as to whether he could explain why they were paying him such an exorbitant salary to sit on his duff and drink martinis at the High Hat all day.

Doyle assured Whitlock he had no idea, but he personally felt he was worth every penny. Then he sat down and typed up some malarkey, handed it in to Whitlock, who scowled from beneath white and beetling brows as he skimmed the crisply typed pages and shook his head.

"Doesn't anyone in this town know *anything*?"

"If they do, they're not talking to the press."

Whitlock didn't say the obvious, that it had taken Nathan all god-damned day to file a story any cub reporter could have turned in his first day on the job. In the old days Nathan would have had his ass canned for that kind of omission, but with the manpower shortage, and the war effort dominating every front page, he had a little room to operate. And, while he wouldn't have previously thought to trade on it, his bloodstained resume gave him a certain amount of clout at the *Tribune-Herald.*

He told Whitlock that since every paper in town was covering the story, he was hoping to get the human-interest angle. Whitlock looked skeptical, and rightly so. Nathan hadn't given any previous indication of anything so unwholesome as an interest in humans, but he contented himself with shaking his head and muttering how he'd always known it was a mistake to hire Doyle.

And then, very off-handedly, he mentioned that the police had been there looking for him—twice.

Nathan stood still. Then he realized that Whitlock was watching him, and he raised his brows. "I can't uncover *all* their leads for them," he said.

Whitlock harrumphed. "Next time meet them at your other office. They bring down the tone of the place." He retreated, muttering, to his lair, and Nathan went to the men's room and splashed cold water on his face.

He needed to eat something. That was the first priority. And then he needed to see what the cops wanted. But, of course, he knew what they wanted. They wanted to know why he hadn't mentioned he was one of the last people to see Phil Arlen alive. They would have found that out right after they visited the Las Palmas Club.

There had never been any question he was going to have to have this conversation with Lieutenant Spain, but it was better to go into it prepared, so he drank some water and headed downstairs to the newspaper morgue where he looked up everything he could find on Lt. Mathew Spain.

There wasn't a lot. He learned that Spain was thirty-five—a few years older than himself—and had been a cop for ten years before he enlisted in the marines, had been hit by sniper fire on Guadalcanal, and he returned to the Los Angeles police force, who were, apparently, so delighted to have him back they'd promoted him to lieutenant.

Mathew. Matt.

It suited him. Nathan stared down at the black-and-white photo. It was a tough face, but an intelligent one. Keen eyes—you could see it even in black and white. A stubborn chin, a full—but grim—mouth. Not a guy who gave up easily—if at all. It was a mouth that looked like it had learned the hard way not to smile too easily. It was an attractive face and it was hard to remember that this was the face of an adversary.

The hungry, restless feeling was on him again. For a few months in hospital he'd hoped—prayed—he was cured, but it was worse since he'd returned to Los Angeles. Much worse. Need was like a fever burning him up, burning up his inhibitions, his common sense, his instinct for self-preservation. Ironically, the war had kept him reasonably sane, reasonably steady. But now he was back to where he'd started.

He needed to give Lt. Mathew Spain a call.

But first he decided to go down to the Biltmore for a couple of drinks.

CHAPTER THREE

"What have you got for me on the Arlen kid?"

Doc Mason shoved a file cabinet closed and locked it. "Straightforward, as far as it goes. There's a bruise on his jaw like someone socked him, but that's the only sign of a struggle. He was shot from the front, from about six feet away. Hands were down at his side when he was hit. That might be significant or not. I leave it to you boys to decide. The bullet lodged in the heart. Didn't exit the body. Here's the interesting part." The coroner moved to the long counter and waved a long pair of tweezers holding a misshapen slug of lead in front of Matt's nose.

Matt's eyes narrowed. "What the hell's that?"

Mason smiled. "That, Lieutenant, is a .17, 4.3 mm ball."

"A homemade bullet?"

"Possibly. But I think it's the real McCoy."

Matt said slowly, "You think the Arlen kid was shot with an antique pistol?"

"I'm guessing a derringer."

Matt thought it over. A reluctant smile tugged at his mouth. "Swell."

"I knew you'd appreciate it."

"When was he killed?"

"Ah." Mason dropped the bullet into a small cardboard container. "Monday evening. I'd say after midnight."

"After the ransom was delivered."

"That's the way it adds up."

"Or doesn't," Matt said.

"They haven't seen Doyle at the *Tribune-Herald* since this morning," Jonesy informed Matt when he entered Matt's office later that afternoon. "He showed up long enough to turn in a story about the Arlen kid floating in the Brea Pit, and they haven't seen him since. I get the impression he comes and goes as he pleases."

Matt raised his eyebrows. "Must be nice."

"They like him over there," Jonesy admitted. "I gave them plenty of opportunity to say otherwise."

"What do you think of Sid Szabo?"

"I've heard things, but nobody ever suggested he ran a crooked joint. That counts for something in this town."

"How reliable a witness do you think Nora Noonan is?"

"On the stand or from my perspective?"

"From your perspective."

Jonesy studied him. "I think Arlen left the Las Palmas Club with Doyle on Saturday night."

"Yeah." Matt sighed. "He lied by omission. I can't think of a good reason for him not to mention he was with the Arlen kid on Saturday night."

"What do you think he was doing out at the Arlen estate this morning?"

Matt had been wondering about that himself. People got skittish in murder investigations—and not always for the obvious reasons. But Doyle didn't strike him as the skittish type. The opposite, in fact, which he thought was proved by Doyle's visit to the Arlen estate.

"That's what I plan on asking him the first chance I get." He smiled at Jonesy's suspicious expression. "What do you know about Nora Noonan?"

"She came to L.A. in '37. Partnered up with Szabo. They started the Las Palmas Club together and it was a hit from the night it opened."

"She's from Denver originally," Matt said. "Used to sing in the supper clubs. She was married to a cardsharp by the name of Stephen Reilly. The story is Reilly used to get drunk and slap Noreen—as she was called then—around, and one night she had enough of it and used a Remington Springfield on him. Claimed she thought he was a burglar. There was a trial, but Noreen was a popular lady, and she was acquitted due to insufficient evidence. She changed her first name to Nora, went back to using her maiden name and came out west where she hooked up with Szabo."

"Cripes," Jonesy said. "The things you pick up. You ever think of joining the police force?"

"Ha."

"Can't see she had much reason for getting rid of Arlen, Loot. Especially when he owed forty thousand in gambling debts."

"Yeah, but did you get a look at how old those notes were?"

Jonesy shook his head.

"A couple of them were nearly a year old. Why did Szabo and Noonan keep extending him credit when he wasn't paying up?"

"I don't see how he could have paid up," Jonesy said. "From what I can make out, he never worked a day in that big office his father gave him at Arlen Petroleum. And according to the brother, the old man had cut the kid off to try and put some backbone into him."

"There was money from his mother, but he went through that in the first year after she passed away."

Silence.

"You want me to bring Doyle in?" Jonesy said.

Matt thought it over. "He can wait. I think I'm ready to talk to the wife now. It sounds to me like, at the least, she took a dim view of his gambling. And see if you can locate the singer, Pearl Jarvis. I didn't like the way she happened to slip out the back door while we were interviewing Noonan and Szabo. If she and Arlen really weren't on speaking terms that night, I want to know why. Either way, I want to know what was between them."

"That dame must have something going for her," Jonesy said. "I get the feeling Szabo's sweet on her too."

"To each his own," Matt said, and thought of Nathan Doyle.

"*I* found some letters from her once," Claire Arlen was saying dully. "Awful things. Violet paper, purple ink...doused in scent." She shivered—although that could have been due to the skimpy silk dressing gown she wore. The apartment was cold, and the only light was the one Claire Arlen had turned on when Spain and Jonesy had turned up at her door.

Someone should have been staying with her, in Matt's opinion. But maybe she didn't want anyone. He hadn't wanted anyone after Rachel.

"And these letters were to your husband?"

She looked surprised, as though the other possibility had never occurred to her. "I thought so at the time. Phil said no. I didn't believe him...but now I wonder." Large green eyes—so pale a green that they looked gray—turned Matt's way. "There was no name, you see. They were just addressed 'darling.'"

"Why would your husband have these letters if they weren't his?"

Claire shook her head. "I don't know. But Phil said they weren't his."

Matt nodded. He was beginning to form a certain ugly idea about Phil Arlen. It had to do with gambling debts no one tried to collect on, and love letters that might not have been his.

Claire said, "I know what everyone thinks, that Phil wouldn't have married me if his father hadn't insisted, but it's not true. We were happy together. Mostly."

"What happened when you went to the Las Palmas Club on Saturday night?"

She stared at him like she didn't understand the question.

"You went to the club and had words with Phil."

"I had words with *her*," Claire said. "I told her that if she didn't stop—"

"If she didn't stop," Matt prompted.

"I…would go to Phil's dad." Her expression was a little defiant. "Mr. Arlen is a very powerful man. He could arrange things so that little floozy would never work again."

Was floozy the kind of job that required good references? Matt doubted it, but he refrained from saying so. "You didn't threaten to kill her or Phil?"

"I might have." She waved that away almost absently. "I got a little hysterical when Carl tried to drag me out before I'd finished. But it was just…talk. I'd had two cocktails with supper, and I've never had a head for strong spirits." She pressed her hands to her temple as though the very thought of strong spirits was making her head spin.

"Do you own a gun, Mrs. Arlen?"

"Of course not!"

"Did your husband own a gun?"

"No."

"Your father-in-law told us that a woman called to say your husband had been kidnapped. Did you recognize the voice? Any idea as to who that woman might have been?"

Claire shook her head dully.

"If your husband and Miss Jarvis weren't lovers, what do you think their relationship was?"

Again Claire shook her head.

"Do you have any idea why the kidnappers would have killed your husband after the ransom was paid?"

"No."

"Do you have any reason to think the ransom might not have been paid?"

She looked up, wide-eyed. "That's just what that reporter suggested."

Matt and Jonesy exchanged looks. "Doyle?" Matt asked. "From the *Tribune-Herald?*"

"That's right. He's a friend of Bob's. Or he was. He was at the club that night too. I suppose he thought I was too upset to remember, but I remember. He was there, and he was plenty mad himself. I know." She met Matt's gaze steadily. "He was smiling, but he was bone white—and his eyes were…glittering." She gave a little shiver. "I don't know *why,* but I do know he was mad enough to kill."

Matt didn't say anything. Then he glanced at Jonesy. "I think maybe it's time to have another word with Mr. Doyle," he said.

*M*r. Doyle had still not returned to roost at the *Tribune-Herald.* The address the paper had on file for him turned out to be his mother's Adam's Hill residence in Glendale.

The house was one of those old-fashioned English-style cottages: red brick with white-trimmed windows and doors. Tidy hedges surrounded the house, and instead of lawn there was neatly trimmed ivy. Christmas lights were draped along the shingled roof of the house.

Mrs. Doyle was tall and thin and fair. She had the elegant bone structure and same light, restless gaze as her son. She took policemen on her welcome mat with remarkable cool, inviting them into an immaculate living room. Matt looked around. Plastic covers on all the lamp shades and antimacassars on the arms of the chairs and sofa. Three pictures of Nathan Doyle at various ages hung in a corner over a large white statue of the Blessed Virgin. Eleven pictures of Jesus at various ages took up the rest of the wall space. A large nativity sat on a long table behind the sofa.

Nathan, Mrs. Doyle informed them, had moved to his own place on Bunker Hill. She offered them tea and cookies, apparently as a consolation prize, and to Jonesy's astonishment, Matt accepted her invitation and made himself comfortable across from the photos of Nathan Doyle. Even as a kid, Doyle had been serious-looking, but then Mrs. Doyle didn't look like a lot of laughs.

Mrs. Doyle carried in a tea tray and set it down on the table. China cups and a lovely china teapot with purple pansies kept a plate of Girl Scout cookies company.

"How is your son adjusting to civilian life?" Matt asked.

Mrs. Doyle fixed him with those cool eyes so like her son's. "Nathan is a realist," she said, which he thought was sort of strange. "Were you in the service?"

Matt admitted that he had been, and she asked him a number of interested questions, and then talked to him about the care packages the church was sending to servicemen all over the world. It was not that she declined to discuss her son; she just managed to answer with as little information as possible. Matt had a fair bit of experience with interrogation, but he suspected Mrs. Doyle could probably hold her own against the SS.

Still, it was interesting seeing the home Nathan Doyle had grown up in. Matt wasn't sure if it would prove relevant, but he didn't regret listening to Mrs. Doyle talk—although he could feel Jonesy's unease. Jonesy took a dim view of Catholics and their arcane ways.

Finally, when they had eaten the last Girl Scout cookie and drunk the last of the tea, Mrs. Doyle said, "I suppose you'll want to see his room?"

She supposed right, but Matt was mildly grateful she'd taken the initiative. Then again, Mrs. Doyle didn't strike him as a lady who ducked unpleasant duty. He accepted the offer, rising, and Mrs. Doyle led them down a short hall and up a short flight of steps—the house was oddly laid out—to a room overlooking the quiet street.

As Matt would have expected, the room was spotlessly neat. A large crucifix of a particularly handsome—but tortured—Christ hung over the crisply made bed. Matt examined the bookshelves. A number of catechism books, tomes on the saints' lives rubbed shoulders with well-worn copies of the Hardy Boys, Tom Swift, and the Radio Boys novels. A large framed map of the world hung on the wall across from the bed—the first thing young Nathan would have opened his eyes to every morning growing up? There were a few class pictures in frames, and a couple of model airplanes. Matt looked around himself, but could get no feel for the boy Nathan Doyle must have been.

He had forgotten Mrs. Doyle was watching them. "He was very badly wounded, you know. They didn't think he would live." She spoke quietly from the doorway, and Matt turned. "I don't think he has quite got used to the idea himself."

"What happened?"

"I don't know. He never speaks of it. They gave him a medal. The George Medal. For civilian bravery. He won't speak of that either. I think he's a little ashamed. Newspaper men are supposed to be neutral, and in the end, he wasn't."

Matt moved toward the door.

She said, "Whatever you think he's done, you're wrong. Nathan is a good man. A man of honor."

Matt said only, "Thank you for letting me see this, ma'am."

"No wonder he went off his rocker," Jonesy remarked as they headed over to Bunker Hill.

Matt glanced at him, but didn't answer.

"From the first minute I saw him, I sort of thought something might not be right with him," Jonesy pursued. "You get an instinct for it."

"I don't see any obvious motive for him wanting the Arlen kid out of the way, but I also can't see any reason for him to have concealed the fact he was at the club. But people hide things in a homicide investigation. They get spooked. It doesn't always mean they've committed murder."

He remembered his father and Jonesy telling him this very thing many years before, but Jonesy looked unconvinced now. And Matt wasn't convinced himself.

Doyle lived in an apartment in one of the original Victorian houses on Olive Street.

Matt and Jonesy identified themselves, and the apartment manager led them upstairs into a chilly room with large bay windows overlooking what must have once been a lovely garden. In the center of the room was an unmade pull-down bed and a table with a typewriter, a half-full bottle of Teacher's blended Scotch whisky beside it.

No pictures and no religious icons. A tall bookshelf stood mostly empty except for a couple of Christmas cards, a parcel wrapped in reindeer paper, and several volumes on travel and history and archeology. The books included a copy of the dialogs of Plato and Thomas Aquinas.

You could tell a lot about a man by what he chose to read, in Matt's opinion. He liked a good Western himself, but it was a long time since he'd read any.

More books were stacked on the table, a couple of medical books, and books on psychology. A book lying next to the bed bore the title *The Homosexual Neurosis.*

"Thanks very much," Matt said to the apartment manager. "We'll take it from here." He turned, nudging the book beneath the bed with the toe of his shoe, and forced the man out into the hall, nearly closing the door on the end of his inquisitive nose.

He leaned back against the door, and realized his heart was pounding hard and heavily, as though he'd barely escaped some terrible threat.

"Couple of bottles of painkillers in the bathroom, Loot." Jonesy poked his head out. "Nothing illegal."

Matt nodded.

"Did you find something?" Jonesy asked him.

"Huh? No." He turned away from Jonesy's curious gaze and opened the drawer of a built-in dresser. A neatly wrapped Walther rested amidst some carefully folded sweaters and corduroys. A beautiful weapon. Modern and efficient. The kind of weapon he personally would choose if he was going to commit murder.

But to each his own.

He closed the drawer again. Rain dripped soothingly from the eaves above the windows. Despite the physical temperature of Doyle's quarters, this room was more alive and warm than the room he had spent his boy-hood in. He could feel Doyle here—feel him too well.

"Nothing," Jonesy muttered from the bathroom, and for the first time Matt wondered if Jonesy was losing his touch. Of course, if it hadn't been for the war, Jonesy would have retired by now. But it was harder than hell to find good men these days.

Jonesy rejoined him in the main room. "I guess he didn't kill Arlen for the money," he remarked as they stared around the monklike setting. "It's like a barracks in here."

Matt nodded.

They went downstairs and spoke to the building manager once more.

"Quiet. Keeps to himself. No problems." The little man licked his lips. "Is there something I should know?"

Matt thought of the book he had shoved under the bed. He had thought of putting it under the mattress, but Doyle was liable to panic when he didn't find it. And the last thing he wanted to do was panic Doyle. Not with a gun in his drawer and a medicine chest full of painkillers.

"No," he said firmly. "This was just a routine check." Like LAPD routinely inspected for dust or something. "Please tell Mr. Doyle to get in contact with us when he has a chance."

The little man nodded doubtfully.

"When he has a *chance?*" Jonesy repeated when they went outside.

"I don't want that nosey parker going through Doyle's rooms."

Jonesy didn't answer.

Matt said, "Let's get a photograph of Pearl Jarvis and show it around."

"Okey dokey," Jonesy said slowly, still looking at him.

$\mathcal{I}$t was quite a while after he'd told Jonesy good night when Matt decided to head over to the Biltmore Hotel Bar.

Doyle's editor had told them that Doyle sometimes went there after work. Matt had hung around headquarters for longer than necessary on the chance Doyle might call, although he hadn't really expected Doyle would make the effort to get hold of him that evening. It was clear to him by now what secret Doyle was guarding.

And Doyle's secret confirmed what Matt already suspected of Phil Arlen.

He tried to put himself in Doyle's shoes, but he couldn't. He thought Phil Arlen was no loss to the world.

Doyle must surely know that they had gone to his workplace—he might even know that they had visited his mother and his apartment. In his position…well, it was hard to picture being in Doyle's position. Matt wasn't sure he wanted to.

The Biltmore Hotel was known as The Host of the Coast, and that night it did indeed seem to be hosting the entire population of California—or at least most of the men in the armed services.

Matt ordered a beer and found himself a quiet table in a corner. It was a beautiful room, lots of warm wood and gold leaf. There were marble floors and hand-painted ceiling frescoes and chandeliers—the kind of thing Matt would have expected to see in a museum—and there was Nathan Doyle way down at the far end of the bar, knocking back highballs with a handsome dark-haired man in a naval uniform adorned with the gold-and-silver insignia of a commander.

Doyle was clearly getting plastered. His face was flushed and his eyes were bright. He was smiling, but it was the quality of the smile that fascinated Matt. He had seen Doyle smile once or twice—always as though he had been caught off guard—but this smile was young and frank and… flirtatious.

He and the naval commander could have been alone in the packed bar; he was oblivious to Matt's presence, let alone his attention. Matt could have been standing right next to him. Instead, Matt stayed in his quiet corner, gently and not-so-gently repelling the advances of a few dames on the prowl, sipping his beer and watching. After some time and a second beer, Doyle and his friend left the bar, weeding their way through the crowd, and Matt rose and followed them out through the lobby with its parquet floors and rich jewel-toned carpets and carved ceilings, down the steps through the arches and columns into the damp night.

Doyle walked with the careful steadiness of the seasoned inebriate. The naval commander was in a little worse shape, stumbling a little and laughing, his voice bouncing back to Matt in the eerily empty street.

Matt dropped back a little. They were making for Pershing Square. Five acres of banana trees, eucalyptus and coco palms. In the daytime, the wide lawns and broad walks were busy with pedestrians, kids feeding birds, and radicals on soapboxes preaching at the top of their lungs about everything from communism to the end of the world.

But at night…at night it was another world. The walkways gleamed white in the moist moonlight, the benches sat empty, the soapboxes were vanished, and the fountain splashed in an echoing silence. And in the underbrush beneath the forest of close-growing trees and plants…

Doyle and his companion disappeared into a copse of banana trees. Matt trailed them still more slowly. He told himself he was simply doing his job, and if he was somehow discovered, he could simply arrest Doyle and his pal—although there was nothing simple about it. The idea sickened him.

But then his own actions sickened him. What the hell was he doing pushing through the stalks and waxy flowers of banana trees in pursuit of these men? He stopped, concealed in shadow and leaves, watching as Nathan dropped his trousers and got down on his hands and knees. The other man unzipped and knelt behind him, momentarily blocking Matt's view.

Matt couldn't move. The scent of decaying leaves and fruit pulp was all around him, and he felt nauseated, almost dizzy. But he had to see, so he stepped cautiously, soundlessly, keeping an eye out for other men twisting and humping in the underbrush.

Pershing Square had always been notorious for this, and now with the military in town, it was worse.

When Matt had repositioned himself, he had a perfect view of Nathan Doyle in a little circle of moonlight on his hands and knees getting fucked like a dog. He was even whimpering like a dog as the other man shoved in and out of him. Helpless, inarticulate cries—was it pleasure or pain or both?

Matt's heart seemed to thud in counterpoint, and he couldn't have looked away to save his life.

Face ricked, Doyle writhed and wriggled back on the huge cock impaling him—the other man's face was in shadow, but his powerful body was beautiful even in this obscene moment as he thrust fiercely, rhythmically into Nathan. His grunts carried through the banana leaves, and Matt wondered if he was imagining the sharp scent of sex mingled with damp earth.

And all the while Doyle kept up that puling.

It was sick and sad, and Matt knew he shouldn't be watching this, but he couldn't look away. He was miserably aware that he was getting hard—rock hard.

Doyle made another of those desperate mewling sounds. He shifted his weight and put his hand to his cock, working himself frantically, trying not to overbalance as the other man continued to slam into him.

He came first and then the other man came, collapsing on top of him, taking them both down to the ground. They lay there in the dampness, breathing hard.

Matt wiped his forehead, surprised to find that it was wet. At last the naval officer moved, rolling off Nathan and pushing up.

They didn't speak. The officer tucked himself back in, zipped up. Neither of them looked at the other as Doyle dressed hastily. The commander said something, and Doyle muttered something back, and the navy whites vanished into the trees. Doyle got up and went the other way, and Matt pulled himself together and followed.

He saw Doyle cut quickly across the cross-shaped plaza. He was making for Bunker Hill and home—making for the Angel's Flight funicular on Third and Hill, and it seemed to Matt that never had public transportation been so accurately named.

Chapter Four

The rumble of tanks and guns in the pitchy blackness, lorries and jeeps bumping along over the shifting sand—no lights allowed but the distant twinkle of the stars far overhead. Clouds of dust drifting ghostlike in the night, the forlorn yips of a jackal, the quiet murmur of voices...

Bam. Bam. Bam.

Nathan rolled out of bed, heart thundering, throat dry, groping for—

He was in a room, four walls, a ceiling, windows—he was crouching on a wooden floor next to an unmade bed. The room was soft with rosy light; the eucalyptus tree outside the window threw gentle brown shadows against the creamy walls. His books were stacked on the floor and shelves, a bottle of whisky stood on the table next to his typewriter.

He was in Los Angeles. He was home.

And someone was banging on his door.

Nathan stood, fighting to get the rush of adrenaline under control. He felt sick and shaky with it—all that fear and energy with no place to go. He sucked in a deep, steadying breath and went to the door.

"Yeah?"

A deep voice floated through the wooden barrier. "Police. Open up."

He closed his eyes, then pulled himself together and unlocked the door. Two uniformed officers stood there.

"Nathan Doyle?"

He nodded.

"You're wanted downtown for questioning."

"Am I under arrest?"

"We can do it that way if you want," the larger of the two cops said.

Nathan shook his head. "Just wondering if I have time to brush my teeth."

"We'll even give you time to pull your pants on." That was the second cop, shorter, younger, more hostile. Nathan stared at him, wondering why he wasn't in the service, wondering if the comment about his pants was intended as a crack.

"Thanks," he said coolly.

He stepped into the bathroom, bracing his hands on the sink and taking a couple of deep breaths, steadying himself.

It looked like he was out of time. He had wasted yesterday—Wednesday—dodging the cops and trying to find Pearl Jarvis. And then last night, giving in to loneliness and nerves, he had gone back to the Biltmore hoping to find the naval officer who looked so much like Lt. Mathew Spain. That had been stupid for a couple of reasons. Stupid to risk going back so soon, stupid to try for a repeat performance, and stupid most of all to acknowledge even to himself his attraction to an LAPD lieutenant. A cop. A married cop at that.

Jesus. What was next? Unrequited love?

Last night he'd found his comfort and companionship in the brawny arms of a senior airman he'd met on the steps of the hotel on his way out.

"Sam." The man had insisted they exchange names. Nathan had used his middle name, "Finan." Named for a disciple of St. Brendan. Finan was supposed to be a patron saint of monasteries, which was a good joke on someone. Sam had fucked Nathan in the banana trees of Pershing Square, and then he had tried to convince Nathan to come back to his flea-bitten hotel, and horrifyingly, Nathan had been tempted. He dreaded the idea of coming back here, of the silence and emptiness of this apartment building at night—just once he'd wanted to spend the night held tight in someone's arms, safe for a few hours, loved for a few hours—or at least pretending that he was loved.

But he'd resisted the temptation, and here he was, safe at home in time for the police to pick him up.

He could hear the cops talking quietly in his bedroom. Nathan turned on the taps, splashed cold water on his face. He shaved, brushed his teeth, ran a comb through his hair, taking no more than three minutes—he'd learned to do this fast and in the dark. His mind raced ahead to what waited for him downtown.

They hadn't tried to put handcuffs on him yet. Did that mean he wasn't being arrested? Surely that was a good sign? But the morning was young.

He dressed quickly, fingers steady, focused on what and how much of the truth he could afford to tell. He would be talking to Matt Spain. That was both the good news and the bad news.

He pushed open the door to the bathroom and the two cops broke off what they were saying to each other and eyed him warily.

The three of them went downstairs, Nathan's landlord and neighbors watching silently from their doorways. He was grateful once again that they hadn't handcuffed him, and if that was due to Matt Spain, he owed him one.

Nathan climbed into the back of the big black Ford. The young cop got behind the wheel, the older cop in back beside Nathan. Nathan listened absently as the officers talked back and forth.

"No Christmas lights at Christmas Tree Lane this year," the younger one commented as they drove down the streets decked in garlands.

The older cop said gravely, "You do know there's no Santy Claus, right, Sullivan?"

The younger cop reddened and fell silent.

Spain was alone in his office when Nathan was shown in. He nodded to Nathan's police escort, who backed out, shutting the door behind them.

"Sit down," Spain said, and Nathan took a chair across from the orderly desk. Spain looked crisp and clean-shaven in a navy suit. The wedding band on his left hand shone brightly.

"Coffee?" Spain asked politely. "Smoke?"

"Thanks."

Spain poured him a cup of coffee from a flask. Nathan sipped, and the coffee, cut with chicory, wasn't bad, though nothing as good as pre-rationing coffee. The lieutenant had a nice set-up here. Nathan's eyes were drawn to the photograph of a dark-haired woman on the bookshelf behind the desk. She looked pretty. She looked like the kind of wife someone like Lt. Mathew Spain would have. The bookshelf was full of books on the law and police procedure.

Spain proffered a pack of Camels. Nathan took one, and Spain leaned forward to light it for him. Spain's hands were large and well shaped. His lashes made dark crescents against his cheekbones. As though he felt Nathan's stare, he raised his eyes—and Nathan couldn't look away.

He stared into Mathew Spain's long-lashed hazel eyes, and he realized with terrible clarity that Spain knew all about him. Knew exactly what he was. Knew it as surely as though Nathan's ugly history were an open file on Spain's tidy desk. In fact…Nathan glanced at Spain's desktop as though somehow the explanation could be found there, because how did Spain know? *How?* Had it become that obvious? Like a scarlet letter branded into his skin—or the mark of Cain?

Hot blood flushed Nathan's face, and just as quickly drained away, leaving him feeling light-headed. He drew back, drawing sharply on his cigarette. He sat very straight.

Spain flicked his lighter closed, put it away. He seemed to be in no hurry.

"Why am I here?" Nathan blew out a stream of blue smoke. His voice was just about steady.

Spain watched him, eyes very direct beneath his straight black eyebrows. "Why didn't you mention you were with the Arlen kid on Saturday night?"

"I wasn't with him," Nathan said. "I ran into him at the Las Palmas Club. We had a drink together." He shrugged.

"Were you with him when Claire Arlen and her brother showed up?"

Nathan hesitated. "Me and half the bar."

"What happened?"

"Claire arrived with her brother, Carl, and asked Phil to come home. He declined. She got upset and said some things. She'd been drinking, I think. Anyway, Carl convinced her to leave. That's pretty much it."

Spain grinned, a white and charmingly crooked grin. All at once he looked a lot younger and a lot friendlier. "Well, that's a very careful, factual recounting of what took place. I bet you're a pretty good reporter. You understand the power of words. Other people we've interviewed have used words like 'screamed' and 'threatened' and 'demanded.'"

"Like I said, she'd had a few drinks. Her brother took her home before she could get into any real trouble."

Spain leaned back in his swivel chair and rubbed his chin. "Listen, Sir Galahad, it might interest you to know that the lady in question didn't mind throwing you to the wolves. She said it looked to her like you were pretty angry with Philip yourself. Like you were mad enough to kill."

"She doesn't know me very well." Nathan studied the ashes on his cigarette.

"Did she threaten to kill her husband and Pearl Jarvis?"

"She might have." Nathan smiled wryly. "I wasn't listening that carefully, to tell you the truth."

"Why's that?"

Nathan said slowly, "I went there for a few drinks and some laughs, but after I got there…I realized that really wasn't what I needed."

"What did you need?" Spain asked—and Nathan, for the life of him, couldn't think of how to answer.

Neither of them spoke. Neither of them looked away.

Nathan's heart was jerking like a marlin on the end of a very short line; he felt as though it was going to slip the hook and go banging around his rib cage.

The door opened behind him, and the tall gray-haired detective Spain had called Jonesy stuck his head in. "Loot, the Jarvis girl never came home last night either," he said.

"Looks like she's lying low," Spain said. "She didn't turn up for her show at the Las Palmas Club last night again."

"You think something happened to her?" Jonesy didn't sound too worried about it.

"Maybe." Spain looked at Nathan. "But according to you, Mrs. Arlen wasn't mad enough to really hurt anybody. And I can't see why anyone else needs to get rid of the late Mr. Arlen's girlfriend. Can you?"

He was baiting Nathan a little, but not offensively so.

"Maybe she knew who kidnapped Arlen." Nathan wondered whether they had already interviewed Pearl and this was merely a follow-up, or if they hadn't questioned her at all yet. He suspected they hadn't questioned her at all, because as far as he could tell, she'd already skipped town.

It occurred belatedly to him that Spain probably knew he'd been trying to find Pearl too.

"Yeah," Spain was saying thoughtfully. "Those kidnappers."

"You don't think he was kidnapped?" Nathan glanced back at Jonesy. He was leaning against the office wall, arms folded. He could feel that Jonesy didn't like him, could feel it in the way Jonesy watched him. He couldn't tell how Spain felt about him.

"I like to keep an open mind," Spain mused. He looked at Jonesy too, although he spoke to Nathan. "So tell me what happened after Mrs. Arlen made her threats and was escorted home by her brother."

"Miss Jarvis returned to her table and friends. Not long after that they all left."

"So she wasn't with Arlen?"

"They didn't speak once as far as I noticed. She doesn't perform there on the weekends, she was there as a guest like anyone else."

"How long after she left before Arlen left?"

Nathan recognized this for the trap it was.

"Maybe half an hour. Phil and I walked outside together. We said good night. He walked east. I walked west. The next time I saw him he was lying in the grass at Brea Tar Pits. Dead."

Spain glanced past Nathan to Jonesy. "Did anyone follow him? Any cars start up along the street?"

Nathan was tempted to lie, to make up a story that might keep them off his back for a while, but he shook his head. "I didn't see anything."

Silence.

Nathan smoked his cigarette, waiting, refusing to indicate by so much as a flicker of eyelash how tense he was. Unless they knew about Phil Arlen, all they had on him was the fact that he'd left the club when Arlen had. It wasn't enough to hold him, let alone charge him.

But if they had already found out how young Phil supplemented his income, then they had him. Spain already suspected what Nathan was—and he could arrest him on suspicion alone.

"Why didn't you tell us you were with the Arlen kid?" Spain asked again, and his voice was a little harsher. "It looks a little suspicious from our perspective, if you see what I mean."

"A lot of people were there that night," Nathan said. "I guess I didn't think I had anything important to tell. I knew you'd find out about it, so it's not like I was trying to hide anything."

Jonesy snorted. Nathan glanced back at him, stubbed his cigarette out, declining to respond.

"Anything else you want to tell us?" Spain asked finally.

Nathan looked up, and knew his surprised look gave the game away, but he couldn't help it. Of course he should have told them he was with Arlen. Of course his actions looked suspicious. Of course he was hiding something. He knew it. They knew it. So what was going on? Meeting Spain's eyes again, he understood that Spain wasn't fooled for one minute, but for some reason he was letting him walk away. For now.

Nathan replied, "No."

"Okay." Spain nodded politely, and Nathan rose, picking up his hat. "We'll be in touch," Spain added.

Nathan nodded and went out. The door swung gently closed behind him.

He expected to be followed, and although he could see no sign of a tail, he took it for granted that he was shadowed. It didn't present an immediate problem. Stopping for breakfast at a diner, he treated himself to eggs and bacon, not because he was hungry but because he knew he had to keep his energy up. He paid with cash and his red stamp coupons—practically the first he'd used since getting back—and then had a cup of real coffee, watching through the Christmas-painted windows as a phalanx of P-38 Lightnings headed out toward the ocean.

Despite his fatigue, he needed to get over to the paper. He felt weirdly numb, but when he thought of the night before in Pershing Square, he knew he wasn't nearly numb enough. And when he *was* that numb, the best thing would be to take that liberated Walther paratrooper Harry Ryan had given him, put it in his mouth and pull the trigger.

He rubbed his forehead tiredly, thought about Mathew Spain. Thought about the look in his eyes and the tone of his voice when he'd said, "What did you need?"

For a minute he let himself believe what he thought he'd seen, but it was too dangerous to kid himself about that.

Finishing his coffee, he left the restaurant. He would go to the paper, and he'd turn in some kind of story on the Arlen investigation, and then he'd try again to find Pearl Jarvis.

"Well, well," Jonesy said. "I think we have a winner."

Matt looked up, distracted from his own thoughts. "Is that so? What do you think Doyle's motive is?"

"It'll turn up soon enough. He's a cool customer, but it'll turn up."

They both knew motive was the least important element in putting together a case. People killed for all kinds of reasons that didn't make any sense to other people. If the means and opportunity were there, you could generally come up with a motive that would serve to convince a jury. All the same, Matt preferred his prime suspects to have strong and compelling reasons for their crimes. He preferred to believe in their guilt as he built his case.

Jonesy said, "He tried to protect Arlen's wife. Could there be something there?"

"No." Matt realized that was too final. "I doubt it." At the expression on Jonesy's face, he said, "We've got plenty of suspects. Don't make your mind up too fast."

"It's mighty convenient him walking out of the club the same time as the Arlen kid. If he wasn't the last person to see Arlen alive, he was damn close to it."

Matt said slowly, "He's not well. Not strong. I'm pretty sure Arlen wouldn't have gone with him without a fight, and I don't think Doyle could have taken him."

"According to Doc Mason the Arlen kid had a bruise on his jaw."

"That doesn't sound like much of a fight."

Jonesy conceded, "I guess if they'd actually tangled, Doyle would be carrying a few bruises. Of course, he could have taken him at gunpoint."

"True." Matt thought it over. "Or maybe the kid wasn't beat up because he went willingly with his kidnappers."

"If there *was* a kidnapping."

The Arlen case was little more than forty-eight hours old, but Matt was already taking heat from above to get it solved. Of course, technically the case was Jonesy's, but from the minute the victim had been identified as Phil Arlen, Matt had been acting as lead investigator. There was too much hanging on it. The Arlens were important people according to Police Chief Clarence B. Horrall, and the least LAPD could do was get the kidnapping and homicide of their youngest son solved in a timely fashion. Matt was treading carefully. Most of the suspects in young Arlen's murder were wealthy and influential people—a number of them also Arlens—and this was the kind of case that could destroy a promising police career if the officer in charge didn't play his cards exactly right.

"A botched kidnapping isn't a bad cover for a murder," Matt agreed with a wry smile. "Especially if the killer walked away with a hundred thousand dollars."

"Assuming Bob Arlen delivered that ransom money."

"Assuming Bob Arlen didn't knock off his baby brother himself."

"He had plenty of provocation," Jonesy agreed. "From what I can make out there was no love lost between those two. Phil was the apple of the old man's eye, and never did a damn thing to deserve it according to just about everyone who ever knew him."

"Bob Arlen doesn't have much of an alibi. He was supposedly home alone Saturday night while his wife was at the ballet enjoying *The Nutcracker* with two other couples."

Jonesy nodded. "He could have waited outside the club for him. Seems likely big brother could get close to Philip without arousing a lot of suspicion, and even with a bum leg, he's a big, powerful guy."

Matt agreed. "And if the wife did get home and discover Bob gone, she'd lie her head off. That dame's crazy for him. Even the muckrakers admit she didn't marry him for his dough. Not that he has a lot of his own. The old man controls the purse strings."

Jonesy scratched his nose reflectively. "All the same, Bob Arlen doesn't strike me as the kind of guy who would fool around with an antique pistol. If he was going to kill baby brother, my guess is he'd just use his service revolver."

Matt nodded to himself. "You're right. We can't forget about that gun. Who the hell walks around packing an antique pistol?"

"Where would Doyle have got such a thing?"

"Where would anybody?" Matt mulled this over. "The old man, Benedict Arlen, collects antiques and western memorabilia. Find out if he's got a gun collection."

Jonesy's eyes brightened. "Now you're talking!"

"Uh-huh. The real question is where is that gat now? If we could find it—"

Jonesy shook his head. "I'm guessing that gun's buried way down deep in the tar with all those dinosaur bones."

"Even if the pistol did come from a collection belonging to Benedict Arlen, it doesn't exactly narrow our field of suspects. Just about everybody *except* Doyle probably had access to it—Bob Arlen, Claire Arlen and, possibly, Claire's brother Carl Winters."

"Winters is supposed to have a hot temper," Jonesy said. "And there have been rumors for years that some of those fancy books he sells aren't the genuine article."

Matt contemplated Jonesy's homely face. The blackmail angle. They couldn't get away from it. Suppose Phil had known—had proof—that Carl faked the fine, the rare and the antiquarian? "That fancy bookstore Carl Winters owns is full of antiques. Let's bring in Winters," he added. "I wouldn't want him to think we were neglecting his side of the family."

Jonesy nodded, turned to leave the office and paused. "You sure you don't want Doyle followed?"

"I'm sure," Matt said.

In a creative fever, Doyle typed up a story from the standpoint of doomed young Phil Arlen and handed it in to Whitey Whitlock. It wasn't journalism—it was more suitable to *Black Mask* than the *Tribune-Herald*—but Whitlock read it, whistled and offered Doyle one of his rare snaggle-toothed smiles.

"Well, it's certainly a new angle," was all he said.

"I thought I'd head over to Griffith Park Observatory and see if I could pick up the trail," Doyle said.

Whitlock considered this and then nodded. Nathan hadn't worked for him long, but he had the kind of track record that inclined Whitlock to give him his head and let him run.

"Thanks," Nathan said, and turned away.

"You all right, Doyle?" Whitlock growled, and Nathan turned back, startled.

"Fine," he said.

Whitlock considered this, not appearing particularly convinced—or particularly concerned—and he turned back to the mountain of paperwork on his desk.

Nathan decided to take his own car to Griffith Park. He kept it garaged and rarely used it as gas was tightly rationed—and tires were even harder to get—but he was thinking he might take a run down to San Diego. Pearl had family there, and anything was worth a try at this point.

Including revisiting the scene of the crime—or one of the scenes.

He didn't expect to discover anything significant at the Griffith Park Observatory and Planetarium, and he was not disappointed. It had changed some since the last time he had visited as a schoolboy on a field trip. Now soldiers were garrisoned in the park, and a large air-raid siren had been set up adjacent to the observatory. Class was being held inside the planetarium for a new crop of navy fliers who needed to learn to navigate by the stars.

Nathan ran upstairs to the east terrace, poked around and found nothing. He stood for a moment staring across the wild hills at the old Hollywood sign, and then he returned downstairs.

Out of ideas, he returned to Pearl's Hill Street rooming house in time to see Sid Szabo leaving it. Szabo carried what appeared to be one of those small women's overnight suitcases. Nathan watched him get into his car—he was alone—and, as Szabo pulled away from the curb, Nathan pulled out after him.

Szabo drove slowly, carefully, clearly having no idea he was being followed. Nathan had no problem tailing him even in the rainy weather. He kept a safe distance, leaving two cars between his Chrysler Highlander and the bright green Oldsmobile.

Szabo turned off onto South Spring Street, pulling into the two-level underground garage of the enormous old Alexandria Hotel. Nathan parked on the street and went inside.

The Alexandria had been built back in 1906, and in its heyday it was the center of Los Angeles social life and the city's crown jewel. But the glory days were gone now and, despite the crystal chandeliers, marble columns and "million dollar carpet," it had a sad, haunted quality to it. It was hard to picture someone like Szabo living there. Nathan would have pegged him for the swankiest, flashiest hotel in town.

The front desk clerk eventually stopped shuffling through mail and greeted him without enthusiasm.

"Sid Szabo?" Nathan inquired.

The clerk sighed, as one much put-upon. "I'll ring him for you, sir."

"Don't bother. I'll just run up and say hello. Third floor?"

"Second floor," the clerk said. "If you think it's really all right…"

He was speaking to the wrought-iron gate of the closing elevator.

Nathan stood in the peeling red velvet hallway outside Szabo's door listening for a few minutes. There wasn't a lot to hear. The murmur of voices, male and female, but that could have been the radio—or another skirt with Szabo.

He knocked and the voices stopped. Footsteps approached, the door opened and Szabo peered out suspiciously.

"What the hell are you doing here?" he said.

Doyle looked down at the brown alligator overnight bag sitting on the floor a few feet from the door. "I was hoping for an interview."

"Some other time." Szabo tried to close the door, and Doyle's foot shot out.

"Just a couple of quick questions."

"I don't have time. And if I did have time, I wouldn't have the inclination." Szabo's eyes narrowed dangerously. "Move your foot or I'll crush it. Don't think I won't."

Nathan withdrew his foot. "You can talk to me or you can talk to the cops."

Szabo sneered, "About what?"

"Among other things, about where Pearl Jarvis is hiding out."

Szabo laughed. "I guess I'll talk to the cops then." He slammed shut the door.

Nathan knocked on the door. It flew open.

"What the hell now?"

"If you should see Pearl, would you ask her to get in touch with me?" He handed Szabo his press card, but the other man made no move to take it.

"She's allergic to reporters," Szabo said.

"It must be catching."

He shook his head disbelievingly. "Why do you want to talk to her?"

"A little bird told me she's got a story worth telling."

Szabo's blue eyes narrowed. "What's it worth?"

"It depends on the story."

Szabo studied him. "Well, if I see her—*if* I see her—I'll let her know."

Doyle went downstairs and parked himself in his car, waiting.

$\mathcal{T}$wo rumors persisted about Carl Winters. The prevailing rumor was that the majority of his income came from his romancing of rich widows. Seeing him, Matt had no trouble believing this. Winters was a walking illustration for *Esquire* magazine, from the soles of his black Blucher town shoes to the velvet collar of his Chesterfield. But the rumor that most interested Matt, the rumor that was little more than a whisper, was that Winters faked a number of the rare and valuable old books he sold. So far no one had been willing to actually come forward and press charges, but that was because many of Winters' clients were the kind of collectors willing to not look too closely at a valuable antique's sales history.

"So against your better judgment you allowed your sister to persuade you to drive her to the Las Palmas Club?" Matt asked, continuing their interview.

"Claire is a headstrong girl," Winters said. "She was going to confront Phil with or without me. I thought that my presence would help to keep their encounter…civil."

"And was it a civil encounter?"

"No. Perhaps if that girl had not been there, it might have been different. Perhaps."

"Pearl Jarvis?"

"Yes. Phil had become entangled with this creature. She doesn't sing at the club on weekends, so I'd imagined it was relatively safe allowing Claire to go there. Unfortunately the girl was with a group of her cronies when we arrived. Although they weren't together, I believe her presence egged Phil on."

"Egged him on to do what?"

"To…behave badly."

Matt made a couple of notes, although he knew all this, had heard from a number of witnesses just how badly Phil Arlen had behaved toward his wife. He'd heard plenty also about how Pearl Jarvis had sat at her own table with her own circle of friends smirking and smiling and making little asides until Sid Szabo had taken her by the arm and gently but firmly removed her from the domestic limelight.

"So your brother-in-law declined to accompany your sister home. What happened then?"

"I saw Claire home."

"Just like that?"

"When she realized that the situation was hopeless, that she was playing to a crowd of spectators, Claire naturally wanted to leave. She felt humiliated."

"You're a man of the world. Do you think your brother-in-law was having an affair with the Jarvis woman?"

"Yes."

"Does your sister own a gun?"

"No, of course not. Claire is terrified of guns."

"Did Arlen own a gun?"

"I don't believe so. I don't believe Claire would have permitted a gun in their home."

It seemed to Matt that Claire had had to put up with a number of things from Arlen that she might not have been expected to permit.

"Do you own a gun, Mr. Winters?"

Winters hesitated. "I'm a member of the North Valley Hunt Club. I own a rifle."

Matt had heard a few things about the North Valley Hunt Club. Fox hunting in Los Angeles. During wartime no less. *Christ almighty.* "No handguns?" Matt asked politely.

"No."

"Any antique or replica weapons?"

"No." Winters looked puzzled. "I own a pair of Civil War sabers."

"Were you fond of your late brother-in-law?"

Carl Winters sighed, as though he had known this question was inevitable. "Not particularly. I didn't kill him, though."

The phone on Matt's desk rang. He picked it up. Jonesy said, "Is Winters still with you? I think we found the murder weapon. A Remington Rider Single Shot Derringer pistol. It was hidden in a large Ming vase in the back of his shop."

Matt's eyes went to Carl Winters' bland handsome face. "Is that so?" he said noncommittally.

"There's a hitch, Loot," Jonesy said. "According to the salesgirl, just about everyone and his brother has been through this shop since Sunday night. Mrs. Robert Arlen was here Christmas shopping yesterday, Claire Arlen stopped by on her way to lunch with her brother, Robert Arlen was here this morning to pick up a book. Sounds to me like anyone could have planted it—including your pal. He was here early Tuesday afternoon."

"My pal?" Matt asked carefully.

"The reporter," Jonesy said. "Nathan Doyle."

CHAPTER FIVE

$\mathcal{P}$earl scrambled out of her cab before it stopped. She darted across the shining wet sidewalk, past the sculptured-fish fountains, spumes of white shooting into the dusk, and disappeared through the side entrance of Union Station. Nathan swore, finally found a parking slot and turned the engine off. He jumped out of the car and loped across the wet and oily lot, following Pearl as he'd been following her since the moment she sneaked out of Sid Szabo's apartment building and into a waiting taxi.

Inside Union Station was a madhouse. Porters hustled, families greeted and friends good-byed, the sheer volume of sound rising from the marble floors and Spanish tiles, soaring up and disappearing into the cathedral-high ceiling and the gigantic iron chandeliers. Nathan scanned the milling crowd for Pearl's hat—a silly little fur doughnut balancing on Pearl's silly little platinum head. But there was no sign of either the hat or Pearl as he avoided small children, animal carriers and stacks of luggage, pushing his way through the mob of holiday travelers and GIs.

In answer to his urgent question, the gateman jerked his thumb toward the wide entrance leading to the tracks.

There were several trains at the platform, but only one was starting to move.

Nathan ran, swinging himself up the steps as the train began to pick up speed. It took him a few seconds to catch his breath. He mopped his face on his rain-damp coat and then set out to find Pearl in the crowded coaches.

He strode through four coaches filled with merry travelers—but no Pearl. He pushed open the door to the dining car. That was packed too, and he almost missed her, wedged in between a steamy window and a fat lady in a bright blue coat. Pearl was mostly hidden behind an open menu, but he spied the fur doughnut dipping drunkenly over the menu.

A steward came forward and Nathan let himself be led to a table, politely insisting on one with a good view of his quarry.

If he'd suspected Pearl knew she was being followed, he was soon reassured. She scanned the menu leisurely, put it down and smiled discouragingly at the friendly overtures of the fat lady.

All at once Nathan was very tired. His side was hurting from his sprint to catch the train. He picked up a menu, glanced it over. He wasn't hungry—he was rarely hungry these days, but he had to keep his energy level up. He watched Pearl over the top of his menu.

She stared determinedly out the window at the sky turning indigo, and the fat lady eventually gave up and devoted her earnest attention to a fashion magazine no doubt full of clothes she would never be able to wear.

The steward came and Nathan ordered a sandwich and a glass of milk. He ate with half an eye on Pearl and half an eye on the rest of the passengers. The sky changed from indigo to purple, Pearl finished her meal and squeezed—with great difficulty—around the cooperative but ungainly lady in blue.

Doyle drained his milk glass, waited a few moments and followed her out to the last car. It was a smoker car, about half-full with passengers. He took the seat across from her, lit up and stared out the window. Pearl's reflection took out a little jeweled cigarette case, selected a cigarette and tapped it on the case. Her gaze fell on Doyle.

He glanced over as though only noticing her. "May I?" he said, pulling his lighter out.

She nodded, leaning toward him, watching him from beneath the foolish hat.

"Thanks."

He nodded politely, snapped his lighter closed and returned to watching her in the darkened window. She studied him appraisingly.

"Say," she said. "Have we met?"

Doyle turned back to her. Cocked his head. "I'm not sure." He offered her his best smile. She smiled back. They always did. He looked unthreatening, like—he had been told by a slightly inebriated starlet—a gentleman.

The conductor was working his way slowly down the aisle, asking for tickets. A gabby old guy stopping to shoot the breeze with just about every passenger.

"I'm sure I've seen you around. You live in Los Angeles?" She pronounced it "Los Angle-less."

"That's right." He expelled a stream of smoke as she worked it out.

"You ever come around to the Las Palmas Club?"

He widened his eyes. "Hey. You're her! The songbird."

She laughed, delighted. Preened a little.

"Nice job you do on that 'I'm Getting Sentimental Over You' number," Nathan told her and listened to her warble on about the rest of her repertoire—and then who she was going to be auditioning for next summer. He let her run 'til she was out of steam, and then he said, "I was at the club on Saturday night. The night the Arlen kid was nabbed."

Her smile slipped. She stared down at her cigarette. "Oh."

"Shame about that."

"Yes."

"So where are you headed?"

She relaxed. "Little Fawn Lodge. Not far from Indian Falls."

He had a vague idea Indian Falls was located somewhere in the Sierra Nevada Mountains. He mimed surprise, and it wasn't hard. "There's a coincidence. That's where I'm headed."

"You're kidding!" There was something funny in her face. "But…the ski resorts are all pretty much closed since the war."

"Well, you see," Nathan confided, "I'm not a skier, I'm a writer."

"A writer," Pearl repeated slowly. She was watching him with narrow eyes. "What kind of writer?"

"Screenwriter. For the pictures." He figured that would impress her, but she remained wary. He'd misstepped, miscalculated either her paranoia or his own recognizability.

"You're kidding."

He shook his head. "I needed to get out of town. Needed some peace and quiet so I could work. Thought of the lodge."

"You'll get plenty of that." She gave him that same discouraging smile she'd given the fat lady. "Well, it's been swell shootin' the breeze." She jabbed her cigarette out, nodded to Nathan, rose and started down the aisle.

"See you around," Doyle said to her back. She didn't respond.

Damn.

"Tickets please," said the conductor, reaching Nathan at last.

"I'll need to buy one from you," Nathan said, pulling out his wallet. "I'm going to Little Fawn Lodge."

The conductor drew the ticket pad from his pocket. "Didn't think it was open. Most of the resorts are closed now. Hope you made reservations. It's not weather to be sleeping out in." He disconnected a strip from the ticket pad, punched it and handed it to Nathan. "Train stops at Indian Falls. You'll have to hire a car."

"That's all right," Nathan said, hoping it was. He didn't kid himself he was up to spending the night in freezing temperatures. He paid for the ticket, considering his finances. He hadn't started the day planning on a ski resort holiday.

The train continued on its way through the deepening darkness. He stared out the window. The black-plum sky had a luminous quality that made the trees and mountains stand out in stark relief.

The wheels of the train clackety-clacked along the rails in soothing monotony. Every so often the whistle blew, sounding through the night, echoing through the pines and slopes.

Now what? He'd found Pearl Jarvis—and the fact that she was trying so hard to avoid being found surely meant she knew something worth knowing—something that might help his own position.

He wondered if Lieutenant Spain would think he was trying to skip town.

"*B*ut you've got your man," Tara protested. "You found the murder weapon in Carl Winters' bookstore. Why haven't you arrested him? Why are you asking so many questions about Nathan?"

Matt shrugged. "You sweet on Doyle?"

"Sweet on him?" Tara flushed and then laughed. "We're just pals." She cast Matt a shrewd look. "Would you care if I was?"

"Marriage could do Doyle a world of good."

"What would it do for me?"

Matt grinned at her expression. "Might do you a world of good too, Tara. Take the edges off you."

"The edges!" She tossed her glossy black curls. "Thanks very much." She contemplated Matt. "You ever going to remarry, Mathew?"

He shook his head regretfully.

She sighed. "I could have gone for Nathan, but he's…"

"He's…?"

"I don't know. Destined for the priesthood or something, I guess." She grinned. "Now I've shocked you, a big tough policeman like you, Lieutenant Spain." She played with her chopsticks. They were having lunch at the Hong Kong Café. "So what did you want to know about Doyle?"

"You said you didn't know him before he went overseas?"

She shook her head. "He didn't work here. He moved to San Francisco right out of college. That's what I heard."

"How's he get along with the other newshounds?"

"He keeps pretty much to himself." She met Matt's gaze. "He's liked. He's good." She grimaced. "He's bored."

"Wants to be back on the front lines?"

She nodded, took out a cigarette. Matt leaned forward to light it. Looking into her dark eyes, he saw instead a pair of light ones, blue-gray eyes with gold-tipped lashes—direct and yet somehow a little shy.

"Why haven't you arrested Carl Winters?" Tara asked. "Off the record."

"Off the record?" He raised skeptical brows, but when she nodded, he said, "That gun came from Benedict Arlen's antique gun collection. The way we figure it, any one of a number of people had access to it."

"Including Phil Arlen?"

She was a smart cookie; he'd always thought so. He could see that sharp brain of hers ticking over. "That's right. And all but one of those same people had opportunity to stash the gat at Winters' bookstore."

"Let me ask you something," she said.

Matt nodded.

"Is Nathan a suspect?"

"He was with Arlen the night he was kidnapped. What kind of a cop would I be if I didn't include him in my list of suspects?"

"Very diplomatic," she said dryly. She sipped some tea from a little porcelain cup. "Nathan wouldn't have access to Benedict Arlen's gun collection." She followed her own line of reasoning. "But he could have got the gun from the Arlen kid, assuming the Arlen kid was carrying it that night, and that Mrs. Arlen hadn't swiped it to shoot him with it."

"It's a possibility."

"Which is? Nathan grabbing the gun from Phil Arlen or Claire Arlen plugging her no-good wastrel husband?"

"Take your choice."

"Well," she said shortly, "I choose not to think Nathan's a murderer."

She was definitely sweet on Doyle.

She said, "Anyway, why would Phil Arlen have taken the gun? I don't think he planned on committing suicide."

"Well, for one thing, it's a very rare piece. Worth a lot of money. There were only two hundred of those Derringer Riders ever made. And the Arlen kid was running low on dough. He'd racked up some sizable gambling debts at the Las Palmas Club, and his old man had cut off his allowance in the hopes of getting him to straighten up."

"You think he planned on trading the gun for his gambling chits?"

Matt shrugged.

"What possible motive could Nathan have for wanting Phil Arlen dead?"

"I don't know. What's his financial situation?"

She said dryly, "I don't think Nathan thinks a lot about money. And if he killed somebody by accident, I don't think he'd try and fix it up to look like a kidnapping." She puffed thoughtfully on her cigarette. "Any line on Pearl Jarvis?"

"We're still looking for her."

"*Cherchez la femme,*" Tara remarked.

"That's what everybody says," Matt replied.

"*D*id it work?" Jonesy asked when Matt climbed into the car after Tara walked away down the busy street.

"I don't know," Matt admitted. "She likes Doyle a lot. I don't know that she'll use anything that throws suspicion on him."

"She's a newshound, she'd sell her granny for an exclusive," Jonesy said.

"Cynic."

"You think she'll quote you, Loot?"

"I hope not."

Jonesy chuckled at Matt's tone. "You want her to do the dirty work. You figure in her efforts to prove her sweetheart Doyle innocent, she'll speculate in print on all the things we can't."

"Yep."

"You think it's occurred to her to wonder why there was so much time between when the ransom was paid and when the Arlen kid was supposed to be released?"

Matt said, "If it hasn't yet, it will."

Jonesy said slowly, "Whoever did that killing was as cold as Christmas. They shot the kid, and then threw him in the tar pit to try and conceal the fact. Maybe they didn't want anyone to know he was dead. Maybe there was another reason, but I've got a feeling it's going to take more than little Miss Tara Renee asking pointed questions in the *Examiner* to shake that killer's nerve."

*T*he train wheels rumbled along the track. Nathan closed his eyes, putting his head back. He had learned to snatch sleep where he could find it, and this seemed to be a safe enough place for a catnap…

A German flare arched high into the night. Machine guns and 40 mm guns opened up, firing from across the dunes, slicing the night with yellow, green, blue and red tracers—pretty, like fireworks. Tongues of colored flame licking out, licking hungrily for the transports high overhead, knocking them out of the sky. He watched them go down, burning. He turned his head and Matt was standing next to him, watching him. Matt's face was shadowed by the fire, little pinpoints of flame in his pupils.

"Where there's smoke," he said, and he smiled that smile that made him look younger and almost affectionate.

Nathan started awake to a surge of new passengers coming down the aisle, taking the seats around him. He sat up, automatically reaching to straighten his tie, and realized the train had stopped. Turning to the window, he peered out, trying to see which station it was. Old-fashioned Christmas lights hung from the station pavilion. Several lights were dead, like missing teeth in a wide grin. A peeling sign read *..di.. .all.*

Hoping it wasn't an omen, Nathan rose, steadying himself on the back of a seat, and made his way hastily down the aisle toward the platform. He found his path blocked by two nuns struggling with a mountain of parcels, and, instinctively, he stopped to help them shove their packages out of the way. It only took a minute, but as he reached the platform, he saw a Ford station wagon sedan pull up at the far end of the pavilion. A familiar tan coat and fur hat slipped inside, and the woody glided away.

Nathan swore under his breath, crossed the platform and walked out onto the street. He looked around himself.

Indian Falls was a resort town, but if it hadn't been for the tatty fake-pine garland strung across Main Street, it could have passed for a ghost town. A steady wall of closed shops stood across from the railroad station—a beauty parlor, a pawn shop, a cigar store, a lending library, a Chinese laundry. Nathan peered at his watch. It was eight thirty.

He went back to the now-deserted station and read the sign on the ticket window. Back in One Hour. *Swell.* He stared at the final twinkling lights of the departing train now vanishing into the pine-thick mountains.

Now what?

One thing for sure, it felt cold enough for snow. He shivered and looked up at the starry sky. Not a cloud anywhere. That was the good news. The bad news…

He walked back out to the street. Far down the block he spotted lights. A corner all-night drugstore. He started walking.

It was warm and bright inside the drugstore. It was also mostly deserted. An elderly woman with a Swedish accent pointed him to a public phone, and Nathan dug for change, wondering if the woman took much heat from idiots mistaking her for a Kraut.

It took time and persistence, but at last he reached LAPD Headquarters, and, to his surprise, with a little more persistence he actually got through to Lt. Mathew Spain.

"Spain here," he answered, still crisp and efficient at eight thirty—no, nine o'clock—at night. Spain worked late for a married man, but that was Homicide.

"It's Nathan Doyle," Nathan said.

There was a funny pause, and then Spain said, "What can I do for you, Mr. Doyle?"

"I've located Pearl Jarvis. She's staying at Little Fawn Lodge up near Indian Falls. It's in the Sierra Nevadas."

"I know where Indian Falls is. I used to camp there," Spain said, sounding almost human. "How'd you find her?"

"I followed her from Los Angeles."

"By car or train?"

Doyle couldn't see why it mattered, but that was a cop for you. They liked all the i's dotted and the t's crossed. No loose ends. Not so different from a good reporter, really.

"By train. I'm in Indian Falls right now, trying to get a ride up to the lodge."

"Why are you telling me this?" Spain asked, and his voice was back to its normal brisk and impersonal tone. "You're unusually cooperative for a newsman."

"Because—" Nathan changed his mind and took a chance on the truth. "I want you to hurry up and solve this thing."

Spain asked smoothly, "Any particular reason? Or are you just a concerned citizen, Mr. Doyle?"

"I…think you know my reason," Nathan said very quietly, although there was no one to overhear him, no one at all in the drugstore now except for him and the little old lady with apple-red cheeks and hair as white as powdered sugar.

There was another surprised silence on the other end of the phone.

Then Spain said, "You're heading up to the lodge, you said?"

"If I can hire a car."

"Try not to spook her."

Nathan snorted. "Tell it to your granny," he advised, and Spain chuckled.

"I'll be seeing you," he said, and rang off.

Nathan replaced the phone on the hook and approached the grandmotherly-looking lady behind the counter.

Twenty minutes later he was on his way to Little Fawn Lake in a battered pickup truck driven by Mrs. Svensson's grandson, a big blond man with a hook in place of his left hand.

"Where'd you stop that packet?" Doyle asked as they left the silent streets of Indian Falls behind, winding slowly up through the mountain roads. Giant pines and incense cedars blocked the waning moon.

Svensson didn't look at him, pushing the car into first gear with the hook as the car began to climb. "What's that?"

"Where'd you lose the arm?"

"Bombing run over Wilhelmshaven." Svensson looked at him.

If you were of eligible age and not in the service, there had to be a damn good explanation, and Doyle made his excuses. "Reporter. I was in Tunisia with the Brits. The Eighth Army." He wasn't ashamed of being a journalist, but by the end of his stint he'd begun to feel strange about recording and observing the free world's struggle for survival without taking part in it himself.

"Where'd you get hit?" Svensson asked, and Doyle shot him a surprised look.

"Medenine," he said, and the other man laughed.

"Mina," he explained. "My grandmother. She can always tell. She nursed a lot of boys in the other one. The first one."

"The War to End All Wars," Doyle murmured.

"Yeah. When you think this one's ending?"

Doyle thought it would be another two or three years, but Svensson believed it would be winding up pretty quick now that the Americans were in, and they passed the rest of the trip talking it over.

The highway grew narrower and steeper, seeming to wind up into the stars. One side of the road was thick forest, and the other a sheer drop into darkness. And then they pulled around an S-curve and the lodge was before them—just waiting for Heidi and the goats to show up.

"That's it," Svensson said. "Little Fawn Lake Lodge."

It must have been modeled on one of those Swiss chalets that populated snow globes everywhere. All that was missing was the snow.

A narrow gravel drive lined with foot-high Christmas trees curved under a trellised porte-cochère, and beneath the dead vines and bare bones of the carport was a door bedecked in a giant holly wreath. The drive itself snaked back to the pine-lined highway and disappeared in darkness.

There was no sign of the woody station wagon, but that was no surprise. Pearl had had quite a start on him.

He paid Svensson and thanked him, and went into the lodge thinking of possible explanations for his missing luggage. He'd picked up a toothbrush and a couple of essentials at the drugstore, but it was going to be hard convincing anyone he'd actually planned this excursion.

The front door jangled cheerfully thanks to a bunch of silver bells. Nathan found himself in a warm, cozy lobby with a high ceiling beamed with rough logs. Colorful woven rugs lay on the wooden floor, and cheerful chintz framed the big bay windows. A twelve-feet blue spruce trimmed in old-fashioned handmade ornaments towered next to a fieldstone fireplace at one end of the long room. At the other end were two arched doorways.

A sign over one doorway indicated the bar, and the second doorway led to the dining room. A staircase wrapped in evergreen started at the back of the room, climbed six steps and veered off into two separate branches.

There was no one at the reception desk. Copper lamps cast mellow light over vases filled with bayberries and holly. Out-of-date magazines littered tables.

Nathan walked over to the front desk and examined the leather-bound register lying there.

The most recently arrived guest was Doris Brown of San Diego.

It crossed his mind briefly that it was possible she'd given him the slip. She had gotten cagey on the train—what if she had hired a car and gone somewhere else? But according to old Mrs. Svensson, there wasn't anywhere else to go—unless she had stayed at the town's only hotel. *Doris Brown* sounded made up, and Pearl Jarvis was originally from San Diego.

He relaxed for the first time since losing Pearl at the station. She was here. He just needed to find a way to talk to her.

Wandering over to the dining room, he glanced in. A waitress came out of the kitchen and began setting the empty tables; apparently they were done serving nobody for the night and preparing for the next day's nonexistent rush.

"Good evening," a voice said from behind Nathan.

He turned. A thin, pale woman with red hair in a painfully tight bun had materialized in the doorway. He knew her hair was painfully tight from the pinched look on her face. Or maybe it was her shoes. Or maybe she'd gotten a glimpse of herself in the mirror—the red hair clashed horribly with the purple polka-dot dress she wore.

"May I help you?" she asked. "I'm the hotel manageress."

"Hello," Nathan said. "I was hoping to find a room."

"In the dining area?"

"Well, no," he admitted. He gave her his best smile, but she wasn't having any.

"Do you have a reservation?"

Since she would almost certainly know if he did, this seemed unnecessary, but perhaps she was short on amusement up here in the snowless mountains. "I made this trip on impulse," he said.

"You must have. You don't appear to have any luggage."

"There was a mix-up at Union Station."

"I see." She smiled a frigid smile that indicated she saw only too well. "If you'll just follow me."

She turned smartly on heel, and goose-stepped back to the lobby, Nathan trailing.

Planting herself behind the garland-decked desk, she examined the key rack behind her, glanced through the register, peered out at the dark night. If a nail file had been present, she'd have probably done her nails. At last she seemed to recollect Nathan.

"May I ask how long you plan on staying? Or will that depend on impulse as well?"

Nathan wondered if the dearth of hotel guests was totally due to the war.

"Just overnight."

She nodded as though she sincerely doubted it, but pushed the register toward him.

Nathan signed his name.

"I see Doris has already arrived," he said with pleasure. "What room is she in?"

Her eyes rested on him for a long moment. "I'll let the young lady know you've asked after her."

"Ah. Of course."

"I'll see you to your room," the manageress said, in the tone of one planning to lock him in for the night.

"I hate to trouble you—" Nathan began.

"No trouble," she said, not bothering to try and make it convincing. She took a key from the rack behind her.

She escorted Nathan upstairs to a pretty little room with pink-flowered wallpaper and two big windows frothed in dotted Swiss. There was a double bed, two white chests of drawers, a little table and a white rocker with pink satin pillows.

"You share a bath with room number seven. However, there is no guest in room number seven tonight."

"Ah," Nathan said.

The key was handed over with the air of one who had serious misgivings, and the manageress departed with the news that someone would eventually be up to make the bed.

Nathan moved to the nearest window. His room was in the center of the hotel. Two dark, apparently uninhabited wings stretched away to the left and right. The night was cold and crisp and clear. A gray Plymouth sat idling under the porte-cochère, exhaust smoking in the frosty air.

There was a knock on the door and the waitress from the dining room entered to make the bed, which she did quickly.

"Not many guests, I suppose," Nathan remarked.

"It's shaping up all right," she said cheerfully. "We just got two more in for the night. Decided they couldn't drive all the way to Santa Rosa tonight."

Santa Rosa by way of Indian Falls? That was a new one for the mapmakers.

"I forgot to ask downstairs, you don't happen to know which room Doris is in, do you?"

"The blonde lady who arrived this evening?"

"That's right."

"Number fourteen. Right down the hall."

Nathan tipped her and she went out.

He waited a few minutes, poked his head out of his room and made certain the coast was clear. He stepped out into the hall and walked quietly down to number fourteen. The light shone beneath the door. He put his ear against the white wood and listened. Floorboards creaked beneath soft footsteps. Doris/Pearl appeared to be pacing the floor.

He considered trying to talk to her again, but decided to postpone it for now. She appeared to be unsettled, and she was already wary of him. He would have a better chance if she ran into him casually downstairs. And if that didn't work, he'd just have to risk knocking on her bedroom door. Not that Pearl struck him as a girl unused to gentlemen knocking on her boudoir door.

Nathan went downstairs to the bar. There were three empty high-backed booths, a row of tiny tables with checked cloths in front of a long built-in—and also empty—wooden bench, and a bar angled across the rear corner of the room. A boy too young to drink stood behind it.

Nathan perched himself at the bar, studied the wall of bottles in front of him and ordered the VAT 69.

"Quiet around here," he remarked.

"No snow," the kid said, which was a refreshing take.

Nathan drank his drink and waited. No one showed up. He ordered another. He thought how strange it was to be sitting here in warmth and light sipping a liqueur-blended Scotch whisky—one of his favorite Scotch whiskies, at that—while on the other side of the world men were dying by the droves.

"I should probably be closing up," the kid said.

Nathan studied him. In about a year he'd be old enough to draft. "One more for the road?"

The kid nodded, poured him another drink.

Nathan sipped reflectively. He didn't think Pearl Jarvis was the kind of girl who would be very happy sitting by herself in her room all evening, but maybe she was worn out from her trip.

He wondered if Spain would drive up himself, and how long it might take him—assuming he started right away. No more than six hours surely?

Abruptly, Nathan was tired. Why not leave it to Spain? He could go up to his room and grab forty winks—which was about all he could sleep these days.

He paid for his drinks, started to rise and then sat back down as two men entered the taproom. He saw the kid open his mouth to protest, and then give it up. He understood why.

They looked like Tinseltown's idea of hoods—or comic relief. One was bald and burly. The other looked sort of like Harpo Marx, blunt featured with lots of light, fuzzy hair. They sat down at one of the high-backed booths. Nathan caught the eye of the bald-headed man. Nathan nodded politely. The man nodded back.

He seemed vaguely familiar to Nathan. He studied the pair; neither man paid any further attention to him, and yet…the hair prickled at the back of his neck, a feeling that had saved his skin more than once.

The youthful bartender went over to take their drink orders, and Nathan nodded good night to him, and went upstairs, conscious of two pairs of unfriendly eyes pinned to his shoulder blades.

At the top of the stairs he waited, leaning back against the wall, safely hidden by the corner.

And waited.

No one left the bar in pursuit of him, and feeling a little foolish, he moved on toward his room. Then on impulse he continued on to Doris Brown's room. The light had vanished from under her door.

He stood there for a moment, and then he headed quietly along the corridor to his own room.

Locking his door, he slipped off his shoes and jacket, removed his tie and lay down on the bed. He lit a cigarette and stared up at the ceiling, thinking.

After a time he stubbed out the cigarette and got up, stepped back into his shoes, shrugged back into his jacket, put his coat on and let himself out of his room. There was no sign of anyone in the hall. He went to the top of the staircase and looked down. The lobby was empty, but he could hear voices from the bar.

He considered. If he went down the stairs and out through the lobby, they were liable to spot him, and even if they didn't, they could hardly miss the cheerful jingle of bells on the front door. He looked down the hallway to where it angled off into darkness. That hallway had to lead to the closed left wing of the hotel. If there was an outside exit, and there had to be, he could probably get out that way and not be seen.

He moved quickly, quietly down the hall, rounded the corner and kept walking as the light from the main part of the hotel faded behind him. It was a long, long hallway. At the far end was a staircase, also in darkness. He felt his way down it, moving as quickly as he could, one hand holding to the banister. No pine garland here. It smelled dusty and closed up.

On the bottom level he found a door. The knob turned and he walked out into moonlight as bright as phosphorus. The cold was like a punch to his lungs, his breath frosted in night air scented with pines and distant snow. It smelled like Christmas, and an odd pang shot through him as he remembered long-ago holidays.

He stuck close to the building, making his way toward the row of garages about a hundred yards beyond the rear of the hotel. They were arranged in an arc around a cement court, and in the center of the court stood a high pole topped by a blazing light. Apparently there were no worries of attracting enemy aircraft up here.

The door of the fourth garage from the left was slightly ajar.

Nathan's footsteps crunched on gravel as he walked toward the garage, the sound sharp in the night. He dragged open the door. The gray Plymouth gleamed in the artificial light. He tried the car door handle, but it was locked. Suspicious minds, he thought with a faint grin. He cupped his hands funnel-style against the glass window, trying to read the car registration, but it was too dark inside the garage.

Walking round to the front of the car, he eased the hood, propped it up and then felt around 'til he found the distributor cap. He unscrewed it, slipping it into his pocket.

That ought to ensure Pearl didn't disappear in the night with the two heavies from the taproom.

He started back for the hotel, walking briskly. He paused long enough to leave the distributor cap in one of the flower boxes beneath the window of a ground-floor room, and then walked on 'til he came to the side entrance.

He opened the door, stepped quietly inside—and the floor dropped out from under him. He plummeted down into darkness lit with red and white flares, tracers and shell bursts exploding around him.

Chapter Six

It was late when the phone call came through. Matt had been leaving for home—or in the process of leaving—for the past three hours. There was no rush to get back to an empty house, and he was not going back to Pershing Square again. He'd had two nights of that insanity. He wouldn't spend another standing in the darkness, hot and sick and shaking inside with a confused mess of feelings that weren't worth analyzing. That he shouldn't have felt anyway.

With Rachel gone it was like balancing on the edge of a cliff—and all the little wildflowers, the netting of grass and roots that kept the cliff from sliding into the sea below, were gone. It was just Matt standing there looking down, waiting to fall.

Even Rachel's memory, the sweet recollection of all they had built, all they had shared, was no longer strong enough to fight gravity. From the moment he had looked across the wet grass and seen Nathan Doyle standing in the shadow of a stone saber-toothed tiger, something had changed inside him. Something battened down had torn free, like a sail taking its first deep breath of sea air.

It terrified him.

And at the same time it exhilarated him.

Which terrified him all the more.

The phone jangled loudly, and Matt reached for it. He had been thinking about the one thing that tied all the suspects in the Arlen case together—thinking about how far people would go to protect their secrets—thinking—because he couldn't stop thinking about it—about Nathan Doyle's secret. The voice on the other end of the line was Doyle's. He sounded a million miles away, like he was calling from the moon.

"I've located Pearl Jarvis. She's staying at a ski lodge at Little Fawn Lake. Up near Indian Falls."

Indian Falls. He and Rachel had honeymooned there. They had gone camping in the mountains there every year until he was sent overseas and Rachel had got sick.

"You're kidding," Matt said. It occurred to him that he might have seriously miscalculated in not having Doyle followed. If he was wrong about Doyle—but if he was wrong about Doyle, Doyle would probably not be calling him to say he had found Pearl Jarvis. He said calmly, "How'd you find that out?"

"I followed her from Los Angeles."

"By car or train?" He found a pen and began to write, listening to Doyle's voice. It was a quiet voice, level. Doyle kept himself tightly under control; at least, that's what Matt would have thought if he hadn't seen him half-naked in the shadows and moonlight of Pershing Square on Tuesday and Wednesday night.

"By train. I'm in Indian Falls right now, trying to get a ride up to the lodge."

"Why are you telling me this?"

Doyle answered, "Because—" And something changed in his voice; he said simply, "I want you to hurry up and solve this thing."

"Any particular reason? Or are you just a concerned citizen, Mr. Doyle?"

He had to press the phone close to hear that weary "I…think you know my reason."

The honesty of it caught him off guard. Shook him even. He wasn't sure he was ready for it. Wasn't sure he could ever be ready for it, because to admit that he understood what Doyle was saying was to admit to something within himself. Something he wasn't sure he was ready to face.

He said finally, "You're heading up to the lodge, you said?"

"If I can hire a car."

"Try not to spook her."

Doyle snorted. "Tell it to your granny!" And Matt had to laugh at the amused affront.

But after he rang off, after promising to send help, he began to worry a little. He thought that Doyle might easily underestimate the fairer sex, and he thought Pearl Jarvis would not have run if she didn't have friends waiting for her—and that those same friends might be waiting for Doyle, as well.

The effort of trying to open his eyes hurt. Nathan postponed it, taking time to place himself. But he was used to that, the freefall feeling of trying to remember where he was and whether he needed to be on alert—even after months in hospital, he still woke with it.

But he wasn't in hospital now. He was lying on a bed—a cot—and he was cold. He didn't seem to be wearing any shoes. He opened his eyes.

He was in a room he'd never seen. The log ceiling seemed a long way away and a little fuzzy. He tried to focus on it. His head hurt. He didn't feel very well. Granted, he hadn't felt truly well for a long, long time, but he felt worse than usual. Quite a bit worse. And his feet were like ice.

He wasn't supposed to get sick. He didn't have much of an immune system left.

"Gin," someone said.

Nathan turned his head. Two men sat at a small table playing cards by the light of a kerosene lantern. One was balder than Cueball, and the other looked like one of the Marx Brothers. He knew them, though it took him a while to remember where. They had been in the hotel bar.

"You're a goddamn card shark, Lawdie," Harpo said.

Cueball grinned widely—like a shark—displaying a mouthful of gold teeth. "No names," he told the other man and glanced at Nathan. His face changed. "Hey," he said, and he nodded at Nathan.

Harpo looked at Nathan. "Well, well. Sleeping Beauty joins the party."

Nathan sat up. It was a mistake. He sat there for a second or two trying to decide how bad a mistake it was.

"Just stay put, newsie," Lawdie pulled out a Smith & Wesson revolver and showed it to Nathan. "Nobody wants any rough stuff."

"That's good to know," Nathan said, and the other two laughed.

The man who wasn't Lawdie scooped up the spread of cards, shuffled them expertly and began to deal again.

"Can I have my shoes?" Nathan asked. "My feet are cold."

This got another big laugh.

"No," Lawdie informed him. "Ya can't." The other man chuckled.

"Can I at least have my socks?"

"Nope."

"Ah, let him have his socks," Harpo said. "We don't need to literally keep him on ice, do we?" He snickered, but Lawdie wasn't amused.

"You gotta big mouth, Hammer."

"Hey," Hammer protested.

Hammer and Lawdie, Nathan noted wearily. He'd have to remember that in case he got out of there alive. "That much I worked out for myself," he said. "You can't be working for the girl, so who? Sid Szabo?"

It had been a shot in the dark, but the two thugs exchanged looks.

"How long do you plan on holding me for?"

"Depends," Lawdie said.

"You talk a lot," Hammer said to Nathan. "It's not a healthy habit."

He was probably right. Nathan lay back down and closed his eyes. The best thing was to shut up and let them forget about him for a while.

He must have actually dozed off because the next voice seemed unnaturally loud.

"Is he still sleeping?"

Nathan opened his eyes. Lawdie was standing over him, staring down. He blinked up at him tiredly, and then closed his eyes again.

"I told you not to hit him so hard," Hammer said. "You probably killed him."

"Shut up, you!"

"I knew a guy died from getting hit on the head just like that. Walked around talking and played a hand of cards and then went to sleep and never woke up. Mike Murphy. Used to run with—"

"He's just playing possum." Lawdie bent over the cot, breathing heavily. Nathan continued to breathe slowly and evenly.

Lawdie slapped him.

He'd pretty well figured that was coming. Nathan groaned and fluttered his eyelashes, then curled over on his side and pretended to go back to sleep.

"Yep," Hammer said with grim satisfaction. "Just like Mike Murphy. Scrawny little guy like that can't take it. Probably got pneumonia too. I told you. The boss didn't want him killed."

"Will you shut your goddamned mouth up?" Lawdie cried. "He ain't dead. His breathing's fine."

"Look how white his feet are."

"You look at his feet! I'm going to hike up to the hotel."

"You're not going to leave me with a stiff!"

"He's still breathing, fer Chrissake! I'll call the boss and see how long we got to hang on to this geezer."

"What's happening with the car?"

"How the hell should I know? I been sitting here with you. I'll find out once I'm up there."

"We got to get outta here before this guy croaks."

"You planning to walk back to Los Angeles? Just stay here and watch him. I'll be back in an hour."

They continued to bicker back and forth for a time, and then finally Lawdie took himself out, the door opening and slamming shut on a gust of frosty air. Nathan couldn't help the shudder that rippled through his body.

His feet felt like ice. His body felt flushed and feverish. Another shiver shook him.

A few minutes passed. Hammer shuffled and cut cards. Then he muttered, "Christ. Leave me here with a croaker."

Nathan heard the scrape of a chair, footsteps, and Hammer bent over the bed. He touched Nathan's left eye—apparently planning to check his pupils—and Nathan bounded up, head-butting him.

Half-stunned, Hammer crashed back on his tailbone, and Nathan sprang on him. He delivered a couple of fast, efficient chops to Hammer's head, and the big man sagged back and lay still.

Staggering to his feet, Nathan searched quickly for his shoes, but was unable to find them anywhere. He sat for a minute on the chair, feeling sick and faint. His head had hurt like hell before he tried head-butting that moose. He straightened up, eyeing Hammer warily, picked up a chair and approached him.

The big man was breathing in stentorian tones. Nathan nudged him, and his head lolled. Nathan knelt, patting him over and finding his gun, a big old Colt .45, which he appropriated. He scooted around, keeping the Colt trained on Hammer, using his free hand to slip his shoes off, one at a time, and put them on his own feet. They were too big, but they were better than nothing.

He went to the window and stared out. Dusk or dawn? Either way there was no sign of Lawdie in the blur of shadows from the close-clustered pines. He checked his watch. Six thirty. It was either early in the morning or the evening of the following day. He figured it was morning.

Easing open the cabin door, he listened. The wind through the pines made a sound like rushing water. The air was cold and clear. Frost powdered the ground. He stepped outside, shutting the door, and sprinted for the shelter of the trees.

He had no idea where he was, but heading back to the hotel seemed like the only option. He couldn't walk all the way to Indian Falls, and Spain and his boys must surely be at the hotel by now.

Hopefully Pearl was in custody already, and Lawdie would have an unpleasant surprise waiting for him when he arrived.

Sticking to the shelter of trees and bushes, Nathan followed the dirt track that led from the cabin to—he hoped—the main highway. He moved quietly and carefully. Lawdie didn't have much of a head start, and Nathan didn't want to run into him.

Every so often he paused and listened. Every sound in the pristine silence was as loud as a shot. Some distance ahead he heard a scrabble of stones or the snap of a twig. That would be Lawdie, he knew.

A bush smacked him across the face and he had to stop. The pain in his head was getting worse. He dropped to his knees, and quietly threw up at the base of a pine tree. He felt a little better then, and, grabbing for the tree trunk, he pulled himself back to his feet. He rested, listening, trying to place Lawdie ahead of him.

It was getting lighter now.

He walked on and the road opened up onto the highway. A deer stood on the opposite side of the road, motionless.

Nathan bent over, bracing his hands on his thighs and tried to catch his breath. His side throbbed. He had no idea which way to walk. Nothing indicated the direction in which the lodge lay.

The deer crossed the road, hooves clopping, passed Nathan close enough to brush him, and then sprang away into the darkness.

From down the road Nathan spotted a pair of headlights.

Christ. Did he take a chance on this? Lawdie and Hammer had at least one ally at the lodge, and it wasn't necessarily Pearl. With their own car out of commission, someone had given them a lift to the cabin in the woods. He didn't believe they had carried him to it, and someone had to have provided the cabin in the first place.

The car was speeding toward him, headlights sweeping the darkness. A solid black Buick bearing down fast.

Nathan stepped out from cover, and raised his hands.

Tires and pads squealing, the car braked sharply, swerved, corrected and skidded to a halt a few yards ahead of him.

Nathan walked toward it slowly. The front passenger door opened and Lt. Mathew Spain stepped out.

"Well, that was a hell of a chance," he said.

Someone turned a powerful flashlight on Nathan as he shuffled in his oversize shoes toward the car. "Who dares, wins," he quoted breathlessly.

"What the hell happened to you?" Spain was peering at him in the white glare of the flashlight. "You're bleeding."

Nathan touched a hand to the top of his head. Gummy. He spared a glance for his fingers. That was blood all right. "It's a long story." He reached Spain, who had walked a few steps to meet him, and a weird thing happened. His knees gave out and he buckled.

Spain grabbed him, two powerful hands closing on Nathan's biceps. Nathan leaned into Spain's broad chest and closed his eyes.

*T*he next time he came around, someone's hands were on him, trying to pull his clothes off, and he made himself start fighting. It wasn't much of a fight, struggling as he was against the extreme lassitude that gripped him, but he made the effort anyway, and a deep, unexpected voice said, "Take it easy, Doyle. We're trying to help you."

His hands were forced to his chest by someone a lot stronger than he was just now, and he opened his eyes against a painfully bright light.

Bewilderingly, he was lying in a room with pink-flowered wallpaper, and two men were leaning over him, holding him onto a bed. One was a big, rawboned man with a shock of iron-gray hair reminding him painfully of Sergeant Yorkie, who had bought it at El Alamein. The other man was Lt. Mathew Spain.

Spain was watching him with those amber-brown eyes—and Spain's big warm hands were covering his own, holding them still.

Nathan mumbled, "What the hell…?"

Spain nodded to the other man, and they let go of him.

"You pack a wallop for a skinny guy." The older ruefully rubbed his jaw.

Nathan blinked at him, tried to sit up, but it wasn't going well, so it was kind of a relief when Spain pushed him flat again.

"Just relax," Spain said. "You're okay. We're at the lodge. There's a doctor staying here and he says you're supposed to take it easy. You've got concussion."

"I'm fine."

"Yeah, we can see that. But it won't hurt to lie down for an hour."

Actually, it sounded like a swell idea. He let his eyes drift closed. Felt Spain and the other cop tugging at him with careful haste, undoing his belt, unbuttoning his shirt. He was going to tell them it wasn't worth it because he was just closing his eyes for a moment. Or…or maybe an hour… He felt like Rommel's panzers had run him over, backed up and run him over again. He ached from head to toe. Which reminded him…

"What happened to the girl?" he asked, opening his eyes. And then, indignantly, "What happened to my shoes?"

"Pearl blew," Spain said grimly. "During the night. Her aunt drove her to Indian Falls, and she caught a train back to Los Angeles first thing this morning." His mouth quirked in a kind of smile. "Your shoes are still on the loose."

He had a nice smile—nice eyes—and Nathan smiled back at him. It was probably a mistake. He couldn't afford to let his guard down with a cop. Even this cop. Especially this cop, really.

Then Spain's words filtered his concussed brain, and he said, "Pearl's aunt? Who's her aunt?"

"Mrs. Hubbard, the hotel manageress. She says Pearl remembered some urgent business back in town and had to leave right away. Had no idea we were looking for her." Spain reached for the waistband of Nathan's trousers, and Nathan brushed his hand away, sitting up fast—which made his head spin and his stomach do an unpleasant flop.

"Suit yourself," Spain said mildly.

Hands shaking, Nathan climbed out of his trousers—acutely aware of how desperately he wanted Spain's hands on him. It was frightening how much he wanted it. He didn't dare look at the other two in case they saw it in his face.

Dizzy, he turned back to the bed and the older cop had pulled the sheet and blankets back sandwich-style. He awkwardly maneuvered onto the mattress, and Spain caught him by the shoulder and quite easily, gently, slipped him out of his unbuttoned shirt.

And there it was: the longed-for warmth of hands on his bare skin, the strength and gentleness that he craved but could never—would never—find except in fleeting, stolen moments.

He crashed down on the mattress, burying his face in the pillow. There were things he should be asking them, things he should be saying, but he was overwhelmed with guilt and yearning and fear and frustration. His body hurt, but his heart hurt more. And he was too tired and too sore to deal with any of it. He closed his eyes, shutting them out, shutting everything out.

The older cop said something, and Spain answered, both of their voices quiet and far away. The lights went out, and Nathan went out with them.

CHAPTER SEVEN

*T*he soothing squeak and creak of a rocker worked its way into his consciousness. Nathan listened to it for a while, lulled by feelings the homely sound beguiled, feelings of safety and peace and well-being.

After a bit he realized that he was awake and that he felt better. His head was no longer killing him, his gut had settled, he was relaxed and warm. He sighed his relief, and the rocker stopped rocking. Floorboards vibrated underfoot, he opened his eyes, and someone was bending over him. Nathan shot upright, dislodging the hand alighting on his brow, and just missing a collision with Lieutenant Spain.

"Jesus," Spain said. "If you ever need a job you could probably find work as a jack-in-the-box."

"Sorry. You…surprised me." He subsided back against the stack of pillows. He wasn't usually this jumpy, but he could hardly tell Spain that it was mostly due to his presence.

"You surprised me too," Spain said. "And you keep surprising me." He sat down on the foot of the shiny pink bedspread and studied Nathan.

Nathan didn't know what to make of that. Spain looked at him with an open directness he found bewildering. If he moved his foot beneath the blankets, he could brush Spain's thigh. His heart sped up at the thought. He was painfully conscious of everything about the other man—his solid muscled warmth, the way Spain smelled of soap and Old Spice, the fine clear texture of his skin, and eyelashes as long and black as a girl's. Nathan liked everything about him. Too much. He searched around for something safe to say. "What happened to Lawdie and Hammer?"

"Hammer? Dewey Hammer?" Spain's mouth curved. "Well, that makes sense. He usually runs with Vince Lawdie. Haven't seen Hammer, but we've got Lawdie on assault and kidnapping." His smile widened into that grin that Nathan liked so much. "We're hoping you're going to be able to substantiate those charges. We were sort of going by your general appearance in the woods, and Lawdie's reaction when we carried you into the lodge."

"You bet," Nathan said. "I'll be happy to press charges. Those assholes cold-cocked me last night. I guess it was last night." He looked past Spain to the sweeps of dotted Swiss framing the windows—and the darkness beyond. "Is it night now?" he asked, astonished.

Spain nodded.

"What are we still doing here?"

"Mostly waiting for you to wake up." Spain didn't seem upset about it, but Nathan couldn't figure it out.

"You all sat around here the entire day waiting for me to wake up?"

For the first time, Spain's man-to-man gaze sheered. "Not all of us. I sent Jonesy and the others back to town this morning with Lawdie. You know who Lawdie works for?"

"I've seen him before. Sid Szabo?"

"Same thing. Nora Noonan. He works at the Las Palmas Club. From what we can make out, their orders were to hold you up here long enough for Pearl to slip."

With a sinking feeling, Nathan asked, "Did your men pick Pearl up in Los Angeles?"

"Either they missed her or she didn't get off the train."

Nathan put a careful hand to his head.

"I know," Spain said grimly, watching him.

Then neither of them spoke.

Spain said, "You and me will have to take the train back. The day after tomorrow."

Noonan's thugs must have really conked him because he just couldn't seem to connect the dots. "The day after tomorrow?"

"Tonight's Christmas Eve."

Nathan let that sink in. *Christmas Eve?* Then he protested, "I don't understand. Why would you—?"

Spain's eyes met Nathan's once more, but there was something funny in his expression. "We didn't want to move you. The doctor said you needed complete rest and quiet."

"The hell with that." And then, slowly, "You could have just left me on my own."

"I didn't want to."

Nathan couldn't seem to tear his gaze away. He wondered if he was still asleep, dreaming maybe. Or maybe what Spain was saying was that Nathan was in custody, that he didn't trust him to come back to Los Angeles on his own.

Or—was Spain setting a trap for him? His heart jerked.

Was there a remote chance that Spain intended what he seemed to be saying with those honey-brown eyes?

"I don't understand," Nathan said at last, huskily, terrified that even this much was giving himself away.

Spain reached over and covered Nathan's hand with the warm strength of his own. "I'm hoping you do."

And after a shocked instant, Nathan turned his hand, intertwining his fingers with Spain. He was almost afraid to look at Spain's face, but when he did, Spain looked as naked and vulnerable as he felt.

He closed his eyes, savoring the hard, calloused strength of Spain's grip. "What about..." With his thumb he traced the gold band on Spain's left hand.

"My wife died last year. Cancer. Not long after I was discharged." Spain said huskily, "Can I tell you about myself?"

Nathan opened his eyes, nodded.

"Feeling this way isn't anything new for me, but…loving Rachel made it easy to ignore." His smile was wry. "Well, maybe not easy, but…I really loved her. We met when we were in high school. I guess she—I guess that's what made the difference."

"That would do it," Nathan said carefully. "You never—?"

"I did. In the service. That's when I realized there were guys just like me. Regular guys, not queers."

Nathan said softly, "They're queers. We're all queers. You think it makes a difference—"

"I do, yeah."

Staring at Spain's earnest expression, Nathan felt an unaccountable desire to cry. And that was funny because if you didn't cry when the Nazis shot you, really what was there left to cry about? Unless it was because they hadn't managed to kill you.

He said, "It doesn't make any difference. If you give in to it—give in to what you're feeling—you're just as vulnerable as someone like me."

Spain's fingers tightened around Nathan's. "That's not what I meant. I don't mean you."

"You do. Even if you don't know you do." But he squeezed Spain back, taking the simple comfort offered by holding hands. He had never held hands with anyone, man or woman.

Spain said, "The Arlen kid was blackmailing you?"

Unexpectedly, Nathan smiled. "I'd have had to pay him in blue stamp rations. No, it happened pretty much the way I told you, except when we left the club that night, Arlen said that if I didn't pay up, he was going to my paper. He'd been hinting around for a bit, and I'd been dodging it, but when he left the club he gave me an ultimatum. I punched him. Knocked him down. Then I walked away. The next time I saw him was at the tar pits."

"How did the kid know about you?"

Nathan didn't look away. "I'm not always as careful as I should be. Since I came home—it's hard. There's not as much to distract me." Spain's face gave nothing away, but Nathan knew how he must see it. Facing disgrace and jail—or maybe a nut house—it wasn't hard to believe that Nathan might kill to protect himself. Not hard at all, considering how warped and desperate he must be to do the things Arlen had seen him do.

He waited for Spain to pull away, withdraw, but he didn't. He kept holding Nathan's hand as he asked, "So the Arlen kid tried to shake you down before?"

"I ran into him a couple of times, but he never hinted he knew anything until a week or so before the Las Palmas Club." Because he hadn't known anything until the night Nathan ran into him at the Biltmore. After that—but he wasn't going to tell Spain that. Wasn't prepared to admit that much.

"How do you figure Pearl Jarvis fits in?" Spain asked.

"I think she knows who killed Phil—unless she killed him herself."

"You have anything to base that on?"

Nathan hesitated. "She's running scared. She's either afraid of being arrested or she thinks she's next on the killer's list."

"And why would she be next? Do you think they were having an affair?"

"I think so. But that wouldn't mark her for murder. Unless the killer is Claire Arlen, in which case I think she'd have started with Pearl. No, I think Pearl was Arlen's business partner. I think she used her connections at the club to find out stuff about people that Arlen could then use to blackmail them."

Spain nodded, as though this confirmed his own thoughts. "I think you're right about the blackmail angle. I know of at least three people in this case who had secrets that some might consider worth committing murder over."

"Carl Winters and the faked antiquities," Doyle said. "Nora Noonan and the Denver murder trial."

Spain's surprise was evident, and Nathan shrugged. "Most secrets aren't as secret as people think."

His own included, he admitted with painful honesty.

"One interesting thing, though. I followed Pearl from Sid Szabo's place. Admittedly, I'm no expert, but I think if he's willing to shield her from the cops during a murder investigation, he must care about her. I can't tell about her. I never paid a lot of attention to either of them."

"She could have more than one beau."

"Yeah." Nathan shifted against the pillows. "Look, Lieutenant, I know how it looks for me, but I didn't kill him."

Spain's eyes crinkled at the corners when he smiled. "You think we'd be sitting here talking if I thought you did?" He looked down at Nathan's hand in his own, looked up and said, "My name is Mathew."

*M*athew pulled rank and persuaded the sour-faced manageress to send up a late supper on a tray. The doctor hotel guest came by while they waited, and he examined Nathan again, pronouncing himself satisfied with his progress and recommending another day in bed, which Nathan brushed off firmly.

The cheerful maid from the night of Nathan's arrival brought a couple of extra blankets and a heavy purple bathrobe that had, she informed them, belonged to the late Mr. Hubbard.

"From Mr. Hubbard's cupboard?" Nathan asked, and she giggled, peeking briefly at him sitting up bare-chested in the bed. She set the blankets on the rocker, and Mathew took the robe, handing it to Nathan.

Nathan eyed the blankets and said nothing, but when the door closed behind the maid, Mathew said, "Don't worry. Nobody's going to think anything about this. I'm supposed to keep an eye on you, according to the doctor."

"I'm not worried." He wasn't, but he thought Matt had an unrealistic idea about the way people's minds worked—which was funny for a cop.

Nathan stood up, feeling a little dizzy, and shrugged into the robe. Mr. Hubbard had been a bit shorter and a lot wider. The robe felt soft and smelled new, and perhaps this explained the tight, pinched face of the hotel manageress.

He walked carefully to the window, resting his hands on the sash, staring down at the moonlit landscape. The frost on the ground shimmered with the eerie glow of the salt flats south of the Dorsale mountain range.

They were playing Christmas carols on a phonograph downstairs, the music faint through the wooden floorboards. "I'll Be Home for Christmas." And he was. Sort of.

"He said you appeared to be suffering from a state of severe nervous tension." There was a smile in Mathew's voice. "He saw you racing around outside the hotel on Thursday night. I think that's what decided him."

Nathan chuckled. "Did he happen to see me get clobbered?"

"He missed that installment of your adventures." Mathew's arms slipped around Nathan's torso, warm through the robe. He held him tentatively, and Nathan knew that he could move away, and Mathew would immediately release him, and everything would end here. But it wasn't in him—not even for Mathew's sake. Instead, he reached up and pulled down the window shade, turning in Mathew's arms.

Mathew was a couple of inches taller; Nathan had to look up. Mathew was smiling—mostly with his eyes.

"The lamp will silhouette us," Nathan warned gently.

Mathew's eyes flickered with recognition.

"Let's eat," he said casually, and he let go of Nathan, but then he rested an unexpectedly possessive hand on the small of his back as they moved over to the little table by the wall.

They ate and talked, mostly about the war—their experiences were so different it was almost as though they'd been in two separate wars—and then, inevitably they returned to the subject of Phil Arlen's murder.

Mathew told him that Nathan was Jonesy's candidate for Public Enemy Number One, and although Nathan laughed, secretly it filled him with dread. His life couldn't take much close examination, and he knew only too well the attention that would come his way if he became a prime suspect in the Arlen case.

"Who's your favorite candidate?" he asked Mathew.

"I haven't completely ruled out the possibility that Arlen was kidnapped."

"Anything's possible." Nathan was being polite, and he could tell from Mathew's grin that Mathew knew it.

"If it wasn't a kidnapping, I think Robert Arlen has a pretty strong motive. From everything I've heard, he's worked his tail off for the old man's approval and spent almost his entire life taking the back seat to Philip—who, by all accounts, isn't fit to black his boots."

"That's true as far as it goes," Nathan said, "but Bob's not the kind of guy who would murder his kid brother. Not even if he didn't like the kid much."

"Is it true the old man forced Philip to marry Claire Winters?"

"Pretty much. Clay Winters was Benedict Arlen's partner in some early business ventures. The Arlens were Claire's godparents, so I think Arlen was trying to kill two birds with one stone—take care of Claire and get Phil on the right track. Claire's been in love with Phil since she was a schoolgirl, don't ask me why."

"What about Robert Arlen? Did the old man arrange his marriage too?"

"No." Nathan smiled at the idea. "No, that was a love match. They're crazy about each other. Ronnie was a navy nurse. She nursed Bob back to health after he cracked his plane up, and they fell in love. I think the old man threatened to disown Bob for a while, but for once Bob stood up to him, and Arlen backed down."

"What's Veronica's background?"

"I don't think it's anything scandalous. Her family comes from some chicken-scratch town in Texas. Poor but honest stock." Nathan's smile was mocking. "One of her grandfathers was supposed to be an Old West gunfighter. In fact, that's probably why Arlen finally acquiesced to the marriage. He's a nut about the old west."

"I noticed." Mathew said slowly, "You were probably too busy tracking Pearl across the state to notice, but we've found the murder weapon." He told Nathan about the Derringer Rider found in Carl Winters' bookstore, and the fact that everyone—including Nathan—had apparently had opportunity to plant the gun there.

"And the gun is definitely from Arlen's collection?"

"No doubt about it. The last time Arlen examined the collection was a month ago, so he wasn't able to narrow down for us when it disappeared or who might have had access to it."

"Maybe he didn't want to narrow it down."

Mathew gave him a funny look but didn't say anything.

When they'd finished eating, they moved over to the bed and lay down side by side, facing each other, studying each other.

Nathan smiled faintly. He thought Mathew had no idea what to do next. He rested his hand against Mathew's face, stroked his bristling jaw. He wanted to kiss him—his belly felt like it was swarming with butterflies at the very thought, but he figured that would be going way too far for Mathew, so he contented himself, brushing his thumb over his full bottom lip.

Mathew caught his hand, held it and leaned forward, kissing Nathan's mouth—soft full lips pressing warmly, firmly against Nathan's—and Nathan realized that maybe he was the one unprepared for this, unready for this. He was shaking when Mathew raised his head.

"You're freezing," Mathew said. "Let's get under the covers."

They sat up, scrambling out of their clothes, pulling back the sheets and blankets, snuggling down into the warmth, rolling quite naturally into each other's arms.

Matt touched the little silver cross Nathan wore about his neck. "Do you always wear this?"

Nathan nodded.

Mathew's fingertips brushed the chain and Nathan's skin and collarbones. He seemed peculiarly gentle. "We've got all night," he whispered. "Why don't you sleep for a while?" He settled Nathan more closely against him, cushioning his body with his own, offering his shoulder as a rest for Nathan's head.

Suddenly Nathan was so tired he could hardly think straight. The temptation of doing just that, of giving in to the forbidden pleasure of sleeping in another man's arms—this man's arms—giving up control, permitting himself to trust for just a little while, was overwhelming. He let his body relax against Mathew's, closed his eyes.

$\mathcal{T}$he light was off when he woke much later, the music downstairs was silent, but he could feel that Mathew was awake, feel his erection probing his belly. His own dick was painfully hard, balls aching—what the hell dreams had he been having?

He pushed his hips forward, relieved when Mathew immediately thrust back. They began to rub against each other, skin on skin, the soft pelt of Mathew's chest hair brushing his own chest, teasing his nipples, rough but somehow sweet. Mathew's hands smoothed up and down his spine, and he was whispering hot things into Nathan's ear. Quiet, but not quiet enough—not nearly afraid enough—not realizing how the squeak of bedsprings, the creak of headboard could give them away.

Nathan knew. He bit his lip hard to keep from making any sounds, all the while wishing he could understand those words breathed against his ear.

Mathew came first, Nathan felt that slick hot spill on his belly, and he wriggled frantically, writhing, panting, gritting his jaw to keep from crying out when Mathew's hand closed around his dick, pumping him. Like he knew Nathan needed this. Not quite the right angle, not quite the right grip, but just the touch was enough to bring him off.

Afterward they held each other while their hearts calmed and their breathing evened out.

It was dangerous to feel this happy, but Nathan wouldn't have traded a second of it.

*M*att's experience with sex—this kind of sex—was limited. Oh, he'd had plenty of experience with lovemaking, and that was probably why. He had loved Rachel very much. Yet in some bittersweet way, this strange encounter with Nathan Doyle in a remote ski lodge was as momentous as any happening Matt had known—up to and including being born.

In a way it was like being born. Like oxygen when your lungs were burning for air, or cold water when you were dying of thirst.

The rushed and harried encounters of marine barracks and showers, the stolen moments in the dry grasses and steamy jungle of Guadalcanal had nothing to do with this, had no reality against the feel of Nathan's wiry warm strength resting peacefully in his arms. He'd never known anyone like Nathan, and he'd known—lived and nearly died—with a lot of guys. Great guys.

He didn't kid himself that this meant anything much to Nathan, and he hoped he was enough of a realist not to let it mean too much to him-self—they weren't starting a romance, for Chrissake—but he was glad that there were still many more hours of darkness, and that they would be staying over tomorrow—and tomorrow night.

Nathan shifted in his sleep, a slight restless movement, and Matt ducked his head, whispering something silly, tightening his grip. Nathan stilled, his breath light and surprisingly sweet against Matt's shoulder.

Nathan was exhausted. Well, he'd had a rough couple of days, and he was the type who lived on his nerves. This breathing space was probably just what he needed. Maybe what Matt needed too—a little distance. From Jonesy, from the press, from Tara Renee, from Police Chief Horrall, from everyone and everything.

*T*oward dawn Nathan woke and they fucked again, slowly, savoring it. And this time Matt was conscious, painfully and pleasurably conscious, of all the ways Nathan Doyle was different from the last person Mathew had made love to: the broad shoulders and hard planes of his chest instead of delicate neck and pillowy breasts; the jut of his bony, narrow hips and the sleek aggression of his cock instead of the soft reception and safe passageway of rounded belly and silky thighs; the roughness of his strong jaw, the bluntness of masculine features instead of fragile bones and feminine face.

Matt liked his strength and his silent intensity. He liked the way Nathan held his gaze while their dicks scraped and stroked in enjoyable friction. Liked the way Nathan's thin, hard fingers dug into the muscles of Matt's arms. And especially he liked the way Nathan woke up randy and ready, just like himself. No coaxing, no sweet talking necessary. Nathan wanted it every bit as much as Matt.

Sensation rolled through him like a tidal wave, leaving him shaken and gasping. He didn't realize he'd cried out until Nathan moved, covering his mouth. "Shhhhh…"

He opened his eyes, staring into Nathan's, and dizzily, Nathan began to laugh, very softly. And Matt laughed too, tasting Nathan's palm clamped against his lips.

"Merry Christmas," Nathan said softly, taking his hand away.

"Merry Christmas," Matt told him.

They had breakfast in their room, the window wide open and the crackling December air clearing out the smell of sex.

Nathan's suit had been brushed and pressed, his shirt and underwear laundered. The late Mr. Hubbard graciously supplied socks. Matt stared out the window at the pine trees and distant snowy mountains while Nathan dressed. He wanted to watch Nathan. He thought his body was beautiful, but he realized Nathan was self-conscious when he stared at him too long.

After breakfast they went for a walk in the woods, not touching beyond the occasional brush of arms or shoulders, but together nonetheless.

"Why do you suppose the kidnappers scheduled things the way they did?" Nathan asked when they stopped to rest on a fallen log. A meadow lark sang in the chilly sunshine. A lone bee zipped past Matt's ear like a miniature Jap Zero.

"They had to wait until the banks were open on Monday."

"But why was there such a long delay before contacting the Arlens? And then why was there such a long delay between when the ransom was paid and Phil was supposed to be released?"

"Well, that last might have been because they wanted to make sure the police hadn't been notified—assuming the intention from the start wasn't to murder young Arlen."

Nathan shook his head. "It still doesn't make sense to me. It's like… they needed time."

"Well, they would, wouldn't they? What's unusual about that?"

"Why'd they wait so long to let the family know he'd been kidnapped?"

Matt knew the answer to that one. "So they'd have no doubt that he really was missing. Apparently Arlen spent more than an occasional night away from home."

Nathan looked unconvinced. "It seems to me that each stage of the kidnapping was spaced so that there was plenty of time in between for the kidnappers to work on some plan they had."

Matt examined Nathan's serious face. He enjoyed watching him, and he enjoyed listening to him. Liked the way his brain worked, liked the easy back and forth between them, liked *him.* Liked him a lot. Maybe too much. Maybe. But he'd never had this before, this effortless give-and-take of equals, not having to guard what he said, not having to sweeten it or soften it because Nathan wasn't someone frightened by the truth—any truth. He said, "Okay, if he wasn't kidnapped, what happened to him? The coroner says he wasn't killed until Monday night. So the kidnapping wasn't faked to cover a murder."

"Maybe not to cover a murder," Nathan agreed. "But it could have been faked."

Mathew stared. "You think Arlen faked his own kidnapping?"

Nathan continued to gaze out over the meadow. His cheek creased in a faint smile. "It'd be nice to talk to Pearl Jarvis, wouldn't it?"

$\mathcal{T}$hey were following a trail up one of the hillsides when Matt noticed Nathan had gotten very quiet. He looked over at him, and he was pale, his jaw very tight. One arm was unobtrusively clamped against his side. Matt put his hand on his arm. "Let's stop a minute."

Nathan slid out from under his touch, and Matt said, "There's no one around. Relax."

He was surprised when Nathan bit out, "You seem to be taking this very much in stride." He eased himself down on a flat-topped rock, breathing heavily.

Matt dropped down beside him. "Would you be happier if I wasn't?"

"I'd feel like—hell. Skip it."

"What?"

Nathan didn't reply, leaning forward, resting his forehead in his hands, breathing fast and shallowly.

"Okay?"

Nathan ignored him.

It was hard not to put his arm around those thin shoulders. "Look," he said. "This is new to me. I guess I have a lot to learn, but one thing I have learned is…it's not what I expected. What I was afraid of. You're not—you're what I used to hope—" It was too difficult to put into words. Too embarrassing. He cut that off. "I wasn't raised by Jesuits or anything, but I don't think God makes mistakes."

"No?" From behind his hands, Nathan's voice was bitter. "What about two-headed calves? What about Siamese twins? You think homosexuality is some kind of deliberate flaw in the design?"

"What?"

"Skip it."

Neither of them spoke for a time. A hawk sailed through the blue silence and vanished—along with the lark song. The wind whispered through the pines around them.

At last Nathan said, "I went to a doctor—in London. I wanted help. Wanted to stop feeling like this. Wanted to be normal." He raised his head and his eyes met Matt's. "I thought I wanted it more than anything."

"What happened?"

Nathan's smile was wry. "He said he could help me. I would have to go into a hospital—be committed, actually. They would give me electro-shocks and cold baths and eventually I'd get better. But it would probably take years."

Matt could feel the hair on the top of his head prickling. "What—did you agree?"

"I did. But then I chickened out." Nathan's grin was sheepish. "I'd used a false name, but I was terrified he'd find me and lock me up. Luckily we were mobilized a couple of weeks later. I wasn't nearly as frightened of Jerry as I was of the witch doctor."

"An asylum would be about right," Matt said. "Christ, you need a keeper, Doyle."

"It'd be nice." Nathan looked away, but there was something in his funny, almost wistful smile that caught at Mathew's heart.

*W*hen they got back to the lodge, they had a drink in the hotel bar with the other guests—there were only a handful, and most of them had been coming to the lodge to celebrate Christmas for years. They were a pleasant enough bunch.

Matt excused himself after a while and commandeered Mrs. Hubbard's office to make a few phone calls.

Nathan finished his drink, made small talk with some of the other guests, and then they all went to eat Christmas dinner served in the dining room. Several tables had been pushed together and covered with red table-cloths. There were candles in polished brass holders and a basket of holly with bright red berries for a centerpiece.

Matt joined them about the time they were all finishing up their soup. He sat across from Nathan in the wide square of tables. Nathan tried hard not to watch Matt too much, but when he wasn't watching Matt he could feel Matt looking at him.

The food was as good as anything before the war—real turkey, stuffing with chestnuts, mashed potatoes and gravy. The yams, corn, green beans and pumpkin for the pie probably came from the hotel victory garden, but Nathan couldn't imagine how they'd managed to come up with the rest of the feast. Hoarded ration books? Black market? He ate more in one go than he could remember consuming in years.

Listening to the others talking about the war, for the first time he was aware of being grateful that he was home and safe—that Matt had made it home safely. And the next time he looked across the linen and candles and met Matt's eyes, he didn't look away, he smiled—and Matt smiled back.

After Christmas dinner they managed to avoid being press-ganged into playing cards, and went upstairs where Matt gave him the bad news that there was still no sign of Pearl. "There's been one development though."

Nathan was resting on the bed. He felt ready to explode from eating too much, but he raised an inquiring head.

"We searched Phil Arlen's apartment and found a wad of five-hundred dollar bills in Claire Arlen's purse."

Nathan dropped his head back on the pillow. He didn't say what he was thinking—that he thought it was a hell of thing the cops were searching women's purses, that none of them had a right to privacy these days.

"She says she doesn't know how the money got there," Matt added.

"Does the money match the ransom money serial numbers?"

"They're checking on that now." And then Matt strolled over to the bed, sat down and stretched out beside Nathan. He yawned widely. "Since we're stuck…"

Nathan shook his head, rose and went to prop a chair beneath the room door.

Matt was already sleeping by the time he got back to the bed.

They napped for a couple of long, peaceful hours, and when they woke they had turkey sandwiches and drinks in the bar with the other guests. They made small talk, sang a few carols when everyone had finally had enough to drink, and then at last it was late enough to retire upstairs, lock the door and turn down the lights. They crawled in between the sheets as though they had been cuddling up together every night for years. For a time they just lay there, breathing quietly, acquainting themselves.

Matt's fingertips brushed the scars on Nathan's side where the bullets had hit him, and Nathan's skin twitched a little. It was Matt's gentleness that he felt in his nerves and bones and blood, although it was nice to be touched, caressed.

"How the hell did you survive this?"

"Just unlucky, I guess."

He was kidding—he thought he was—but Matt raised his head. Nathan couldn't read his expression in the darkness, but he heard his tone. "There are about a hundred thousand guys who'd have given anything to trade places with you."

Nathan grimaced. "I know."

But Matt couldn't let it go. "You know how rare it is to survive getting hit by machine-gun fire?"

"I know."

"Seems to me like that kind of—"

"I know," Nathan said again, and this time he couldn't keep the irritation out of his voice.

*W*hen, at last, they began to fuck it was very good and Nathan bit back his desire to ask for more—this was all new for Matt and Nathan didn't want to shock him or scare him off. It would be easy to do. It was clear to him that Matt had more enthusiasm than experience. It didn't matter. He was willing to trade a lot for the pleasure of sleeping in Matt's arms again, and when they had finished, pleasure echoing through him like the last vibrating note of a choir of angels, he turned to Matt and folded close.

Matt's lips pressed against his forehead. Nathan could feel he was smiling.

He'd never slept as well as he had in the past two nights.

On Sunday morning they were driven down to Indian Falls in the hotel station wagon, and they caught the first available train back to Los Angeles. There was no chance for further intimate discussion, so they talked trivialities, and somehow those seemed newly significant.

As the mountains flattened out, and the pine trees gave way to cactus and desert and then houses and gardens, Nathan began to dread the swift approach of Los Angeles.

He could feel Mathew's withdrawal, although each time their eyes met, Mathew smiled fleetingly, and the knowledge of what they had shared was in his eyes.

In Union Station, things happened very quickly, and they were out front on the pavement while the never-ending flood of passengers and friends and family parted around them.

Nathan said, "Can I drop you somewhere?"

"There's a car coming for me," Matt said.

Nathan nodded. He knew he shouldn't ask, already knew what the answer had to be, but he asked anyway. "Will I see you again?"

Matt said brusquely, "I'm not leaving town."

And that pretty much answered Nathan's question. He nodded, turning away, and Matt caught his arm. He immediately let him go, and said quietly, painfully, "It's not that I don't—I'm a cop, Nathan. It's…too dangerous."

Nathan nodded. Smiled. "I know. Nice to have had a taste of…what it could be like. That's more than I ever thought I'd have."

Matt's face twisted as though Nathan had said something terrible, and Nathan wanted to reach out and reassure him that he meant it, meant every word. That he was truly grateful for these few hours, that it was the best Christmas ever. He had no regrets at all, despite the fact that he wished he hadn't woken up this morning, that perfect happiness would have been to have gone to sleep in Matt's arms and never opened his eyes again.

But of course he couldn't say that, and he couldn't reach out. He could never touch Matt again.

Instead he said softly, "Take care of yourself, Mathew."

Chapter Eight

"How'd you make out?" Jonesy asked, as Matt climbed into the car.

Matt grunted. In his mind's eye he was watching Nathan's long-legged stride across the Union Station parking lot, hat dipped at a rakish angle, apparently not a care in the world. Nathan was fine—so why was Matt's gut knotting in anxiety?

"How's Mr. Doyle?"

"Good as new," Matt replied. "He just needed a couple hours' sleep."

"Didn't do you any harm either," Jonesy said.

"Who are you, my mother?" But Matt grinned. Jonesy had known him since he was in short pants. Then the flicker of curiosity in the older man's eyes caught his attention. "What?"

Jonesy shook his head. "Were you able to get anything out of him?"

"He's not our man."

"No? He's sure as hell hiding something."

"Everybody's hiding something, Jonesy. Even you, I guess."

Jonesy chuckled. "Mebbe so, mebbe so."

"Still no sign of the Jarvis woman?"

"Near as anyone can tell, she stepped onto that train and vanished into thin air."

"Swell," Matt said gloomily. "You're watching her place and the Las Palmas Club?"

"Yep, and we're watching Sid Szabo's apartment, but I don't think she'd be dumb enough to go back there." Jonesy turned south on Alameda, pausing for two jaywalking ladies laden with Christmas parcels. He gave a low whistle, and Matt shook off his preoccupation long enough to notice the women.

Nice-looking women. He realized with something like shock that he was missing Nathan—it was like a pain you couldn't quite put a name to. Maybe it wasn't so strange after spending almost forty-eight hours in each other's company, but he missed the sound of Nathan's voice, and his quiet laugh. He even missed the smell of him.

He shook off the feeling, and said crisply, "Tell me about the dough you found at Claire Arlen's."

Jonesy put the car in motion. "The five hundred dollars she claims she didn't know anything about?" He smiled. "Well, sorry to disappoint you, Loot, but that money didn't match up with the serial numbers on the ransom money."

"So where'd the money come from? Old man Arlen cut the kid off, and I didn't get the feeling Arlen's wife was the thrifty kind."

"She stuck to her story. Said she didn't know anything about the money. Had no idea how it got in her handbag."

Matt's eyes rested on the Christmas garland stretched across the street. Funny how bedraggled Christmas decorations looked the day after Christmas. "Let's bring Carl Winters in again," he said. "In fact, bring Claire in too. Let's have a brother and sister act."

Nathan went home to his apartment, collected the gift he'd bought weeks ago for his mother, and headed over to Glendale and the house he'd grown up in.

His mother must have had a lonely Christmas on her own, although he didn't see how that would be possible what with her church dinners and all her church friends and her church activities, but she hugged him as though she'd never expected to see him again, and there were tears in her eyes when she finally let him go.

There were more tears when she opened his gift, a fuzzy pink cardigan. He felt foolish at the impulse that had prompted him to buy it. She didn't wear fuzzy things or even pink.

"Oh, Ma," he said. She was not an emotional woman, and this rare display of sentiment made him uncomfortable.

She wiped her eyes. "When you didn't come yesterday I thought maybe…maybe something had happened to you."

"Like what?" He felt vaguely alarmed at the way she wasn't meeting his eyes.

But she brushed that quickly aside, insisting that he stay long enough to eat a sandwich and drink a glass of milk. "We had real turkey at the parish Christmas dinner," she told him proudly.

"Good," he said, swallowing a lump of dry bread and dry turkey. She had never been much of a cook—or even much of a sandwich maker, but then neither of those things was required to get into heaven.

He thought of the turkey and stuffing and mashed potatoes at Little Fawn Lodge. It all seemed like a dream now. His eyes fell on the nativity meticulously arranged on the long table behind the sofa. The only time she'd ever slapped him was when she once found him playing with the nativity—he'd had a couple of those handsome hand-carved archangels holding earnest discussion with a couple of the tin reindeer requisitioned from the Christmas tree.

She chattered on about midnight Mass and Father Brennan's sermon, and then she jumped up and brought him a small gift from beneath the fake miniature Christmas tree perched on the dining room table and decorated with tattered ornaments he'd made through his school years.

He put the sandwich aside and took the parcel. She stroked his back as he opened it, and he felt another flare of nervousness. He couldn't remember her ever being so demonstrative since he had been a very small boy.

The present was a pen, a very nice, expensive pen. A Parker Blue Diamond.

"For the novels you're going to write one day." She swallowed hard as though she were ready to start weeping again. And, as he stared at her red-rimmed eyes, he realized she had been afraid that he had killed himself.

"Thanks, Ma," Nathan managed. He stared at the pen, and then he hurried through the rest of his sandwich, telling her that he had to get over to the paper right away.

They were still celebrating at the *Tribune-Herald*. Several bottles of homemade hooch—mulled wine and that sort of thing—were circulating with a couple of trays of Christmas goodies—everything a little less sweet than it used to be because of sugar rationing.

Nathan had a couple of drinks—fortifying himself after the visit to his mother—and spent the next few hours doing a little research and dodging his editor.

"Sid Szabo," he asked at large, remembering that overnight bag Szabo had toted away from Pearl's rooming house. "He any relation to the Szabo Alligator Farm out in Lincoln Heights?"

There was a bit of debate on this point—a few people holding out for the theory that Sid was more likely to be related to a snake farm if there was one available—and in the end Nathan took his coat and hat and left them still debating.

Supposedly the Szabo Alligator Farm had only been around since the early 1900s, but it could have been from the Stone Age. Nathan parked beneath low-hanging trees in the empty parking lot and entered the park through a long white stucco building with a slim, two-story columned por-tico. The gift shop—offering baby alligators for sale—and ticket booth were closed, but he climbed over the turnstile and walked along the shaded path, crossing a small wooden bridge over a large dank pond filled with sleeping alligators.

According to the sign out front, there were supposed to be over one thousand alligators and crocodiles, some more than two hundred years old, inhabiting over twenty miniature lakes.

He wondered if the alligators ever climbed out of their swimming holes, and if they were able to scale the slopes leading to the deeply shaded pathways. Stepping on one of those three-hundred-pound babies would be an unpleasant surprise for everyone involved. Glancing over the side of the bridge at the slithering tangle of reptiles, he decided they looked pretty tired; it was probably a little cold for them this time of year. Cold for him too. He missed the warmth of North Africa.

Over the murky scent of wet earth and slimy water, he could smell wood smoke. And through the dense foliage of weeping willows, he could see the twinkle of lights: a farmhouse in the back of the park. He picked up his pace, footsteps sounding dully on yet another little wooden bridge.

It was a creepy place, no doubt about it, and it was hard to picture Pearl Jarvis in her high heels and faux furs trotting along these rustic bridges and uneven dirt trails. But she was hiding somewhere and, Nathan had to admit, this was a pretty good hideout. Especially off-season.

He came out of the woods, and there was an old house behind a new and sturdy-looking chain-link fence—probably to keep the alligators and crocodiles from paying a social call. Several yards behind the house was a large empty field. Two men stood beside a pickup truck, and they appeared to be digging a deep hole.

Nathan watched them, then he reached over the substantial-looking gate, lifted the bar and let himself in. He closed the gate firmly behind him.

He went up the paved path to the house and knocked.

Nothing happened.

He knocked again. After a time, the door swung open and Pearl Jarvis, in dungarees and a man's sweater, stared back at him. She was holding an old Webley revolver, and it was pointed at his chest.

"You can't hold me," Claire Arlen was protesting for the *n*th time. "I'm an *Arlen*. I'm Philip Arlen's *wife!*"

"Well, you were," Matt replied. "Now you're his widow. We're trying to figure out if that was by accident or design."

The door opened and Carl Winters was ushered in—none too happily—by Jonesy. Jonesy raised his eyebrows at Matt, and Matt said, "Sorry for the inconvenience, Mr. Winters—"

"This is harassment," Winters interrupted furiously. "How many times am I to be subjected to police interrogation? I've answered all your questions. Again and again! I didn't kill my brother-in-law, and the fact that you would drag my sister—his widow—out, when she's ill—"

"It's all right, Carl," Claire said, although she'd been saying pretty much the same thing herself since she had arrived.

"I didn't realize you were ill, Mrs. Arlen," Matt said. She didn't look particularly well, but there could be a number of reasons for that—including guilt.

She said coldly, "I'm expecting a baby. And when Benedict Arlen hears the way you've treated me, and endangered the life of his grandson—"

There was what might be appropriately called a pregnant pause.

Matt fixed his gaze on Claire Arlen with the sensation of having been sucker-punched. He could feel Jonesy's eyes, but he didn't dare look at him. This was a bad oversight on their part. He knew how Jonesy felt, but that couldn't be helped now.

"Congratulations," he said. "Did Phil know about the baby?"

"Of course he knew!"

There was something odd about the way she said that. Matt couldn't put his finger on it. Had Phil known and not been happy about the pregnancy?

But a baby would have improved things with old man Arlen, of that Matt was sure. The first grandkid? The first child of his favorite son? Yeah, that would have softened old Benedict up, probably convinced him to reinstate the black sheep's allowance—or maybe even increase it.

"I guess the family was pretty happy about the news?" he tried.

"I suppose so," she said stiffly.

Huh.

"Why are we here?" Winters demanded. "I can't believe that I and my sister are your only suspects! What about organized crime? The mob? What about that reporter, Doyle? He was there that night. Perhaps he's your kidnapper. Reporters have all kinds of unsavory underworld contacts."

"What would his motive be, Mr. Winters?"

"Phil must have been—well, how should I know? I'm sure Doyle needs money. He's been around asking all kinds of strange questions. Why aren't you questioning him?"

"We have questioned him," Matt said. "Now we're questioning you." He turned to Claire. "Speaking of money, have you had time to remember where you got that five hundred dollars we found in your purse?"

"How is that your business?"

"*I* gave her that money!" Carl Winters was white with fury. "*I* put that money in her handbag on Saturday night. You mean *that's* why you dragged us down here?"

"If that's the case, why didn't you say so?" Matt asked Claire evenly. He was starting to get mad. Why hadn't this obvious explanation been explored? What the hell kind of background checking had Jonesy and his men done that they hadn't uncovered Claire Arlen's pregnancy or the fact that her brother was occasionally financing her household? This was supposed to be Jonesy's case, and Jonesy had as much or more experience as anyone on the squad. Some bad mistakes had been made with this investigation, obvious things had been overlooked.

"I didn't know!" Claire was raging. "I never left the house or looked inside my purse until your apes pointed that money out to me."

"Claire, honey." Winters patted her shoulder awkwardly. "You mustn't get so upset. It's bad for the baby." He turned to Matt. "I slipped that money inside her purse because they were broke, and Phil wasn't capable of taking care of her. He couldn't take care of himself!"

Something wasn't adding up.

"Why didn't your husband's family…if they knew you were going to have a baby?" It was like feeling his way in the dark. He was very much aware of how delicate this situation was, and that his own career might be riding on how he handled the next thirty minutes.

Claire flushed. "They didn't know about the baby until Sunday night. I told Phil first, of course. I was hoping…I was giving him a little time to adjust to the idea…before I told Dad. But then when they told me he'd been kidnapped—"

"Wait a minute," Matt said. "Are you telling me the kidnappers didn't call *you?*"

"Why would they call me? I don't have any money. Phil didn't have any money. They called Dad."

The kidnappers had known for a fact that Claire Arlen would be unable to meet their ransom demand. Knew the Arlen family's domestic arrangements so intimately that they had gone straight to the old man right off the bat.

"So you never heard the voice of the woman who called with the ransom demand?"

She shook her head.

The office was silent.

"You think I would have recognized her voice," she said slowly.

Carl Winters was looking from Matt to Claire bewilderedly.

"Let me ask you something," Matt said. "Say your husband wasn't really kidnapped. Say the kidnapping was just an excuse to bump him off. Who would you say had the strongest motive for getting rid of Phil?"

"You can't ask her to answer a question like that!"

"I *am* asking her," Matt said.

Claire said, "Phil's brother, Bob. I guess Bob had plenty of reasons to wish Phil was dead."

$\mathcal{H}$aving barely recovered from the last time he was filled full of lead, Nathan was keen not to repeat the experience. And he didn't trust the way Pearl Jarvis held that Webley. Her hand shook, and she had a wild-eyed look.

He said—not moving his gaze from the dead eye of the revolver aimed at his chest, "And here I was afraid it was you they were burying out back."

Amazingly, she laughed. Her voice wobbled a little as she replied, "They're burying Big Al. He was the granddaddy of a lot of these gators. He was two hundred and fifty years old."

"That's a good long life."

"His hide is so tough they can't use it for anything. But they're keeping his head. And his claws."

"Is that so?"

She nodded tightly.

"You found yourself a great little hideout," Nathan said. "That's for sure."

"Hideout? You make me sound like a criminal!" Her eyes narrowed. "I didn't *do* anything wrong."

"Well, I know you didn't kill Phil," Nathan said, "because you're frightened to death of whoever did. You've been running scared since it happened."

The gun wavered, and he reached out and gently redirected her aim away from himself. She lowered her arm, finally taking a step back, letting Nathan into the house. "You're that reporter, Doyle. Sid told me about you. He said you were trying to find me. You followed me to Little Fawn Lodge."

"And Sid's boys followed me."

Her gaze slid away from his. "Sid's just trying to look out for me."

"Who's he trying to protect you from?"

She swallowed hard. "Want a drink?"

"Sure." He followed her into an old-fashioned parlor, pausing on the room's threshold. There were lamps made from alligator feet, stools and chairs upholstered in alligator and crocodile skin, and a mounted alligator head on the wall.

Reading his expression correctly, Pearl said, "Yeah, and you should hear them bellowing at night. The alligators, I mean, not Sid's folks. B flat, I think." She dropped the revolver on the wine cart with a clatter that did nothing for Nathan's nerves and poured two thimblefuls of sherry from a small decanter. She offered a fragile amber glass to Nathan and made a face. "It's all they have here. Funny Sid coming from a family like this!" She swallowed the sherry in a gulp.

Nathan took a mouthful of sweet sherry and controlled a shudder. "You know," he said, "the safest thing for you to do is tell me exactly what you know. Once you've spilled your story there's no incentive for anyone to hurt you."

"You don't think so? You think that wife of his wouldn't like me to pay for stealing Phil from her?"

"Is that what happened?"

She nodded, tears filling her eyes. "We were going away together. We were going to Buenos Aires."

"After Phil's dad paid the ransom."

She stared at him, and Nathan almost laughed.

"Well, nobody can find any trace of these kidnappers before or since Phil was nabbed. You and Phil set it all up, didn't you? So you'd have money to run away together?"

She nodded.

"What happened?"

She gnawed her lip. "Everything went fine. Phil picked up the money at the Observatory. They must have followed our instructions just like we'd planned. He was supposed to meet me in the back of the park. I was waiting in the car. He came hurrying along the path holding a bag, and I remember I turned the engine on, turned the headlights on so he could see. It was so dark and muddy. But a few feet away he stopped and turned around like he heard someone following him. Like someone called his name. And a man came running up the path behind him, and Phil stood there, and he shot him." She stopped and covered her face. "Just like that. Shot him dead."

"What did the man look like?"

She looked up out of her hands, and her face was horror-stricken. "I couldn't tell. Tall, thin. He was wearing a black raincoat and a black hat pulled low. I didn't recognize him, his face was just a pale blur. He fired at me—at the car—and I threw it into reverse and drove away. I should have run him over! But I panicked and I drove away."

Personally, Nathan thought retreat had been Pearl's best bet. Phil's killer had been cold and steady as steel. "You're sure you didn't recognize this man?"

"I didn't get a clear look at him. First Phil was standing between us, and then—" she gulped, "—all I saw was the gun."

CHAPTER NINE

*W*hen he heard Nathan's voice on the phone, Matt felt a warm rush.

He'd been *wanting* to hear Nathan's voice, missing him, wanting to know that he was okay, wanting to tell him about the problems in the Arlen case. His men had made some serious mistakes in the investigation. *Jonesy* had let him down. Matt's career might be on the line. He wanted to talk to someone he could trust. He wanted to talk to Nathan.

But in the very next instant, that warm rush gave way to chilled alarm. Didn't Nathan understand? Was he that lost to common sense? They hadn't been starting something—those two days at Little Fawn Lodge were all there could be between them, thinking anything else was crazy. Dangerous. They were neither of them the kind of men who wanted to go that route. They had careers, families, responsibilities; they weren't the kind of guys who gave in to that kind of thing. Where was the future in it? There *wasn't* any future in it.

It wasn't logical thinking, it was just Matt's instinctive response to the pleasure he felt at hearing Nathan's voice—because he felt too much pleasure, he knew that much. So he said crisply, "What did you need, Doyle?"

There was a too-long pause, and then Nathan said deliberately, "I'm trying to tell you. I found the Jarvis girl."

Matt's face flamed. He'd been so busy panicking that he hadn't heard a word Nathan had said, and he could hear in Nathan's voice that he knew it.

He didn't know how to back away from his mistake, so he just said, "Where?"

And Nathan told him where, crisply and concisely. "I wouldn't take too long getting here. She thinks she's being tracked by whoever killed the Arlen kid. She's liable to pull another flit."

"We're on our way," Matt said. And then, awkwardly, "Will you be there?"

He wasn't even sure why he'd asked it, but Nathan said, "No. She's got a couple of brawny gamekeepers here to keep her safe, and I've got a story to file."

"Right. Thanks for the tip." He should have hung up, but for some reason he couldn't. He wanted to correct the mistake he'd made when he'd first picked up the phone. He'd realized how stupid he was to think that he and Nathan couldn't be friends, couldn't work together as much as the press and the police could work together. As long as they both understood that it couldn't go any further than that, he wanted to be friends with Nathan. In fact there was only one thing he wanted more. So he said tentatively, "See you around."

And Nathan said shortly, "I'm not leaving town," and hung up.

*S*everal hours later, sometime after midnight, Matt followed Nathan and his newest swain—a big bruiser in a khaki uniform—down the steps of the Biltmore hotel, watched them run across the street and disappear into the jungle of Pershing Square. Matt followed silently, cursing himself—and Nathan—every step of the way.

Who was the unhealthy, neurotic one here? Himself or Nathan? Nathan was at least—assumingly—getting what he wanted out of this. What the hell was Matt getting? Other than ill with jealousy and anger and something too close to despair.

He was the one who'd told Nathan that any kind of relationship between them was impossible. That the risk was too great. The incredible thing to him now was that he had expected—believed—that Nathan would understand that the risk to himself was too great, as well. That he would belatedly exercise wisdom. That he would make the same sacrifice Matt was having to make.

Why not admit it? He had believed that what they had shared was so special that Nathan wouldn't cheapen himself by settling for something else, something less.

But here Nathan was, not even waiting one goddamned night before he was back in the jungle with the other animals.

None of which explained what the hell Matt was doing down here again. And if he hadn't seen Nathan, hadn't tracked him like radar illuminating a target, would he have been trying to find someone of his own to spend a few hours with?

He didn't know.

He was afraid to consider it too closely.

He crept through the grass and brush until he heard them, the harsh panting, crackle of dead leaves and twigs, and he pushed aside the branches and found them—found Nathan down on the ground fighting for his life while his erstwhile lover tried to brain him with a short and solid tree branch.

As Matt watched, the man kicked Nathan, and Nathan cried out and stopped fighting, lying there stunned. The man bent over him. Matt took his gun out, stepped through the branches and hit the guy hard with the butt of his revolver across the back of his head. The man slumped over Nathan's supine body. Matt dragged him off.

He knelt beside Nathan, dragging his boxers up, pushing his flaccid dick inside, possessive and angry about that soft warmth, Nathan unaroused but asking for it—he had asked for it and he had got it—and Matt wanted to kill the other guy. And he wanted to kill Nathan.

"Come on, get up," he told Nathan, locking hands on him, drawing him up, and Nathan staggered to his feet, peered at him and then looked ready to fall again when he saw who his rescuer was.

"Christ, pull yourself together," Matt hissed, and then tried to soften it. "Nathan, come on. We've got to get out of here." He was trying with all his might not to let his anger through because Nathan had been hurt enough for one night. And as angry as he was with Nathan, he was also frightened for him.

Nathan hadn't said a word. Not one word. He reached out to steady himself on a banana tree, and then looked down at the man who had tried to kill him.

Matt collected his coat and hat. He put an arm around Nathan, and Nathan reeled against him and dropped his head in the curve of Matt's neck and shoulder. Matt pressed his cheek to the softness of Nathan's hair. He gave Nathan a moment—he thought he might be crying, but then he realized, no. Nathan was just breathing deeply, exhaustedly, as though he'd run and run to get to this instant, and now there was nowhere else to run.

"Can you walk?" Matt murmured. He had to walk. Matt couldn't carry him, but he asked anyway.

Nathan nodded. He pulled away from Matt and reached for his coat, and almost overbalanced. Matt grabbed him, helping him shrug into the coat, putting his hat on him.

The man on the ground moved, groaned, and Nathan's foot lashed out. He kicked him with the strength and accuracy of a mule and then almost fell over again.

Matt put an arm around him and led him through the trees, keeping to the deepest shadows, Nathan stumbling along like he was drunk or blind.

When they reached the plaza, Nathan straightened up.

"It's better if we don't walk across the square together." His voice was flat.

And that was true. Matt said, "I parked on Seventh Street. Wait for me at the intersection."

He didn't know if Nathan heard him or not. Nathan walked out of the bushes across the pavement, and he stood straight and moved briskly, swiftly, with no sign of what had just happened.

Matt watched him go, gilded in moonlight, crossing the square, and suddenly he couldn't bear it. Couldn't bear for Nathan to have to make this particular journey on his own.

He started after him and caught him up quickly, walking beside him, within arm's distance but not touching, and bitterly damning to hell anyone who watched them and dared to think anything.

They crossed Olive Street and walked north. There was no traffic, no one at all.

And then they were on Seventh Street. Matt took Nathan's arm, ignoring the initial resistance, and guided him along 'til they came to Matt's car. He put Nathan inside, and he was gentle now, careful with him. He slammed the door and went round to his own side, sliding inside. He rested his hands on the steering wheel.

"Are you—how bad is it?"

"I'll live," Nathan said dully.

"He could have killed you. You know that. He could just as easily have bashed your brains out."

Nathan stared out his window, not answering.

Matt started the car engine. He didn't even think about it, he drove straight to his own house, taking Nathan home. He parked in the back, turned off the lights and came around to Nathan's side. Nathan got out slowly, as though he hurt, and Matt put a supporting arm around him. Nathan tried to shrug him off, but Matt wouldn't let go, so instead Nathan walked stiffly, rejecting help without saying a word, making Matt feel silly for that protective arm wrapped around straight shoulders and a ramrod spine.

Up the tidy walk, past the flower beds that Rachel had planted, beneath the trellised carport with roses heavy with perfume even in December. Matt unlocked the side door and put Nathan inside before stepping in himself and turning on the light.

Nathan winced at the light, raising a protective hand.

"You better let me take a look at you," Matt said. "You might have a couple of cracked ribs. He could have ruptured your spleen or your kidneys." He was getting angry again, thinking of it. Nathan could have died there tonight. Died an ugly, pointless death in the underbrush of Pershing Square—and for what?

Nathan lowered his hand, frowning. He said slowly, "You must have followed me. I don't guess you went there for sex."

"I followed you," Matt agreed.

Nathan peered at Matt as though he was viewing him from a distance, as though he was having trouble making him out.

"Can I take a shower?" he asked, abruptly.

Unspeaking, Matt got him towels, showed him the shower. He poured himself a drink while he listened to the water raining down from the bathroom and the resounding silence from within.

Gradually the red glare faded from his brain, his heart slowed back into a normal rhythm. He felt depressed, anxious. Nathan was taking a long time in the shower, probably dreading facing Matt as much as Matt dreaded facing Nathan.

The door opened and Nathan came out, his hair wet, combed back. He had re-dressed in his mud-stained clothes.

And for the life of him Matt couldn't think of a word to say. He was overwhelmingly, abjectly grateful that Nathan was alive, in one piece. The intensity of his feelings overwhelmed him.

But his silence seemed to confirm something for Nathan, whose face grew stiffer and more closed. "I appreciate what you did tonight, but I'm fine. I should be going."

"Drink this." Matt pushed a whisky into his hand.

Nathan hesitated, then he drank. He avoided looking at Matt—looking everywhere but at Matt. He drained his glass, spotted Rachel's photograph on the piano and picked it up, studying it.

"This is her? Rachel?"

Matt nodded. He felt protective of Rachel's picture, prepared for Nathan to say something cruel about her although Nathan had never shown any sign of cruelty. He looked up from Rachel's smile and said, "She looks like she laughed a lot."

Matt's eyes stung. "Yeah. We laughed a lot." He took the photo from Nathan—careful not to look like he didn't trust Nathan with it—studying it. Rachel's photographed face—more glamorous than she'd ever looked in real life—smiled back at him, her eyes shining with love and trust. He looked at Nathan, who was watching him.

He tried to imagine what Rachel would make of this, what she would make of Nathan. Rachel was kind and intuitive. He thought she would have been frightened for Nathan too—and frightened for Matt.

Nathan put his whisky glass down, walking around Matt's living room, as though he were too restless to sit—or expected to be invited to leave shortly. He didn't look at Matt. Matt could have not been there at all.

Matt watched him, telling himself to tread softly, but the words came out harshly anyway. "You know you could be arrested. You keep on the way you're going, you will be."

Nathan had paused at the window, staring through yellow frilled curtains at the garden fenced in white pickets. He nodded, not seeming to notice Matt's aggressive stance.

"If you're not killed first."

At the frustration in Matt's voice, he looked over.

"I know."

"Then why? Why are you taking such a chance? You're not stupid. Why are you risking...*everything?*"

Nathan's face changed. Came back to life. "Because I'm not like you! I can't live my life like a goddamn priest. I need…something, even if I can't have some*one*." He began to cry. It was painful to watch, painful to hear, Nathan fighting it every step of the way, and sobs tearing out of his chest anyway.

"Don't." Matt pulled Nathan into his arms, roughly, overcoming his resistance, holding him fiercely. He could feel sobs racking the thin, hard body, and he kissed his neck, his ear, his hair, any part of him he could find—a tear-streaked cheek, the corner of a wet eye, his trembling mouth. "Don't, Nathan. I love you. Don't cry."

He was shocked to hear his own words, but hearing them he knew them for the truth. He loved Nathan. It didn't make sense, but it was true. From the first minute he'd laid eyes on him.

All the fight went out of Nathan. He went still, then he shook his head, wiped his face on Matt's shoulder, tried to pull away. "No. Don't." He made another attempt to mop his face on his arm. "Don't." He sounded a little calmer.

"It's the truth. I do love you. I can't…bear this. That's God's truth."

"I can't bear it either," Nathan said tiredly. "Let's forget it."

He put Nathan into his bed and lay down with him, wrapping his arms around him and pressing his face against the back of Nathan's head, feeling the softness of his hair against his face. It smelled sweet, like summer, like grass, like Nathan.

Nathan lay unmoving, waiting for something—for Matt to fall asleep perhaps—but then he began to relax…muscle by muscle, nerve by nerve, losing the battle—whatever battle this was—sliding without a word into a deep exhausted sleep.

Matt held him, cradled him and tried to think what the hell they were going to do.

*H*e woke to the feeling of Nathan's taut ass pressing back against his groin. His cock stirred and filled, and he opened his eyes. The room was hushed and hazy with the dawn's early light. Nathan's skin was smooth and brown, and the nape of his neck looked vulnerable and boyish, with the glint of silver chain against his skin, and the pale hair. Nathan pushed back against him, and Matt's dick slid along the crevice between his firm buttocks.

He said, "You can't want this…after last night."

Nathan said, staring forward, "I need it. Need it more than ever now—and I always need it." He added, not in apology exactly, but helplessly, "It makes me feel connected. It makes me feel…alive."

"And it doesn't matter who or how?"

Nathan's head turned. He heaved himself, facing Matt. "It matters. Of course it does. I want it to be with someone I love. With you, Mathew. But if I can't have that, I still have to have it." He met Matt's eyes. "It's a sickness, I know. I wish I could be strong like you and just not need it, but I do." He turned back on his side and pushed himself against Matt's rigid cock, humping back in delicate invitation, weak and wanton. "Please, Mathew," he whispered. "Please."

…someone I love. With you, Mathew…

Matt said, "I—haven't done this before."

And Nathan froze, stopped those tiny urgent movements that were making Matt crazy, rolled over and sat up.

In other circumstances Matt might have laughed at his wide-eyed expression. "No? But I thought…"

"Not this."

"But you want to?"

Matt didn't have to think—he'd already had too much time to think. He nodded, and surprised relief flooded Nathan's face. "Yeah? Sure?"

"I'm sure already," Matt growled.

Nathan grinned. "I was afraid—" He bit off the rest of it. "Do you have some kind of lotion? Or oil?"

"Petroleum jelly in the bathroom. Lie still." Matt rose, went into the bathroom and found the jar. Carrying it back into the bedroom, he swallowed hard at the sight of Nathan lying on his belly, brown and relaxed in the sheets. Matt sat down on the bed.

Nathan turned his head on his arms and watched him. "It feels good," he said. "You'll see."

Matt nodded.

"You're not betraying anyone. It won't...take anything away from her."

Matt smiled faintly. "I know. Now you're thinking too much about it." He unscrewed the lid of the petroleum jelly, handing it to Nathan's reaching hand, watching—unable not to watch—as Nathan scooped a glob of glistening jelly and reached behind himself. Nathan closed his eyes as though even this was somehow pleasurable.

"How do you want me?" he asked, and Matt caught his breath on an unsteady laugh.

"Let's do this," Nathan said after a time, and he sat up, getting on his hands and knees while Matt readied himself. Nathan waited for him, his body relaxed and beautiful.

Matt got behind Nathan, the bed dipping beneath his knees, and his cock was huge as he positioned himself. He took himself in hand and guided himself at the rosebud center of Nathan's ass, prepared for resistance and pain—his own and Nathan's. And there was a moment of resistance, and Nathan breathed, "Yes, please...Matt..."

Matt pushed, felt that ring of muscle give, and then he was enveloped in dark heat—a black-velvet kiss.

Nathan moaned. "Oh, Jesus, Mathew." He sounded broken. Matt held very still and Nathan gasped, "Don't stop. Please..."

Matt thrust once. Felt Nathan's body clench around him—and he began to understand why, once experienced, it might be hard to forget this, why it might even be worth the risk. Was it as sweet on the receiving end? He couldn't tell, Nathan was breathing unevenly, pushing back against him, making that little keening sound.

"Is this what you want?" he asked.

Nathan whispered, "I want you to fuck me, Mathew. I need you to."

And Matt let go, beginning to move inside Nathan, slowly, then faster, lancing in and out, swift and slick, Nathan rocking back against him, begging him for more, urging him to fuck him harder, to take him, to make him feel it in his belly, his chest—naked, shocking, broken phrases that excited Matt more, allowing him to shake off his inhibitions, his fears. He thrust hard, and he enjoyed the roughness of it, the sweet slap of skin on skin, knees brushing knees, thighs against thighs.

He remembered the first time he'd watched Nathan, and he reached beneath his taut abdomen, finding Nathan's rigid cock—Nathan whimpered in a kind of relief—and Matt worked him while he pounded frantically against him.

Nathan came first, biting off a cry as hot sticky wetness filled Matt's hand—it was like he was bringing himself off, he felt Nathan's release as keenly as though it were rippling through his own body—and then exquisite relief was surging through flesh and bone…

*H*e felt tears fill his eyes. He closed his lashes against them, but maybe

Nathan heard something in his breathing. He said, troubled, "Are you sorry, Mathew? Do you regret it?"

Matt moved his head negatively against the muscled warmth of Nathan's back.

Nathan kept trying to reassure him. "It doesn't have to mean anything. Not to you. You can forget it, if you'd rather."

Matt listened to Nathan's heartbeat, fast and light like a deer flashing through sunshine and shadow. "Listen, Nathan…"

Nathan was silent, but Matt could feel the immediate tension down his spine.

"I loved Rachel with all my heart. You're right, nothing changes that. But—I never wanted her the way I want you."

Nathan slid out from under him, rolled over. His face was different, grave but sort of lit from within in a way that gave Matt a funny pain in his chest.

"Though I don't know what the hell we're going to do," he admitted.

Nathan slipped an arm around him, lowered his head to Matt's chest. "Maybe the Japs will solve it for us. Maybe they'll drop a bomb on us."

Matt raised his head. Nathan's eyes were closed.

"Don't," he said.

"No? Sorry."

"It should make a difference, Nathan."

Nathan opened his eyes. "It makes all the difference in the world. I mean that." His smile was self-mocking. "It's a long time since I've had anything to lose. I guess I'm scared."

Matt bent his head and found Nathan's mouth. He tasted sweet and sleepy. "Me too," he said. "But I don't regret it."

CHAPTER TEN

When the alarm went off about an hour later, Matt jackknifed up, hair in his eyes, and Nathan sprang up beside him, pulse hammering in the base of his throat.

"Christ," Mathew said thickly, raking a hand through his hair.

Nathan sat back, watching Mathew carefully. Dawn and all its rosy promises seemed like a lifetime ago. Matt was straightforward. Direct as a bullet, he wasn't going to adapt well to any kind of subterfuge, and Nathan knew then that he wasn't doing him any favors by falling in love with him. Mathew had been a lot safer mourning the gentle ghost of his childhood sweetheart.

They rose and dressed, and neither had a lot to say.

"Did you believe Pearl Jarvis's story?" Mathew asked as they stood eating toast in the sunny kitchen. It seemed to Nathan that Matt kept one eye on the window over the sink all the time, as though he thought someone might be watching them. Maybe Matt's neighbors were the interested kind.

"Didn't you?"

"I did."

"But?"

And Mathew told him about the interview with Claire Arlen and Carl Winters, about Jonesy's carelessness—or forgetfulness—in asking some crucial questions, about the money Carl Winters had given his sister, and about the baby that changed everything—the baby that Pearl Jarvis hadn't known about. That no one had known about until Sunday night, a few hours before the ransom was paid.

It turned out that this was something he could actually do for Matt—just listen to him.

And Nathan listened without moving a muscle as all the pieces fell into place. And it occurred to him that there was one more thing he could do for Matt.

$\mathcal{T}$here was a black wreath on the elegant front doors of Benedict Arlen's mansion in Mandeville Canyon, and Nathan remembered that Phil Arlen had been buried that morning.

He was shown through to a formal drawing room. There was a portrait of a smooth-faced woman with two little boys over the fireplace.

The family was busy drowning their sorrows in dignified fashion. They were all there, all formally dressed in black. Claire sat by the fireplace, looking wan. Carl was examining the leather-lined bookshelves; Bob was pouring drinks with the air of a man fulfilling his manifest destiny. Veronica stood a little apart, watching the others as though her season theater tickets were proving a bad investment—that was probably due to the fact that Benedict Arlen was holding center stage. He broke off what he was saying as Nathan was shown into the room.

"Mr. Doyle," Benedict said, and the lack of pleasure in his voice was mirrored in the faces of the rest of the family.

"Nathan," Bob said, uncomfortable and unhappy that Nathan apparently didn't know better than to crash a family funeral. "This isn't the time."

"It's the only time left," Nathan said. "Lieutenant Spain and the police will be here within the hour to make an arrest."

There was general distress at this. Nathan let them work it out of their systems, and then Veronica said steadily, "Who do they plan on arresting?"

"I'm not in their confidence. I can't guarantee that they'll arrest the right person. They might simply arrest the most obvious suspect." He saw her gaze flick to Bob, who merely looked bewildered.

"And I suppose you know who the right person is?" Carl Winters said.

"I think so. Would you like to hear my theory?"

"No," Claire said. "I think someone should throw you out."

"We may as well hear it," Veronica said.

"Yes," Benedict Arlen said. "I want to hear what he has to say."

Bob stared at his father, and then at Nathan. He seemed surprised to find a drink in his hand, and he brought it to his lips, tossing it off in one gulp.

Nathan said, "The police located Pearl Jarvis yesterday. She had an interesting story to tell."

"I don't want to hear it," Claire protested. "Dad, please!"

"Hush, girlie," Benedict Arlen said.

Nathan said slowly, "I guess you could say that Philip's murder was a crime of passion, but not in the ordinary sense. Plenty of people felt passionately about him, all right. Mostly they hated him, and mostly they had good reason."

"How *dare* you!" Claire said.

Nathan ignored her outburst. "And in a way Phil set up his own murder. He faked his own kidnapping so that he'd have the money to run away with his girlfriend to Buenos Aires."

"That's not true!" Claire cried.

"It is, you know. The irony is, if his murderer had understood that he was running away—that it wasn't just another scam, another grift—his death might not have seemed necessary. Maybe *necessary* is the wrong word, because this was more impulse than premeditation."

"What are you trying to say?" Carl Winters demanded.

"Yes, Nathan," Veronica said. "What *are* you trying to say?"

"That someone was clever enough, or shrewd enough, or just watched Phil operate long enough, to see through the kidnapping scheme. I think this person was tired of watching Phil manipulate and use everyone around him, and I think this person was especially tired of seeing Bob Arlen treated like a second-class citizen by his father."

Bob said uncomfortably, "Oh, hogwash. Where do you come up with this stuff, Nathan?"

"Now see here," Benedict Arlen began.

Nathan ignored this too. "And I think the final straw was when this person found out that Claire was going to have a baby. Because that baby meant that Mr. Arlen would reverse his earlier position. He'd reinstate Phil's allowance, he'd try once again to get him to take his rightful place at Arlen Petroleum, he'd shower him with presents and stock bonuses—none of which really changed Bob Arlen's position much, it was more the—the affront of it, I think."

"It's not true!" Claire cried. "None of it is true! He wasn't leaving with her! He wouldn't have, now that the baby was on the way."

"I don't think Phil was ready to be a daddy," Nathan said. "I don't think he had any intention of changing his plans because of this baby. But no one else could know that, except maybe Pearl. Everyone else would assume that Phil would recognize that baby for the ticket back into his father's good graces."

Phil's father said unsteadily, "This is…poppycock. Phil was a good boy. A good son."

No one seemed to have the heart to contradict him.

Bob said stiffly, "Why wouldn't this person…kill Claire and the baby in that case? Even if Phil did leave, the baby would still be a—a rival for my father's affections—and money."

"Because this person didn't hate Claire or the baby. Didn't blame them—maybe even saw them as fellow victims of Phil's ruthless and selfish behavior. Probably thought they—and everyone else—would be better off without Philip."

No one said anything. Nathan moved over to the case against the wall with the miniature display of the Battle of the Little Bighorn. There was a mirror over the case and he could see them all sitting frozen in shock— with one exception. And he knew he was right. And if he was right about that, he figured he was probably right about the rest of it.

"Of course there were other reasons somebody might have wanted Phil out of the way. He had a bad habit of stretching his pocket money by blackmailing his friends and acquaintances—or trying to, anyway—and maybe he knew something about this person's past as well. I don't know. That's speculation, but once I'd worked out that Phil arranged his own kidnapping, I realized I only had to look for people who didn't have alibis on Monday night, and there was only person who didn't have an alibi for Monday night."

Nathan glanced at Bob. "Well, two people. Bob was in the vicinity of Griffith Park when Phil was killed, but his bum leg rules him out as the person who ran after Phil and shot him in front of Pearl."

"I was here," Claire said. "I was here the whole evening, waiting 'til Bob got back with word the ransom had been delivered."

"I know," Nathan said. "You were here with Mr. Arlen. And Carl was at the theater. So that pretty much left only one person." He looked into the mirror over the miniature case and Veronica stood in the doorway, one hand on the light switch, one hand holding a pistol pointed at his back. He took a deep breath, but then the side doors next to him flew open, and Mathew and a number of uniformed cops were rushing into the room.

He glanced back in the mirror in time to see Veronica's hand move on the light switch, and the room plunged into darkness. He saw the reflected flash of muzzle fire, there was a loud bang, and the mirror splintered next to him, tiny shards of glass dusting his face. Screams were followed by the sound of crashing furniture, and he was knocked to the ground hard. There was another shot.

Someone who weighed a ton was lying on top of him, and Matt breathed into his face, "No, you goddamned well *don't,* Nathan. You don't get out that easy!"

And the next minute the lights were on again, and everyone was picking themselves off the floor. No one seemed to be hurt, though Clare was sobbing her fright. Matt got up, dragging Nathan to his feet, hands fastened in Nathan's shirt like he wanted to punch him. His face was furious. He gave Nathan a little push, turning away to where Veronica stood with two police officers holding her arms. There was a gun at her feet. Her black hair spilled loose over her shoulders. She looked as wild as her outlaw grandfather must have.

"Ronnie," Bob gasped.

"W-what is the meaning of this?" That was the old man, looking every one of his years.

Mathew strode over to Ronnie. He said curtly, "Veronica Thompson-Arlen, I'm arresting you for the murder of Philip Arlen…"

"*A*ll kinds of things pointed to Ronnie once I started looking," Nathan said. "She was on a bunch of committee boards, including one for the George C. Page Museum."

"The Brea Tar Pits," Mathew said automatically. They were sitting in a small café on Wilshire a few hours after Nathan had nearly got his head blown off playing Master Detective at Benedict Arlen's Mandeville Canyon estate. Nathan was busily rattling off his reasoning, but he didn't fool Matt. Matt knew guilt when he saw it, and knowledge was sitting in his guts like a lump of cold snow.

"She knows how to handle firearms, she's physically strong, cool under fire—"

Mathew said quietly, "Just so we're clear—you ever pull a stunt like that again, I'll kill you myself."

Nathan broke off what he was saying. Color rose in his face. "Look—"

"No, you look. One thing I never figured you for was a coward."

The color faded right out of Nathan's face.

"The entire goddamn world's at war. We might not any of us be here a year from now. You don't think you can hang on long enough to see how it turns out?"

"That's not fair—" Nathan was getting angry now. That was fine by Matt. He'd been mad ever since he opened the door to Benedict Arlen's drawing room in time to see Nathan calmly setting himself up to get shot.

"Don't." Matt cut across, his voice very quiet, and though no one was paying any attention to them, Nathan threw an instinctive look over at the table nearest them. "Don't. Because we both know you'll be lying, and whatever else happens between us, at least let's be honest with each other."

Nathan's jaw tightened. He nodded curtly.

"I didn't look for this. It's the last thing I was looking for, but…I don't regret it. You understand?"

Nathan nodded again.

"I don't know how we're going to work it out. I just know…it's worth working out. It's worth it to me anyway."

"You don't know—"

"Neither do you, Nathan. Neither does anyone. I can tell you what I do know. Love…doesn't happen every day. It doesn't happen at all for some people."

Nathan ducked his head. Mathew watched him fight for control, eyelashes flickering, mouth unsteady. "Don't do this to me," he whispered.

Matt ignored that. "We're, what, three—four days from the New Year? You can focus on the end, or you can focus on the beginning, that's up to you. But I'll tell you what I want. Assuming you decide to hang around and hear it."

Nathan sucked in a sharp breath, nodded. At last he looked up, meeting Matt's eyes.

"I'm not leaving town," he said.

Acknowledgments

Out of the Blue:

"Varlik's toast" is from "The Song" by Eric Wilkinson. The author also wishes to acknowledge *High Adventure* by James Hall and *Fighting the Flying Circus* by Eddie Rickenbacker as primary source materials for this work of fiction.

Thank you to author Clare London for the Brit check.

The entire collection:

Thank you to Sasha Knight, Judith David, Lynne Anderson, Deborah Nemeth and Keren Reed.

ABOUT THE AUTHOR

Author of over sixty titles of classic Male/Male fiction featuring twisty mystery, kickass adventure, and unapologetic man-on-man romance, JOSH LANYON'S work has been translated into twelve languages. Her FBI thriller *Fair Game* was the first Male/Male title to be published by Harlequin Mondadori, then the largest romance publisher in Italy. *Stranger on the Shore* (Harper Collins Italia) was the first M/M title to be published in print. In 2016 *Fatal Shadows* placed #5 in Japan's annual Boy Love novel list (the first and only title by a foreign author to place on the list). The Adrien English series was awarded the All Time Favorite Couple by the Goodreads M/M Romance Group. In 2019, *Fatal Shadows* became the first LGBTQ mobile game created by Moments: Choose Your Story.

She is an Eppie Award winner, a four-time Lambda Literary Award finalist (twice for Gay Mystery), An Edgar nominee, and the first ever recipient of the Goodreads All Time Favorite M/M Author award.

Josh is married and lives in Southern California.

Find other Josh Lanyon titles at www.joshlanyon.com, and follow Josh on Twitter, Facebook, Goodreads, Instagram and Tumblr.

For extras and exclusives, join Josh on Patreon.

Also By Josh Lanyon

NOVELS

The ADRIEN ENGLISH Mysteries

Fatal Shadows • A Dangerous Thing • The Hell You Say
Death of a Pirate King • The Dark Tide
So This is Christmas • Stranger Things Have Happened

The HOLMES & MORIARITY Mysteries

Somebody Killed His Editor • All She Wrote
The Boy with the Painful Tattoo • In Other Words...Murder

The ALL'S FAIR Series

Fair Game • Fair Play • Fair Chance

The ART OF MURDER Series

The Mermaid Murders •The Monet Murders
The Magician Murders • The Monuments Men Murders

OTHER NOVELS

The Ghost Wore Yellow Socks
Mexican Heat (with Laura Baumbach)
Strange Fortune • Come Unto These Yellow Sands
This Rough Magic • Stranger on the Shore • Winter Kill
Murder in Pastel • Jefferson Blythe, Esquire
The Curse of the Blue Scarab • Murder Takes the High Road
Séance on a Summer's Night
The Ghost Had an Early Check-Out

NOVELLAS

The DANGEROUS GROUND Series

Dangerous Ground • Old Poison • Blood Heat
Dead Run • Kick Start

The I SPY Series

I Spy Something Bloody • I Spy Something Wicked
I Spy Something Christmas

The IN A DARK WOOD Series

In a Dark Wood • The Parting Glass

The DARK HORSE Series

The Dark Horse • The White Knight

The DOYLE & SPAIN Series

Snowball in Hell

The HAUNTED HEART Series

Haunted Heart Winter

The XOXO FILES Series

Mummie Dearest

OTHER NOVELLAS

Cards on the Table • The Dark Farewell • The Darkling Thrush
*The Dickens with Love * Don't Look Back • A Ghost of a Chance*
Lovers and Other Strangers • Out of the Blue • A Vintage Affair
Lone Star (in Men Under the Mistletoe) • Green Glass Beads (in Irregulars)
Blood Red Butterfly • Everything I Know • Baby, It's Cold
A Case of Christmas • Murder Between the Pages • Slay Ride

SHORT STORIES

A Limited Engagement • The French Have a Word for It
In Sunshine or In Shadow • Until We Meet Once More
Icecapade (in His for the Holidays) • Perfect Day
Heart Trouble • In Plain Sight • Wedding Favors
Wizard's Moon • Fade to Black • Night Watch
Plenty of Fish • The Boy Next Door
Halloween is Murder

COLLECTIONS

Stories (Vol. 1) • Sweet Spot (the Petit Morts)
Merry Christmas, Darling (Holiday Codas)
Christmas Waltz (Holiday Codas 2)
I Spy...Three Novellas
Point Blank (Five Dangerous Ground Novellas)
Dark Horse, White Knight (Two Novellas)
The Adrien English Mysteries
The Adrien English Mysteries 2

www.ingramcontent.com/pod-product-compliance
Lightning Source LLC
Chambersburg PA
CBHW050954180726
48291CB00006B/1815